1919:

The Metamorphosis Of Hitler

by Larry I. Barron

In Einstein's time, Germany was the promise and later the nemesis of the world, the country that had a decisive bearing on world politics and where, for a moment that seemed a lifetime, the moral drama of our era was enacted.

- Fritz Stern

You do not alter the destinies of nations in kid gloves.

- *Mein Kampf*

Adolf Hitler was the greatest villain of the 20th century. This novel looks at his life in the year after World War One. During the war Hitler served with Jews and even respected some; a year later, he wanted them all hung or banished from Germany.

1919 saw Hitler metamorphosize from despondent army corporal into leader apparent of the Nazi Party, discovering inside himself an ability to convince others, through his mesmerizing powers of speech, that transformed him into the idol of zealots and the scourge of civilized peoples.

While Hitler was the dark star of the 20th century, another German, Albert Einstein, was the light. In 1919 he became famous as his Theory of Relativity burst upon the world. It was exciting and exotic, and came to represent the best of science and the pursuit of knowledge. And while Hitler preached hate, Einstein pushed for peace.

The best and worst of the 20th century were hatched in Germany in 1919. It was toleration and logic versus master race and blood. And though the former eventually prevailed, in 1919 the Nazis were on the rise.

Contents

1919

Red Rosa

Under the Lindens

It was downtown Berlin, early December 1918, three weeks after the armistice that ended the First World War. This was the beginning of the German interregnum known as the Weimar Republic, destined to last a decade and a half before Hitler swept it all away. The Unter den Linden, the showcase avenue of imperial Berlin, is lined with stately palaces, magnificent hotels, a renowned university, and other edifices of grandeur built mostly since the second Reich was born in 1871, just half a century before. The linden trees that grow up and down this broad boulevard named for them had shed their leaves in the autumn and were bare and frigid, reflecting the general mood of the time. At the west end of the avenue stands the Brandenburg Gate, a Romanesque columned structure under which vehicles moved and armies paraded. On top of the gate, in a wondrous sculpture, is a female warrior on chariot drawn by four magnificent beasts, hooves thundering eastward. Looking west, the broad avenue enters a green and forested park, the Tiergarten, a former royal hunting preserve in the middle of which stands a lone column rising high into the air, with a majestic stone lady, winged victory, erect atop. After World War Two, the Brandenburg Gate divided East and West Germany; but that was thirty years away. In 1919 most people could not imagine another great conflict engulfing all Europe. But there were those on the losing side who were already swearing themselves to another throw of the dice in ten or twenty years' time.

The Berlin streets were frequent scenes of anarchy. Armies returned from the Western Front, first to Berlin to parade through the Gate, then to be disbanded and sent home. But many had nowhere to go, no jobs to return to, so they stayed in the capital, looking for what they knew not. Crowds of ordinary folk and disillusioned war vets marched up and down the streets behind that German minstrel of the Red revolution, Karl Liebknecht. He, like Rosa Luxemburg, publisher of the *Red Flag*, had just been released from prison. Liebknecht, the only Reichstag member to have opposed the war from the beginning, was back on the streets inspiring revolution such as had happened in Russia the previous year.

Except for the lands west of the Rhine, as well as some bridgeheads on the east side of the river around Cologne, Coblenz, and Mainz, extending to Frankfurt, Germany was not occupied by the Allies. There were only German troops in the rest of the country, although wealthy land and business owners were forming private armies to protect their properties from the scavenging hungry and Red revolutionaries who sought to redistribute the wealth.

Still, it was no fun to be in an officer's uniform. The ordinary people, disgusted by the lost war, continued to suffer from hunger and cold, due to the continuing Allied blockade, even after war's end, on food and fuel. Officers had badges of rank and hard earned medals torn from their arms and chests by ordinary folk, so they took to banding together for protection. With truckloads of soldiers and revolutionaries cruising the streets, and guns aplenty, the powderkeg was set.

To cap it off, scores of people wore masks over their mouths, not to hide their identities, but for protection against the great Swine Flu epidemic sweeping the world. Around the globe more people died from the flu than the war. In many cities, some in America, it was a crime to cough in public. But at least in the Allied nations there was food, warmth, and hope.

A cab pulled up outside the luxury Adlon Hotel, a block east of the Brandenburg gate, on the south side of the Unter den Linden. Albert Einstein and Fritz Haber stepped out onto the cobbled pavement. Einstein sported dark hair and a mustache on a head that seemed a little too big for his body. He was the larger of the two, which was not to say much. Haber, bald as a billiard ball, with a mustache and tiny wire-rimmed glasses, was all of five foot five. He was about fifty, Einstein a decade younger and a few inches taller. And Haber was impeccably dressed while Einstein sported his usual rumpled look which today included a bow tie slightly askew. He had on a grey sports jacket with black slacks and scuffed black shoes. Putting his nose to the air, he took a draught of the chill November breeze floating down the avenue. He longed momentarily for some sunny Italian shore; then, cold reality intruding, he stared wistfully at the stone and steel building that stood across the sidewalk from him.

The Hotel Adlon was new, in fact the newest and nicest in Berlin. It was planned before the war, but didn't complete until just after the conflict was done. And only the wealthy, those with American and English currency now, could afford its hospitality. Common folk could but envy its grandeur and lush opulence. And certainly this applied to the two soldiers in worn battle fatigues leaning against the lamppost a quarter block away to the east, sullenly eyeing the gleaming new structure which stood out amidst older surroundings with dirt and soot clinging to them. And these soldiers were hungry and cold, though the stubble of their beards looked no more than a day or two old. Oddly, their uniforms, though worn and tattered, were surprisingly clean. The two had rifles slung over their shoulders, and one had a cigarette drooping lazily from his lips. The other soldier's eyes, blue and piercing even at a distance, strayed toward the cab in front of the hotel as another passenger disembarked. Perhaps it was the long, sculpted heels followed by exquisitely carved legs in sheer black hose that held his gaze.

Emerging from the cab behind the two scientists, the young woman to whom these legs belonged was dressed smartly in a slim black dress which clung nicely to her sleek figure. Liesl was thirty-two years old, of auburn hair that behaved itself for the most part, mysterious green eyes, seductive lips, and a small, slightly upturned, not-quite-button nose. Her cheeks were pink and ruddy; but her general skin tone, which would darken to olive in June and July, was light in the German winter, except for a few freckles left over from last summer. Luxuriant brown hair draped itself around her shoulders as she strode towards the lobby entrance. Just then, the massive glass doors swung open, and a mustached man in his late thirties, in pinstriped suit and dark blue overcoat, came hurrying out towards them. He extended his hand.

"Albert. Fritz. How are you doing?"

He had black hair, mostly intact though thinning in front. His eyebrows were generous, and his skin tone was darker, of a south European variety. He was solidly built, yet slender, and his open features revealed a vibrancy beneath. He surveyed the three visitors, eyeing each in turn, then quickly focussed upon Liesl.

"I'm so glad to see you," he smiled, and leaned forward to kiss her.

She deftly turned so that his lips met her cheek which, warm though it was, wasn't quite what he wanted. Her perfume, the aroma of her hair, enticed him achingly. Hypnotic memories of past pleasures roused themselves, stinging him now by their long absence.

"Wolf, how are you," she replied, icily pulling back.

They had been sweethearts when the war began in 1914, but their relationship was now another casualty of the conflict. Politics had killed it. Though the attraction endured, their points of view separated. Liesl couldn't continue her relationship with someone whose idea of honour veered so far from her own. At least that was how it had started. Somewhere along the way, though, plain stubbornness took over, and now it was hard to forgive or forget. All that remained was a wrecked romance, but still, she couldn't stop yearning.

"When did you get in," asked Wolf. "How's Munich? Your parents? Dunken?"

Dunken, her brother, was supposed to be in Kiev, deep in the Ukraine, doing business, a safe place while still under German occupation; but now that the war was over, the troops were coming home. Russian Reds or Ukrainian partisans would then rule the roost – not too safe for German nationals. All the same, Wolf didn't intend to worry Liesl about it.

"Coward! You damned deserter! What are you up to here, in the capital? No good, no doubt!"

The cry came from one of the soldiers leaning against the lamppost up the block. It shattered the otherwise calm of the morning, rising above the din of the street traffic, the sounds of tires running over wet pavement, and the slight rustle of the winter wind as it funnelled down the cavern of multi-storied buildings along the avenue. And the breeze was blowing in their direction, which only amplified the perfidious barrage even more. As Einstein and his party turned to look in their direction it appeared as if, in his animated rage, the soldier was yelling at one of them. Then, with a vicious, crooked look splashed across his face from ear to ear, blue eyes ablaze, he suddenly lurched away from the pole he was leaning against and strided urgently towards the party, his surprised mate following hesitantly after him. Cursing, howling about cowards and deserters, he unslung his rifle as he hurried forward. His mate tried to restrain him as they neared the four civilians. Onlookers gawked, but no one came to their aid.

Damn, thought Wolf. What is he doing here?

Liesl and the others were alarmed. Very frightened, in fact, if the truth be known. Einstein saw what appeared to be an armed madman, only half a block away now, hurrying straight for their party. His rifle was pointed in their direction as he methodically shoved cartridges into the chamber.

Liesl, instinctively, turned to Wolf, grabbed for his arm. He moved quickly to place himself in front of her, to confront the attacker. What is he doing here, Wolf wondered to himself again. Thoughts raced through his head at light speed. This soldier, he knew him from his old regiment. A loner – and not particularly bright. The fanatical type, Wolf recalled. Just the type to worry about now that the war was lost and over.

Wolf quickly regretted that he had no weapon. Mentally he calculated his chances of successfully rushing his armed adversary. They weren't good any way he figured it. He turned and smiled briefly at Liesl.

Suddenly Fritz Haber, the smallest man in the group, stepped forward, thrusting himself in front of the two soldiers who were now within a couple yards of him.

"What is the meaning of this, Corporal," he barked, eyeing the bars on his shoulder. "I am Captain Haber. Fritz Haber! How dare you accost us in this manner?"

The soldier stopped short. His jaw dropped, and his eyes bulged in surprise. Einstein, Wolf, and Liesl displayed much the same reaction. Wolf later recalled noticing the sun, to the south in the winter sky, overlooking the scene as if out of the Old West. Liesl was now squeezing his arm. He looked at her face, at the red hue from fright lighting up her cheeks.

After a long moment, the soldier gulped, and stepped back. Then he looked at his companion, and at Wolf, and finally at Haber again.

"I know of you, mein herr. How is it that you are in the company of this snivelling coward," he exclaimed, nodding towards Wolf Warburg, "who ran out on his countrymen early in the war? He should be shot down like a dog!"

Haber looked first at Warburg, with disdain, as if to say "You brought this on yourself", and then back at the soldier whose hands were fidgeting on the rifle.

"Your name, Corporal. Immediately! Come to attention and sling that rifle!"

He did so automatically, without delay.

"I am Corporal Adolf Hitler, of the List Regiment, mein Captain."

"Where is your regiment based?"

Haber, eyes stern through his spectacles, barking questions with authority, had the situation completely under control. Liesl's initial fright wore off. The aura of danger was gone, and as the cause of the trouble sunk in, a deep and painful hurt resurfaced.

"In Munich," she said, in reply to Haber's question to Hitler. "Herr Warburg here did indeed transfer out of it," she added in disdain. Three years after the event, Liesl hadn't gotten over it, even though she understood it now, and even, deep down, agreed with it. Maybe Freud could explain – but he was in Vienna.

"Ach, I should have known," said Haber, looking at Wolf and Liesl.

Haber wasn't confused. He knew Wolf wasn't a coward – there are other reasons for wanting to get away from the Front. But he was tired of defending his friend to others. He'd had enough of it. Now the fighting was finally over, but still the insults continued. Blood rushing to his face, Haber clenched his fists and turned on his heels towards the soldiers. His eyebrows arched and his mustache twitched as his lips pursed to speak.

"The war is over, whether we like it or not," he said in a finely clipped tone that brooked no nonsense. "Herr Warburg lives here, and there is little you can do about it.

Now, be on your way home to Bavaria. What are you doing in Berlin anyway?"

Hitler sported a miserable look.

"We're just passing through, from the military hospital in Pasewalk, north of here. I was just released two days ago and we're headed south," he pleaded, suppliant as a puppy looking for a pat.

"What were you in the hospital for," asked Albert Einstein, feeling a touch of empathy for the suddenly forlorn-looking soldier. It was amazing, he thought, how quickly Hitler had gone from ferocious to pitiable. But so many people displayed behaviour nowadays that before the war would have seemed strange and remarkable. Now, sudden mood shifts were common. People were jumpy by nature, and serenity was a luxury.

"Recovering from a British gas attack that I got caught in about five weeks ago."

Einstein cast a knowing glance at Haber, and said, "Well, Fritz, it seems your contribution to the world calamity has come home to roost on our own fighting men."

Haber looked at him furiously. The focus was on him, rather than Wolf – Haber's own skeleton from the war was now front and center, or so Einstein had just made it. Fritz reacted, instinctively, savagely, but close to the mark.

"At least I, unlike you and Herr Warburg here, was not a *pacifist,"* he spit the word out, "hoping for a victory by the enemies of the Fatherland."

No one said anything for a long while. Hitler and his mate expected someone to object; but no one did. It was kind of a defining moment. Everyone knew that Haber was right. But now that Germany had surrendered, Einstein and Wolf could both admit it without fear of arrest. To Hitler and his mate, and to Haber, it displayed the pitiful depth to which Germany had sunk.

Haber finally turned to Hitler.

"Enough of this," he said with a limp wave of his forearm, in a tired tone of resignation. "Be off now, before I have to have you arrested. Return to your homes in the south. There is nothing more you can do here."

The look on his face was not to be brooked, so Hitler and his companion reluctantly turned and slunk away. Casting a venomous glance back, Hitler vowed to himself, not for the first time, that he would settle accounts one day with all the traitors and slackers who cost Germany the war. And, as was the case with Liesl von Schlieffen at that same moment, his steely blue eyes were fixed particularly on the frowning visage of Wolf Warburg.

The party was left standing on the pavement outside the Hotel Adlon. An awning hung overhead, and a red carpet protruded from the front doors out over the sidewalk. The sun shone dimly now through a light cloud. The streets and sidewalks were wet and grimy from snow melt caused by the busy vehicle and pedestrian traffic. It was a gray and dreary scene, especially now that the excitement of the armed encounter had passed.

Haber had lost his appetite for the meeting. It was never his idea in the first place. He and Albert had been lecturing at the university down the street that afternoon, and Liesl had joined them for lunch. When Einstein told them he was going to meet Wolf for a drink that afternoon, to catch up on his recent trip to New York, they accepted his invite to tag along. Now that the war was done, perhaps Liesl and Wolf could put differences aside. But after the escapade moments before, Haber mused to himself that he sympathized with the soldier – Wolf had left the Front early in the war, left all the fighting to other Germans. Some resentment still resided in Haber, even while he saw clearly the German folly in not pursuing a settlement in the West much sooner.

"I have to be getting back to the institute. Nice to see you, Wolf," he said wryly. "Liesl, coming or not?"

He turned to summon a cab. Now it was her turn. And, like a broken record, the same battered tune played itself out. She knew Wolf had been right – Germany should have sought peace early on. But she couldn't admit it.

"I'll go with you," she replied to Haber, with a sneer towards Wolf, her nose turned up and her eyes half closed. His teeth gritted, but he closed his mouth to disguise the hurt. After all, he'd gotten used to it over the past few years.

Haber and Liesl looked over to Einstein.

"Well, that just leaves you and me, Wolf," Albert said. "Two confirmed old pacifists."

There was an awkward silence as Einstein stared momentarily straight into the eyes of Haber and Liesl. Even though he held the same pacifist views as Wolf, they didn't resent him as they did the latter. Einstein had been for peace from the start – he didn't come to it partway through war when the going got tough. Haber and Liesl waited a moment, then turned together and walked towards a yellow cab which had just pulled up to the curb. Without a look back Liesl slid into the rear seat, followed by Haber. The cab pulled away in the traffic, heading east half a block before pulling a U-turn and to head back west, so that Wolf caught a last glimpse of Liesl through the car window as it passed by them, on its way through the Brandenburg Gate and beyond to their destination southwest of the city. If he could have peered closer, he would have seen her long lashes fluttering, and a few tears flowing down her cheeks. Fritz Haber, who did notice them, sat sadly silent.

Einstein and Wolf finally turned from the street and made their way through the lobby doors into the hotel. The lobby itself was chilly at that time of year. Einstein frequently booked a room in town, as did certain other professors who thought they would be kept late lecturing at the university down the street, and didn't want to make the half hour trip out to Dahlem, where they lived due to its proximity to the Kaiser Wilhelm Institutes where they mainly worked. On this occasion, the two men headed for the hotel lounge.

"I could use a drink after that row outside, Wolf."

He wasn't arguing. They sat down and ordered drinks. Wolf was still tense and shaking a little; his cheeks were still flushed, and his dark, thinning hair, usually on the curly side, still bristled on end.

"I don't like being called a coward. I never liked it during the war, and I don't like it now. Especially since you and I were right all along, Albert! They should be apologizing to us."

But he knew human nature better. People aren't quick to admit mistakes. This latest episode with crazy Adolf shook him. His hands worked themselves over the frosty glass pint. He began to relax. The waitress, a young redhead in a clinging green dress that reached her knees, brought their drinks and smiled as she left.

"I do hope you and Fritz can patch up your differences. I hate to be the cause of a problem between you."

"Oh, don't worry about it," replied Einstein with a smile. "You know that we've argued about this war from the beginning. We always get over it. Did you know that it was Fritz who recruited me to work at the Institute just before the war?"

Einstein's eyes looked across the room out towards the lobby.

"Just a moment. I think I saw Ulrich."

He got up from the table and hurried across the room, out into the lobby and around the corner where Wolf lost sight of him. Wolf cupped his hands round his mug, leaned back in his chair to wait, and viewed the lounge patrons. They were all clean, well-dressed, and seemingly affluent, including a couple of senior Allied military uniforms mixed in the bunch. Generals no doubt. It all contrasted with the unruly crowds he had seen on the streets since his return from New York. The theatres and cabarets featured sexy, avant-garde musicals and bawdy humour. The former German Establishment, including the Kaiser and his circle, the Junkers of East Prussia, the General Staff, and the rich weapons makers, were all objects of revile and scorn by the rest of the population; and the butt of biting, oft-repulsive jokes, cartoons, songs and skits. The new government had neither the resources nor the inclination to enforce censorship of any sort regarding insults to the former elite.

A couple minutes later Einstein returned, accompanied by a slight middle-aged man with wire rim spectacles and a light grey goatee that matched his receding hairline. Over a dark three-piece suit he wore a heavy leather coat with fur-trimmed collar. He sported a fur hat as well, beaver in fact, a gift from friends at the former Russian Imperial Court during his days there. Count Ulrich von Brockdorff-Rantzau was now the new German foreign minister. He smiled broadly as he looked down upon Wolf, who quickly extended a hand towards him.

"How goes it, Ulrich?"

"Passable. And you, Wolf? You must tell me of New York. It must be a very different mood there. Celebrations, victory dinners, and the like. One non-stop party, I imagine. So, why haven't you looked me up yet? You've taken time to see Albert here."

Count Rantzau continued talking even as he bent and set his briefcase on the floor, took off his coat and hat, and sat down next to Wolf.

"Hey, wait a minute," Rantzau said excitedly, turning towards him, "Liesl's in town, did you know? Doing some business with Haber."

"That's a bit of a sore point," Einstein interjected. "Fritz blew a gasket just before you got here."

Rantzau took a pipe from his suit pocket and stuffed it with a pinch of tobacco from his pouch. Putting it to his mouth he lit it and settled back in his chair.

"Oh, do tell," the Count replied, smiling. "I can chat for a few minutes anyway, though I'm wanted at the Chancellery. I don't really want to go, if the truth be known. The atmosphere over there isn't quite so pleasant. They're under a bit of a siege, as you can imagine. Karl Liebknecht has his minions marching up and down hollering for the Marxist revolution to be completed. It seems that a Republican government is not enough for him He is intent on having a second revolution, like Lenin and Trotsky carried out in Moscow a few months ago."

"As a matter of fact I'm supposed to meet with Karl and Rosa later this week," Wolf informed the Count. "Meantime, have you heard anything about what's going on in Russia right now? Liesl's brother is still in Kiev."

"I understand there's fighting on the Polish-Russian border," the Count replied. "The victors in Paris have just resurrected Poland, a century after it was snuffed out. Now Poland's eager to take some more land from Russia. And from Germany, if we let her."

"Seems only fair, wouldn't you agree, Ulrich," Einstein interjected. "What goes around comes around."

"Still can't get over Wolf?" inquired Fritz Haber of Liesl, relaxing in the back of the cab as they rode back to Dahlem, on the southwest outskirts of Berlin. "He is so exasperating. Both him and Albert."

The cab headed west, through the Brandenburg Gate which had armed men atop, a ragtag militia that Liesl and Haber guessed were part of Rosa Luxemburg and Karl Liebknecht's red hordes. There were no organized Republican troop formations to be seen, even though lots of soldiers, their units disbanded, wandered the city looking for work, wondering what awaited them back in their hometowns. The cab travelled west through the forested Tiergarten, then jogged south onto the Kurfürstendamm for the drive to Dahlem, by Lake Havel in the Grunewald Forest, where Einstein loved to sail. It was late afternoon, with the lights of the shows and shopping district not yet lit. The cabarets and clubs were already busy, though the ex-soldiers and munitions men, now suddenly jobless, had little cash for liquor, women, and song. But still they spent their last marks. The currency lost value by the day, so money spent now got them more than tomorrow.

And the shows themselves were magnificent. Sprung loose from the shackles of an oppressive Prussian prudishness, Germany's playwrights and directors strove to outdo each other in cleverness. Weimar decadence was born, lasting gleefully until 1933 when the Nazis swept it all away.

"Maybe it's we who are wrong, my dear," said Haber. "Look at that sign there. 'Lords of the Trough'. That is how they portray Ludendorff and Hindenburg. Disgusting!"

The two German generals were cast as pigs, complete with snouts. They were in General Staff uniforms, with riding crops to direct underlings. Their porky ears stuck out above their caps, and stubby brown tails sprouted behind. The hooves at the end of their forepaws somehow managed to grip long-stemmed glasses, while they instructed on the 'proper Prussian way to *swill* champagne'. It was advertising for a comedy.

"That would have been criminal before the armistice," Haber ruminated, "a hanging offence. Now we, the old leaders, are blamed for everything."

Liesl had no reply.

"Ach," Haber grunted, with a sigh and a frown. He stroked his close-trimmed beard. "We all thought it would be a six-week romp through the provinces of eastern

France. Modern industrial warfare. Total war! We had no idea. Only a fool would want more."

Haber stared out the window at piled snow along the roadway, troubled, chewing hard on his cigar. Destitute folks trudged along, their worldly possessions in carts or wheelbarrows behind them; and soldiers in ragged uniforms in small groups returning from the lost war in the west. In contrast the gleaming automobiles of the wealthy sped past, Mercedes, Daimler, Olds, pulling into opulent homes and stores and theatres. The looks of desperation and envy of the former for the latter: just his imagination, he hoped, for such were the roots of Red revolution.

He turned to a more pleasant topic. Fritz Haber was a romantic at heart. He thought of his own young wife awaiting him at home in Dahlem. Even now he envisioned her naked before him, long, thick, dark hair draping her head and shoulders. He knew he was a lucky man.

"So you miss Wolf dearly, despite your differences."

"Oh, Fritz," Liesl paused, then replied, "I miss him every day. But when he got that transfer from the Front, I just couldn't get over it. A coward!"

"Come, Liesl," Haber said, taking her hand, "you don't believe that. He served in combat for over a year before the transfer. And he was never accused of cowardice in battle."

The urban landscape had now turned semi-rural, with snow-covered plots and farms as they left the city proper. In a few minutes the cab would reach the budding community of Dahlem, an otherwise green suburb in which the Kaiser Wilhelm Institutes were the most prominent fixture.

Liesl's head drooped and she stared down into her lap.

"Maybe that's what so shocked me at the time. And since then I've pushed him so far away – how can I ever turn it around," she sighed.

"It's a shame about Liesl," said Count Rantzau, back at the Adlon, as he nursed a Cointreau.

Wolf sighed. "I hoped she'd understand after a fashion."

"Seems that few appreciate the common soldier's dilemma," commented Einstein, sipping his tea. "Even if he wants to quit fighting, he can't. There's just no place for him to run. He can't go home; so the only option is surrender, and if he's not shot in the process, he spends the duration as a prisoner in some wretched camp."

"That's it in a nutshell," Wolf replied. "After that first year, a lot of my fellows in the List Regiment felt like I did. We'd had enough killing – enough to last forever. But they couldn't face their families or a firing squad if they deserted."

In Wolf's case, though, Cousin Max pulled some strings to get him transferred to headquarters to draft occupation ordinances.

Count Rantzau had a warm fuzzy feeling in his gut from the liqueur he had been sipping. He looked Wolf in the eye.

"I can feel for you, my friend. But there's only one person whose opinion really matters."

Wolf looked up from his mug into Rantzau's face, frowned and nodded slowly.

Einstein suddenly looked over to Rantzau.

"Didn't you have to be somewhere, Ulrich?"

"Oh, my, Ebert and Scheidemann will have my hide," said the Count, pulling out his pocket watch to check the time, while chastising himself by boxing his ear with his other hand. "I'd better head right over to the Chancellery."

He rose and pulled on his coat and hat, bent to pick up his briefcase, and said to Wolf, "Call me after you talk to Rosa and Karl."

They waved goodbye as Count Rantzau finished his liqueur, licked his lips, and rushed from the room.

"When do you see Rosa," Einstein asked.

"Tomorrow if possible."

"A very clever woman, I'm told."

"You ever run into her, Albert?"

Einstein smiled. "No, my path doesn't cross much with the disciples of Karl Marx. But she certainly writes well."

"It strikes me that you should be writing more about your brainchild theories."

"Oh, that's not such a loss. There are those that explain them much better than me."

"But none that understand them. This *Relativity* theory is supposed to shake up the universe like no one since Newton – although I must admit I still don't really follow it."

"We shall see. Anyway, you'll be attending Haber's little soiree on New Years Eve?"

Wolf laughed. "That's a month away. I suppose we'll be over our little spat by then."

"I suspect Liesl will be there."

* * *

The offices of the *Red Flag* were a few blocks south of the Adlon Hotel, in the heart of Newspaper Row on the Kochstrasse. It was over a week since Wolf's encounter with Hitler. Karl Liebknecht and Rosa Luxemburg were busy provoking a revolution, and it had been difficult catching up to them. The offices were a beehive of activity, everyone wearing frazzled, yet happy, looks. It was a good time to be a Red. Their fortunes were rising. All they had to do was to keep the revolution, which had already produced the fall of the monarchy and the establishment of a Republic, going further in the same direction, ever to the Left.

Whether the course of the Russian Revolution only a year before would now repeat itself in Germany was the big question at the end of 1918. In February 1917 the Tsarist regime had fallen in Russia, to be replaced by Kerensky's quasi-democratic government; eight months later the Bolsheviks seized power and installed the Dictatorship of the Proletariat. The same second revolution could now happen in Germany, and all signs pointed in that direction. Liebknecht and his Spartacist League were inciting mass demonstrations by workers and soldiers. In the center stood the new Republic, espousing capitalism and private property while nationalizing some businesses, but taking care, to its later detriment, not to plunder old money and industrial fortunes.

Rosa Luxemburg had a certain shine to her face, an inner light that came from surviving, with mind intact, years of wartime imprisonment, for her own protection according to the government.

"I discovered tranquillity, Wolf," she told him after they retired to her office in the rear. "There was nothing I could do, so I accepted fate."

"But she paid a price," put in Leo Jogiches, her lover years ago, and now co-editor. "Before prison her hair was jet black."

Wolf remembered vividly, and saw for himself how grey it had gone.

"The cuisine was not what it could have been," Rosa smiled, then added, "but no one, except for the Kaiser and the rich, and the General Staff, were eating well. Leo, tell him what they discovered in the warehouses beneath the Imperial Schloss."

Wolf looked towards him.

"Obscenity considering that commonfolk and soldiers hadn't been eating much of anything except soup made of sawdust, and cats and dogs and other delicacies. When the Sailors Division occupied the palace right after the Kaiser's abdication they found in the cellars huge supplies of meat, poultry, soups and sauces, eggs, coffee, chocolates, dried fruit, biscuits and the like. Sacks of flour stacked to the ceiling. And the liquor! Hundreds of beer kegs; racks of vintage wines. With those they had quite a party," Jogiches concluded his inventory.

"Tell me about the Sailors Division," Wolf asked.

"It's made up mostly of ex sailors who took part in the mutiny in Kiel, a few weeks before the war ended. Some came to Berlin and formed this division. After the abdication, they occupied the Schloss because they had to sleep somewhere."

The Schloss was a few blocks east, the biggest building in Berlin, a huge, old castle built up over many generations by the kings of Prussia on an island in the Spree River.

"The heart of the old empire," commented Rosa. "And the Kaiser now resides in a bungalow in Holland, fretting he'll be handed over to the Allies and paraded through Paris in a cage. Fitting, don't you think?"

"I like the bungalow," Wolf replied. "The cage may be going a little far."

"Both Karl and I lived in cages for years on the Kaiser's orders, or those of his government, Herr Warburg," Rosa sneered.

Leo looked at her crossly.

"I think Wolf knows that better than most, Rosa."

"Forgive me, Wolf," she said, the colour fading quickly from her face. A touch embarrassed, she silently recalled his many visits to her in jail.

"It's forgotten," Wolf quickly replied. After all, he knew better than most (considering he hadn't actually served time himself) what she had been through.

He wanted to change the subject anyway.

"So tell me, what is your take on the current situation here?"

Rosa rose from her chair and paced the room in thought for a moment.

"On the right are the industrial and business cartels, the Junkers, the old Establishment: they all want to turn the clock back. We on the Left want a Marxist society, a true democracy reflecting the will of us all. And then there's the current bastard government in the middle. Ebert thinks he can have it both ways: maintain private property rights while at the same time giving to the former have-nots. You can't do both."

"So you would nationalize most industries?"

"Exactly."

"And who do most people support?"

"Not us, not yet. They want to be rich themselves."

"So how do you expect to succeed with your new Order? A dictatorship, like Lenin and Trotsky in Moscow?"

"They've gotten carried away," Rosa replied carefully. "The people must be led, forcefully at first. But the secret police, the terror – well, we would never do that."

Wolf eyed her sceptically with raised eyebrows.

"But you maintain contact with the Communist Party in Russia. Many here say that you receive your instructions from Moscow."

Rosa bristled.

"That's a lie," Leo snarled from behind the desk. "We're independent."

"What about Karl Radek? I heard he's back in town. I expected to find him here now, to be honest. Isn't he still the Moscow connection?"

"You seem to know so much about Comrade Radek. Why don't you tell us," Leo replied.

Wolf couldn't think of any reason not to.

"It was Radek who negotiated the transit through Germany of Lenin's sealed train back to Russia a year and a half ago. And didn't he arrange financial aid from the

Kaiser for the Bolsheviks when Lenin guaranteed that he'd overthrow Kerensky and pull Russia out of the war?"

Rosa and Leo remained silent.

"Isn't Radek the Jew who told one journalist that he'd like to 'exterminate', I think the term was, all Jews? But to be fair, I suppose, he just said it to prove what a good godless Marxist he is."

Wolf paused. Rosa and Leo weren't smiling.

"My information is that Radek was sent here within the last few days with instructions from Lenin to encourage workers and soldiers to boycott the elections in January. And to overthrow the government. Sound familiar? Another Bolshevik coup, just like Russia a year ago."

"You're certainly not shy, counsellor," Rosa finally replied, then added, "While it is true that Comrade Radek has come from Moscow to offer advice, neither he nor Lenin himself is in charge of the German Communist movement. We are completely independent of Moscow."

"Then who funds you," Wolf shot back.

"The common folk, Herr Warburg. Is that so hard to believe?"

"Yes. They have no money."

"Well, you believe what you will. We cannot convince you otherwise if you don't wish it. But mark my words: we are the wave of the future," Rosa replied determinedly. "You can't stop the people from coming to power. Our time is here. Or just around the corner. We already control Bavaria, under my old friend Kurt Eisner."

Wolf knew about Bavaria. He'd grown up there and still called it home.

"So, Wolf," Leo Jogiches said, "what have you come for today? Just to catch up?"

"Yes. I've only seen you once since you were released," Wolf replied, looking at Rosa. "Though there is something else I wanted to talk about. Where's Karl?"

"Out marching, probably," Rosa said. "It keeps him out of our hair. So how are you, Wolf? Forgive my manners."

She stood up, bent over, and kissed him lightly on the cheek. She was still grateful for all he had done, or tried to do, to gain her release.

"And how is Liesl? Are you making any headway yet?"

Wolf frowned.

"Ah, give it time. She'll come around," Rosa said, gently stroking his arm. After a moment, she asked, sitting down, "So what else have you come about? You must be busy."

"I'm assisting Hugo Preuss drafting a new Constitution for the Cabinet to consider. I want your input. We don't have much chance of a consensus without Leftist input."

Rosa frowned, then replied, "We aren't interested in your new Constitution. Communism is coming to Germany, and it's just around the corner!"

"But Rosa, be reasonable," Wolf argued. "We have to do something to maintain order. Surely you must want some say in how the country is governed while you wait for Marxism to arrive."

"No. I'm sorry," she replied firmly. "We've decided to boycott Ebert's government in order to hasten the Red revolution."

* * *

The next month passed with Berlin growing increasingly tense as the Allies continued their blockade of food and fuel, both to punish Germany and to force her to sign a formal treaty of surrender to replace the temporary armistice of November 11th, 1918. Soldiers returning from the Western Front, along with refugees from the battlefields of eastern Europe, from Poland, Galicia, the Ukraine and Russia, swelled Berlin's population as never before. A malcontented, misery-ridden mass continued to starve or freeze, or to die from swine flu or typhus, amidst an abundance of weapons. As Christmas descended, Wolf Warburg heard rumours of a situation developing at the huge and gaudy state palace, the Imperial Schloss. It all started when the government negotiated a deal to pay the occupying sailors to move out of the palace and into a building across the street. Two days before Christmas the sailors came to the Chancellery, just around the corner and down the street from the Adlon Hotel, for their money. When told they would have to wait, they grabbed Otto Wels, the official picked to deliver the good news, returned to the Schloss, and threw him in an underground cell.

The first Cabinet of the new Republic consisted of three moderates and three members who were farther left. The moderates, including Chancellor Ebert, intended nevertheless to show that the government had control of Berlin. The leftists wanted the Sailors Division left alone. Ebert agreed, for the time being.

But this wasn't good enough for the German General Staff, who saw slipping away from them a perfect excuse to smash the renegade sailors. On a private line to Ebert's office, General Gröner contacted him later on the night of December 23rd.

"Herr Chancellor, the field marshal and I are at the end of our patience. Your persistence in this eternal negotiation is breaking down the fighting spirit of the last troops faithful to the officers. We are determined to hold to the plan to liquidate the Sailors Division."

"But you can't do that, General. Half of our Cabinet will resign if you do. They are sympathetic to those sailors!"

Ebert's voice was breaking. Gröner thought he might cry. Despicable! And this was the new Reich leadership.

"You can't do that, General. We do not approve your request to storm the Schloss."

"Well, I must tell you, Herr Ebert, that the orders have been given and the troops are marching. You asked for our support a month and a half ago, after the armistice, and you begged for it again earlier today, when those cursed sailors had you trapped in your own Chancellery. Now you must back us, or the army will fall apart. And then so will your government."

"You must call back your troops," Ebert shrieked into the phone.

Gröner waited a moment for him to calm down.

"Unfortunately, Herr Chancellor, it may be impossible to relay those instructions to the troops in time. Once a major military operation has begun it is difficult to abort midstream. You should have thought of this before you begged for our assistance."

"But that's outrageous! The army's not in charge!"

"That may be," Gröner replied, barely containing his glee, "but it doesn't change the fact that the troops are marching. Tomorrow morning at dawn they will attack the Schloss. I suggest you support us, since you might find it difficult to explain an army mutiny and still retain power."

Ebert hung up in defeat. He knew the general was right. To his fellow moderate Scheidemann he said, "I don't know how we're going to tell Haase and Barth," leftists in the Cabinet, "about it. They'll resign for sure."

"And if they leave, they'll likely walk straight over and join forces with Rosa Luxemburg and Karl Liebknecht. The army is playing into their hands," Scheidemann wailed.

But neither man could bring himself to call their Cabinet colleagues.

It was early morning on the day before Christmas. He had just sat down to breakfast when the phone rang.

"Hello."

"Wolf. Thank heaven I caught you."

"Hugo? What's up?"

"We need you right away. It's urgent!"

Hugo Haase was Wolf's former law partner, from a few years previous when they both did some criminal law. Hugo moved into politics for the most part, while Wolf drifted to litigation. When the war came, their paths separated further. But they still helped one another in a pinch, and collaborated to free some of the more 'political' prisoners.

Wolf looked at the clock on the wall. It wasn't even eight o'clock yet.

"What's up?"

"They're about to attack the Schloss. He's already given them an ultimatum. He says they'll attack at eight sharp!"

"Slow down, Hugo. Who's going to attack the Schloss? You mean attack the sailors inside?"

"Yes. Yes. The army. A General Lequis, I think he called himself."

"Who gave the order?"

"No one, as far as I know. We, I mean the whole Cabinet – we all agreed only yesterday that we would do nothing for now."

"Have you talked to Ebert this morning?"

"I can't reach him. No answer at his house or at the Chancellery."

"Maybe he doesn't want to be reached," mused Wolf.

"That's what I'm thinking. But maybe not. Either way it's a bad situation. Either Ebert has double-crossed his own Cabinet, or the army is in mutiny."

"What can I do for you, Hugo?"

"Tell them they're breaking the law. That they can be arrested and tried…you'll find something to threaten them with."

"But you can do that, Hugo."

"Maybe. But the more of us, the stronger we look. Anyway, I don't know who else to call. Can you come down right away?"

"I guess so. But there's no way I can get there before eight. It's almost that now."

"Just hurry."

Wolf pulled on a jacket, patted the dog, and left to warm up the car. In the cold weather that took a few minutes, so he surprised himself by arriving in downtown Berlin by eight-twenty.

The streets were quiet as he cruised east across the city core, heading for the tiny island in the middle of the River Spree where the Schloss was located. He noticed the pedestrians with their collars turned up and scarves wrapped around their necks against the icy wind, their breath drifting upward in the cold morning air. The buildings had light coverings of frost, and snow remained on the ground, although there had not been a fresh fall in days.

Boom!

Wolf flinched and the car quivered. The sound of cannon, from the general direction of the Schloss. He noticed he wasn't alone in his surprise. Pedestrians peered over their shoulders towards the Schloss. Some hurried away, in the opposite direction of the noise; others, more inquisitive, hurried towards it. The area was aquiver with anticipation: would there be fighting between the army and the Reds?

As he approached the island, the traffic thickened. Empty troop and artillery transports littered the way; on the island itself, the approaches to the Schloss were choked with civilians and soldiers.

Wolf abandoned the car and hurried on foot towards the sound of shouting. He rounded the corner to the front of the huge castle, and at once encountered a huge army deployment: troops with cannon, howitzers, and some smaller munitions. A heavy, odorous smoke wafted through the air, though the cause he couldn't see. Then he caught sight of Schloss itself.

Wolf stopped dead in his tracks, and gasped aloud. The massive wooden doors had been blown clean off the cavernous front entrance. That much was obvious. They were lying in shattered pieces on the ground. Great splinters hung from the huge iron hinges still attached to the building itself. Cannon had been used, and now a gaping, smoking hole stared back at him from the front of the palace.

"You there!"

A trooper poked a bayonet in his direction.

"Stop! This area is restricted!"

"I'm looking for Hugo Haase. I am here officially," he replied, flipping his wallet quickly open to a Chancery identity card, and then withdrawing it before the soldier had a chance to examine it. He moved forward quickly, leaving the trooper standing, and threaded his way through to the front line, where he stared briefly across a small no-man's-land to a line of civilians massed in front of the debris-strewn entrance to the Schloss. Out in front of the army line, 20 feet forward and facing the crowd, was a heavy-set officer atop a black stallion. A sword pointed skyward from his right hand, while his left held the reins.

Wolf stood speechless as he caught sight of Hugo Haase standing eye to eye with the horse. Emil Barth, his cabinet colleague, stood beside him. Wolf blinked, shook his head, and hurried across the open space, cautiously skirting the horse and approaching his friends from the rear.

The officer looked down on Wolf; the horse acknowledged him by flaring its nostrils.

"Wolf, finally! Tell him. Tell this, *soldier*," Hugo Haase spat it out, "that he can't do this. It's illegal! He can be arrested for it!"

The general looked down at Wolf, who stared back. Through both their minds ran the same thought: who the hell was going to climb up there and arrest him?

"What is going on here, Hugo," Wolf replied. "Who are all these people," he added, glancing at the crowd gathered behind them.

"They're all brave citizens who rushed here to stop a massacre of the sailors inside!"

Wolf looked at the Schloss, at the open archway where people massed solidly; and there way behind them, the sailors gathered far back in the entrance hall itself, cautiously peering out, fearful lest they make themselves easy prey for a sharpshooter.

"The General here is proposing to clear the entrance, one way or another, so that his troops can go in after the sailors," Hugo Haase continued. "He wants a bloodbath!"

Wolf looked up at the bulky figure on the horse again.

"It might be nice if you stepped down to talk to us, Herr General. What is your name?"

"My name's Lequis, commander of the Berlin garrison. You'd do well to remember me."

Newly appointed. Wolf didn't recognize him.

"General, my name is Wolf Warburg, and I am counsel for the government. What's the problem here?"

"There is no problem. I have my orders directly from General Gröner."

"That mutinous dog," Emil Barth exclaimed.

The general's horse nudged forward, almost trampling Barth. Wolf grabbed the horse's bit and turned the animal aside.

"Maybe you should check with your Cabinet colleagues," Lequis snarled. "Perhaps they've been lying to you. I have my orders from Gröner, and Hindenburg himself."

"You're lying," Haase exploded. "I order you to pull back your troops!"

Lequis smiled.

"I receive my orders through military chain of command. Your colleagues will have to talk to my superiors. But I don't think they're going to have time."

With that he turned to his troops.

"You'll be the scapegoat for this," snapped Wolf. "Ebert and Gröner will both blame you!"

At that the general paused. What Wolf said was plausible.

Wolf quickly turned to Haase.

"Get the crowd to move in closer," he whispered. "Right up to the troops."

"Citizens!" Haase turned and shouted. "These troops mean to attack and kill our brothers who have taken refuge in the palace. Have we overthrown the Kaiser only to have the generals rule us?"

The crowd hesitated at first, not knowing what to do. It was the German Wehrmacht that Haase urged them to challenge, the remnants of the mighty army that had almost conquered all Europe, and took the whole world to wrestle to the ground. In the Kaiser's day it would be unthinkable for commonfolk to challenge such power – they knew they would be crushed.

Then, in silence, one old man in an old black suit shuffled slowly forward. He had no tie, but he had dignity. He moved slowly at first, on his own, towards the army lines. Then an old woman followed, in a long coat with a kerchief wrapped round her head to blunt the wind. She might have been his wife. A young soldier, sweat beading down his face, clicked the bolt on his rifle. The sound jarred the otherwise silent scene. The man paused – then moved forward again. And then other civilians followed. Involuntarily at first, they were drawn by the brave boldness of the old man's gesture. Very slowly and very deliberately, the mass of citizens moved towards the army lines.

General Lequis sat aghast, high atop his mount. Then he shook his head free, and raised the sword in his right hand over his head.

"Troops – take aim!"

Wolf leaped forward.

"Think carefully, Lequis," he shouted. "If you fire on these people, you'll hang in effigy!"

The general looked down at Wolf, then sneered contemptuously and looked to his troops.

"Ready!"

Wolf pulled a gun and pointed at him.

"If you bring that sword down, General, it'll be the last thing you do."

The general hesitated, his sword high in the air, ready to slash down in a signal to fire. His horse reared, straining to go forward as he held it back. General Lequis was nervous. He felt the pressure in his head building, and sounds increasing, like a steamwhistle warning that a boiler is about to explode. He had to make a decision: to order the troops to attack, the cannon to explode in the crowd – or to stand down.

In the past, protests had been broken, the protestors killed, arrested or chased away. Though the mighty Wehrmacht had been chased out of France by the Allies, it still asserted cohesion and authority at home. But at this watershed moment for the infant German republic, the merest and meekest – old men and women yet – were standing in open defiance. Surely the army must bat them down. And if not, what then? Optimists saw democracy; pessimists only chaos. Being a pessimist, General Lequis now felt horror should the army abdicate its authority.

But he never gave the signal to fire. Paradoxically, his decision avoided chaos. For that day, at least.

The troops wavered, their demeanour and confidence visibly shattered; and then – in what seemed like the very next instant – the braver protestors enveloped them, hugged them, grabbed their guns and tore off their badges of rank. The rest of the crowd right away followed suit, and the army lines crumbled. Chatter and laughter swelled through the crowd.

"Wait! Stand your positions! I order you to hold your posts!"

Too late now, General Lequis turned to rage, his face beet-red, his sword arm still held high in the air. But his bellowing was useless. His troops could not hear him above the din; and none would have obeyed if they could. Even their commanders were now melting off into the crowd.

"Give it up, General," shouted Wolf, putting his gun back in his jacket. "Don't you know when you're done?"

Lequis looked down, contempt splashed across his face.

"You think this is good?" he yelled back at Wolf. "Don't you know you're just helping the Reds?"

Wolf thought for a moment. "It's not that simple," he finally replied.

"It is to me," said the General. He then lowered his sword and put it back in its scabbard. "The Reds have taken over Russia, and now you'd hand them Germany."

All around, troops melted away. Without further words, General Lequis turned his steed around and rode slowly through the disorganized throng, back through the remnants of his vanished brigade.

Wolf stood there watching in amazement. Hugo Haase stood at his side, observing the square as it slowly cleared of both soldiers and civilians. Wolf noticed again the smoky odour, rising from the smouldering remnants of the castle gates. He thought how ironic it was that the pitiful shattered remains themselves seemed to personify

Germany itself at that moment. Not having suffered enough in the world war, Germans would now tear the country apart fighting amongst themselves. The war after the war.

"What just happened," he asked his companion.

"It seems we were successful," replied Haase.

But at what price?

More than a few hardy households were lighting holiday candles at the end of 1918, the first Christmas season at peace in five years. The streets of Dahlem glittered as well. Some houses sported reindeer, sleighs and elves on their lawns, to the delight of the passers by, and the appreciative smiles of neighbours in warm boots and fur coats, walking freshly groomed dogs or children. The affluent suburb southwest of Berlin had a light, fluffy covering of snow to complete the mood. Strolling along the sidewalk a couple blocks from his own Victorian-style abode, Wolf turned into No. 5 Haberlandstrasse, an upper scale apartment building.

"Hello, Elsa," he said, as the door opened to admit him. A pleasant looking woman about his own age, with light brown hair tied in a bun, smiled as he entered.

"Where's Albert?"

"In the living room waiting for you. He wants to hear all about your adventures at the Schloss."

Wolf made his way down the hall and entered a comfortable room with walls papered in dark green. On one wall hung a portrait of Frederick the Great. A bust of Schiller stared across the room at a similar bust of his mentor, Goethe. Comfortable older furniture strewn with books and magazines, pillows and a blanket, filled the room. Einstein was seated in an oversize stuffed chair that looked immensely inviting, while on the antique sofa beside him sat Count Rantzau.

"Hello, Wolf," acknowledged his host. "Ulrich has paid a special trip over this evening, just to hear your tale."

"On Christmas Eve yet. I'm honoured."

"I imagined you would be," Rantzau replied with a smile.

Wolf sat down in a large old chair across from Einstein and the Count. Elsa handed him a cocktail, and he commenced to recount the morning's events. Count Rantzau soaked it all in.

"Your account is much better than any I've heard today," he told Wolf after the latter had concluded his tale. "General Loquis provided us with a much different story. And Hugo Haase wasn't around to challenge him. It seems that Hugo doesn't trust his Cabinet colleagues right now."

That came as a surprise to no one.

"What does it mean when imperial German troops turn tail and flee from unarmed civilians," Wolf mused.

Rantzau didn't wait long to reply.

"It means that the quality of German troops has sorely declined. I can't imagine a German military unit breaking ranks and running from anything. This was rabble."

"You don't think it's possible that the troops finally saw the light," countered Einstein. "That they decided there was already enough killing during the war?"

"No. To them the people supporting the sailors are traitors. Or at least they'd think so if the officers had had time to prep them. No, this sounds like the work of a rookie battalion. Unfortunately it only confirms what General Gröner has been saying: we have no reliable troops to put down an attempted coup by the Reds."

"I think Ulrich's right," agreed Wolf. "Among the troops was my cousin Max's boy, Eric. He came up to me after it was all over, scared as a rabbit among coyotes. The crowd had taken his helmet and rifle. He didn't know where to go or what to do. He's only eighteen; it was his first engagement. When he was called up earlier this year, before the war ended, he had no idea he'd be hoisting his bayonet against German civilians the day before Christmas."

"Where is he," asked Elsa.

"I put him on a train back to Hamburg. He's likely home by now."

Home for Eric was the magnificent Warburg estate at Kösterberg, overlooking the Elbe River on the outskirts of Hamburg.

"I've heard of Max," said Elsa. "He's got some brothers, too? And they're all bankers, aren't they?"

"Yes. Max, in Hamburg, is one of the most prominent in Germany. But that's partly due to his Wall Street connections. His brothers Paul and Felix are both New York bankers with partnerships in Kuhn Loeb, a top-tier firm there. Paul even sat on the board of the Federal Reserve, their central bank, so to speak."

"Isn't Kuhn Loeb the firm Jacob Schiff controls," asked Rantzau.

Schiff had been a high profile, powerful presence on Wall Street for a quarter century. He'd also stepped occasionally into international politics, particularly concerning Russia, which was where Rantzau knew him from.

"Yes, that's right," confirmed Wolf. "Felix married Schiff's daughter. It gets pretty convoluted, though. Schiff himself had married Solomon Loeb's daughter. Years later, actually it was just a few months after Felix's wedding, his brother Paul married Loeb's much younger daughter Nina. So Paul is actually Schiff's brother-in-law while Felix is his son-in-law."

"And that makes Paul and Felix in-laws as well as brothers," chuckled Einstein. "Weird. Are there any Loeb females left for you?"

"There's still only one woman I'm interested in," Wolf replied dejectedly, his features drooping.

"And have you spoken to Liesl today," asked Elsa, smiling sympathetically.

"I called her at the hotel, but she hasn't called back," replied Wolf. "Isn't she supposed to be attending Fritz's for Christmas dinner tomorrow?"

"Fritz is out of town at the moment. Didn't you know," asked Einstein.

Wolf shook his head.

"Yes, the talk around the Institute is that he was scared of being arrested as a war criminal and paraded through Paris. There were Allied investigators poking around the Institute just before he left. And no one really believes that he's gone off to see a sick relative."

"Any idea where he is?"

"They say Switzerland."

"Makes sense," said Rantzau. "I heard that Ludendorff grew a beard and started wearing sunglasses in the last days of the war, and that's how he escaped to Sweden. Do you think our illustrious Haber grew a beard and put on dark glasses," he asked, chortling.

"I'm sure Fritz will be back by next week," Wolf stated with certainty. "Can you remember the last time he missed his own New Year's Eve party?"

Der Kaiser's Legacy

"Elsa, it's so nice to see you again," Charlotta Haber greeted her as she and Albert entered the house. Elsa was Einstein's cousin and constant companion.

"And you," Elsa replied. "How's the old goat," she asked jokingly.

Charlotta was at least twenty years younger than her husband. She had been a hostess at his private club before his first wife's suicide.

"Fritz is always fine on New Years Eve."

"How was Zurich? Albert is taking me there next month when he goes."

Einstein wandered off down the hall in search of his host. A few minutes later Wolf arrived.

"Wolf, come over here," Fritz Haber called as he spotted him, their spat forgotten. "Albert needs our advice. He is still waffling over the terms of his divorce. He needs to get it over and done with. That's what I keep telling him."

"Well, Mileva is willing to wrap up the settlement if I agree that she will receive the prize money if I'm ever awarded a Nobel."

"She's an astute lady, Albert. She could live quite nicely for years on that."

"True enough, Wolf. But what if I don't win? Anyway, I want it all settled before I leave for Zurich at the end of the month."

Albert Einstein didn't love anything about Berlin except Lake Havel in the Grunewald Forest, just west of Dahlem, where he liked to sail. What kept him there was the incredible concentration of scientific talent in fields related to his. The Kaiser, a dinosaur in so many ways, was visionary when it came to supporting applied science, like his sponsorship of his namesake institutes in Dahlem. The

Nobel Prizes were instituted in 1901, and from then until 1933 Germans received thirty percent, more than any other country. Of those, German Jews won nearly a third, and in medicine it was half.

In the large formal living room were a number of professors from the Institute and the University. Max Planck was seated on the sofa. His discoveries were the basis of quantum mechanics which, along with Einstein's *Relativity*, were the twin pillars of 20th century physics. Formal, well dressed, with rimless glasses, in 1906 he had been the first prominent scientist to divine Einstein's genius. In the next few years he lobbied to have him offered a position in Berlin. In 1913 Planck finally made him an offer he couldn't refuse: full professorship at the university, Director of Theoretical Physics at the Kaiser Wilhelm Institute, and a seat at the Prussian Academy of Science. They were all well paid positions.

By limiting his lecture time and concentrating on solitary research, by 1916 Einstein had expanded his Special Theory of Relativity, published in 1905, into the General Theory. In doing so, it explained what gravity is, replacing the classical theory of Isaac Newton.

"What do you hear of the eclipse tests, Albert," Planck asked.

"Not much. Eddington's had no direct contact with me. I've never spoken to the man."

"Who is he?"

"An Englishman, an astronomer with the Royal Astrological Society. Since that debacle in 1914, when our team got stranded in Russia when war broke out and couldn't get photos of the eclipse, this will be the first attempt."

"Too bad it's not a German team that's going to prove you a wunderkind," drawled Haber.

"Makes no difference to me. In fact, no one has to verify it. There's no doubt in my mind that it's correct."

"When's the eclipse," asked Planck.

"The end of May."

"Where are they going to take the photos from?"

"Two locations, both somewhere near the equator, where the eclipse will be full," continued Einstein.

"So tell me what the tests will prove."

"Quite simply, that light has weight, and that its path is affected by the mass of large objects," replied Einstein. "That Relativity theory is valid.

"Do you think the public will understand?"

"Well, they will understand one thing," Haber interjected. "That Newton has been toppled from his throne by a German. The English will not lightly accept it."

"But that's the beauty of the laws of nature," said Wolf. "They always prove irresistible in the end."

"Politics are for the present, but an equation is something for eternity," declared Einstein.

"Tell that to the British," replied Haber. "They may still be too hostile to surrender anything to a German."

He looked at Einstein, who was about to answer him back, and said, "It won't do any good to blame me, Albert. That's just the way it is."

By 1916, his stature ever growing as inventor of a method which vastly increased German production of nitrates for both food fertilizer and explosives, and as director of the Kaiser Wilhelm Institutes, and himself possessed of a burning desire to aid his country in the war effort, Fritz Haber became head of the Chemical Warfare Service, which under his personal guidance produced mustard gas in 1917. Haber introduced Phosgene as the poison gas agent. It was more toxic than Prussic acid. A single inhalation was lethal. Green-cross and blue-cross gases were both mustard gases. Blue-cross was a strong irritant and could partially penetrate gas masks; green-cross was a typical poison gas. When combined, it would force the soldier to tear off his mask, and then be exposed to the poison gas.

Germany claimed the British were the first to use poison gas, and the Brits say it was the Germans. In any event the victors sought out Fritz Haber as a war criminal, although never prosecuted. Of all the Nobel prizes awarded, Haber's was the only ever contested. The French Nobel winners refused their awards at the end of 1919 when Haber received his. But there was other fallout personally to Haber from his involvement in the poison gas program. His first wife, Clara, committed suicide because he wouldn't get out of it.

Wolf left the huge living room and wandered towards the rear of the house. He had heard a rumour that Liesl was somewhere to be found. Strolling into the den he found Count Rantzau in conversation.

"Hello, Wolf, I'm glad you're here. There's someone I want you to meet. Well, you may already have. This is Gustav Noske," the Count said, nodding to the man beside him.

Noske, a barrel shaped man about five foot ten, with a balding head and a large, walrus mustache, grasped Wolf's hand in his own. It was big and Wolf noticed the solid grip. Noske was a former Social Democratic member of the Reichstag. When serious Red anarchy broke out in some of the Baltic ports at the end of the war, the new government sent him to restore order and prevent a communist coup. He was successful.

"I heard you were back in town, Gustav. You've come to restore order to Berlin, no doubt."

"Someone must be the bloodhound of the revolution, and I am prepared to do it. I know I won't be loved, but I can live with it. Let's not forget that those damned sailors are still holding Otto Wels."

The past week had seen a flurry of events. After the troops at the Schloss broke and fled the day before Christmas, crowds surrounded the Chancellery demanding Ebert's resignation. A couple of days after Christmas, Hugo Haase and the other leftist members of the Cabinet resigned, believing that Ebert had double-crossed them and ordered the attack on the Schloss. The remaining Cabinet, afraid to be seen in public, took to meeting in secret. The first order of business was to call Gustav Noske back to Berlin.

"Hugo Haase tells me he intends to run against Ebert in the election next month," Wolf related to Noske and the Count. "He doesn't intend to join the Communists, though he says he can't speak for all his supporters."

As 1918 ended Rosa Luxemburg and Karl Liebknecht led the formation of the German Communist Party, and many of Haase's supporters did indeed migrate there.

"Did you hear Karl Radek hollering from up top of the Brandenburg Gate today," asked Noske. "He was exhorting the workers to fight a decisive battle along with the Red armies of Russia against capitalist oppression in Germany! He's inciting an armed coup against the government, and we can't even silence him! We've no reliable troops."

"But you intend to do something about that," asked Wolf, already knowing the answer.

"Rest assured, mein herr," replied Noske, stroking his massive mustache with his left forefinger.

Wolf left the group, and nursing a cocktail wandered about hoping to run into Liesl. Passing the doorway to Haber's library, he glimpsed long, light, blonde, flowing hair surrounding a familiar face.

"Hella?"

If she was here, Liesl had to be close by. Wolf ambled into the room. Hella von Westarp was Liesl's closest friend. They had known each other since childhood. She was from an old Munich family. Her brother Kuno was a politician, a leader in the Conservative party. Wolf had run into him a few times in the last couple of years, Kuno supporting the Kaiser and Wolf opposing the war.

"Countess, you're looking radiant this evening."

"Charming as ever, Wolf," Hella replied. "How nice to see you."

She was appalled by Wolf's pacifist tendencies, but liked the man nonetheless. It was more that she couldn't understand him, because she knew he was no coward.

"The Countess von Westarp is present. Fräulein von Schlieffen must be close by," Wolf said hopefully.

A waitress dressed in a short French maid outfit came into the room carrying a tray full of glasses.

"Midnight approaches. Champagne?"

At that moment Liesl walked into the room on Einstein's arm.

Wolf melted inside when he saw her. She was dressed in a beige chiffon evening gown, low cut in the chest. It was eerily similar to the gown she had worn at the Münchener's Ball when she and Wolf had first met a decade before. He had never forgotten that night, and the feel and aroma of her soft auburn hair as his tongue brushed against her ears, for he swore later that that was when he had first fallen in love with her. Their paths had been star-crossed. Though they had a torrid affair for a year, it was already in Wolf's mind to move to Berlin for awhile. For four years they conducted a long-distance love affair. But through her work as a journalist she managed to spend time in Berlin, and Wolf came back frequently to Munich.

Hella von Westarp, Liesl's best friend, had been there from the beginning. She had been at the ball when Wolf and Liesl first met. And she had been there for Liesl when Wolf moved away a year later. She had supported Liesl when, after Wolf obtained his transfer from the Front a year into the war, Liesl refused to speak to him anymore. Now another four years had passed.

Midnight arrived amidst cheers, whistles, and New Year's resolutions.

"How are you, Wolf," Liesl said casually, almost disdainfully, as they stood together. "So nice to see you here," she added rather icily.

"Are you really glad to see me?"

"No," she replied quickly. "You shouldn't even be allowed in the country."

It all seemed involuntary. She acted towards him the exact opposite of how she felt.

As for Wolf, his eyes moistened, and a miserable expression crossed his face.

"You're right. I see I shouldn't have come this evening," he said slowly, his voice breaking. "It hurts too much. I need to forget you."

He couldn't look at her. Eyes downward, head drooped, he turned to leave the library. Liesl responded instantly. Without hesitation, she caught him by the shoulder and pulled him around. She threw her arms around his neck, pulled his face to hers, and kissed him passionately. Then just as suddenly she pulled away. Wolf stood in shock, a dazed look splayed across his face, as she turned and strode quickly from the room.

* * *

Every time he thought about it he could taste the bile. That common soldiers and civilian rabble should dare lay their hands not just on him, that was bad enough, but on the general himself. That was outrageous! And though Schleicher was actually of the new school, the pride of the German General Staff raged through his veins. Major Schleicher was recalling the trip back from Staff headquarters a couple days before the armistice. That was the first indignity: travelling by public train. But most of the German rolling stock was at the frontier. So they had been forced to travel by ordinary means to Berlin for their meeting with the chancellor, Prince Max of Baden. The general and he were minding their own business when drunken scum burst into their compartment, attacking the general himself, trying to tear his epithets from his uniform. Gröner, more amazed than hurt, his face beet-red, sputtered that he'd have them all shot. But Schleicher then drew his revolver and fired a shot out the window, and the motley crew retreated from the berth.

Sitting now astride his horse, on January 3rd in the new year at Dahlem, in a large field within sight of the Kaiser Wilhelm Institutes, he vowed, not for the first time, that the army's place and dignity would be restored. Insulting officers would again be a crime for all Germans.

"I say, Schleicher, did you hear the Minister?"

"I'm sorry, sir, what was that?"

"You're daydreaming, Major," said his mounted companion. "Is it about the armies we managed to bring back intact from France to Berlin, and march through the Brandenburg Tor, only to then be forced to disperse them?"

"And where are they now, when we need them to fight the Reds?"

"We all sympathize, Major," said Gustav Noske, the new Minister of Public Safety and Defence, seated in the touring car parked next to them. "But who could have known that Liebknecht and those other fanatics would behave so recklessly. Nothing will satisfy them but a Red dictatorship."

"We are all moderates here," General Gröner replied with a sly smile. "So tell me, Herr Minister, how do you like our first Free Corps? Will such as these save your Republic?"

Noske surveyed the marching columns spread over the open field before them, stroked his thick walrus mustache first on one side, then on the other, before replying.

"I am most impressed, General. They appear well drilled, precise in movement. You see what sure grips they have on their weapons! General, do you have any doubts about your ability to retake control of the city streets, and without much bloodshed? We don't want a bunch of citizens killed. That would only play into the Reds' hands."

"Herr Minister, there is no doubt that troops such as General Märcker's Free Corps here can crush those amateurs," Gröner replied. "As to how many might be injured in the process, that is hard to predict. It is up to Liebknecht and his Red provocateurs, and how much they are able to involve the public."

"You really must do something about those fanatics, Noske," Schleicher interjected. "You underestimate them, and we'll see that second revolution here."

"So what would you have me do, Major?"

"Let us go after them. We've got fanatics of our own who will root out the Reds quickly enough."

"Oh, I'm sure you do, Major," Noske replied wryly. But he managed to put aside his misgivings, and said, "Tell me more."

Following the armistice a few commanders, with the assistance of large landowners or industrialists seeking to protect their property, had secretly kept intact some of the battalions. They supplemented these with more men and weapons, including tanks and even planes. Not being under government scrutiny, the units were easily broken down and hidden from the Allies. It was Schleicher's idea to use Free Corps to back up what little remained of the army in Berlin.

"Schleicher, that's young Ludendorff, isn't it," asked Gröner, pointing across the field. "What's he doing here?"

"It looks like he's with Captain Canaris. But as I recall, his name is Heinz Pernet. He's the General's stepson. There were three of them. Two were killed in the war."

"Ah, yes, that's right. Both pilots, weren't they? Fetch him here."

Pernet rode up accompanied by a naval officer and a captain of the Horse Guards unit.

"General," said Schleicher, "I think you know Captain Canaris. Minister, the Captain here is the chief liaison between the army and the Free Corps units regarding the joint operation to re-establish order in Berlin."

They greeted each other, and then Noske eyed the other officer.

"Captain, what is your position," asked Noske.

"Chief of Operations of the army Guards unit stationed a few miles southwest of here in Potsdam, Minister."

"Heinz, what do you hear from your father? How is he," Gröner cut in.

"He's still in Sweden." Heinz paused, then went on, "But he seems to be wrestling with demons from the war still. He says he's got to return to Germany to fight our true enemies."

"And they are," asked Gustav Noske.

"Reds, Bolsheviks, Jews..."

A month before the war ended, Ludendorff was finally dismissed from co-command of the Wehrmacht, which he had ruled together with Hindenburg. And if Ludendorff was the true genius of the two, he was also, by the last year of the war, the crazed fanatic. Partly deranged, he believed in ancient German warrior gods, and raged at Jesuits, the Catholic Church, international Jewry, Reds, and capitalist materialism.

With Ludendorff fired, Hindenburg bore sole command, and hence sole responsibility, which was not to his liking. So he had Gröner appointed the new Quartermaster-General; and the first task Hindenburg saddled him with was to break the news to the Kaiser that he must abdicate.

The knock on the Kaiser's door came on November 9th, 1918.

"Yes, Gröner, what is it now? I still won't agree to it."

"You should have a seat, All-Highest. I have bad news."

"Well, spit it out," Wilhelm barked.

"All-Highest. Prince Max informed me a few minutes ago that he had no choice. He had to make the announcement."

"What do you mean?"

"All-Highest. For the good of the nation, to avoid bloodshed and revolution, he has announced your abdication."

Wilhelm was stunned. He couldn't breathe for a moment, like the air had been sucked out of him. He reached out for the desk with his left, gimpled arm, which nearly collapsed under him. Gröner hurried over and helped him to a chair.

"How, how…"

"For the good of nation," Gröner repeated. And repeated.

"You had no right," argued the ex-Kaiser.

"It is done, All-Highest, and cannot be called back. You must now consider your own safety."

"What do you mean?"

"Is it safe for you to remain in Germany, All-Highest? The new government, when it is appointed, will be looking for a scapegoat to blame the war on. And the army may not be in a position to protect you."

He had become Kaiser at age 29 when his father died young, and the most powerful army in the world personally pledged him allegiance. He reigned pompously and passionately for three decades, surrendering little power to the elected Reichstag. And he constantly pressed the Russian Tsar, Nicholas, to follow the same course.

That was the image Adolf Hitler saw and admired, even with its blemishes, as a child growing up. It was German martial might with a strong leader. Something Austria was sorely lacking, he ruminated.

Tsar Nicholas was forced to abdicate in 1917; a year later, it was Wilhelm's turn. Within hours of Gröner breaking the news to him, his train pulled up to the Dutch frontier where he formally presented his sword to the border patrol and requested asylum. The guard was so surprised he didn't know how to respond. The Kaiser would please wait while he sought instructions. So began the permanent exile of the last King of Prussia.

Friedrich Ebert was the leader of the Social Democratic Party of Germany, the largest in the Reichstag. Prince Max, the last Chancellor appointed by the Kaiser, named Ebert Chancellor immediately after the Kaiser abdicated, calling upon him to form an interim government to sign the armistice with the Allies, and then frame a constitution and hold elections. On November 11th, 1918, the armistice took effect, ending the war. Ebert was working in his office in the chancellery late that night when a telephone rang that he had trouble locating at first.

"Hello. Who is this?"

"General Gröner. I am calling from Staff headquarters. To whom am I speaking?"

"This is Friedrich Ebert."

"Herr Ebert. Good. I am calling on a secure line. Let me get to the point. In these troubled times, the General Staff wishes you to know that the Wehrmacht will support your new government against Rosa Luxemburg and the Red rabble which threaten you. We require assurances, however, that you intend to fight Communism."

"But of course, General…"

"That you will not betray us later, and give in to the Reds as they did in Russia."

"I can assure you, General…"

"Then you have our support."

* * *

The Reds more or less controlled the streets of Berlin as 1918 ended and the new year began, just over a month and a half since the end of the war. It was not possible to keep completely hidden from them the huge military buildup going on in the Berlin suburbs and outside the city, so their leadership knew that a test of strength was near. Street fighting began in Berlin as the Reds moved to strengthen their control of the downtown core. Karl Liebknecht, anticipating the showdown to come, without the knowledge of Rosa Luxemburg or the rest of the Central Committee formed a Revolutionary Council to direct the armed overthrow of the Ebert government.

Berlin police headquarters was on the Alexanderplatz, a town square two blocks east of the imperial Schloss, on the other side of the Spree River from the Unter den Linden. Across the square from the police station was city hall, the Berlin Rathaus, and on the afternoon of January 6th, key members of the Central Committee were meeting in the mayor's top floor office, which they had appropriated for 'purposes of the revolution'.

"You had no right, Karl! This matter involves us all. We aren't going to take over the government by force. The people must want us!"

"Do you think they'll just hand over power to us, woman? You're mad if you do," Liebknecht replied, pacing the floor, glancing out the window at the crowds in the square below. "The people have to march and take power. And it looks like they're ready to do it!"

Karl Liebknecht was about five ten, with dark brown hair and a full, well-manicured beard to match. He was dressed in a dark, well-worn, three-piece suit and tie.

"You want a civil war?" Rosa yelled back. "Because that's what you'll get. German killing German."

"And what of it," asked Karl Radek, seated in a chair against the far wall. "You're not even German."

Radek, a lean figure, sported a black goatee under a black sailors cap. His black leather jacket looked quite new. With his dark, devious eyes it all made him look rather devilish.

"And that makes the killing okay?" she shot back. "You're just spouting what Lenin wants you to, anyway. Wolf Warburg was right. All of us here know truly whose words you speak."

"Warburg? That capitalist wolf in sheep's clothing? We must act now," intoned Karl Radek. "Look at the size of those crowds! I can't see the end of them."

The previous day the Central Committee had plastered posters around the city calling for a demonstration the next day, a Sunday, to protest against Ebert's government. There was much to complain about, what with the continuing shortage of food and heating fuel due to the continuing Allied blockade, the unemployment brought about by the end of the war, and the extra half million refugees and former soldiers in the city looking for food, shelter, and work. Sunday dawned clear and cold, and crowds began to gather around the Rathaus in the early morning. By mid-morning, Karl and his cohorts found that the rally was exceeding expectations, the massive throng stretching west all the way to the Schloss.

"There are so many out there that only those in the square can hear the bullhorn," Liebknecht exulted. "Now is our time. We must take advantage and march on the Chancellery and the Reichstag today. Now!"

"No," thundered Rosa, rising from her chair behind the mayor's desk. "I'll not have blood on my hands. I won't start a civil war, with mass killing like we hear coming out of Russia now."

"This is unprecedented," said Wolf as he surveyed the scene from the lobby of the Adlon Hotel, near the western end of the Unter den Linden, a long block away from the Brandenburg Gate. "There must be fifty thousand people out there."

"Now aren't you glad that I called you down here," asked Count Rantzau, looking out on the street with him. People continued to gather, spreading ever farther west down the Unter den Linden, past the Crown Prince's Palace and the Armoury, the Tomb of the Unknown Soldier and the State Opera House, past Humboldt University.

"They're past the statue of King Fritz now," observed Rantzau.

"The Cabinet must be terrified," commented Wolf. "Not that they shouldn't have expected it."

"No. But we're not strong enough yet to challenge the Reds. Just look at all their supporters! What's to stop them from marching on the Chancellery? Noske says he needs a couple days more."

Still the crowd grew. By mid-afternoon, it sprawled relentlessly down the Unter den Linden, crossing the Friedrichstrasse, spilling past Wolf and the Count at the Adlon Hotel. And still the imperial avenue continued to fill, the crowd surging west past the British Embassy and the Interior Ministry. By dinner they had enveloped the Brandenburg Gate itself, continuing west into the Tiergarten, the former royal hunting preserve, now a huge park. A block to the north of the gate, the crowd surrounded the Reichstag; to the south, down the Wilhelmstrasse and in the distance, the human sea circled the Chancellery itself, inside of which the government leaders cowered in fear.

"I tell you, there's over a hundred thousand people out there," exulted Karl Liebknecht from his perch on the balcony of the Rathaus, over a mile to the east.

"You can't see them all from here," Karl Radek noted. "There may be twice that number. It's the largest crowd this city's ever seen."

"We must storm the Chancellery," yelled Liebknecht as he stepped back inside.

"No!" Rosa still would not budge. "We will not take over the government by force. Over my dead body!"

Radek looked at her with a sly smile. "It won't be us who shoots you, my dear Rosa. Ebert and that new goon of his, Noske, that's who'll put a bullet in your back."

1919

Trench Warfare

> This preservation of favourable individual differences and variations and the destruction of those which are injurious, I have called *Natural Selection*, or the *Survival of the Fittest.*
>
> - Charles Darwin

"I'm just another casualty of the war. I've been brutalized by four years of killing people, where life is worth no more than vermin. In an instant I would kill a few more now, if it was for a good cause."

The woman appeared shocked. But when the other men at the table, veterans themselves, murmured approval, her expression softened.

"But aren't you tired of all the killing by now?"

"I was tired of the sawdust dinners and eating rats and cats, of living for months in a wooden dugout in a trench, of cold and wet. Of trench foot and trench mouth and trench fever and trench rot. I didn't like being gassed. But I could go on killing. Yes I could. It's the easiest thing in the world now. All I have to do is pull a trigger. But don't get me wrong," the soldier added after a momentary pause. "I don't look forward to more killing for the sake of killing. I'm not so far gone as that – except where the enemy is concerned. No, I wouldn't be at all squeamish about gutting all of them."

"But the war is over. So there isn't an enemy anymore."

And at that last remark by the waitress, the entire table burst into laughter.

"And the Kaiser reigns in Berlin! Sure," muttered Sgt. Max Amann. "Are you about ready to head back to the barracks, Adolf," he asked the first soldier, the one who had been speaking.

"Yes, anytime."

"And how about you, my dear fräulein, can we escort you somewhere?"

"No, another time, perhaps. But you boys go straight home, no raping and pillaging along the way, just because you miss the war. You mind me."

They left the Gasthaus and turned north along the Türkenstrasse heading in the direction of the barracks. Ernie Schmidt, Adolf's wartime buddy, strolled with them. They had been through thick and thin together, both among the handful of soldiers of their brigade who originally signed up in 1914 to have survived the war. Max Amann was their sergeant.

It was December 1918, in a cold Munich winter. The sergeant turned up the collar on his overcoat, and leaned over to speak to his companion.

"Adolf, there's a few of us getting together again on Wednesday night. Come along."

"Well, if you think I should."

"Yes. I enjoy hearing your views. Where did you go to school?"

"I gained my education in the streets and libraries and newspapers of Vienna. And four years in the trenches: that is an education that can't be taught. The armchair soldiers at home try to understand what it's like. But the most horrible things can't be conveyed by words or pictures. How can one know what it feels like to rip a man's innards out with a bayonet just by watching someone else? You must gut the man yourself! And it's only in war that a man's true nature comes out. You can't hide at the Front. You can't just shout bravely and think that will impress people. You must put up or shut up! Cowards are quickly exposed, and you know who your true friends are."

"Not like here, that's for sure. Who can you trust," Ernie Schmidt joined in. "You can't tell a Red from a Republican. And sometimes you can't tell who's who in your own brigade. I meet pacifists and traitors in our own barracks."

"But when the Red plague has swept the country," said Hitler, "then it's too late. Under a Red dictatorship, they'll realize how they surrendered Germany."

"The war is over," asked Sgt. Amann. "Like hell it is! Not if we have anything to say about it."

The group made its way up the Türkenstrasse, past the fires in trash barrels on street corners, as derelicts and the displaced sought warmth from the winter. Past the occasional fresh corpse, not from a bullet or shrapnel, but from swine flu. Still it wasn't all bad. In the beer halls, in the stores and streets, everywhere they passed by that element so lacking at the Front: women. Women everywhere. In long, clinging negligées, and legs that ran on forever, beckoning them in for an hour's pleasure. Ernie Schmidt was positively elated.

"Let's stop for awhile," he suggested, licking his lips. "The ladies look friendly enough."

Hitler, though titillated, was disturbed and reserved. Deep memories returned, of dilapidated streets and back alleys in the olden quarter of Vienna – dark thoughts of dark places. Max Amann, practical by nature, had his mind at present squarely fixed on politics, and didn't appear to notice at all. They ignored Ernie's plea and started to trudge on. He stood for a moment, staring lustily at the curvaceous figures in the doorways and windows, torn by their siren calls.

But then he heard, "Come, Ernst. Leave these whores to the Red swine. Have some pride! You can do much better than this. You're a German soldier!"

Hitler tugged at his friend's sleeve. It was during moments like this that Hitler's quirky nature really irritated Ernie. Why did he have to be such a prig? But this wasn't new; he'd seen it before. So finally, with a shrug, he turned and ambled on after his friends.

At the barracks Ernst and Hitler made their way to their bunks, where a few soldiers were gathered in talk.

"What have you got to lose, Helmut? What property of yours would be lost to the 'collective' under Communism? It's only those that have something that should be quaking in their boots," said a soldier seated on a nearby bunk.

"But if I did get something, I wouldn't want to have to share it with everybody. I want some things for my own. I don't plan to be poor all my life," Helmut replied.

"Well, be stubborn, but the Red wave is sweeping Germany whether you like it or not."

Adolf and Ernie listened drearily to the familiar rhetoric. The same swill they had heard, at first only in whispers, for the last year.

"But the Reds aren't doing too well in Berlin, are they, my Marxist friend? Rosa and Karl and their mob. Why should we here in Munich hitch our wagons to such a band of losers," enquired Helmut.

"We aren't allying ourselves to the Berlin Reds at all," his companion, one Anton Giesbrecht, replied. "We want an independent Bavaria. Why, I'd rather be joined with Austria than continue under the yoke of the *Saupreissen* from Berlin."

Saupreissen, 'swinish Prussian', was a term of endearment by which Bavarians expressed their appreciation for having been incorporated into the German empire under Bismarck in 1871, after centuries of independence as a separate kingdom under the Wittelsbachs, a line older than the Kaiser's Hohenzollern heritage.

"Traitorous scum! Whelp of a dog," cried Hitler as he suddenly hurled himself at Giesbrecht, taking two steps before launching himself through the air and crashing into the other man's chest.

The latter was knocked to the ground with Hitler on top, raising his fist and smashing Giesbrecht several times before he was dragged off. Anton lay stunned on the floor. Ernst and Helmut held Hitler, restraining him as he raged on.

"You can insult the German army, for now. It is disgusting and corrupt and weak and lifeless. It will recover, though not with the likes of you. You can even spread your filthy Red propaganda to whoever is stupid enough to listen. But don't ever try to destroy the unity of this Reich! Don't ever try to separate one part from the other. Let Austria, country of my birth, join the Reich. But never speak of splitting Germany. Never!"

It was going to be a rough night, no doubt about it. His head was throbbing, his eyes burning around the sockets. He lay on his bunk in the dark, ruminating on the evening, seething in anger and frustration. The more aggravated Hitler was, the worse he slept. The headaches, the burning around the eyes, the raspy throat, all after-effects of the gassing, returned with a vengeance. The war haunted his dreams as he drifted off to sleep.

* * *

Hitler's mind drifted back a year, to the previous March on Western Front, and the eve of the spring offensives. He was a courier, running orders between division headquarters and various units, and he was good at it. He was proud of his reputation for bravery and dependability. He could have risen higher than a corporal just by virtue of having survived four years of war in fighting condition. But he liked his job. It kept him with his old regiment, and near headquarters where the orders came from, but also allowed him to travel constantly throughout the battle zone.

Hitler's unit was about to go into action for the first time since the previous autumn, in the campaign to end the war. The Russians had collapsed; now the British would be crushed. That is, if the Reds or the soldiers returning from the Eastern Front infected with the Lenin virus didn't cripple the war effort in the meantime. Just two months ago, the munitions workers around Berlin staged a general strike that had a terribly demoralizing effect on troops and workers. And imagine the foreign headlines: "Germany facing revolution! Victory of the Allies inevitable!" They had no appreciation of the *Reinkulter*, the pure culture of the front line soldier, a blend of bravery and brutality. He remembered the speech that Lieutenant Guttman gave them the evening before they went into battle.

"Loyal Germans, take heart. We are about to embark on the final offensive of the Great War, to drive the British into the sea and the French back to Paris. You've heard the Americans are coming? Our subs are sinking them as they cross the Atlantic. Fight on!"

The troops split off into units. Sgt. Schmidt gave his final instructions.

"We must first breach the British lines to separate them from the French, and then push them back on the Channel. With the British beat, and the Americans unable to help, the French will surrender before we destroy Paris, and the war will be over. Long live the Kaiser!"

In the spring of 1918 the German Empire was run by Generals Hindenburg and Ludendorff. Ludendorff was the planning and strategic genius while Hindenburg, recognizing the talents of the smaller man, was content to contribute his impressive appearance and reputation. While the Kaiser was the final authority in the Reich before the war, by 1917 that power was taken over by the generals. When Russia surrendered in late 1917, and the generals promised victory with a massive offensive in the spring of 1918 before America could intervene, the nation followed them.

Ludendorff, short and balding, with a mustache and monocle, had a gift for organization. His credo was to conquer quickly with great force; he didn't favour wars of attrition. He had three stepsons, all fighter pilots. Franz was killed in September 1917, shot down over the channel by a Brit.

"You can't imagine what a heavenly feeling it is when all the day's fighting is successfully over," Franz had written to his mother weeks before, "to lie in bed and say to one's self before going to sleep, `Thank God! I have another 12 hours to live.' The certainty of the thing is so pleasant."

Winston Churchill awakened just after 4 a.m. in his billet in the town of Nurlu on the Western Front on the morning of March 21st, 1918. As British Minister of Munitions, he was on an inspection tour. The day before he had met with General Haig at his headquarters in Montreuil, before visiting his old division, the 9th, under the command of General Tudor at his headquarters at Nurlu.

"We know the attack is coming. Maybe tomorrow morning, or the day after, or perhaps next week," the general said, "but it's coming."

Churchill lay thinking in his bunk. It was very quiet, except for the rumble of artillery fire in the distance. He reflected on the fact that more than half of the enemy forces, and most of their firepower, were concentrated against the British on the northern half of the Front, as opposed to the French who held the south. And the Germans had the numerical advantage on the Western Front for the first time in the war due to the forces transferred there after the Russian surrender. But they had limited time before the Americans arrived en masse, so the attack would come quickly.

He couldn't help thinking how quiet it was.

Then the silence was broken by six or seven loud, heavy explosions several miles away. He thought they were 12-inch guns, or mines. And then, within a minute, there began to build the loudest crescendo of cannon fire he had ever heard. Ludendorff had launched nearly six thousand Krupp cannon and three-quarters of a million troops on his 'final offensive'. It all concentrated upon a forty mile stretch of the Front, intending to punch a gaping hole in the British line, severing the link with the Allies to the south.

Hitler had slept little. As a dispatch courier he had been running messages to various gun emplacements, artillery and infantry divisions, since well before the German guns lit up the sky in the early morning hours. The initial bombardment lasted about four hours, a cannonade of incredible fury, accompanied by heavy discharges of mustard gas.

Then came the storm troopers. From well behind the lines these elite units came hurtling forward in trucks to front attack positions, leapt from their vehicles and headed at a run for no-mans-land at the same time as the shelling ceased. The storm units were new, having seen action for the first time the previous year in an attempt to break the four-year-old stalemate of static trench warfare. Their job was to neutralize enemy communications, lookouts and machine gunners. They wore dark, pliable clothing with reinforced knees and elbows made for crawling quickly over rough terrain; balaclavas and black toques replaced helmets. They used light submachine guns and mortars, and knives when they had to kill silently.

"Out of the way", the *stürmtruppen* shouted as Hitler was pushed aside in their rush for the front. It was over the tops of the trenches and into no-mans-land, with the German armies close behind. The effect on the British was devastating. The conflict was continuous as the British retreated for five days, falling back thirty miles. After a pause of a couple days, the Germans attacked again. Finally, the Allies refused to retreat further, for to do so would cost them their chief supply line.

"Every position must be held to the last man," ordered General Haig "With our backs to the wall and believing in the justice of our cause, each one of us must fight on to the end."

Corporal Hitler came round the corner of the trench and collided with a young, dirt-covered soldier in full retreat. He was followed by another in similar haste. Two teenaged, terrified raw recruits.

"Hold on there, soldiers, where are you going?"

"Away from the guns, they're killing everyone. We can't get by them."

"But where are you running to? The machine guns aren't following you, are they?"

"No sir, but if we stay, we'll be ordered to try to get by them again."

Hitler was disgusted.

"Cowards! You turn around and head straight back to the line. Your mates are putting their lives on the line to silence those British guns. There must be sacrifice so that the Reich may conquer."

"You do it. I've noticed how easy it is for officers to send us common soldiers forward, with no protection but our uniforms against bullets and shrapnel. How brave are the ones giving the orders?"

Hitler struck the youth across the face with the back of his hand.

"Insolent punk! Impertinent puppy! How long have you been at the Front?"

"Two months, Corporal," the unlucky recruit wailed in response.

"Then come follow me and I'll show you how it's done."

With that Hitler unshouldered his rifle and with the other arm pushed the two recruits forward in front of him towards the sound of the machine guns.

By the fourth year of the war the art of laying out machine gun positions had developed well. Fewer nests with longer, unrestricted views of the alleys which the enemy must swarm down, accompanied by advances in gun sighting, dependability and speed of fire, made it a deadly business to attempt to run at an entrenched gun. Contrasting this was the lack of shielding given the individual soldier. Generals on both sides seemed to callously order young men to run straight at machine guns firing hundreds of rounds per minute, with little more than a light helmet for protection.

Hitler had orders for the commander of the advance unit in D sector and would not be stopped from delivering them. The two recruits that he was pushing on in front of him towards the front line were whimpering audibly.

"Come, all your comrades will be proud. You'll be heroes if you live," Adolf assured the two.

That only caused them to whimper louder. The machine gun fire, with grenade and mortar explosions mixed in, was almost on top of them now. Bloodied corpses lay strewn, piled one on top of the other, on both sides of the trench as they made their way westward. Groans and occasional shrieks of pain surrounded them.

"Are you ready to run at the guns, my young friends," asked Hitler. "We are almost there. Just around the corner is the forward trench. Then I have to push on to the advance group to deliver their orders. That means I have to get by the machine gun nest that's still blocking our advance in this sector. Your brigade is trying to take that nest out right now, and you're going to help them. Understand?"

The two trembling troops nodded reluctant assents.

As they rounded the corner the sound of the machine gun reached a crescendo. A continual rapid fire rat-tat-tat with an ear-splitting decibel level was punctuated only by the screams of German soldiers as they charged the dug in, fortified British nest two hundred yards down the alley. Then they saw bodies littering the way. Comrades crawled and pulled their wounded brethren back down the alley, towards the German trenches and away from the razor fire.

"Listen to me," Hitler told his young charges, "when you're up and running, you can't stop for an instant. Delay is fatal!"

The two recruits were terrified and near sobbing.

"Snap out of it," Hitler barked at them. "When more than one person is running at them, there's more of a chance of breaking through. Or at least getting closer to the gun nest. The gunner hesitates a moment deciding who to aim for. So the three of us are going to race down that alley all at once."

He saw the horror in their eyes. Did they comprehend?

"Understand?" he shouted.

They nodded jerkily.

"Alright. Spread out. Let's keep as far apart from each other as we can. Tougher on the Brit gunners."

They slowly shuffled into position. Damn, thought Hitler. This is what I have to work with.

"On my signal, up and over," he shouted. "And I'll shoot whoever hesitates!"

He peeked up over the mound of dirt, surveying the terrain. Then he raised his arm and looked over at his companions. Bringing his hand down, he pushed himself up and over, and with a brief look sideways to confirm that both the recruits were with him, raced zigzag down the alley. Stepping over and around bodies he got some forty yards before diving behind another mound of dirt. Turning to eye his companions, he noted they were both still on their feet spread out but coming forward. One ran straight ahead, head down, stumbling over dirt and bodies before tripping and sprawling forward in a heap. The second came slower, more hesitantly.

"Dive," yelled Hitler. "Hit the ground!"

The soldier looked up at him. Then the bullets ripped across his chest in a horizontal line from one side to the other, knocking him rearward, down, dead.

The remaining recruit was about fifteen yards behind and to the right of Hitler, who motioned for him to crawl forward. The soldier, hypnotized by his friend's corpse, did not acknowledge Hitler, who shouted and shouted in vain.

Zing! Zing! – Hitler shot at the dirt a yard to the left of the soldier, who sprang away.

"Get over here now, or the next one will get you!"

The soldier was bawling so bad he couldn't see straight as he crawled towards Hitler. With machine gun bullets kicking up the dirt around him, he finally made it to Hitler's side.

"I have to get these orders through," declared Hitler. "You're going to have to draw their fire over there," he pointed right, "while I make a dash for it down the left side."

The recruit looked uncomprehending. He managed a weak "How?"

"You run over there, down the right side," he pointed to it again, "in a zigzag fashion. You want them to notice you, right?"

The soldier's jaw dropped. Make them notice him? But the crazy corporal wasn't joking. He'd shoot him if he didn't do it.

"Ready, lad," Hitler asked him.

The recruit nodded assent, but inside he was saying goodbye to his loved ones. A Lutheran, for the first time he crossed himself as his Catholic friends did. Then he looked over at Hitler, jumped up from behind the dirt, and ran zigzag diagonally up the alley towards the right hand side. After a moment, when the dirt began kicking up round the recruit's feet, Hitler dashed down the left side. Machine gun bullets momentarily strayed to the middle of the alley as the gunner instinctively swung the barrel towards Hitler. An experienced Brit, he immediately corrected and swung the barrel back in a sweeping motion. He caught the recruit across the gut, ripping his uniform apart and exposing his innards. He would run no more interference for Hitler. There were hundreds of dead Germans at this site alone. But the guns could not be overwhelmed. The Germans were mown down in heaps, and the offensive ground to a halt. Hitler survived unscathed to deliver his orders; the recruit bled slowly to death staring at his own intestines.

Two days after the launch of his 'final offensive', Ludendorff's youngest son, Erich, another fighter pilot, was shot down and killed like brother Franz.

Hitler woke in a sweat. Ernie Schmidt had hold of both arms and was shaking him.

"Adi, Adi, come out of it. You're raving. You're back in France by the sounds of it. Wake up, man! We all want to get a little sleep."

His eyes steadied, opened fully.

"I'm alright. I'm awake now. Let me be."

"Where were you, man?"

"It's like you said, Ernie. I was back in France. About to spear some Brits with my bayonet."

"Well, so long as you're alright. Pleasant dreams, then, but keep the noise down."

Hitler drifted off to sleep again, back to the spring offensives.

Once the initial battles in the north died down, the Allies spent the next month wondering where along the Front, from the English Channel all the way to the Swiss border, the next blow would fall. On the morning of May 26th a German officer and a private were captured by the French in the Aisne sector, midway along the Front. They were interrogated at the Army Corps Intelligence centre, and the results sent on to French Staff Headquarters.

Major Esterhazy descended down a circular metal staircase at headquarters. A guard stationed by the door below admitted him immediately. Dim lighting was provided by a low-wattage bulb on a fixture hanging low over a map table placed in the middle of the room.

"General Petain. Sir," he said saluting the French commander who was peering over the map table.

"What do we know, Major?"

"Well, sir, the German Lieutenant, Müller, at first denied any knowledge that an attack is planned in this or any other sector. When told that his fellow captive, Private Heydrich, still maintains that an attack is imminent, Müller said that Heydrich will say anything if you just promise to feed him enough."

"So what exactly did he tell you, Major? Get on with it, quickly!"

"Yes, sir. An attack is scheduled to take place tomorrow morning beginning at 2 a.m. It will be a drive southward in the Chemin des Dames area, between Soissons and Rheims. Twenty German divisions, supported by almost four thousand cannon."

"May God help us – there is no one else to," intoned Petain.

It was almost suppertime; the attack was due in a few hours. There was no time to move reserves to the area; there were none, anyway. General Petain commanded a sector held by only four French regular and two reserve divisions along with three refitting English ones sent there to recuperate from the battles in the north. A disaster was now imminent, and there was nothing anyone could do except wait for the hammer to fall.

Adolf Hitler was warning everyone around him to keep their voices down. There were no guns firing, no shells exploding; just a calm, pleasant late-spring night. It was just after midnight and Adolf was running messages to the forward units that would follow the *stürmtruppen* across the open ground between the opposing trenches at the appointed hour.

"They know nothing of this attack, it is to come as a complete surprise," Hitler told all who would listen. "The surprise of the Chemin des Dames. With this stroke, we will win the war! They aren't even expecting us to attack in this sector. We will overwhelm them. Paris is only a stone's throw away."

Within the hour four thousand Krupp cannon commenced bombarding a twenty mile wide sector in the Chemin des Dames. A couple of hours later the bombardment changed to a rolling barrage. Led by the storm troopers, eighteen German divisions descended upon the four French and three British holding the sector. The two French reserve divisions quickly joined the fray, but all to no avail. Within hours the Germans overran the Chemin des Dames and crossed the Aisne. By the first afternoon they had already moved the Front fifteen miles south, a record advance.

The situation couldn't be any more desperate for the Allies. Now the danger was not that the Allied armies might be split and the British driven back to the sea. The prize was a clean breakthrough to Paris. If enough men and material could be forced through this breach before the Allies could reinforce, then the great city lay open. So the British and French divisions stood their ground, continuing to hold their positions or dying to the last man. Regiments were wiped out or reduced eighty percent or more. By June 1st the Germans were on the Marne. Paris was forty-four miles to the west, unprotected except for the few troops attempting to assemble a new line of defence by the village of Chateau-Thierry.

Hitler and his mates were ecstatic. Not since September 1914 had they been this close to Paris; nor since that time had they held the ground gained in the last week. Rich, well-provisioned farmland. The retreating French troops and villagers could not bring themselves to destroy what they could not take with them; not even the bridges over the Aisne had been destroyed, which aided the Germans in their swift advance southward. Their advance units had sighted the Eiffel Tower; their nostrils quivered as they scented victory.

For the French troops, the surviving remnants of which were now finally in retreat, life couldn't be worse. Many were beginning to think death preferable to losing finally, disgracefully, after so many years of sacrifice. France once again humiliated by the *Saupreissen*. The French peasants, townspeople and civilians all blamed their soldiers. They had held the line for four years, and now were turning tail to run.

"Cowards and traitors! Stand fast and die for France as your countrymen have done!"

These were the slogans thrown their way, spit in their faces by disgusted peasants during the retreat south and then west. But France was bled dry of able-bodied males, and by 1918 there were no more to call. It now seemed inevitable that, after holding on for so long, all must end in defeat. And so it was at first with a sceptical curiosity that they noticed a hint of freshness wafting through the air.

Reversal of Fortune

> Like Siegfried, stricken down by the treacherous spear of savage Hagen, our weary front collapsed.
>
> - Erich Ludendorff

Adolf Hitler was running on empty. The German army continued to chase the French troops and civilians who were beating a hasty retreat westward towards Paris. So long as the Germans were just chasing the retreating French, in effect sweeping them along in a direction that they were already moving, things were alright for the Germans. But it was a real question whether the German troops, fully extended as they were, with little sleep after fighting their way southward without stop for 20 kilometres before swinging west for the last run to Paris, had the strength to overcome any further obstacles put in their path. Then again, they didn't expect any further obstacles.

Hitler first heard the news, more of a rumour, from soldiers of one of the forward reconnaissance units that he was running dispatches to at Chateau-Thierry, on the Marne, about forty-five miles from Paris. They were speculating about the recruits that were being thrown into the new French line that was being hastily fashioned only a mile to the west.

"They spoke English; but they didn't have that usual dour English discipline. They were loud, brash. And they were young. But not teenagers. They were in their early twenties, prime military age."

"But I'll tell you what was worse," a second soldier added. "There were lots of them."

They knew who they were.

The French peasants and townsfolk, in the fifty mile wide area between the fighting Front and Paris to the west, who were retreating ahead of the receding Front, at first heard a very faint sound in the distance to the west and south. As it became louder it sounded like singing. But not sad, mournful dirges; rather, they were upbeat, happy tunes. As the peasants continued walking or riding west towards the music, it became apparent that the singers were coming towards them as well. And then, from up ahead on the tree lined road, came strong, throaty, vibrant voices with loads of energy to burn.

"Over there, Over there, send the word, send the word over there. That the Yanks are coming, the Yanks are coming. We're coming, so beware!"

In the hearts of the French men and women encountering the advancing Yankees a first slender ray of hope rekindled. The first upbeat note since the disaster that had unfolded a week ago had sapped their innermost reserves of hope and faith. At first it seemed more of a lark, as a single lorry of brash, bubbling, disgustingly prime and healthy American troops passed them. But when a second passed, and then a third and a fourth, all headed towards the Front to defend their lands and lives, the tiny flickers of hope began to swell.

The Yankees with their boisterous chants and shouts flung ringing challenges to an exhausted Europe, an entire continent whose spark and zest had been snuffed out by four years of death and the destruction of the better part of a generation.

"Take heart, Frenchmen, we are here to stand with you. The retreat stops here! We have news for the enemy: We have come to fight! We have come to kill Germans! We have come to hang the Kaiser!"

More lorries passed. The narrow, tree-lined roads were now becoming clogged with Yankee troops moving east past the French civilians travelling in the opposite direction. And real hope burst forth. People began to believe. A breath of springtime after the stifling oppression of the spirit brought about by the German advance.

Hitler and the other troops of the Reich had been assured by their leaders, by the Kaiser and Ludendorff and Hindenburg and the other senior commanders, that the Americans would never get across the ocean, that the U-boats would destroy their transports in the Atlantic. And a few American troops didn't worry them. They were inexperienced, raw recruits who would turn tail at the first sight of blood. They had shot at dummy targets only, and possessed no experience shooting at live, moving bodies. But that had not turned out to be the case. The Marines proved to be excellent shots. The Americans were the ones throwing themselves into the lines, sealing gaps, breaking the rushes of the *stürmtruppen*. In hand-to-hand fighting their initial shock at the first serious injury was not to turn tail; rather, they became enraged at the enemy and turned on them, coming at them either with rifles and grenades or with their bare hands.

The Germans, living under the most horrible conditions in their dugouts in the trenches since 1914, malnourished and eating scraps laced with sawdust and other concoctions to "give it body and texture", underweight and losing muscle mass, prone to illness, exhausted by continual fighting since March 21st, despondent and discouraged to find a new enemy after breaking through what was supposedly the last line of French defences before Paris, could not cope. The healthy, fit, young, energetic, primed and pumped American manhood was in the springtime of its enthusiasm for the war. They had not trained for months, crossed the ocean, been told that they were there to rescue an exhausted France from the Hun invasion, marched bravely to the sound of the battle, witnessed their friends and comrades being blasted and torn and shot to pieces due to their inexperience, only to turn around and retreat along with the exhausted *poilus*, the soldiers of France.

No, the Yankees were there to fight and to kill. The Germans would advance only over their dead bodies. And the Americans had seemingly inexhaustible supplies of hope, fortitude and courage. The German forward units returned with tales of being hurled back by ferocious Yanks who fought like wildcats as the Germans tried to overrun their hastily-laid new defensive lines, and of Americans overrunning German positions. Their fighting spirit could not be crushed; it was young and still indomitable. The Germans had no reserves of morale or élan. They had been promised that Paris was just over the horizon, that they had made the final breakthrough, that no more defences stood in their way. That the Yankees would not arrive in time.

On June 3rd, on the main road running east from Paris to Chateau-Thierry and Rheims, just over forty-four miles east of Paris, the U.S. 2nd Division disembarked from their transports. The division consisted of an army brigade that deployed itself in a line stretching south from the road for about six miles; and a marine brigade that spread itself out in a line stretching north for six miles. French artillery supported them.

Retreating French troops ran into the line as it was being formed, the last line of defence before Paris.

"Captain, who is in charge here?"

"I am, sir. Captain John Walsh, U.S. Army 2nd Division. And you are?"

"Major Dupuis, French 9th Army. Captain, what are you doing here? You should be falling back."

"Falling back? We were told to form a line across the highway here; that unless we did the Germans would have an easy drive to Paris."

"Captain, I don't know who gave you your orders, but they're ill-informed. This whole sector is falling. The Hun is attacking in overwhelming numbers. Order your troops to pull up on the double, or they'll just be killed or taken prisoner. *La guerre est fini*, Captain. Retreat!"

The captain was dumfounded. *The war is finished*, did he say? Not bloody likely!

"Retreat, hell. We just got here!"

The Germans came out of the woods and across the wheat fields. The French artillery opened up first, raining shrapnel on the German transports advancing up the highway towards them, and the columns of infantry advancing on both sides of the road. The shrapnel appeared as patches of white daisies, little puffs of smoke, amidst the Reich troops. The Germans began to run towards the Yankee lines, which at first remained silent. Walsh thought that some of his troops might have difficulty restraining themselves waiting for his signal, but none did. So just as planned, on cue and on target, both the marine and army brigades opened fire with machine guns and rifles, with an accuracy and intensity that shattered the enemy advance and scattered her troops. Any that made it to the American lines to engage the Yankees personally found themselves outmuscled and overmatched by the sheer physical strength and ferocity of the vibrant, healthy, robust arrivals from the New World.

Sgt. Max Amann stumbled back into camp and collapsed to the ground. His greatcoat was covered with blood, mud, and artillery powder. He had a gash across his cheek with dried blood caked on. Hitler stooped and lightly lifted the sergeant's head.

"What is it, Max? My god, what is the matter?"

Max opened his eyes, and coughed slightly.

"Ah, Adi. Adi…It is over. They lied to us."

"What do you mean, who lied?"

"The generals. They told us that we had won the war when we broke the lines at Chemin des Dames a week ago. They told us it was now a victory march to Paris, some mopping up along the way. They told us we had broken the last of the French armies between us and the capital. "

"So what is wrong? So there are a few more troops brought up from elsewhere, but there can't be many. There just aren't any more Frenchmen to stop us anymore. We've killed them all over the past four years! I know it. You know it. We both lived through it."

"But there are more, Adi. The Americans are here. The Americans. They've come! They've arrived!"

Sgt. Amann began flailing out, beating at the air. Hitler restrained him.

"Easy, Max. So there are a few Americans. We'll scare them so bad they'll run straight back into the ocean."

The sergeant calmed down, lay back, and stopped struggling. After a moment, he said, "No, Adolf, you are wrong. Just like the generals. No more illusions. We are at the end of our strength. We are stretched to the limit, and breaking. We needed to take Paris now or lose the chance forever. There are too many, Adi. They are too many, too fresh and brimming with hope, too strong."

Imperceptible at first, it finally dawned on both sides that the German advance was halted, forever; there was no prospect of it ever being successfully taken up again. They could not break the Allied lines. From now on the Allies would steadily build an ever greater superiority of both men and supplies.

Only three American divisions entered the fray against the Germans at Chateau-Thierry but they were enough to break the German advance and turn the tide. The German drive was halted on June 4th.

Ludendorff was secretly terrified. He finally realized that American troops were pouring into France at the rate of over 10,000 per day, with a million already in France either training or, increasingly, at the Front. Another million were expected to arrive by the autumn of 1918. Even if Germany survived the year and made it to the winter break in fighting, how could she survive next year against the expected arrival of even more troops from across the ocean, planting themselves across the road to Paris. The die-hards in the Kaiser's armies continued to believe the stories fed them by their commanders, who were fed them ultimately by Ludendorff and Hindenburg. The war would still be won, the commanders cried. The Americans were too few; the Germans were too strong. But in June U.S. troops drove the Germans out of Belleau Wood, a forested area near the Marne. A stubborn Ludendorff, now committed to the last gamble, ordered German forces to cross the Marne on July 15th. The Allied commander, Ferdinand Foch, ordered a counterattack three days later.

French and American troops, beginning at Chateau-Thierry and swinging north, crushed the Germans in a stunning counterattack. The Germans ran for the Aisne in an effort to cross it and avoid capture.

The Allies remained on the offensive for the rest of the war.

On August 8th British and empire forces to the north opened a drive along the Somme River. A surprise assault by almost 500 tanks led the way, overrunning the trenches and causing havoc in the German rear. The Canadian Corps drove forward eight miles on the first day, the greatest advance for the Allies on a single day in the war. The Germans, their lines breached and enemy soldiers rushing through, took two weeks to seal the gap. But by then they were also in full retreat. In late September almost a million American troops took part in the beginning of the last great offensive of World War One, in an attack in force along the Argonne Forest and the Meuse River.

After four years of trench warfare, the Western Front was finally about to crack open. Both sides sensed it. But the German leadership had prepared neither the army nor the public for the possibility that it might be its own side that cracked. So as the first snows fell in the late autumn of 1918, Adolf Hitler, among millions of others, received quite a rude shock. And many Germans, in their angst and despair, felt betrayed. But by whom?

Hitler awoke with a start. He was sweating, back in his bunk in Munich. The room was dark and quiet, except for a couple of men snoring. It was chilly, and after a few minutes he started to notice it. He wasn't perspiring anymore. He got out of bed, pulled on his pants and sweater, slipped his boots on, leaving them untied, and headed for the common room down the hall. When he entered only Seth Hoffman was there. He was having a cup of soup broth. He looked up.

"Oh, hi Adi. You couldn't sleep either. Want a cup? I heated enough for two."

"Thank you, Sarge."

"So, Adi, how's it going? Any idea where you're headed?"

"I suppose no more than the rest of us. How about you, Sarge?" And after a pause, "I suppose you'll find some business position somewhere."

"Oh, I don't know. It's pretty difficult right now. No businesses are doing well at the moment. What with the inflation, nobody can afford to buy anything."

"But you must know some people with money. You're Jewish."

"Oh, yeh, that's true. But I happened to luck into a poorer family. We just didn't seem to have the knack for making the loot, you know."

"One of the few, I suppose," said Hitler. But then, after a moment, another thought dawned on him. "So why aren't you a Commie, then?"

"A what?"

"You know, a Communist, a Red."

He had known Hoffman for the past three years, had fought alongside him, and he knew that he wasn't a Red. In fact, that was one of the reasons that he could stand him. And he was damn brave. Never left a wounded mate out on a crater-pitted battlefield, even if it meant getting shot at more himself.

"Why is it one or the other, Adi," Hoffman smiled. "My family is neither rich, nor Red. We're struggling and suffering along with most everyone else. I wish there was a rich relative out there."

"So you won't be voting for that rabid Red, your countryman, in the election," Hitler inquired, smiling at the sergeant.

"No, I will not be voting for Kurt Eisner. Even though I like the red in his hair, I don't like it in politics. But what about you, Adi? Let me guess. The Fatherland Party all the way, right?"

"But of course the Fatherland Party. How can there be any other choice? Now more than ever, we must stand up for Germany! You must be able to see that. You fought for the Fatherland, after all."

"Yes, but I'll likely vote middle of the road, Democrat or Social Democrat. Fatherland Party is too far right for me. Wasn't it our wonderful and reactionary Admiral Tirpitz, along with our most esteemed Quartermaster-General Ludendorff, who formed the party a couple of months before the war ended? And what did they want at the time? Oh yes, I remember. That we refuse any offer of peace from the Allies that required us to surrender either Belgium or any of the huge chunks of Russian territory, including most of the Ukraine, which we extorted from Trotsky at Brest-Litovsk."

"Ah, yes, the Jew Trotsky."

"Oh, don't start, Adolf. Lenin isn't Jewish, and he's the man in charge over there."

"That's true, Sarge, but Marx was a Jew, and he really started all that Red swill."

"He converted from Judaism. He was less of a Jew than Jesus was. Jesus was a rabbi. Haven't we had this conversation before?"

Adolf finished his soup and shuffled off back to bed. Trouble was that he liked Seth Hoffman. His type made it difficult to pigeonhole all the Jews. Just when you thought that they were all either Reds in league with Moscow or rich, money-grubbing misers along came some like Hoffman. The Aryan blood was definitely winning out over the Jewish running in his veins.

Besides, there were greater enemies than the Jews. Take the Americans, for example. That mongrel nation had no business mixing into a European war. America, the only nation in the world to come out the big winner in the whole affair. America, which had let the other civilized countries of the world batter themselves senseless for almost four years before sending in her own boys to feast upon the spoils of nations. Especially on the carcass of Germany. Uncle Sam was the big winner in this war.

Uncle Sam, Lenin and the Reds, the rich, the Jews, France, Britain, the Poles – he was running out of fingers to count on. A world full of enemies picking at Siegfried's bones. And his eyes still hurt from that damn British gas! Hitler wrapped himself in the blanket, tightly in his bunk, and drifted off to sleep again.

Nipped in the Bud

Whatever her motives were, Wolf wasn't questioning them. He was just glad that Liesl was accompanying him to meet Rosa. Other than the danger. But she claimed it would be a coup to get an exclusive on the female leader of the Reds in Berlin, who were threatening to take over the government. Her editor had already told her so. It was only a couple of days after the huge rally in downtown Berlin, and Defence Minister Noske and Count Rantzau had requested that Wolf meet with Rosa in an attempt to avoid bloodshed.

"She trusts you, Herr Warburg," pleaded Noske, "and there's no one else outside of those Red extremists around her that she would talk to."

"I won't be just a government mouthpiece," he warned.

Liesl coming along was the bonus. He felt so good that he felt guilty. But he warned her of the danger; and it was an important story.

Her long legs stretched out in front of her on the passenger side of the Daimler roadster. It was cold out and, beneath a long skirt, delicate silk hose covered her legs down to the ankles. It was now over a week since their rendezvous on New Year's Eve, which Liesl remembered in detail. Wolf had followed her from the library, after she had impetuously kissed him full on the lips at the stroke of midnight. She was already at the front entrance and out the door, into the chilly night air, before he caught her. Putting both hands on her shoulders from behind, he spun her around and gripped her tight to him, pressing his lips immediately to hers. Her mouth opened involuntarily, and his tongue entered. Thus they met in a charmed embrace, the intervening years melted away by an undeniable chemistry which rekindled instantly. They held each other for a time, both refusing to allow the moment to end. Finally they separated long enough to whisper a few words to each other.

"Where do we go from here," Wolf asked.

"Perhaps nowhere," Liesl replied, a familiar coyness returning to her voice.

"Is that all this is about," Wolf asked, exasperated. "Do we still have to play that miserable game? Why tease me? Haven't I suffered enough?"

She looked at him, a look of grief casting over her features, finely etched as they were in the moonlight of the new year

"I didn't mean that," she whispered. "It's all coming out wrong."

Wolf stroked a tear from her cheek.

"Are you ready yet for us to try again," he asked.

She looked into his eyes, put her lips to his.

Liesl sighed contentedly as her thoughts returned to the present, seated in the roadster beside Wolf.

"So why didn't the Reds storm the chancellery when they had the chance," she asked, returning to matters at hand. "What could have stopped 200,000 people?"

"You can ask Rosa that yourself in a few minutes," Wolf replied. "But I'd say it was simply that they couldn't get their act together quickly enough. No one dreamed so many would turn out, and marching on the government is a big step. But now they may have missed their chance. Did you see the signs Noske is posting all over town? Take a look," he said, reaching for a poster lying folded on the back seat. Liesl took and unfolded it.

> 'Citizens! The Reds now fight for complete power. The government wishes to hold an election later this month, but the Reds oppose this. The people are not permitted to speak; their voices are

> suppressed. The newspapers are seized and traffic is paralyzed. There is bloody fighting in Berlin! Some neighbourhoods lack water and light. Food depots are stormed. The government is taking the necessary measures; decisive force is coming! Have patience a little longer. The hour of reckoning is near!'

"Not too subtle," she commented. "How do they plan to enforce it?"

"You saw some of the troops in Dahlem," Wolf replied. "I'm told there are over twenty thousand surrounding the city."

They were travelling east along the Französische Strasse, a couple blocks south of the Unter den Linden and running parallel to it.

"What was that," Liesl shouted, as the car suddenly shook.

"Sounds like the fighting has begun. Feels like mortar, close by," Wolf commented, remembering the sickening sensations of the trenches again.

He sped up, continuing east until they reached the Spree River and the island in the middle, with the royal Schloss. The shaking hadn't repeated itself. He turned north and drove a block to the front of the Schloss, where the huge wooden doors still lay in splinters from cannon fire the day before Christmas. Across the street to the north was their destination, the Lustgarten, a tiny oasis of green under the shadow of the cathedral and the Old Museum.

"It's open and neutral," Wolf explained. "Rosa trusts me but not the government; she thinks they'd try to ambush her indoors. I told her that I'd just as rather meet somewhere outside too. I don't trust Radek and the Moscow group, and vice versa."

They parked the car and hurried across the street.

"Liesl. So nice to see you," Rosa smiled and greeted her a few moments later.

The plants surrounding them were bare for the most part. Still, the vegetation in its wintry state was much prettier than the drab inside surroundings that most Germans had to endure that winter. And the air was cool and invigorating, though not too cold. Her heavy overcoat, reaching almost to her ankles, along with a wool scarf and mitts, kept her comfortable against the frost. As her exhaled breath floated visibly upward, Rosa looked tired but resolute.

"You know Leo Jogiches. This is Eugene Levine," she said, pointing to her second companion. Wolf hadn't met him before. "You said you wanted a German."

Levine was just under six feet, with brown hair and a clean cut face. He had on a loud brown suit with wide yellow pinstripes, under a green overcoat.

"We're trying to avoid a civil war," Wolf replied. "I thought that might have more of an impression on a fellow German rather than one of Radek's Russian gang. Remember that it's in their interests to stir the pot here."

"And how is that," Rosa asked.

"Lenin wants an international revolution to help him stay in power. More foreign aid to prop up his faltering regime."

"Comrade Lenin is going to win that war," Leo replied, jerkily lighting a cigarette. He was annoyed by Wolf's suggestion. "This year. Wait and see."

"That's not the issue," said Wolf. "Why won't you take part in the elections? We were all leftists when the war began, because none of the right wing parties ever stood up to the Kaiser's browbeating. But now that he's gone, and the government isn't going to be chosen by the Kaiser anymore, why won't you help us? What have you got against democracy?"

"Because the system is fixed," replied Rosa. "The Kaiser was just the hat worn by the rich. By tossing off the hat you don't sever the head. And that's what we have to do. Chop it off. Start not just with a new government, but a new system. A Marxist one."

"Exactly," chimed Levine and Jogiches.

"But the Kaiser was more than a hat," Wolf objected. "The new Cabinet will be responsible to the Reichstag, the peoples' reps. Give it a chance. Elections are in ten days."

"It's only cosmetic," Rosa replied, shaking her head. "The rich industrialists, the bankers, the generals, the Prussian Junkers – they all remain at the levers. Right now they're building an army to crush us. And my old colleagues in the Social Democratic Party – Ebert, Scheidemann, and now Gustav Noske – they're helping them! This is still a battle between rich and poor. It's as simple as that. Only a Marxist society can do away with such inequity."

"But you'll guarantee a civil war," Wolf argued. "You can't expect people to roll over and let you take all their property."

"Talking about yourself, Wolf," asked Rosa. "You can't stomach the thought of your family giving up its wealth?"

"That's right," he replied. "At least not all at once. You've got to move gradually. One step at a time so people can get used to it. And not all of our property, thanks."

"Our opportunity is now," exclaimed Levine. "If we let the army get control again, things will never change."

"Rosa," Wolf pleaded, taking her hand. "Unless you stop this, we're headed for bloodshed."

"That's not fair," she replied, gripping him hard, in a clasp he would remember in the days and months ahead. "I have forbidden Karl to build an army like Lenin and Trotsky have done in Russia. But Ebert and Noske are raising one here to crush us. We will oppose you; but we won't take up arms."

"But you've shut the electricity down; even the water supply in some neighbourhoods. We can't live like that."

"I won't surrender my principles, Wolf. Or our opportunity to form a Communist state here and now. But we won't take up arms."

"And what about Karl Liebknecht, and Radek," asked Wolf.

"He'll not get my help," she replied. "But when the troops fire on us, who knows what they'll do? I can't control everyone."

Unfortunately, Wolf knew she was right.

"We've tried to make a deal with those radicals," General Baron Lüttwitz hollered at the rows of troops assembled in front of him as he stared down over them from his mount, a huge, dark brown mare. "But all to no avail. And now they've hoodwinked the people, ordinary folk like your families, your own sisters, brothers, fathers, mothers – they're spreading their poison throughout the population. And you see the result. Electricity cut, no water, sewers backed up. And it only gets worse! Well, the time has come to put an end to it. Now, they'll probably turn tail and run at the first sight of disciplined troops, so you needn't worry for the most part. But there will be some stubborn ones. Reds from Moscow. They're the ones you need to root out. But be warned: they'll try to hide behind women and children. That's the type of cowards they are. So listen up: I don't want you shooting good German folk. You pick out the Reds and kill them, but don't harm our brethren who've just been hookwinked by these traitors. Now go to it, lads. Happy hunting!"

The government troops and Free Corps units were better equipped and better commanded. In straightforward confrontations on the streets, they blew apart the Red barricades and routed or shot the opposition. Then women manned the barricades and the troops hesitated.

"We have no choice, Captain, if we are to retake control. Get on that bullhorn," the major ordered.

"You there, behind the barricades," Captain Ehrhardt barked over the horn, "women included, listen up! We mean to clear this street, and then these buildings. You have ten minutes to disperse. After that we're going to blow your blockade apart, and then go through those buildings. I expect to see the hallways clear. Anyone getting in the way will be arrested. And anyone pointing guns at us will be shot! Man or woman! So clear away from those barricades and return to your homes!"

Ten minutes later, Captain Ehrhardt announced over the bullhorn that his troops were coming in. He ordered his unit forward, an elite Free Corps of naval and army veterans just pulled together over the last three weeks to deal with the Red threat. A different kind of battle, he thought, from the trenches in France where the enemy wore uniforms, not street clothes, and women weren't aiming rifles at you across stacks of overturned furniture and junk. Not that the women had actually fired at them…

"Get back," she shouted from behind the barricade. "I'll do it. These are our homes, our streets, and we won't surrender them to this government. You're no better than the Kaiser before you. Listen to me! Turn your weapons on your oppressors, and come join us," she shrieked nervously.

"I have my orders, ma'am," the trooper yelled. "Back away, I'm going to knock this wall down."

He bashed on the wall with his rifle. His mate joined him as they pushed against it now with their shoulders. It started to cave in, and in reply came a series of shots whistling through the wood from the other side, just to the outside of each of the troopers.

"The next bullets will be dead center," the woman cried. "Leave now."

They turned to look at their commander.

"You there," Captain Ehrhardt cried, pointing to half a dozen troopers. "Assist them."

They rushed forward, and the entire group rushed the barricade. Shots rang out from other side, and two troopers fell back.

"Bastards!" Ehrhardt shouted, watching periodic red gushers spurt from their chests. "Clear away," he cried to the remaining troops. "Where's my mortar? Blast them!"

Into the neighbourhoods of central Berlin, south of the publishing district around the Schützenstrasse, retreated the Red forces, into districts and amongst peoples sympathetic to them.

"I think it's cowardly of them to hide there," opined Liesl as she and Wolf drove through the district a few days after their meeting with Rosa.

"What did you expect," asked Wolf, "that they would continue to expose themselves to the big guns? Baron Lüttwitz was firing Krupp cannon at barricades made of plywood. Yes, he had to crush the resistance. But he didn't have to enjoy it so much. And I don't see why they have to follow the Reds into these neighbourhoods. Leave them be for now and let things die down."

"But the problem will just resurface," replied Liesl. "We have to root it out now once and for all."

"It's going to keep surfacing for a long time no matter how the Right wing attacks it. But you don't solve the problem of rich and poor by attacking with cannon. You just create hate and more violence."

"Stop here," Liesl cried.

Wolf slammed on the brakes in front of an older wooden apartment block where a Free Corps unit was deployed and appeared ready to attack. Liesl opened the door and jumped from the roadster, running towards the scene with camera in hand. She stopped twenty yards behind the line of troops. Then she noticed, suddenly, that close to a dozen lay sprawled on the stairs leading up to the door from the pavement, riddled with bullets holes! Her camera hand dropped to her side and she stood there in stunned consternation, her gaze transfixed upon the bloody red spots snaked across their faces and chests.

The officer barked his message.

"You have thirty seconds to surrender. Otherwise, you die. We'll not be rushing the building again," shouted Captain Ehrhardt to those inside.

The time elapsed with no reply. Ehrhardt stated, softly, "Fire!"

From a howitzer tilted at the appropriate angle a shot flew directly forward and into the open doorway of the building. The rear of the structure detonated in the next instant, smoke, tinder and ash emerging from the front doorway as well as the roof above. But there were two front entrances to the building, and stationed in front of the second one, about forty yards to the north, was another trooper, this one with a nozzle in his hand that ran via a hose to the tank upon his back. After a long minute the door opened, and two or three people briefly stuck their coughing heads out.

"You'll not murder more good German soldiers," an infuriated Captain Hermann Ehrhardt yelled at them. "You have just ten seconds to surrender. Come out now or die."

After the time had passed, he stated softly, "Burn them."

"Wait," shouted Liesl, who had moved directly behind the trooper aiming at the door, "there's someone coming out!"

It was too late.

A gusher of flame erupted from the nozzle held by the trooper closest to the stairs. It shot up and into the open doorway, a solid vortex of fire engulfing the entire hallway as far back as Liesl could see. Screams issued from within the inferno, and then flames, in the shapes of human beings, came running from the building, diving to the pavement, rolling over and over. Mercifully the soldiers shot them quickly. After a moment the smell of black, smoking flesh overwhelmed Liesl.

"I, I'm sorry, I couldn't help it," stuttered the trooper, his eyes and mouth both open wide, the colour drained from his cheeks, terrified that he had just murdered fellow Germans.

"There's nothing to be sorry for, soldier," shouted Captain Ehrhardt.

He rode up, surveying Liesl with a leer.

"And who are you, my sweet one? Not another Red bitch, I hope."

"She's with me, Captain," said Wolf, emerging from the Daimler roadster. "We're on government business. Under Noske's protection."

Wolf produced a folded paper from his vest pocket.

"Oh, pity," mumbled Ehrhardt. He liked unfettered control. "The party here is over, anyway. But I lost a dozen good men," he added, eyes narrowing and a dark, mean, determined look crossing his face. I won't make that mistake again, trusting those damn dirty Reds. Never again! I'll blow the suckers up before I try to get them to surrender next time. No more dead German soldiers."

"And where're you off to now, Captain," asked Wolf a few moments later as they stood watching the remainder of the building burn, while Ehrhardt, hands gesticulating wildly, shouted orders at his men. "You look like you're in a hurry."

The remaining troopers were already beginning to load their dead and wounded comrades into their transports, along with ammo and weapons.

"That's right, counsellor. We're off to liberate the government newspaper offices of the Red trash that's been occupying it the last few days."

Then his eyes drifted to Liesl, and he added, smiling darkly, "Want to come along for the show?"

But they'd seen enough; and the smell of burnt flesh and gunpowder still wafted through the air. Close to a thousand Reds had already been killed in Berlin. It was all over but the mopping up.

Wolf was feeling guilty again. Here he had the best of everything due to the crisis. Liesl had finally seen enough of people dying horribly so that she was starting to admit that maybe Wolf hadn't been so despicable getting transferred out of the trenches during the war. She was also feeling weak from the odour of people roasting. So when Wolf suggested that they get a room at the Adlon, instead of making the drive out to Dahlem, she acquiesced easily.

He tried to take her mind off the events in Berlin, all the killing, and they talked about Munich, how it was so beautiful even in the winter, with the Bavarian Alps to the south.

"We must take a trip to Garmische this winter. How long's it been since you last skied? And a hot tub? And the evergreens all around us! We won't even think about Berlin."

He actually had her smiling how. Liesl was stretched out on the sofa, a couple of glasses of wine under her belt, prepared to admit that she had been wrong all these years about Wolf, that she wanted to make it up to him now.

"All the wasted years," she whispered, a tear trickling down her cheek, which he stroked away lightly with his finger.

"Only smiles now," he whispered back.

He moved his hand to her blouse, undid the top button, and then the next, and the one after, encountering no resistance. The blouse fell to the side, and she bent forward to embrace him, enabling his hand to reach behind her back and unclip her bra. Wolf moved to stretch out on the couch beside her, pulling her body close to his, caressing her face and neck with his wine-tainted breath. The aroma wafted through her nostrils; and the air sent shivers as it tickled her inner ear. She groaned and gasped lightly, her legs wrapping themselves around him. Her actions declared that all was forgiven, that she wanted him to make love to her…

So why was he still feeling guilty?

Partly it had been the phone call from Hugo Haase who managed to track him down through the switchboard.

"Wolf, you must talk to Noske and Ebert," implored Hugo. "White terror rages here exactly as it did under the tsarist regime in Russia before the revolution there." The Whites were the government forces. "Even under the Kaiser at least an attempt was made to make it appear that the law was followed. But now, brutal force rules. Government troops break into apartments at night, make arrests without warrants. Did you know they searched Oskar Cohn's apartment the day before yesterday? He's a Reichstag deputy, for pity's sake! He escaped only because he was out of town. His property was confiscated. Ebert and Noske and their cohorts, who try to pose as the guardians of the law, let the hordes of brutal soldiers do as they like!"

"But what can I do, Hugo? They're trying to stave off a coup by the Reds. Or at least that's what they claim. Nothing I can say will stop them."

"But you must try, Wolf. Otherwise, someone will be murdered. Rosa, Karl, myself, maybe even Ebert or Noske themselves. They must stop this brutal rule of the soldiers now."

"I'll try, Hugo. But Karl Liebknecht, and Radek, had better keep their people in line, too."

By the time he got off the phone, any romantic mood had left him. He switched from wine to scotch for a couple of belts, and then sat down, lifting Liesl's legs as he squeezed under them on to the sofa beside her. Moaning about the rotten state of the world, but feeling her body against his, in a short time he really felt like life wasn't so bad after all. And that got him feeling guilty again.

The open fighting was at an end in any event. Early the next morning the attack turned to police headquarters itself, stronghold and last bastion of the armed elements of the revolution, which fell to Maikäfer Free Corps the next day. Even the Sailors Division, wisely recognizing the reality of overwhelming force, vacated the Schloss and dispersed throughout Berlin before they could be confronted by the army or Free Corps units. And finally Gustav Noske, with Philip Scheidemann at his side, marched at the head of his Iron Brigade, two thousand strong, from Schöneberger High Street to the Potsdamer Platz, within view of the Chancellery itself.

The final scene of this opening act of the German civil war took place at the offices of the Red's own newspaper, the *Red Flag*, where the few remaining Red leaders at large, including Rosa and Karl, were thought to be holed up. Under a white flag those inside made their way out, in the face of Captain Ehrhardt's rifles.

"Keep those guns trained on them," shouted Ehrhardt. "The slightest wrong move, they twitch the wrong way, and you blast them!"

"Those murdering slime," he continued, this time under his breath, as the Reds began to file out. He was remembering his dead mates in the army and Free Corps units, fired at point-blank by women and old men who they trusted. Put up to it by such as these. And the mutilated bodies of good German folk found in the buildings that had been occupied by the Reds. Charred, burned, torn apart by flying metal, shot. Sometimes by Ehrhardt's own men, he knew, in their frenzy to get at the Reds. But these were the leaders of the Reds, those responsible for all the carnage. Good Germans dead; and these Red backstabbers were likely going to walk away with a slap on the wrist because, he knew, the new civilian government had no guts!

"Wait," Ehrhardt shouted, as he suddenly realized it, "where is Rosa Luxemburg? I don't see her here."

It was true; there were no women in the group.

"Tell me where she is," Ehrhardt raged, shaking his riding crop up and down. "She is still hiding inside?"

"No, Herr Captain," one of the group shouted "The leaders are not with us."

"You lie," he shouted, savagely striking the man down with the crop. "Tell her to come out, or I'll shoot the lot of you!"

"She's not here," they shouted desperately.

"You have ten seconds to surrender yourself," Ehrhardt raged at the building. "Just ten seconds," he hissed.

The time passed and no one else emerged. Ehrhardt raised his crop. "On my signal," he directed the gunner, and as his arm dropped machine gun bullets tore into the group, ripping them and their white flag to shreds.

Eugene Levine, at the tail end of the group, caught two bullets in his left calf as he ran for cover. Jumping behind a parked car, he survived, to crawl away, lick his wounds, and make his way south to Munich with his tale of Free Corps butchery.

* * *

Rosa and Karl had been forced underground, but they were not silenced. The next day the *Red Flag* somehow appeared on the street, in a limited edition with messages from the Red leaders:

"A final and lasting victory in this moment could not be expected," Rosa wrote. "Was, therefore, the fight of the last week an error? Yes, if it had been an intentional putsch. But what was the cause of the fighting? A brutal provocation by the government! The revolutionary classes were forced to take up arms to repel the attack."

"The Red cause crushed? Steady!" added Karl. "We have not fled, we are not beaten. And even if they throw us in chains – we are here and here we remain! Victory will be ours."

"Provocation," cried Gustav Noske, upon reading the broadsheet. "Still they try to make trouble. They must be silenced, Herr General."

"What more would you have us do," asked General Baron Lüttwitz in return. "I am uncomfortable ordering my troops to continue breaking down doors and searching peoples' homes. Already it is affecting their discipline. It is a job for policemen, not combat troops."

"We have no choice, General. Where the Reds Luxemburg and Liebknecht lead, their minions follow."

"Do you really think we can shut them down by arresting or killing the leaders? What has happened to all you good gentlemen of the Social Democratic Party, who used to scream bloody murder when the Kaiser occasionally tried to censor you or read your mail? Now that you give the orders, you think nothing of ordering the Wehrmacht to break into peoples' homes!"

Ironic, but necessary, the Minister thought to himself. The Kaiser never faced a revolution, and Noske really was too busy right now to give moral considerations any more attention.

"You just keep doing what you're doing, General, until you capture Rosa and Karl."

"I tell you, they've been captured," cried Hugo Haase over the phone. "You know that I wasn't supporting them any more than you were, Wolf. Leo Jogiches just called me, but I told him that I'm not a Cabinet member anymore. I resigned after the affair at the Schloss the day before Christmas. But I told him that I'd call you. Don't let them kill her, Wolf."

"What about Karl? They have him too?"

"Yes. They were hiding in the bedroom closet, apparently. The troops knew just where to look for them. Walked straight in there. Someone sold them out."

"What can you do," Liesl asked him after he hung up the phone.

"Probably nothing," he replied. "And I'll tell you, I'm scared to get involved. One of those Right wing fanatics might decide to put a bullet in my back for trying to help any Red, let alone Rosa Luxemburg."

It was a late afternoon in mid-January when Wolf entered Noske's office at the Chancellery. Count Rantzau was seated inside with the Minister of Public Safety and Defence, Gustav Noske, who was seated behind his desk. He rose to greet Wolf.

"Do you have her, Minister," Wolf enquired, after shaking his hand and sitting down.

"My assistant is checking into that now."

"You don't know yet," he asked sceptically, his tone hardening. "I talked to you over an hour ago."

"These things take time."

Sure.

"You were quick to call me when you wanted my help," Wolf countered. "Why can't you be truthful now? Just tell me if she's still alive."

Noske looked away from Wolf, over to Rantzau, and to Wolf again with a blank look.

"The Count doesn't know anything," Wolf told Noske. "He wouldn't lie to me about this. But you're lying to him."

Rantzau stared hard at Noske.

"Where is she, Minister," the Count demanded, his hand gripping hard the handle of his folded umbrella.

Noske gulped. Then his eyes, which had been wide open in a look of feigned innocence, returned to normal, and his face relaxed. He had decided to come clean.

"She and Karl Liebknecht are being held at this moment in a safe location. Both alive. But they are incommunicado."

"And why is that? I'm her counsel," Wolf barked. "She has a right to talk to me."

"And eventually she will. But not now. It's too dangerous."

"Don't you care that both the newspapers and the courts will jump on you after this is over," asked Wolf.

"I must do my duty to our fledgling Republic now, Herr Warburg," replied the Minister. "If I don't, it will fail and the Reds will triumph here as in Moscow."

Noske truly believed it.

"But why won't you even let her talk to me," implored Wolf. "What is so dangerous in that?"

"Because their words cause harm. They cause other people to follow them," he continued, looking down, at the same time toying with a pen in his hand.

"Who is 'they'," asked Wolf.

"Communists," Noske replied, and then, "Jews."

"What?" cried Wolf.

"Don't take it personally, Herr Warburg," the Minister continued. "It has nothing to do with anti-Semitism when one points out that the 'Marxists' of east European Jewish background have a special aptitude for transforming Socialism into a dogma and changing popular views into confessions of faith."

In particular the Pole, Rosa Luxemburg, of course.

"Karl's not Jewish," Wolf replied desperately.

"Perhaps not Karl Liebknecht. But how about Karl Radek, the one from Moscow? And what has religion to do with it anyway?"

"You brought it up!"

Rosa came from Poland, and most Jews today are descended from Polish Jews. What was incredible about this Jewish sub-culture is that as far back as the mid-1500's there was an almost one hundred percent literacy rate, women included! Since Jews could read, write, add, and subtract, whereas most Poles could not, Polish nobles leased their lands to Jews who acted as tax collectors and overseers. In good times they lived well; in bad times, it was the Jews whom disgruntled peasants blamed and took out their frustrations upon. In the industrial and political revolutions of the 19th and early 20th centuries, when literacy became more necessary than ever but was only beginning to spread generally, these ingrained skills thrust many Jews into leadership roles. In the West many became wealthy capitalists; in the reactionary East, they became revolutionaries.

"How long are you going to keep denying it for," asked Captain Pabst. "You are Rosa Luxemburg, former Reichstag deputy, and currently leader of the Communist Party of Germany, more commonly known as the Spartacist movement. Admit it and let us get on with things that I don't know."

Rosa looked up wearily from the armless wooden chair in which she was bound by rope around her midsection, with arms tied tightly to her body. There was slight bruising around the right side of her mouth. But they had beaten her mostly about the body, so that her face would still photograph well for government propaganda purposes.

Still, Pabst couldn't resist the occasional slap across the face as her filthy mouth continued to spew forth disrespectful, evasive and unresponsive answers.

"Herr Captain, I am Rosa Luxemburg. That is all I wish to say now."

Pabst stepped back, looked straight at her, and smiled.

"Ah, now we are getting somewhere, former deputy Luxemburg. But our conversation is just beginning. I require much more information from you. Then you can go your way."

Rosa looked back at him, bewildered.

"Are you saying that you will release me if I answer your questions?"

"But of course, my dear. We do not wish to harm you. We only wish to defuse a tense situation."

He smiled as he gritted his teeth.

"I am not so far gone as to think that I shall be released anytime soon, Herr Captain. I have no information for you."

The smile vanished from Pabst's countenance, replaced by a scowl.

"Ah, and I thought we were starting to get somewhere, madam. This is disappointing."

With that he suddenly pulled back his right arm and then threw his fist with all the force he could quickly muster into Rosa's ribcage, just under her left breast. She pitched forward, falling to the floor with the chair still tied to her, coughing and gagging.

"Bitch! You're not in a position to argue. Who do you think is going to help you now? Karl Liebknecht, that fierce Red warrior? He's whimpering like the Jew coward he really is. Or perhaps Lenin and Trotsky?"

Pabst smiled maniacally as he smacked the palm of his left hand with his short riding crop.

"Let them come, my dear Red Rosa. Let them come. We are preparing a little surprise for all the little red devils out there."

"For the record, Karl is not Jewish. What has religion to do with anything?"

Rosa was willing to discuss anything that would distract Pabst from seeking the specific tactical information she possessed.

"You are all Jews! Don't argue with me! The time for arguing is over! Now, when are your Moscow comrades planning to launch their invasion of the Fatherland?"

Rosa thought for a moment about telling Pabst the truth again, that there was no planned invasion, that Lenin was more worried about the White Russian counterattack than invading other countries; but she knew it was to no avail. And she did not have the strength to hold out against the continuing beatings.

"If you will bring me a little water, Captain, I'll tell you what I can of Comrade Lenin's plans for the invasion of Germany."

Karl Liebknecht's interrogation went just as smoothly. He too first denied his identity. But Captain Pabst would have none of it.

"You are Karl Liebknecht, German radical socialist leader and founder of the Communist Party of Germany. "

Karl moved his head from left to right, back and forth, in denial.

"You were born August 13, 1871, in Leipzig, the son of Wilhelm Liebknecht, who was co-founder of the illustrious Social Democrat Party of Germany. Our current government!"

At this last statement Pabst laughed uproariously at himself.

"Isn't that rich? Your own former comrades are now the government, and they have ordered me to arrest you! Ha, ah ha ha ha!"

He continued, "You studied law and then became involved yourself in the Socialist movement. In 1907 you were sentenced to 18 months in prison for anti-government writings. While still in prison, you were elected to the Prussian House of Deputies. In 1912 you moved to the national stage and were elected a Reichstag deputy. Ah, 1912," Pabst continued, "the year the Socialists won a majority in the Reichstag. Well, no matter, it didn't help you or your comrades to gain power, did it?"

Liebknecht said nothing.

"With your fellow Socialist Rosa Luxemburg you formed a radical faction of the Social Democratic Party, which came to be known as the Spartacists, because you signed the pen name Spartakus to a series of articles calling for revolutionary opposition to the war. As the first deputy to break party solidarity and oppose the war outright, on January 1, 1916, you were expelled from the Social Democratic Party and soon after you were convicted of high treason for leading an antiwar demonstration. Traitorous dog that you are, you were rightly sentenced to two years in prison and loss of civil rights. Unfortunately, you were released in October 1918 as a result of the general amnesty of political prisoners near the end of the war. Right so far, 'Comrade' Liebknecht?"

Karl smiled weakly back at Pabst.

"Ah, you still have some lip left in you, you filthy traitor," Pabst smiled. "We still have time to play. And at the end of the game, zpf!"

He made a slicing motion across his neck. The interrogation commenced again.

"In November 1918 you led the Communist rabble rousing against the government. In December 1918 you and the Jew Rosa Luxemburg formed the Communist Party of Germany. In January 1919, just days ago, you led the attempted overthrow of the lawful government of Ebert and Scheidemann. That is all correct, is it not, Karl Liebknecht?"

"I told you, I am not him."

In reply Pabst kicked him in the face, knocking him and the chair to the floor. The back of his head hit the smooth wooden surface so hard that his eyes rolled around momentarily before, mouth agape, he passed out.

In his unconscious state Karl remembered back, back to when Kurt Eisner, his former colleague in the Social Democratic Party before the war, had come to Berlin from Munich at the end of November 1918, to tell of the revolution that had already taken place in Bavaria. Earlier that month Eisner and some comrades had led the south German state in the first successful revolution at the end of the war, on November 9th booting out the Wittelsbach monarchy and instituting a provincial republic. Eisner was interim president, a flaming revolutionary with red hair to match his political views. Surprisingly, he urged Liebknecht to moderation.

"Move slowly," he counselled. "Berlin may not be as ready as Munich for a change of government so quickly. Remember, it is the seat of the old imperial power, which Munich was not."

But Karl answered that the whole system first had to be pulled down, and everything constructed anew.

He returned to consciousness to hear Pabst droning on.

"...so the charges against Karl Liebknecht are," he said, reading from the sheet in front of him, "that you caused the deaths of over two hundred officers, the looting of shops, and the distribution of money among soldiers to incite them to revolution. For all these crimes you are subject to summary execution. This can be commuted if you cooperate with the government against the rest of the traitorous scum," Pabst concluded, staring down at Karl.

He, in turn, looked up, smiled slightly, and said nothing.

"Your comrade, Liebknecht, has already cracked, and is singing loudly the whereabouts of the other traitors, and when Trotsky's army is set to invade. He is to be granted immunity. He is turning on you! What have you to say about him?"

Rosa's face was covered with welts and blisters. The right eye was surrounded by black, bruised skin. The eye itself had a red background rather than white, blood vessels within it having ruptured from concussion.

"I have just about reached the end of my patience with you, Rosa Luxemburg," Pabst shrieked. "Either give me some information I can use or I will put you out of your misery."

Rosa thought to herself that Karl was either silent or leading them on a merry chase through the fantasy of a Russian invasion. All she cared about was not betraying the revolution before she died. But Pabst really had had enough by this time. Convinced he would hear nothing further, he grabbed her by the hair, throwing her to the floor. Dragging her by the hair, he opened the door and made his way down the hall. The chambermaid he passed by could only stare, aghast, at the bloodied woman trailing along the carpet behind him.

"Herr Minister, I do not believe there is any more information to be gained from either of them. They will die before they betray anymore to us. Besides, I'm not sure that everything they've said up to know is reliable. Liebknecht claims eight divisions are on their way by boat from St. Petersburg. But can they get by the Allied blockade even if they really are coming?"

After a pause, "Yes, Herr Minister, I will take care of them. Nothing will happen to them. Unless they try to escape. Yes, they are to go to Moabits prison tonight. Yes, I understand. I will look after the arrangements myself. Goodnight, Herr Minister."

Captain Pabst hung up the phone and called for his adjutant.

"Who is to escort the two prisoners to Moabits?"

"Lieutenant Vogel is in charge of the escort."

"Send him to me. I wish to instruct him myself."

Vogel appeared a few minutes later. After the door had closed, leaving them alone in the room, Captain Pabst spoke.

"Lieutenant, I have instructions from the very highest levels of the government. These orders are from the Chancellor and the Defence Minister concerning the radical revolutionaries Rosa Luxemburg and Karl Liebknecht."

Pabst finishing writing the orders.

"You are to be entrusted with their transport from this location to Moabits prison, where tomorrow they will be visited by their lawyer, who is already demanding to see them. This will entail a journey tonight through the Tiergarten. Here are your instructions. They are confidential, only to be relayed to your immediate subordinates as is necessary to carry out their tasks."

Private Runge was only acting upon orders given him by his superior, Lieutenant Vogel. The only problem for Karl Liebknecht was that one of those orders involved him. As Karl emerged from the rear of the building for the trip to Moabits, Runge, waiting just outside the door and to the side, clubbed him in the head with the butt of his rifle. The savage blow knocked him out immediately.

When he came to, he was in the backseat of a car, with Private Runge on his right side and another trooper to his left. Lieutenant Vogel and a driver sat up front. Trees surrounded them on both sides of the roadway; Karl thought that they must be driving through the Tiergarten. All of a sudden, at one particularly dark and lonely spot, Vogel ordered the car stopped.

"Out, traitorous dog. Out to face your fate," barked Vogel.

Private Runge pulled him out the car door.

"What should I do, Lieutenant," he asked Vogel.

Vogel motioned for Runge to release Karl and to push him away. Runge did so. Karl didn't understand at first.

"What do you want me to do," he asked, confused.

"Leave, traitor, just make sure that you don't come back to Berlin. Get out at once!"

Liebknecht couldn't believe his ears. He was free?

"You won't shoot me?"

"Not if you leave now and never return," Lieutenant Vogel barked.

Karl looked at him, and at the other soldiers. He really had no choice – if they were going to shoot him, they would do it whatever he did. So he turned, paused, and started to walk away without looking over his shoulder.

Then came the shots.

His body was delivered to a local mortuary. Two bullets were dug from his back, another from his head. The mortician knew him only as an unknown man found by the roadway in the Tiergarten.

They continued to knock Rosa down and drag her through the hotel. Finally they lifted her to her feet and escorted her out the rear exit. Private Runge was again waiting off to the side as she came out. He clubbed her in the head, the blow so hard that it was heard inside the hotel, and her unconscious body then stuffed into the back seat of the car and driven off.

Lieutenant Kurt Vogel did not go through the motions of forcing his prisoner to attempt an escape; rather, he had

Rosa shot in the head while still in the car. They then made their way to the Landwehr Canal close by, as it snaked its way through the city, where her body was weighed down with stones and dumped in.

The headline in the government paper proclaimed 'Order reigns in Berlin', and said that a mob had stopped the car Rosa was in, taken her from her army escort and torn her to pieces.

"'Order reigns in Berlin'? You stupid lackeys," Rosa screamed from the grave in her last article, a prescient piece written days before, and which ran in the *Red Flag* the morning of her death. "Your 'Order' is built on sand. The revolution will raise itself up again clashing, and to your horror it will proclaim to the sound of trumpets: I *was, I am, I shall be!"*

"That is not what I ordered!"

Gustav Noske was livid as he bellowed at Captain Pabst over the telephone from Ebert's office.

"Don't tell me that you nipped the problem in the bud. I didn't authorize Rosa's murder!"

The killers needn't have worried, though. Most judges were sympathetic to the Right since they, like most of the civil service, had been appointed by the Kaiser's ministers well before the war. They tended to prefer the status quo, since their job security depended on it. Private Runge was sentenced to two years; Lieutenant Vogel received four months; Captain Pabst was never convicted, and lived to a ripe old age.

The murders of Rosa and Karl ushered in an era of political violence in Germany that lasted until the end of the next war a quarter century later. They also drew a line of blood and mistrust between the centrist parties, including the Social Democrats, and the Reds who thought that the centrists had abandoned them to the terror of the extreme Right. So just over a decade later, the Reds adamantly refused to form an alliance, even to keep the Nazis from power.

In May, four months after her murder, Rosa Luxemburg's emaciated corpse washed up on the bank of the Landwehr Canal that flowed through the middle of Berlin.

> Red Rosa now has vanished too.
> Where she lies is hid from view.
> She told the poor what life is about.
> And so the rich have rubbed her out.
>
> - *EPITAPH, 1919* by Bertolt Brecht

Munich

Viennese Tramp

> We must see to it that we never again fall too low, but also that we don't rise too high.
>
> - Eric Warburg

The Jewish problem came to Austria-Hungary by way of Poland and Russia, and then filtered its way into Germany. Hitler, coming from Austria, absorbed much, which he carried with him to Munich.

Austrian Empress Maria Theresa protested that she did not want Poland partitioned. "Trust and faith are lost for all times," she cried in the late 18th century; but she joined in anyway. Of the three countries which partitioned Poland amongst themselves, Prussia received the fewest Jews, perhaps ten percent. Russia got about half, and the Austro-Hungarian empire the rest, over a quarter million. They were all located in Galicia, an independent principality which became part of Poland during the 1300's, and stayed that way till it came under Austrian rule as a result of the Partitions.

Throughout the 19th century Jews steadily gained civil rights in Austria-Hungary so that they were barred only from the civil service and military, which were open if one converted. Galicia came into the empire at the same time as railways and steamships opened up a new age of mass transport over the plains and rivers of Austria-Hungary. Vienna's Jewish population was about 5000 by 1850. With the aid of steam and rail, it exploded to 70,000 by 1880, and approached 200,000 by WW1. As Galicians Jews flocked to Budapest and Vienna, the overall image of Jews got confused. The native Viennese Jews and those from western Europe dressed and looked like the rest of the population. But the Galicians stood out, clinging to their old-world appearance, the males in long black coats and beards.

* * *

So disgusted were they with the atmosphere in the barracks when the arrived back in Munich after the war, Ernst Schmidt and Adolf Hitler jumped at the opportunity to serve as guards at the de-commissioning prisoner of war camp at Traunstein, sixty miles southeast of Munich. It was almost in the mountains, close to Salzburg and Berchtesgaden.

It was the end of January, still winter, with snow on the ground. In the higher altitude, just a few miles from the mountains, it was cold. It wasn't so bad in the daytime, in the sunshine, as on this day, when Ernst Schmidt and Adolf Hitler left the camp and headed southeast till the road forked. The main route swung north to reach Salzburg on the Austrian border, while the other branch, which they took, headed south to the alpine slopes and lake at Berchtesgaden.

The travellers were deep in the mountains now. The Bavarian Alps towered above as they approached the Obersalzberg, a couple of miles from Berchtesgaden. There they passed the ancient Augustine monastery which the Wittelsbachs had at one time converted to another royal residence. Just beyond the town to the south was the Königsee, a sliver of a lake wedged between the almost-vertical Watzmann and the Kahlersberg, two of Germany's highest peaks. And there, in the middle of the lake, the tiny island of St. Bartholomö, and its red-roofed chapel.

But the two did not go beyond the town. Instead they took the cable lift up the Obersalzberg, about 3300 feet, there to explore the mountainside and its magnificent scenery.

"A step up from that hell-hole of a camp, eh, Adolf, my friend? Life is still beautiful, isn't it," Ernie said, looking around at the vista spread out before him.

"Yes, it is quite a sight," replied Hitler. Pointing north, he added, "Look, you can see Salzburg there."

Ernie looked in the direction his companion indicated, and then at the Salzach River in the foreground. Then his head swivelled from side to side, his eyes sweeping the wide open vista surrounding them.

"Sure is peaceful here," he said.

"Yes, I swear, I would love to have a house in the mountains here," cried Hitler, his face aglow, his arms reaching out. "Truly, Siegfried must have walked these mountaintops!"

"Why, Adolf, you amaze me sometimes," said Ernie, a smile on his face. "You haven't got this excited since we stormed the Marne last summer. There's hope for you yet."

Hitler looked at him, his expression turning sour.

"Don't confuse this momentary appreciation of nature in any way with the true joy of fighting for the Fatherland against alien aggressors. And if I haven't smiled since the war ended, is it any wonder? The magnitude of our loss is a catastrophe beyond compare. We have yet to feel the true consequences. Wait and see! A pretty view from a hillside will not make up for that."

"Oh, lighten up, Adolf. You're still mad at those Russian loudmouths back at the camp. Well, forget about them. They'll all be gone soon, anyway."

"Yes, but look at what they're doing in the meantime," retorted Adolf. "You know the poison they're spreading. And it's infecting our soldiers, too. And any civilians that they come into contact with. They spout all that Red filth about community property and rule by Soviets. About everyone being equal. It's even worse than western democracy!"

Hitler looked at Ernie, momentarily pausing for him to reply. But Ernst did not. He remained silent, hoping his friend would cool down. But Hitler was not done.

"They spit at us, Ernst! They show no respect. We crushed them on the battlefield. We forced them to accept a humiliating peace. We did that through our strength in arms. And yet, now, that is all taken from us; and they are counted among the victors! Instead, these Russian swine laugh at us. We have to feed them, while our own people starve!"

"Such are the fortunes of war. Lighten up, Adolf. You don't want to get another headache, do you?"

"No, I suppose you're right. By the way, I don't suppose you brought an extra pair of sunglasses, did you? My eyes are getting sore again. That snow is bright."

"Here, take mine," Ernst replied, handing the glasses over, recalling the gassing that Hitler had suffered only three months before. He knew it stung the eyes and throat the worst.

"So, Adi, tell me about what it was like growing up here."

"Actually it was north of here, in a little border town called Braunau. It was on the Inn River, the border between Bavaria and Austria. My father was a customs official for the Habsburg government but he was posted to Passau, here in Bavaria. And, you know, even though I was very young, I loved Germany. I became infected with a love for the mighty German Reich..."

"We're on holiday, Adolf," Ernie cut in, dreading the prospect of another dreary lecture. "You can give it a rest. Besides, the war is over."

A wild look momentarily danced across Hitler's eyes.

"The war is not over," he said softly but emphatically. "It will only be over when the flag of the German Reich flies over central Europe."

There was a pause, then he began to speak again.

"When I was six or seven my father resigned from the customs service and retired, along with all of us, to Linz, back in Austria. There was me and my older half-brother Alois, and my half sister. Both losers, I'll tell you. He ran away from home early, about fourteen as I recall. My father used to beat him up pretty good. Papa liked to drink, and he had a temper. Maybe that's why I don't drink. Anyway, Alois has been in trouble with the law a few times, from what I hear. We haven't kept in touch."

"How about your sister? What's her name?"

"Angela. No, she was quite a bitch, I'm afraid. She and her husband decided that I was wasting my life trying to be an artist or architect. A civil servant was what I should be, according to them. Like my father. I don't miss her."

"Anyone else? What about Paula?"

"Well, you know about Paula."

"She's a half-sister, too?"

"No, actually, she's my full sister. And the only family I'm close to."

"When was the last time you saw her?"

"Last summer. I've been meaning to go to Linz ever since I got back to Munich, but I haven't been well enough."

"I know. But tell me more of your childhood. You say your family moved to Linz when your dad retired? So what did you do as a kid there?"

"Well, he bought a farm, but then he didn't like that one, so we moved to another. I'll tell you, the first thing I really remember was singing in the church choir, believe it or not."

Ernie laughed, and Hitler continued.

"Papa was almost sixty when we moved to Linz, and we didn't always see eye to eye. After my brother ran off, I got all the beatings. He was one mean son of a bitch when he got drunk. Which was nightly. But such is life, eh, Ernie? After having been through the war, how can one think much of childhood whippings? German youth need to be toughened up for the fight ahead. Don't you agree?"

"I don't expect another war in the near future, Adolf."

"Oh, it will take at least a decade. But this shameful defeat will not go unavenged!"

"So what was school like," asked Ernst, changing the subject.

"I was a very good student to begin with, but my grades dropped off after the first couple of years. I got bored. Well, actually, we were having more fun with our own explorations. I remember reading the German and Norse mythology. You know, Siegfried and Wotan, and all that stuff. And the German tribes against the Romans. Caesar Augustus bawling when the Germans destroyed his legions and stole their banners, their 'eagles'. But my history teacher, Dr. Pötsch, caught my interest. He introduced me to the pan-German movement. He told me about the *Sudmark,*" Austria, "and the need to protect our citizens of German blood from being overrun by this damnable democracy. That was when I started to have arguments with my father."

"So what did you fight about," asked Ernie.

"He supported the Habsburg's multi-ethnic mongrel state. I was a pan-German. You know, one Germany for all Germans. We wanted all of German Austria to join the German Reich. Instead we were trapped in that Austro-Hungarian monstrosity in which ethnic Germans accounted for only a fifth of the population. The rest were all either Slavs or Magyars of one variety or another. Or Jews."

"So what was the problem? The German Austrians were in control."

"That was until democracy came along," Hitler grimaced. "When that damn parliament assembled in Vienna, and our esteemed Habsburg emperor started surrendering his powers to it, we were lost. The will of the superior people was replaced by the superiority of numbers. It was then that we knew that empire was doomed. That's why I decided to leave as soon as I could."

"When did you come to Germany?"

"I was twenty-four. It was after I'd spent some years in Vienna, during my 'artist' days. At the time that was all I wanted to be."

"An artist? Is that right? I remember you doing some painting during the war once or twice."

"That's why I went to Vienna in the first place."

"How old were you?"

"Seventeen. My father had already died, but he left mom a small pension, so we got by. I had a friend, Gustl Kubizek. He was into arts as well, so we went to Vienna together. He ended up getting accepted into the Academy of Music. Did very well. I've lost contact with him, though. The war does that."

"How did your mom take to your being an artist?"

"Oh, she supported me," replied Hitler. "She was the best mother in the world."

He meant it. The expression on his face changed to sadness. He was thinking of her. Then pain coursed through his eyes. He screamed in agony.

"What's the matter, Adolf," asked Ernst, alarmed.

Hitler was clutching his head with both hands.

"My eyes are on fire," he rasped.

He thought of his mother again, how she died, in agonizing pain. Jews. No. It wasn't Dr. Bloch's fault. It was the cancer. He couldn't blame that on the Jews. Still…

Dr. Bloch had been Jewish, but then, what doctor wasn't in Austria? And he was one of the better ones.

Hitler's mother had been diagnosed with a lump in her breast. The only chance was to try to burn the malignancy out.

"Ow! Ahrr, it hurts," he cried.

His head was on fire now. He remembered his mother when they applied the Iodoform to her breast. He even smelled the burning flesh, as if it was just happening now. He grabbed snow from the ground, slapped it onto his forehead. The freezing feeling helped for a moment. Then the memories returned.

His mother received forty-seven treatments. He would never forget it. The Iodoform was applied straight to the tissue of her breast, and burned its way through the tender flesh to the lump. He could smell it sizzling away; he could see his mother biting the pillow, trying not to scream.

For the better part of a year the cancer dragged on. At one point his mother appeared cured, but then it returned. Finally, a few days before Christmas, she died.

"In all my career I never saw anyone so prostrate with grief as Adolf Hitler," Dr. Bloch would later recall.

After the *Anschluss* between Germany and Austria in 1938 Jews were forced to sell their possessions to the state for next to nothing before leaving the country. Dr. Bloch, however, was given the choice to stay and continue practicing medicine or to leave the country. When he elected to emigrate, he was given fair compensation for his property.

"Favours were granted to me," he said later, "which I feel were accorded no other Jew in all of Germany or Austria."

No, the Jews were responsible for many things, thought Adolf. But not for his mother's death. His headache began to ease off.

"After my mother died I moved to Vienna permanently. Gustl followed me there a few weeks later, and we shared a room. Gustl did well. He got into the Academy of Music right away. Took that city by storm."

"How about yourself, Adolf? What did you do?"

"Me? Well, I had intended to attend the Academy of Fine Arts. I had some talent drawing."

"So what happened?"

"I submitted some of my drawings, but the director felt that my talents lay more in architecture. So I went away and began to explore the city and to draw its magnificent buildings. Ah, Vienna was in quite a renaissance at the time. Ernie, you should have been there in those early days. I was in my best clothes – an overcoat and hat, even a walking stick with an ivory handle. Kubizek and I took trips around the Ringstrasse. We saw St. Stephen's Church, and St. Maria am Gestade. And the theatres. They were what we lived for. The Städtheatre, the Peoples Opera, the Royal Opera. We inhabited them all. I couldn't get enough Wagner. It was heaven on earth."

He was lost in rapture as Ernst looked on. That was fine. At least his head didn't look to be hurting.

"Anyway, I submitted more drawings to the academy, but they said that the perspective was off, or something. They told me to work on it some more. Trouble was, my money was beginning to run out. I had a small inheritance, and it carried me for a few months, but that was about gone. And I couldn't borrow any from my aunt when I wasn't actually attending the academy. So we moved to less expensive rooms. But Gustl was becoming successful and I wasn't. So when he went home for a Christmas visit, I used the time to move to a cheaper room on my own. And so began my descent into the underbelly of Vienna. That Jewish town was killing me slowly! I had to sell my nicer clothes. Where I was living, anything nice would get stolen anyway. I went from the Stumpergasse to the Kaiserstrasse, where I slept out on the street during the summer. I began to sell drawings to make a living. I was pretty good at watercolours and India-ink or pencil. I did pictures of the parliament, the old Burgtheatre, the Auersperg Palace, the Minorities Church, the Prager; I sold pictures for advertising. And we explored the city, the despicable, ugly depths of the Leopoldstadt district. Jewish slime in all its splendour."

Hitler paused, looking off in the sky.

"Well, I can remember it all too clearly," he continued. "I didn't drink, you know. I got thoroughly loaded one night in Linz, when I was just a lad, and that was enough. Woke up the next morning outside on the lawn. Couldn't remember falling asleep there. I swore that wouldn't happen again. But Gustl and I decided to explore the Leopoldstadt district one night. We would see what that infernal den of iniquity, that Hookers' Row, was all about. We were young, and entitled to explore."

Ernst's interest was piqued now.

"It was Leopoldstadt, the Second District of Vienna. An old Jewish ghetto."

"But tell me what you saw there, Adi. What sorts of things were going on? Did you sample anything?"

Adolf turned on him, with a horrified look.

"What do you mean, did I sample anything? It is a lie! Anyone who says differently is a Jewish swine. I tell you only what I saw. I did not do anything there!"

"All right, Adolf, simmer down," Ernie said soothingly.

"It was a repulsive visit, if you must know. We walked through the alley, and saw and heard men grunting and women squealing. Really the most disgusting things. Fortunately you couldn't see much in the dark. But you could smell the dankness, the disease. And then every so often some miserable creature would come at you from the shadows, like a vampire, ready to devour you. And she would breathe heavily and ask if you want some company, or she quotes a price for her services. Well, wouldn't you know it? Gustl couldn't resist further and when a dark haired temptress approached us out of the shadows and cast her silk negligee over his head, so that the scent of the perfume overwhelmed his nostrils, and he could smell nothing else but her hot, musky odour, he gave in to temptation and let himself be led, against *my* entreaties, into this vixen's lair! "

Hitler went silent. Ernst waited for his friend to take up the story again, but nothing happened. Hitler was looking off into the distance, across and down the broad mountainside, at the snow surrounding him on the higher elevations, and the green area close to the town in the valley below.

"Yes, so what happened next, Adolf?"

Hitler was thinking to himself.

"That bitch. She did something to him. He couldn't bring himself, at the last minute, to perform for this Jewish whore, and she laughed at him. He came out a few minutes after he went in, his tail between his legs, so to speak. We got out of there in a hurry."

"How do you know, Adolf? He told you this," asked Ernie, somewhat sceptically.

Hitler looked back at him.

"What is that supposed to mean," he asked defiantly. "He told me so, of course." And then after a moment, "My head is starting to hurt again. There, see what you've done."

"In truth it was the Jews themselves that were so repugnant to me in the Leopoldstadt district, and everywhere else in Vienna," continued Hitler. "You know, I can't remember many Jews in Linz, or at my school. I don't even remember having heard the word from my father, though he may have cursed them and I didn't notice. But when I was through wandering the Leopoldstadt, I knew the Jew, and a cold shudder ran down my back. Here was the creature, dressed in a long caftan and wearing black sidelocks. I remember that I couldn't help thinking: is this a German? But here he was, the devil in flesh incarnate. Here was the cold-hearted, shameless, and calculating director of the scum of the big city in the revolting vice traffic. Here was the Jew in his natural element!"

Hitler was standing, his fist thrust into the air. He was animated, his features aflame even under the sunglasses. Ernst looked on, enthralled.

"But I digress," Hitler continued, calming down, his body appearing to shrink. "It was shortly after that that I got into the Männerheim. It was a hostel about a half mile from the Danube. New at the time, and very nice. It could sleep five hundred. Built by some guilty Jewish philanthropist!"

"What happened with your architecture? Did you give the school some more drawings?"

Hitler's expression turned to a scowl. Ernst knew he had brought up the wrong topic.

"Those Jewish manipulators were determined to keep me down," raged Adolf after a moment.

Then he cried in pain, and quickly gripped his head with both hands; digging his fingers into his temples, he started rocking from side to side.

* * *

The term 'Anti-Semitism' was coined about 1879 by Professor Wilhelm Marr in Berlin. It was a supposedly scientific term for a scientific age. All the same, it meant disliking or even hating Jews. If in centuries past a religious motive was the chief cause of anti-Semitism, during the Industrial Revolution it became an economic one. As peoples' jobs and livelihoods were threatened, many tended to blame the Jews.

By virtue of their literacy, clerical skills, and familiarity with urban existence, the Jews became the chosen people to lead the mass of society into the changes accompanying the industrial revolution. This headstart allowed Jews to take the forefront in all the new occupations. They were traders, clerks, and managers in corporations and banks. The Austrian railroads were pioneered by the Rothschilds. As in America, Jews rose rapidly. On the eve of WW1 almost three quarters of Vienna's financiers were Jewish, as well as two-thirds of the industrialists, lawyers, and doctors, and over half the journalists. Most of the leading Viennese newspapers were owned or edited by Jews. The banks, press, theatre, all lay in Jewish hands. This was the situation Hitler encountered in Vienna.

Karl Leuger was the most successful politician in pre-war Vienna. "We are friendly toward all Christian classes and nationalities; we only do battle with one nation, the Jews, not because of the religion of this tribe, but because the Jew seizes with thieving hands all we hold sacred – Fatherland, nationality, and finally even our property. Anti-Semitism is a purely ethical movement."

But he was quick to add, "I decide who is a Jew."

"Anti-Semites unite!" was the slogan Leuger's party used in the 1895 elections for Vienna municipal council, when it won a majority. Vienna became the first and only major European city to have an openly elected anti-Semitic administration. In the last general election before the war, two-thirds of German Austrians voted for parties which supported anti-Semitic laws.

* * *

Ernst had to wait for a few minutes. He said nothing and let Adolf cool down. When Hitler resumed his story, he related how he had been turned down again when he had applied to the Academy of Fine Arts. He had to face the fact that he was unlikely ever to gain entry.

"But I was learning lots of life's little lessons back then," the future Führer reminisced. "We used to discuss politics in the meeting room at the Männerheim. I was in my element, I'll tell you. I loved to teach, to show others where they had gone wrong in their thinking. I was always a leader, right back to my schoolyard days. And I remember getting into an argument with some of the workers who came to sleep at the hostel. There were two transport workers who were defending the Reds as true friends of the working man. I pointed out that socialism, like democracy, would allow Slavs to rule the country because there were more of them. German leadership would be lost. Then I left for the bathroom, and the two goons followed me in. They said I had too big a mouth and had to be taught a lesson. They proceeded to teach me. I learned then that politics is not only about who can give the best speech. You have to be able to protect yourself too. I'll never forget that. If I ever do speak in public again, I will have the goons by my side, not across the table."

He paused a moment, looked out upon the snow covered mountainsides surrounding him, and continued.

"I had a large chair by the window in the reading room. Everyone used to leave it for me. They respected me in the Männerheim. Even the director would come chat with me, something he never did with the other tenants. But he knew that I had a brain; that I was just biding my time."

"What were you waiting for, Adolf?"

"I don't really know. I'm still waiting. I spent time visiting the Austrian parliament, and that was an experience. The most useless institution I've ever seen. The best speakers go there to make speeches. But they never get heard. Or, to be more exact, what is heard is what the press reports."

"What do you mean?"

"The real power in a democracy is the power of the press. Who else distributes the message to the common people? Whatever the press reports that the minister or whoever said is what the people hear. The battle for public support is fought out in the press."

A few moments passed as the two gazed again out at the scenery.

"Do you think that coffee might still be warm," inquired Hitler.

Ernst checked the thermos and poured cups for them both.

"So then I checked into who owned the newspapers and who wrote the articles; and do you know what I found?"

Ernst guessed what was coming.

"Jews! Jews owned them all," Hitler thundered. "I began to compare what I had heard myself in Parliament to what the newspapers reported. It was so skewed that at first I thought it was about a speech I'd missed. But the same thing kept happening. That was my wake up call to the 'objective' reporting of the press. And that wasn't all. Those Jewish caftan-wearers, they controlled art, literature, the theatre, business, the professions. And was there any form of filth or profligacy without at least one Jew involved in it? The fact that nine tenths of all literary filth, artistic trash, and theatrical idiocy can be set to the account of a single people, constituting hardly a hundredth of the population, could not be talked away; it was the plain truth."

"Are you sure you're not exaggerating, Adolf?"

"Exaggerating? Exaggerating?"

Hitler appeared to go wild. He jumped around in the snow, and then rushed to a nearby bush and tore off a sapling.

"Exaggerating am I?"

He rushed forward at Ernie, the stick held high to strike him.

"Adolf, what are you doing," cried Ernie, covering his head with his hands. "Have you lost your mind?"

Suddenly a blank look crossed Hitler's face; his hand dropped to his side, and the sapling fell to the ground.

"I'm sorry, Ernst," he said quietly. "Ever since the gassing, and the news of the surrender – I just don't seem to be able to control myself sometimes. Rage gets the better of me."

Ernie looked at him, then said, "And the war. Don't forget the war itself, Adi. We were ordered to do the most horrendous things to people in the name of the Fatherland. We were ordered to kill in a frenzy, without mercy; and now we're supposed to become peaceful and lamb-like on a moment's notice. You're allowed to lose it once in a while."

He waited a moment, then smiled and added, "Just take it out on somebody else besides your old friends."

Neither said anything for a short while. Then Ernie ventured, "But was it just Jews, Adolf? Surely there were Red leaders who weren't Jewish?"

Hitler thought for a while before replying.

"Well, yes, I was willing in those days to admit that there must be good Jews, who put Germany first, and were true Germans at heart. And during the war, I saw a number in the front lines. And they were brave. I shall not dishonour our army by making false accusations of cowardice. But as a people they cannot be trusted. They will betray us."

"Why do you say that?"

"Because of the Zionists I encountered. They had their headquarters in Vienna. Their leader, Herzl, was a Viennese journalist. He looked German, like so many of the better Jews do. But if you just listen to them, they tell you up front that their loyalties are to Palestine. They want to gather the remnants of the Jews there. They are not loyal to Germany."

Ernst was getting bored with the topic.

"So what else happened to you in Vienna?"

"There's not much more to tell," Hitler replied. "I stayed there, at the Männerheim, for a few years. I couldn't get work; Jews could, of course, because their tribesmen owned everything. But because my father had been a civil servant, I was able to draw a small orphan's pension till I turned twenty-four; not much really, but it helped. And I was giving my sister part of my benefits, so I couldn't really leave earlier. But I was just biding time till the benefits ran out. So, a couple of weeks after my twenty-fourth birthday I packed my few belongings – my artists supplies and some books – and left Austria for good. Next stop, Munich. It was May 1913 when I arrived. And that's where I was when the war began the year after. A true German city, not like mongrel Vienna. My city!"

Bavarians & Barbarians

> How naïve we were, even as men forty years old!! I can only laugh when I think about it. Neither of us realized how much more powerful is instinct compared to intelligence.
>
> - Einstein reminiscing
> a quarter century later

From the Sahara a warm breeze flows north, crossing the Mediterranean and then the Alps before descending upon Munich, in southern Bavaria. The Föhn, as it is called, makes some folk moody and irascible, while in others it draws out the artist. The Wittelsbachs, Bavaria's ruling house for the past millennium, displayed both and left a legacy of lavish palaces and art collections. They were an older line by far than the Hohenzollerns in Berlin or even the Habsburgs in Vienna. But during the 19th century, while the latter two battled for German leadership, mad King Ludwig II built storybook castles throughout the countryside. Declared insane in 1886, still in his early 40's, Ludwig drowned himself a week later in the Starnberger See, a lake a few miles southwest of Munich.

From its headwaters in the Alps fifty miles to the south, the Isar flows northeast through Munich on its way to the Danube. The city is green with parks and woodlands abutting both banks of the river. The Aubinger Lohe contains sacrificial sites from Celtic times. Upriver sits the Hellabrun Zoo, whose residents became food during the blockade. The Englischer Garten sprawls on the west bank of the Isar near mid-town, one of the oldest and largest urban parks in the world. A cultured city in love with music, Munich introduced the waltz to the world in 1740.

Magnificent palaces date from the 13th century, young by Egyptian or Chinese standards, but ancient compared to imperial Berlin, a post-1870 creation. On a narrow island in the middle of the Isar sits the Deutsches Museum, with the world's first car. And Munich has a fine university, by the Siegestor, the triumphal arch that marks the northern end of the Ludwigstrasse, north of which lies Schwabing.

The Einstein family moved to Munich from nearby Ulm in 1880 when Albert was a year old, by coincidence the same time Max Planck was beginning to teach at the university. From a quarter million at that time, by 1919 the city's population almost tripled. Albert's family stayed until 1894, when he was fifteen. His father's electrical business failed and the family moved south over the Alps to Genoa. He stayed to finish high school, but left for Italy six months later without a diploma.

In good times in Munich there was weinerschnitzel, dumplings, cheese, paté, breads from poppy seed to dark pumpernickel; there was weinerwurst, liverwurst, brotwurst and weisswurst, the white sausage of Munich rumoured to contain a good portion of brains and best tasting when washed down with a beer before noon. Bavarians drink more beer than anywhere else in the world, they claim. But in 1919, what with the blockade, there was little of anything for most. Still, life went on at places like the Circus Krone, north of the railway yards, and in Schwabing, its heart the Leopoldstrasse, Munich's home for artists and entertainment. The *Simplicissimus* was its most famous club; in 1919 Bertolt Brecht performed there, and Dietrich Eckart could be spotted in the audience.

"Yes, Schwabing's become decadent by pre-war standards. Not as bad as Berlin, though, from what I understand."

"But disgusting, nonetheless," his companion replied. "They should burn it down and start over, wouldn't you agree, Willy?"

"That doesn't sound like the Franz I used to know," Wolf Warburg interjected from across the table. "I do believe you've become an extremist," he added with a smile.

"It doesn't seem much in the context of the last four years," Franz Gürtner replied with a melancholy stare.

"True," Wilhelm Frick agreed. "But where would we go for more risqué entertainment then? The atmosphere in this town right now is dreary enough as it is."

The three were having lunch at the Vier Jahreszeiten, a hotel in downtown Munich on the Maximilianstrasse. It was mid-February, 1919, and the weather was cold and blustery.

"And how is your love life, Wolf," Gürtner inquired. "Are you seeing anyone? What do you hear of Liesl?"

"As a matter of fact, I'm seeing Liesl again."

"That's wonderful," Frick replied, smiling.

"I'm astounded," said Gürtner. "How did this come about? She doesn't hold that transfer against you anymore?"

"Liesl's finally gotten around to the view that perhaps fighting and killing aren't the only true measures of manhood. She saw a little blood herself in Berlin last month."

"If those who criticized you served a little time at the Front themselves they'd soon shut up," said Frick.

"And the war would have ended quite quickly," Franz Gürtner added, "if the Kaiser, Krupp and Ludendorff had served a little time in the trenches."

Wolf and his tablemates had known each other since 1905, when he had returned from university in Heidelberg to practice law in Munich. Gürtner was a young prosecutor with the Justice Ministry; Willy Frick was a neophyte lawyer and prosecutor newly employed by the Munich police department. The three became aggressive adversaries inside court but good friends out. Wolf moved to Berlin in 1910 but kept in touch with Gürtner and Frick, who both remained at their positions throughout the intervening years. And having foregone military service themselves, they refused to judge Wolf's choices during the war.

"Tell me about Munich as the war ended," said Wolf. "You were both here. What really happened?"

Frick remembered it vividly.

"There was little the police could do but get out of the way as a hundred thousand people marched through the streets intent on throwing out the old government. It was November 7th, mid-afternoon. Workers, ex-soldiers, and other Red sympathizers gathered first at the Oktoberfest grounds and then marched on the city center, even invading the palace grounds themselves."

"So what did the royals do?"

"The old king grabbed a box of cigars, climbed into a touring car with the four princesses, and fled," recalled Frick. "So ended over 800 years of Wittelsbach rule in southern Bavaria – not with a bang, but a whimper."

Within a day, the rest of Germany's ruling houses followed suit, and the day after, the Kaiser himself crossed the border into Dutch exile.

"And who was at the head of this 'Peoples' Revolution'? Why, none other than that distinguished socialist, the drama critic from Berlin, Kurt Eisner. You can imagine how thrilled the Munich establishment was about that," concluded Frick.

"The chief complaint was that his governing experience was a little sparse," added Franz Gürtner. "And most people weren't thrilled to be part of the new Bavarian Socialist Republic. The only thing that kept the army, and the police, from marching over there and throwing him out was his promise to hold elections by the middle of January," explained Franz Gürtner. "So rather than start a small war in the streets, we decided to put up with Eisner until the elections last month."

"Who commands the army locally," asked Wolf.

"General von Mohl overall; General Lossow commands the 7th Division; Colonel von Epp is chief of infantry troops," replied Gürtner.

"That's in addition to his Free Corps brigade," added Frick in a low voice. "But the real one to watch is Epp's new adjutant. He put the brigade together, and our sources say he's stockpiling weapons and looking for veterans to form several more."

"What's his name," asked Gürtner.

"Ernst Röhm. An obscure captain."

"Why, Wolf Warburg! How are you," the voice boomed.

A dapper man in a light gray suit stood by their table.

"Willy, Franz, don't get up."

"Ernst," Wolf replied, rising to shake the other man's hand. "It's been a while. Have a seat."

Ernst Pöhner was Wilhelm Frick's boss, chief of the Munich police.

"How long have you been back, Wolf? And how long are you here for?"

"Haven't you heard, Ernst? He's back with us permanently. Enough of living among the Prussians," said Frick.

Pöhner raised an eyebrow as he looked at Wolf.

"You've moved back to a hornets nest."

"Can't be any worse than Berlin."

"Maybe not, but just as bad," said Pöhner. "The lads here must have filled you in. We don't even know who to take orders from. Is Eisner's government really legal? His Cabinet is still handing out orders, but there's no legitimacy anymore, since he did so badly in the election last month. And the situation here is desperate."

"How so?"

"The electricity, water, light problems. Coal, oil, and food shortages, so people are starving and freezing. And there's the flu epidemic. Is that enough?"

"Quite."

"And there's massive resentment towards the Allies," added Frick.

"And Jews," noted Wolf.

"It's those damn Reds," Pöhner stated. "They've got everyone terrified, and so many of their leaders are Jews. It's no mystery."

"But why not more resentment towards Prussia," Wolf argued. "That's who led Germany down the garden path and into the minefields."

"You may be right," Pöhner replied, "but the Prussians are not a particular threat to peace and order in Bavaria right now. The Reds are! And there must be no civil war here. That is the reason no one has gone after Eisner and thrown him out forcibly. The transfer of power must take place legally, so that all will follow once a new government is installed."

"So everyone is patiently waiting for Eisner stepping down," Franz Gürtner noted, "but it's been a month now since the January election. The legislature is finally due to meet in a couple of days, and everyone expects him to resign then."

"He had better," muttered Wilhelm Frick.

"Or what," asked Pöhner, looking at his lieutenant. "Do you know something I don't, Willy?"

"It's just that we may not be able to control the popular anger towards Eisner and the left if he refuses to resign."

"Someone should have a talk with Eisner and make sure he understands the stakes," suggested Pöhner. "If he refuses to step down, who will the army obey? And my police?"

He looked over at Gürtner.

"Any advice from the Ministry of Justice?"

"We would have difficulty supporting a government so decisively defeated in elections," Gürtner replied. "If not a civil war, Bavaria would still suffer from a nervous breakdown."

* * *

"The perfect cap to a perfect night," she purred to Wolf as he cradled her naked body to his.

"Yes. I rather enjoyed it myself," he replied, whispering in her ear from behind.

She was facing away from him as they lay in bed.

"And it was wonderful to have dinner with Hella and Kuno tonight, just like old times," she added.

Countess Hella von Westarp was Liesl's closest friend, and her brother, Kuno, was the leader of the German Conservative Party in the Reichstag in Berlin.

"Yes, it was nice," Wolf agreed. "Now, you were going to tell me all about your interview with Kurt Eisner today. I only got part of the story at dinner tonight."

"I didn't want to go on about it too long," Liesl replied. "You know how much the man upsets Kuno and Hella."

"I'm not too thrilled with him, either," remarked Wolf, "but I still want to hear what he said."

Wolf held Liesl close as she related their meeting earlier in the day. Wolf already knew something about Eisner, and had met him while Eisner was writing for the Social Democratic Party newspaper, *Vorwärts*, before the war. When its editor was Rosa Luxemburg. Eisner was also a drama critic who, at age forty, left a wife and four children to move to Schwabing in Munich. He was a small, thin, bird-like man who sported a gray beard, frizzled hair, a pince-nez, and thick steel-rimmed glasses, all topped off with a big floppy black hat. In Munich he got involved in peace activism, and spent the first nine months of 1918 in jail. And Eisner was Jewish.

"I think he intends to step down when the legislature reconvenes in a couple of days," Liesl replied.

"But he didn't say so for sure?"

"I don't want to talk about politics anymore. You were going to tell me about your phone call with Albert today. When's he coming to visit us?"

"When the weather gets warmer. Later this spring, he says. Did you know he got his divorce a few days ago? He had to appear in court to answer some questions. Haber went with him."

"Albert must have been devastated," Liesl said sadly. "And what of his boys? How are they taking it?"

"Pretty bad. They're in Zurich with their mother. But it's not like they just separated. They did that back in 1914, just before the war. She couldn't stand Berlin."

Liesl was silent for a moment.

"What are his plans now?"

"Nothing new. He's waiting for the eclipse later this year. If it confirms his theory of Relativity, I suspect he'll become famous. But it would mean lots of travelling, even to America, to give lectures and the sort."

"What's his story, anyway? I know he grew up in Munich."

"Yes, but his family moved to Genoa after his father's electronic business failed. He was fifteen at the time. A year older than me. We never knew each other since he went to a different school. I think it was the Luitpold *Gymnasium*," or high school, "down by the train station. He stayed here with relatives, friends of my parents as a matter of fact, to complete school. That's when I first met him. He really missed his family. I wasn't surprised a few months later when he was expelled."

"For what," exclaimed Liesl.

"Being too bright. Or disruptive, depending on your point of view. The instructors couldn't teach him anymore since he knew more than them. But if you ask Albert, he'll tell you they were more like drill sergeants. He says his years at the Luitpold Gym were his only military service."

"What then?"

"He joined his family in northern Italy, which he really loved. A couple years later he left for Zurich and the Swiss Polytech. Which is where he met Mileva," his first wife.

"How did Albert and Elsa meet," Liesl asked.

"They're distant cousins, and he knew her a bit growing up. They got close again a few years ago, but broke it off when he moved to Prague. Then he moved to Berlin, and separated from Mileva in 1914 just before the war. Elsa would come over and clean up the house for him, cook a little. But a couple of years ago he got really sick. Liver and gut problems. So Elsa moved in and nursed him. They've been together for the most part since."

Again they were silent.

"What's wrong, Liesl," he asked a few minutes later, as a tear rolled off her cheek onto his.

"It's Dunken. I can't help worrying about him."

It had been over six weeks since they'd heard from her brother.

"If he got out of Kiev with our troops last month, we should have heard from him by now. Oh, what's happened to him," she whimpered softly in Wolf's ear.

He knew he'd left it too late. Through the blowing flap covering the back of the truck in which he was riding, Dunken von Schlieffen could see the enemy vehicles, mainly old trucks and battered armoured relics, in the distance trying to gain on them. The German soldiers with whom he was riding had the advantage in that they were on the road itself, whereas some of the enemy were in the fields and moving slower. But the ones on the road were keeping up with them. It was his own fault; why had he waited until the last minute to leave?

At least he'd made the right decision in leaving with an army unit instead of driving west from Kiev on his own. The Partisans would have picked him off easily by now. The retreating Germans had been worried about possible attacks by some Red units; they weren't even thinking of the Ukrainian Partisans. Until half an hour ago, when their convoy was almost ambushed, and would have been if a scout hadn't managed to sound the alarm. The Partisans were closing, within a kilometre when the warning came, and the convoy sped up in reply. They raced west now, a half dozen army trucks and semi-armoured vehicles ahead of twice as many pursuers, trying to reach the safety of the bulk of the German army heading home. These last stragglers faced the greatest danger.

The problem was that they were barely thirty miles outside Kiev, and the last big armoured group heading home to Germany was at least a day's travel to the west. Could the tiny convoy outrun the bandits chasing them for that length of time? As if in answer explosions rocked the fields by the roadside ahead of them. There must be enemy mortar or tanks hidden in the brush up ahead! The Germans had been herded into a trap that they would now have to fight their way out of, and the odds were against them.

There were several side roads, and woods off to the right. Another shell struck, this time close by, shaking the truck violently. Then Dunken felt the vehicle turn sharply to the right, and saw through the rear flap that they had left the convoy. In a few moments, trees rose on both sides. They raced ahead, but where they were headed for, Dunken had no idea. Ten minutes later they entered a village. The truck rolled to a halt on the edge of town and the soldiers got out. There were just three of them.

"We must hide. If Partisans come through here and we're caught...," warned the supply sergeant with a slicing motion across his throat.

"Herr Schlieffen," he said to Dunken, "we thought our chances were better than with the rest of the convoy. I'm sorry that you're mixed up in this."

"Where will we hide," he asked, bewildered.

"Split up, and find a barn or something."

"Then what?"

"I don't know, mein herr. Make your way back to Germany somehow. Without being caught by the Partisans, or the Reds, or the Poles. But there's less of a chance of getting caught if we split up. And get off the road!"

With that he waved, and headed off up the road before there was a chance to argue. Dunken stood there stunned. Then he heard a muffled noise. He cringed and turned to see a peasant leading a horse and wagon up the road. Relief – at least it wasn't a Partisan. The wagon was loaded with hay and large ceramic milk jugs.

"You are German," asked the peasant in a language that Dunken recognized, a form of German bastardized over the ages by eastern Jews: Yiddish.

"Yes. A businessman. Just trying to go home."

Perhaps it was the terrified look in Dunken's eyes that the other man noticed.

"Climb in under the hay. A patrol is coming up the road."

Dunken scrambled onto the wagon and under the hay, pulling his bag with him. The Jew then urged his horse forward.

"I don't even know your name. And where are we," Dunken called out.

"My name is Jonah, and we're in the village of Fastov. Now keep quiet, or you'll get us both shot!"

* * *

Adolf Hitler had had just about as much of the Russian POWs as he cared to. The camp at Traunstein, southeast of Munich, was losing its appeal, and he yearned to be back in the city itself, whether or not it was rife with Red swine. It couldn't be much worse than he had to put up with as a guard at the camp, waiting for prisoners to be shipped back to Russia. The same trains that disgorged German troops returning from their occupation of the Ukraine and the east were on their return trips slowly ferrying Russian POWs to the frontier; but it all took too long, Hitler lamented. In the meantime the Russian swill spewed forth the Lenin virus into the German population.

On the other hand, it hadn't been a total loss. Maybe there was something to what some of the Russians were saying. The ones that weren't spouting the Red poison. The White Russians. At first Hitler was sceptical when they claimed Germany never beat Russia – that it was the Jews.

"How," Hitler asked them, wide-eyed.

"Because the Jews created the Reds. Marx was a Jew, and all the Red leaders are too! Trotsky's a full Jew and Lenin's got some buried deep down. And those rich western Jews are funding them. That's what brought down Russia. Not you damn Germans."

Hitler's rifle butt smashed the man's cheek, knocking him down.

"And now the Jews have beaten Germany as well," the Russian finally replied, rubbing a bruised jaw, sitting up on the floor. "Unless you believe that the mighty German Wehrmacht lost the war with the West on the battlefield."

"Do you think it's possible, Ernie," Hitler asked a few days later, "could that Russian have been right? Is it really the Jews behind it all?"

"You know best, Adolf. You're much more informed in these matters than I am."

Ernst Schmidt was learning not to argue with his friend. What was the point – he risked upsetting Hitler, and Ernst didn't care much about politics anyway.

"But it had to be someone," Hitler continued, animated, eyes blazing. "The British and French, even with the Americans, could never defeat Germany. No army in the world could! It was the Red traitors, the defeatists – but I didn't imagine the Jews were behind it. Yes, a lot of the Red leaders are Jews. But there were loyal Jews in the German army."

Hitler was pacing up and down the barracks floor. Ernst read a magazine as the snow fell outside.

"At least I thought they were loyal," Hitler muttered.

Ernst continued his reading.

In Munich on the same snowy, blustery afternoon, in a conference room in the Hotel Vier Jahreszeiten a meeting of the Munich branch of the Thule Society had been called to order twenty minutes before, with two dozen members and a couple of guests present. The secretary, the enticing Countess von Westarp, had just finished reading the minutes of the last meeting. Now the discussion shifted to the January election results in Bavaria.

"It's been over a month now since Eisner lost. When is he going to step down?"

"That is the question, Herr Drexler," the presiding member replied. "He keeps saying that he will, but it hasn't happened yet. How long do we put up with it for? We've already threatened him publicly. If he doesn't go soon, we have to remove him, if only to maintain our own credibility."

The Thule Society had circulated a handbill after the election telling Eisner to step down, or else! The society, which drew its name from Ultima Thule, the mythic birthplace of the German race, was an offshoot of the secret *Germanenorden* Society which had been formed in Berlin in 1912 by the likes of Admiral von Tirpitz, creator in the years before the war of the German navy that so enraged the British. The navy camouflaged it as a literary club about German history and customs, and its membership included nobility, right wing politicians, military officers and police. It owned and operated the *Volkischer Beobachter,* a local newspaper. And it secretly participated in intelligence work, infiltrating Red organizations, maintaining arms caches, and its own *Free Corps Oberland.* It also helped finance other Free Corps units such as the Ehrhardt Brigade, which displayed reverse swastikas on their helmets, a symbol originally used centuries ago in German tribal worship.

"We're all in a hurry for Eisner to step down," noted Ernst Pöhner, chief of Munich police. "But who is there to vote for even after he's gone? There isn't a decent political party running in Bavaria. They're all either Red or Republican."

"That issue was to be addressed later, but perhaps we can hear it now if Herr Eckart is ready."

The presiding member looked over to the left side of the room, where a couple of men sat in chairs by the window. Dietrich Eckart, in a cream-coloured suit, was in his fifties, his face weathered by whisky and smoke. Son of a Bavarian lawyer, he viewed himself as a sometime journalist, full-time intellectual, and man of the world when it came to women; he was also an alcoholic and morphine addict with a heart condition. He looked slightly perturbed; he'd been called upon early. But he shuffled to his feet.

"As you know, I've been working with Herr Drexler," he motioned to his neighbour, "on this. And so far we can't find a party that represents our interests. So we must form a new one. But we can't be openly linked to it or its leader. He has to appeal to both workers and veterans, so he can't be some aristocrat, or a general such as Ludendorff – the people are fed up with the old leadership. He has to be a man of the people. With us pulling the strings, of course."

Liesl von Schlieffen, from a chair at the back of the room, sat listening quietly. She was trying to remember as much as she could without taking notes. As a journalist, it was a skill she at times found essential.

"You know Dr. Gottfried Feder," said Dietrich Eckart, nodding over towards the man sitting closest to Liesl at the back of the room. He had dark hair and a small mustache that was clipped so that it grew just under his nose and didn't extend over the full lip, just like the Tramp in Chaplin's silent movies, at the time a top box office draw. Feder was an engineer by trade, but an economist at heart who had founded an obscure organization called the German Fighting League for the Breaking of Interest Slavery.

"Along with Dr. Feder this afternoon is Dr. Karl von Müller," continued Eckart, "a professor of modern history at the University of Munich. They have been drafting a platform for the party."

Feder glanced at Müller and stood up.

"Ours is a simple platform. We stand against international Jewish loan capital, the Jewish loan market. It turns us into slaves of the Jews. Easy to understand, easy to follow. Don't borrow from Jews. It doesn't help Germany. It only makes the Jews rich! Are there any questions?"

"Dr. Feder, is it all right to borrow from German Jews," Liesl asked. "Then the money stays in the country."

"Oh, don't you believe that, my dear. It goes out of the country, to London and New York."

There was applause from most of the room. Feder sat down, and his companion Müller took the floor.

"Do you not realize that the Jews own New York, and New York now owns the world! It is so simple that I am surprised you do not see it. Heed the words of Heinrich von Treitschke, the Berlin history professor who warned that year after year the Jews pour from their Polish cradle to dominate our stock exchanges and newspapers. Among the most educated Germans we hear the cry, 'The Jews are our misfortune!'"

"Hear, hear," said Dietrich Eckart, clapping loudly. "But there's something more. A Jew cannot change into a true German just by joining the Lutheran church. It is in the blood!"

Here was a new type of hatred of Jews. No more simply based on religion – now it was racial, blood-based. There was no way to convert to avoid persecution.

"That is exactly right," the presiding member confirmed. "If in the past we did accept the occasional patriot who had converted from Judaism, the loss of the war has now made us recognize the Jewish menace. Which is why we have denied membership to Count Arco-Valley. He has Jewish blood, even though he seems a true German."

The presiding member was referring to the next matter on the afternoon's agenda.

"The Count is waiting outside. He insisted on coming here today to argue his case in person."

The presiding member turned and whispered to Hella von Westarp, who appeared lost in troubled thought. She got up reluctantly and opened a door leading to an adjoining room. Embarrassed by what was about to take place, she admitted Count Arco-Valley, who entered wearing a scowl.

"You all know me," he began. "I am Austrian by birth. Nevertheless, my first love is a greater Germany that would include German Austria. I even served in the German army in the war with the 1st Bavarian Heavy Cavalry Regiment on the Russian Front where I was decorated for bravery. As you can see from my leg, I was badly wounded. I am a German through and through," he shouted, raising his fist in the air. "I served the Fatherland with bravery and distinction. But all this is not enough for you! My mother is half-Jewish, and so I am denied membership in this society. What can I do to prove myself," he screamed.

No one replied at first, then Ernst Pöhner asked, in jest, "Can you kill your countryman, the Jew Eisner? Then I might believe you."

Dietrich Eckart snapped quickly, "That matters not! Even were he to, he couldn't join the Thule. He's a Jew, and it's in the blood."

Everyone was silent. Then came the vote. All to no avail—the majority turned him down.

"I'll show you," he raged, eyes ablaze. "I'll show you all!"

With that he stalked from the room.

The stateliest street in Munich, the Maximilianstrasse begins in the Max Joseph Platz, with the statue of the monarch seated in the middle of the square by the Royal Residenz, with the National Theatre and its magnificent stone eagles looking on. Travelling east one passes the Vier Jahreszeiten Hotel on the left, with the Kammerspiele art gallery across the street. A couple of blocks further east a green boulevard of grass and trees commences running down the center of the street, leading farther along to a statue of Maximilian II. The grand avenue then crosses over the Isar, under the gaze of Athene, goddess of wisdom, who watches over the bridge at mid-span. The Maximilianeum, home of the Bavarian state legislature, sits on the eastern bank surrounded by a soothing greenery.

It was to the Maximilianeum that Kurt Eisner was strolling, along a downtown sidewalk with his ever-present bodyguards, on this late February morning. Eisner was wearing his trademark black floppy hat with long, straggly hair spilling out underneath. Liesl von Schlieffen walked with him.

"It was because I needed time to consult the other parties, to see if they would join a coalition government. That's why I didn't resign immediately after the election."

"And what is the result now?"

"I think you know, Fräulein von Schlieffen. Neither the Communists nor the majority Social Democrats will support me. I'm too far right for the Reds and too far left for most Social Democrats."

"Which is kind of interesting since all the papers label you a Red anyway."

"Based on what? My politics or my religion? Or just my hair?"

"All three," Liesl observed. "In any event, since you've got no support from any other party, and since your own party only won three seats in the last election, you really have no choice but to step down as Minister President today."

"You wish to scoop the other papers," Eisner accused her with a wan smile. "I can relate. I too was a journalist not so long ago. And will soon be again, no doubt."

Liesl was dressed in black, a long coat reaching down below the knees, with black dress and hose underneath. Her hat too was black. It was all in sharp contrast to her skin tone, that of a Munich winter. The light of the day was etched around her finely chiselled facial structure, her small though patrician nose; large, green eyes framed by long lashes gazed out from under the wide rim of her hat.

"Can I take that as a confirmation that you will be stepping down this morning?"

"Ah, Fräulein von Schlieffen, you will have to be patient to…"

As Kurt Eisner and his companions shuffled along the sidewalk Count Anton Arco-Valley, hidden in a doorway vestibule, came out behind him, and without hesitation raised his gun, took aim, and shot him in the back and brain.

Before his stunned guards moved, Eisner hit the pavement face-forward, dead.

One guard then lurched into action, pumping five shots into the Count, and a mob then trampled and stomped him. Left for dead, Arco-Valley would survive to be sentenced to five years.

Liesl stumbled away from the scene, wandering in shock in the direction of her apartment. Upon arriving there, she felt suddenly weak, and her legs began to buckle, so that she had to lean against the sandstone exterior. Once inside, she struggled up the stairs to her second floor suite, double-locked the door, and took off her clothes. She threw her coat and hat away, not content just to clean them, covered as they were with bits of Eisner's hair, scalp, brains and blood. Then she ran a very hot bath, climbed in, put her hands to her face and began to cry.

Wolf made a rare trip to the legislature that morning just to hear Eisner speak, and only heard about his assassination when he arrived. Striding along a concrete pathway bisecting a wide snow-covered lawn with the yellow grass of winter poking out along the edges, he noted scores of angry people with loads of weapons milling about. Hurrying through the stately entrance and down a broad foyer, Wolf made his way to the gallery where he snagged a seat near the front, and settled in to wait for the show to begin.

The session was called to order and the Interior Minister, Erhard Auer, rose to speak in place of Eisner. He was now head of the government. He thought Eisner had been too far left, but he eulogized him as a loyal Bavarian.

"Woe to the coward who cut him down in the street like a dog," Auer thundered. "Now, let's have a unanimous show of hands in support of the motion currently before us praising Kurt Eisner as a Münchener and Bavarian of the first order!"

Wolf looked round the room. There was loud clapping from some pockets, but most of the legislators simply raised their hands in silence. And then there were those who were booing instead. Or worse.

"Auer, you hypocrite," shouted an Eisner supporter from the gallery, "you're glad he's dead. Admit it!"

"That's slanderous," Auer screamed, and the shouting grew. Wolf, sensing danger, slid from his seat and made for the door. From the corner of his eye he saw someone surge through the crowd, and then a rifle being drawn from beneath a long coat.

"You murdered him, all of you! This is for Eisner!"

The rifle spoke, and Erhard Auer fell dead to the floor. A brave major jumped to his aid, only to topple likewise. Firing erupted around the chamber and Wolf dove down, ruminating on how Bavarian politics had suddenly become a Wild West show. And this was just the opening act.

A Passing Rule of the Jews

> The Jews are without any doubt the strongest, most tenacious and purest race now living in Europe.
>
> - Nietzsche

> Eisner's death only hastened the development and finally led to a dictatorship of the Councils, or, better expressed, to a passing rule of the Jews, as had been the original aim of the instigators of the whole revolution.
>
> – *Mein Kampf*

Albert Einstein and Count Rantzau kept Wolf well informed as to what was happening in Berlin after the deaths of Rosa Luxemburg and Karl Liebknecht in mid-January. And the personal accounts through their letters were so much more interesting than the newspaper reports which he'd already read. The essentials, though, were that national elections were held less than a week after the brutal murders, with the lion's share of the vote going to the centrist democratic parties including the Social Democrats. Things then calmed down in the capital for a few weeks until the Reds, realizing that they couldn't confront the government by force, called a general strike. Their posters exhorted their supporters to avoid violence, but the Reds couldn't control their more radical elements like the Sailors Division.

As March 1919 began, with winter still in the air, the Free Corps attacked the Alexander Platz and the Berlin subway, and then the Marstall, where the Sailors were, across from the Royal Schloss. All fell by the 5th. The next day, using planes, trench mortar, howitzers and flamethrowers, they took back the main police station. Five policemen were killed by the Reds, but the number was inflated by the government.

"The brutality and bestial behaviour of the Reds fighting against us oblige me to issue the following order: From now on, any person who bears arms against government troops will be shot on the spot," declared Defence Minister Noske.

"Anyone found with arms in his possession will be shot without trial," was the Order of the Day issued by the Division of Horse Guards.

"You are ordered to disarm and disband," the Defence Minister told the Sailors Division. When the unarmed sailors arrived to collect their mustering-out pay, almost 30 were killed outright by Free Corps who claimed they were gathering to attack the government.

Free Corps formations then moved to cleanse the city of any Red resistance. A few days later the city was quiet, with more than 1500 Reds and 'sympathizers' dead and 10,000 wounded. The Free Corps units which had their trial of fire in Berlin then moved on from city to city across Germany, stamping out Red resistance wherever it surfaced. They were brutally successful in every case. Allied governments, grateful that they didn't have to send in their own armies, cheered as the forces of 'Democracy' triumphed over Communism in Germany.

On the personal side, Einstein, concerned about Liesl's state following Eisner's assassination, promised to visit Munich sometime in the spring, perhaps the beginning of May when the weather improved.

Wolf lay back on the couch and thought of Liesl, who lay beside him. They were at her apartment in Munich, close by the Isar. Her spirits were slowly recovering now, a month after witnessing Eisner's death. For her the war, at least in terms of seeing death actually inflicted, had only begun after the world war ended. Up to then she had seen many wounded, even amputated, soldiers who had returned from the Front. But since late December 1918 she had actually witnessed people being shot or burned or blown apart in front of her, first in Berlin and now in Munich. And now she wondered that it had taken Wolf so long to leave the army back in 1915.

Now she was experiencing what he did back then, visions of human limbs and guts and brains splattered about. How could she have been so wrong? How could her whole country, and the whole civilized world?

And she had sabotaged her relationship with Wolf.

Sitting up on the couch, Wolf reflected on Munich now that Eisner was gone, with Erhard Auer blasted the same day by a deranged apprentice meat cutter. He recalled diving for cover as shots erupted in the chamber, and the melee as members and panicked spectators alike rushed for the door. But the crisis passed, a new leader was chosen, and a measure of calm returned to München.

In March the yearly Fasching festival took place for the first time since before the war as people donned outrageous costumes and partied for a week. Ash Wednesday arrived and the party ended, and the ugly business of politics raised its head again. Senior Reds arrived from Moscow and Berlin, and to demonstrate their strength strikes were organized. By late March, Munich was paralyzed.

In a meeting hall in Schwabing, a group of those who happened to hate the Reds were gathered.

"Ah, Herr Rosenberg. So glad you could make it," said Dietrich Eckart.

A young man in his mid-twenties took off his scarf and jacket. He returned the greeting in an accent that was unmistakably Russian. But it was fluent German; he was obviously familiar with the tongue. In fact, Alfred Rosenberg came from Estonia where he received an engineer's diploma and studied architecture before fleeing the Russian Revolution.

It was a boisterous meeting, with many frayed and heated tempers despite the plummeting temperatures outside. The outspoken Rosenberg fit right in with the fanatical Red and Jew bashers who increasingly dominated Thule policy discussions.

"I'll never forget the first thing he said," Dietrich Eckart regaled the group. "There's this knock at my door; it's late at night and I'm getting ready for bed. I'm nervous about opening it because it might be a Red come to shut me up. But I'll be damned if they'll make me scared to open my door," he shouted to the applause of his companions.

"So I open it, and there's this tramp on the landing. He's got on an old hat and overcoat that he'd worn all the way from Russia. I ask what he wants, has he come to rob me? And the first thing he says is 'Can you use a fighter against Jerusalem?'"

There was laughter around the room.

"Well, we've been fast friends ever since," Eckart declared, slapping Rosenberg on the back. "And since then, we've had some very enlightening conversations about the Jews."

Jews were in the forefront of the German economic expansion of the mid 19th century and pre-eminent in banking and the stock market. Jews as well flooded into law, medicine and journalism. In Berlin, two-thirds of the dailies were Jewish-owned.

"Perhaps never before in Europe had a minority risen as fast or gone as far as did German Jews in the 19th century," observed Fritz Stern.

Karl Marx, son of a line of rabbis, was highly anti-Semitic himself, expressing the same bitterness towards Jews which Luther displayed when they didn't flock to his Reformation. When Jews did not embrace Marxism, they became to him the embodiment of vulgar and cruel capitalism.

"What is the secular cult of the Jew? Haggling," declared Marx. "What is his secular god? Money. Well, then, an emancipation from haggling and money, from practical, real Judaism would be the self-emancipation of our age."

The spectacular success of the Jews in Germany in the 19th century might have continued down a sunlit path had it not been for the massive influx of *Ostjüden*, eastern Jews. During the 1870's thirty thousand left Russia. After the pogroms following the Tsar's assassination in 1881 emigration shifted into high gear. Still, by the war Jews formed less than 1% of the German population, and Berlin's Jewish population was just a third that of Vienna. But WW1 saw millions of Jews from the battlefields of Galicia, Poland, Lithuania, and the Ukraine streaming westward, with nearly 100,000 winding up in Berlin. It made little difference to their detractors that over 100,000 Jews had fought for Germany during the war, and that a third had been decorated for bravery.

"Gather your arms!"

Adolf Hitler was standing on a chair in the middle of the common room of the Turkenstrasse Barracks in downtown Munich , hollering at his fellow troopers. It was March 23rd, and news was filtering in from Budapest. There had been a Red coup in Hungary the day before.

"They've nationalized all industrial and commercial enterprises, banks have been expropriated and newspapers banned. They're led by Bela Kun, a Jew trained in Moscow," shouted Hitler.

He was reading from a newspaper.

"How long will you wait," he wailed to his listeners. "There's only Austria between us and the Red hordes now!"

Müncheners were terrified that Austria would fall and that Bavaria would then face a Red monolith stretching all the way to Moscow.

"Do you see him," asked Captain Röhm to the civilian standing beside him.

"See him," asked Dietrich Eckart in an exaggerated fashion. "I can hear him clear as a bell, across the din of a crowded room. He's like a bullhorn!"

The two stood silently for a moment, observing Hitler gesticulating excitedly as torrents of words gushed forth.

"What's his background?"

"He's an Austrian," Captain Röhm replied.

"But that's great," smiled Eckart, squeezing his arm. "They hate Jews much more than the average Germans does. This Hitler fellow confirms that. They've been overwhelmed for a couple generations now by Jews from the east. It just takes one trip to Vienna or Budapest to see it firsthand."

"Yes, well, I have a little job for him to test your theory," commented Röhm. Then he shouted across the room, "You there, Hitler! Over here, on the double!"

"Yes, Captain," came the answer along with a sharp salute as Hitler arrived in haste, puffing.

"Corporal, I noticed how concerned you are about the Red Jewish swine from Moscow who have swept over Hungary. We need your help to protect the Fatherland. Can we count on you?"

"You have only to command," Hitler gushed, saluting boldly.

"Corporal," said Captain Röhm, "I want you to keep an eye on who is a Red or a Red sympathizer in the barracks, and who we can count on. It's of the utmost importance.

Make a list of the traitors, Corporal, and prove yourself truly loyal to your adopted country!"

It was still unseasonably cold, with a late winter hanging stubbornly about. On April 1st, a foot and a half of snow fell on Munich. The municipal employees stopped taking the emergency money that the city was printing, so a lot of the streetcars, water, sewer and phones went dead. On April 4th, the heaviest snowfall in years blanketed the city with twenty inches, but the political scene heated up nonetheless. Drawing on the momentum of the Communist coup in Hungary two weeks before, Red delegates in Munich braved the snow on the night of the 4th to make their way to the Lowenbräukellar, a beer hall a few blocks north of the main train station, to read aloud a resolution calling for Red revolution.

A couple of days later the Union of Revolutionary Bavarian Internationalists was formed, led by Ernst Toller, a young poet from Berlin. From the Queen's bedroom in the Wittelsbach Palace they declared a Soviet republic in Bavaria. Now there were two Bavarian governments, Republican and Red. The first, the one elected in January, fled terrified to Bamburg in northern Bavaria.

Toller spurned the support of the senior Reds from Moscow and Berlin. His inner circle were inexperienced revolutionaries who thought themselves visionary. His foreign minister, Franz Lipp, was a former mental patient who liked to write to Lenin.

"My dear Colleague: I have just declared war on Württemberg and Switzerland because these dogs did not send me 60 locomotives immediately. I am certain of victory."

Silvio Gesell, the new minister of Finance, espoused a "free-money clique", and Gustav Landauer, the Commissar for Public Instruction, opened Munich University free to all

Bavarians over 18. And then declared that 'history, that enemy of civilization, is suppressed.'

The new regime proved incompetent. Businesses and property were seized. Money and credit were freely spent on luxuries while essential services were ignored. The true Reds from Russia, and the dedicated ones from Berlin, bided their time, embarrassed, knowing that the circus under Toller could not last.

"But it's not only the true Reds who are gagging on this perverted regime," Liesl was saying to Albert Einstein over the telephone. "Just imagine what the Right wing is feeling now. The army, the business leaders, the establishment – my father. They're scared to death that their property will be expropriated. Everyone waits for an army to liberate Munich. It's not just that they're Marxist – they're such thieves and bunglers!"

Wolf heard the one side of the conversation from his chair a few feet from Liesl.

"What do you intend to do about this nonsense, Willy?"

"Dr. Pöhner assures me that a force is massing to the north, and will march to liberate Munich within the next few days," Wilhelm Frick replied from his chair across the room from Wolf.

They were at Liesl's suite in downtown Munich in the late morning.

"Do you believe that?"

"It makes no difference," Frick shrugged and then smiled. "Give this regime a week and it'll fall apart on its own."

But Toller was deposed in a palace coup by the senior Reds from Berlin and Moscow. The next thing they did was appoint a young 23 year old radical by the name of Rudolf Egelhofer as commander of the new Red Army of

Bavaria. And he began to assemble the best paid mercenary army in the country. The Reds were for a short time unchallenged in Munich, and certain of their leaders took the opportunity to institute a reign of terror, which allegedly included mad sex orgies involving Egelhofer. Perhaps the Reds had a premonition their time was limited, so they decided to enjoy it to the hilt. They had heard of events north of Bavaria. In mid-April Free Corps units put down a Red coup in Dresden, and four days later they crushed a revolt in Brunswick.

Defence Minister Gustav Noske proposed sending to Munich the Free Corps von Epp along with two other crack, battle-tested divisions to break the Red yoke. But the Bavarian government, now hiding in northern Bavaria, declined the offer. Federal help wasn't necessary; Bavaria could solve this on her own. So 8000 Bavarian troops faced off against Rudolf Egelhofer's Red army of 30,000 mercenaries. In this first Battle of Dachau, just north of Munich, the Reds smashed the Bavarian force. The government finally turned to Noske, who ordered 20,000 Free Corps, including the Epp and Ehrhardt Brigades, to Munich to join the local troops. By April 27th they ringed the city, setting the stage for the second Battle of Dachau on the outskirts; then would come the storming of the city itself.

Albert Einstein and Fritz Haber were on a southbound train to Munich. It was the last week of April and they were determined to visit Wolf and Liesl before continuing on to Zurich, their ultimate destination. Albert remembered the Munich of his youth. His family moved there from Württemberg in 1880, when he was just a year old, and stayed until he was fifteen. The family was not religious, neither attending synagogue nor Hebrew school, nor observing Jewish diet and festivals.

“We lived in a big old house in Sendling, surrounded by maple trees and lots of shrubbery. And Mama had a garden too. I liked spending time there. Maybe that’s why I learned to speak so late. It’s true you know. I couldn’t speak until three and I wasn’t fluent until nine or ten.”

“It didn’t seem to do you any harm,” Haber mused.

“No, to the contrary, I think my slow development caused me to think about such basic things as time and space later in life than most people; and so I gave it a more mature and systematic study, since I was already almost grown. Naturally, I could go deeper into the problem than a child of normal abilities.”

“Sheer drivel,” said Haber.

From age five to ten Albert attended a Catholic school near his home, and then transferred to a *gymnasium* or high school by the Hauptbahnhof, the central train station.

“That school was a perfect example of the use of the educational system not to teach, but to indoctrinate our youth with a Prussian worship of authority. The teachers were like drill sergeants. And their foolish faith in authority was the worst enemy of the truth!”

Haber, who had been with the German army on the Western Front as recently as the spring of 1918, was more respectful of the need for discipline, particularly working within large organizations. And if by 1933, with Hitler coming to power, even Haber's enamourment with regimentation and authority had worn thin, in the spring of 1919 he was sure of one thing.

"The revolution in Germany was only an indictment of the Kaiser's system of government, and not of capitalism," he lectured Einstein. "The Reds should know that most Germans are, at their core, capitalists."

"Now what's the problem up ahead," asked Einstein, as the train shuddered to a halt.

They were just north of Munich, on the outskirts of Dachau. Haber looked out the window of their private berth and up the track. He could see troops but little else. A few minutes later a knock came from the door, and a young Free Corps officer entered.

“There is Red insurrection inside Munich, and federal forces are currently engaged in an action to relieve the city. For safety’s sake, no civilians can currently cross our lines. You will have to remain on the train at least overnight.”

"What is your name, Captain," asked Haber, standing up. "I am Professor Haber from Berlin. You have heard of me, of course? We wish to get into the city."

"I am Captain Hess. I'm sorry, mein herr, but I don’t recognize your name. I have my orders. No one is allowed in."

"But that's preposterous! You must have heard of me. I run the Kaiser Wilhelm Institutes in Berlin.”

"You'll have to take it up with our commanders," replied Hess. "They're from Berlin, just like you. Stubborn Prussians. And their orders are to not let anything through!"

"So how are we supposed to get into Munich then," asked Haber, exasperated. "Surely they're letting some people through."

Einstein looked out the window to see troops from the Epp and Ehrhardt brigades manning a checkpoint that stretched across the track and the roadway beside it.

"Unless you have some good connections, mein herren," replied Rudolf Hess, "you might as well get comfortable. You may be here awhile. Besides, it's for your own good. We've received some horrible reports. Believe me, you don't want to be inside the city right now."

Exactly which act of violence begins the cycle is often hard to determine. What is more certain is that atrocities don't generally happen in a vacuum – they usually come about in the midst of an atmosphere of general lawlessness and violence. In that setting the event seems not nearly so amazing as it does years later when the violence of the moment, captured and frozen, is judged in the harsh light of history. For our purposes, the starting point is a stone quarry just outside the city limits, where a group of Russian POW's, still waiting for transport back home, were being guarded by a squad of Red troopers. It was their bad luck that the particular Free Corps battalion that ran into them first was not a veteran unit, and it became jumpy upon encountering so large a group of Reds. Or maybe it was a veteran battalion that was bearing a grudge. The result was a massacre of 52 Russian POWs along with all their Red guards.

Word leaked back to Reds all over Munich of the massacre at the stone quarry. The local population knew that Free Corps and federal army forces were now ringing the city, poised to rush in and do who knows what. More incidents like the stone quarry, but on a larger scale?

"We must root out the Republican leaders and their cohorts inside the city now," muttered one Red strategist, "before they can order our ambush."

"And we need hostages," wailed another nervous Red.

And so there commenced a slew of arrests.

Adolf Hitler was still asleep, tossing and turning in the throes of another nightmare. His eyes were burning, his fingers clawing at them through an imaginary gas mask. But then he was awakened by arms tugging him, pulling off his blanket and yanking him out of bed.

"On your feet, scum! Aren't you Corporal Hitler?"

Three Red troopers surrounded him, one poking with a bayonet.

"I said, on your feet, swine!"

Hitler was now standing. It was seven in the morning, and he was in his longjohns.

"Sleeping a little late this morning, aren't you," asked one of his tormentors.

"He's a pitiful sight, isn't he, comrade," laughed another, poking Hitler in the ribs with his rifle tip. Luckily his weapon didn't sport a bayonet.

"What do you want of me," Hitler asked meekly.

"We're rounding up all the imperialist spies. We're going to have a roast. And you're invited! Ha, ah, ha ha ha."

Hitler's face was white.

"I'm going to faint," he said. "Please, I must sit down."

"What a sorry sight. How did you survive the war, you pitiful excuse for a soldier!"

They pushed him to the floor and started kicking. He curled up in a ball.

Endure, he thought. You survived four years in the trenches, you killed enemy troops who made these Reds seem laughable.

"Please, I don't feel so good. Could you get me some water from the bathroom."

They were all laughing at him now. One asked where the bathroom was, perhaps it would be a good place to drown him.

"No, we were sent to arrest him, comrade. They'll be no drowning now. But be patient. I'm sure you'll get the chance later!"

Adolf edged closer to the bed, crawling slowly across the floor.

"Where are you going, slime?"

"Back to my bed, sir," he replied.

He was almost there. They didn't make a move towards him as he pulled himself up onto the bunk. They still made no move as he reached down on the far side of the bed, where they could not see.

"So where the hell is his rifle? It's not in the closet here."

Almost immediately they heard the bolt clicking and turned to see Hitler, weapon cocked and aimed, sitting on the bunk before them.

"You laugh and degrade me? You rank amateurs. Now I should kill you!"

He had the drop on them, and the Reds went white.

"No sudden moves, my dear comrades," Hitler said. "So you've come to arrest me, have you? I'll say this but once. Leave now and I will not shoot you where you stand."

The Reds looked at each other, then turned and left the room. He followed them into the corridor, in his underwear, rifle aimed at their backs.

"Just keep on going!"

He would have shot them then and there, but he didn't know how many of their comrades were lurking about. Then he quickly donned his tattered uniform and skipped out a side window of the barracks. Walking down the freezing alley, glancing over his shoulder for Red troopers, he discovered he'd forgotten his overcoat and hat. And he couldn't risk going back.

The Reds knew that the federal army and Free Corps forces had now joined the local troops surrounding Munich. A showdown was imminent, and the Red leadership was not optimistic. The Free Corps had been brutally successful in every city that they had turned their attention to. The Red leaders desired insurance against the Free Corps and forces of reaction.

Countess Hella von Westarp was a favourite of the Thule Society membership. She hadn't been there long, but then neither had anyone else. On this morning Hella and her best friend Liesl von Schlieffen happened to be walking down the Briennerstrasse, just east of the Odeonsplatz with its *Feldherrnhalle*, Generals Hall. In the distance the Obelisk stabbed the sky in the middle of the Karolinenplatz.

The women were bundled up in overcoats and scarves, sheltered against the wind and cold. What little snow remained was strewn across otherwise bare and icy streets. Little auto or truck traffic could be seen. The city was bracing for a firestorm. The Free Corps counterattack was expected any time. Leaflets were beginning to appear, informing Müncheners that a federal army was on the way to lift the Red yoke from the city.

Most of the town waited apprehensively but optimistically. The Reds were a nightmare. Egelhofer and his orgies, either supported or given a blind eye by the senior Reds, Levine and Axelrod; the sheer waste of resources on government largesse; the outrageous salaries paid to the Red Army mercenaries. And still the city did not function! Trams didn't operate, phones were intermittent, garbage piled up, sewers backed up, and electricity failed. In a way the atmosphere was almost festive: the Reds celebrated as if there was no tomorrow; and the rest of the folk smiled in anticipation of the comeuppance in store for Egelhofer and his gang.

It was about eleven in the morning. An old jalopy drove slowly down the lonely roadway. Liesl was beginning to wonder how good an idea it was to be out walking. Hella was unconcerned: she had always known her place in Munich society, and was proud of it. It was not just her family or her title; she was beautiful and stylish to match. A fine combination in a civilized society.

But Munich was not civilized at the time. The truck passed the women slowly and then did an abrupt U-turn in the middle of the street. A comrade jumped out of the passenger side as the vehicle screeched to a halt. His carbine was levelled at them.

"Up against the building, up against the wall! Now! Schnell!"

He was an unsavoury, unkempt character, who hadn't shaved for the last few days. His uniform was tattered with occasional patches, and he bore a red armband. And since he had a rifle and bayonet, the women obeyed. The Reds searched the women – slow and methodical, feeling underneath the women's coats for guns.

"Ooh, I recognize you," drawled the comrade who was searching Hella. "That's why we stopped, you know. You're one of those Thules. We've been on the lookout for you. Who's your friend here?"

Neither of the women answered. The comrade who was holding Liesl closed his fingers tightly around the right side of her waist, squeezing and pinching. She gasped and moved away as far as she could. But he had her pinned.

"So what is your name, my lovely fräulein," her tormentor asked.

"Liesl," she said. "Liesl von Schlieffen."

"Never heard of you. Are you a Thule too?"

"No," she replied quickly. "The Countess and I are old friends."

"Hmm," said the other comrade. "Well, it's not safe for you to be walking the streets alone. You might get kidnapped by one of those Free Corps fellows. You'd better come along."

"Where are you taking us," asked Hella, as they drove down the Briennerstrasse, past the Obelisk and continued further west to the Königsplatz, and left down the Luisenstrasse. They saw Red machine gunners on the second level of the Propyläen, on the western side of the plaza. They reached the Hauptbahnhof, and turned east for a block to the Luitpoldstrasse. They pulled into the Gymnasium parking lot. This was Red headquarters.

The women were hustled up the stairs and through the entrance, then down a hall, and then another. Liesl quickly lost track – she was growing increasingly scared. They were nearing their destination, and she could hear mad shouting at the end of it. Finally they entered a large room: the school auditorium. There were lots of people there – a couple Red leaders, some armed comrades and, in a large group in a far corner of the room, other hostages. A hundred or more, it appeared, a huddled mass of shivering, terrified, sometimes sobbing souls. Into this enviable scene Liesl and Hella were now plunged.

Just to the north of Munich, in the village of Dachau, the battle was getting underway. The Free Corps attacked in force; the Red defenders replied with dumdum bullets and poison gas.

"Disgusting," opined Einstein, from his seat in the railcar at the Dachau train station. "Fritz, we have people like you to blame for this."

Here we go again, thought Haber. Would it never end?

"What are you talking about, Albert?"

"The gas. Once the genie is out of the bottle, you know," continued Einstein. "If you had never invented it in the first place, it would not be turning up here. And who knows how many will die from poison gas in the future."

"But how about atomic energy, Albert? What if someone makes a bomb out of that? Should we blame you because you first divined the incredible power of the atom?"

* * *

Avoiding the streets, roaming alleyways, looking for someplace safe to hole up, Adolf Hitler finally made his way to the Englischer Garten to hide out in the woods. He settled in amongst the grass, tree roots and brush, and tried to sleep. It had been a rotten month, what with news of the Red coup in Hungary, and then the catastrophe in Munich itself. And to top it all off, just a few hours ago he was almost arrested, probably to be taken away and shot. Would the nightmare never end?

1919

Here he was – a war veteran, a hero! Awarded the Iron Cross 1st class. His thirtieth birthday was just days ago – and this was his life: hiding out in the local park, coatless and hatless. Damn those Reds! Those Jews!

Stabbed in the Back

The acrid odour drifted into the train car, causing Haber to react immediately. He rose from his seat, pulling Einstein along with him.

"Come Albert, we must hurry. And try not to breathe."

Einstein was already tasting the gas. The two left their berth and headed down the corridor, through one door and then another leading to the dining car. Haber moved to a table, grabbed a napkin and soaked it in a glass of water. He handed it to Einstein.

"Put this over your eyes and mouth, Albert. And get down on the floor, below the gas!"

In the middle of Munich, a certain corporal suffered other torments. Unwilling to risk a return to the barracks, he ended up hiding out in the Englischer Garten by the river Isar, lying down among the bushes. He had no coat, nothing to cover himself with, nothing to rest his head on except a cold rock or the hard ground. In misery, his dreams dredged back to the previous year, to the dying days of the war, when his regiment was ordered back to Flanders where they had sacrificed so many times before. They dug in below Ypres, by the town of Comines, near Werwick, among hills and fields. Hitler was back in the chow line with Ernie Schmidt on a night in mid-October, awaiting some sort of sawdust and paste concoction for dinner.

"How long has this damn shelling been going on for," muttered Ernie. "Sounds like it's getting a little closer."

"Not close or loud enough to force me back inside that trench, like a rat seeking shelter in a grubby little burrow."

"Did you hear that? The thuds." Like shells not exploding.

And then a pause before Hitler answered, "Gas?"

Alarmed, they both ran through the mud left by the rains, reaching their dugout and diving into the wooden shelter, grabbing their masks and drawing them hurriedly over their faces; then settling in for the long, tedious wait, first for the attack to halt and then for the gas to dissipate.

Pungent clouds commenced drifting through the trenches. This was mustard gas; unlike chlorine, it actually burned throat and eye tissue rather than merely irritate it. Soldiers were compelled to keep their masks on for hours as the night passed, the air inside them becoming dense and stale. One brave recruit finally doffed his mask, gingerly sniffing the air, tentatively breathing in. His mates looked on through goggled eyes, first with relief as he gulped the air – but then in horror as he fell to the ground, retching, gurgling, gasping, then choking to death.

By dawn the gas had dissipated and shelling resumed. Hitler doffed his mask and sucked in oxygen mixed with the scent of high explosive. But not poison. The respite was brief, though, before there were more thuds amongst the explosions.

"Gas! They're gassing again!"

Hitler scrambled to put his mask on, but caught a whiff of the gas. He thought it sweet, though some found it acrid. He could breathe now inside the mask – but his throat burned, and his eyes stung so he squeezed them shut! He started to tear the mask off to wipe his eyes – but caught himself in time. For the next minute he did nothing but try to calm down. Then he cautiously opened his eyes to inky blackness. Was it a moonless night, or was he dreaming? He stumbled to his knees, terrified. A few moments later he began to grope blindly forward.

Of those left alive, one soldier could see faintly. Another grabbed onto his coattails, and another grabbed onto his, and so on, and so on, so that this one led all the others to safety. Hitler's face was puffed up and his eyes swollen shut. They felt like glowing coals, stinging, burning, pain radiating from them. For the first time in years, since early in the war, he felt real fear, for now he was truly helpless. All he could do was cling to the coattails of the other victims as the blind, pitiful column of cripples made its way to the first aid station at Linnselle.

* * *

He waited as long as he could, but Wolf still hadn't heard from Liesl by the time he had to leave. He was due to meet Haber and Einstein out at the Dachau terminal since the Free Corps surrounding Munich weren't letting any trains into the city. So instead of the short trip from Liesl's suite downtown to the Hauptbaunhof, the central train station, he now had a forty minute drive out to Dachau ahead of him. Normally no problem, but these weren't normal times. Which was why he was so worried about Liesl. Where was she and why hadn't she at least called? She was supposed to go with him to meet the Berliners.

As he steered the Daimler roadster through the streets heading northwest on the Dachauerstrasse he ruminated on the deteriorating situation. The Reds knew they were likely to lose to the Free Corps, and that a heavy blood debt would be extracted by the freebooters. Their reputations preceded them. So the Reds were partying and panicking at the same time, knowing there was likely no tomorrow. Literally. They could easily find themselves strung up in a public square by morning. After all, there was already fighting going on at Dachau. And there was now no escape since Free Corps ringed the city. Civilians were easy targets for the armed Reds carousing through the streets on their last night in control. And there was much talk of Red units breaking down doors in search of Free Corps and Republican supporters.

So as Wolf neared Dachau, Liesl weighed heavily on his mind. But the boom of cannon and howitzers focussed him on the immediate. He began to encounter Red military units hurrying to and fro. A few minutes later the military traffic became thick as he approached the rear of the Red line. Finally he hit his first roadblock, a Red army cargo truck turned sideways, blocking half the road. But it turned out that the troops there were more interested in keeping other Red troops at the front line and preventing them from fleeing back towards Munich, rather than stopping anyone foolish enough to be going towards the line. So Wolf sailed around the truck and continued up the road. A mile later, it became impassable. A sea of Red troops was fleeing towards him, towards the city. He turned the Daimler sharply to the left and pulled off the road, waiting for the flood to pass.

A half hour later there was a lull in the traffic fleeing south from the Dachau battlefield. The Reds had passed but the Free Corps units hadn't yet caught up. Wolf backed the Daimler onto the road and continued towards Dachau. He reached the train station on the outskirts, where he ran into the first Free Corps formations. And there on the platform stood two familiar figures.

"Albert, Fritz, so good to see you," Wolf said, shaking the visitors' hands as they loaded their luggage into the roadster.

He quickly bundled the two in and started back towards the city in haste.

"Why the hurry, Wolf," asked Einstein. "We haven't even told you about getting caught in the gas attack."

"I'm sorry – you were what," he replied, distractedly.

"We were gassed, Wolf, didn’t you hear," Haber growled. "What's the matter with you, boy," and he slapped Wolf on the back. "And where's Liesl?"

That was the nub of it, Wolf explained – where was she?

They returned to her suite downtown and Wolf made some calls. It turned out that several Thule members had vanished in the last few hours, and there were rumours of some being kidnapped off the streets in broad daylight. To be used as hostages, or tortured in revenge.

"But where have they taken them," Einstein inquired as Wolf hung up the phone once again.

"To one of their strongholds, an old school down by the Hauptbaunhof."

"Which one," inquired Albert again. "I probably knew it as a lad."

"It's on the Luitpoldstrasse, I think," Wolf said. "At least that's what Hella's father tells me."

"Well, I'll be," replied Einstein. "The Luitpold Gymnasium. My old high school!"

"Well, get your books together again," Wolf replied, leaping from his chair, "because we're going there!"

"You might want to take a weapon or two along as well," suggested Haber.

Shansky was actually a Jew, a professor at the University of Munich. He had been mistaken by the Reds for a Thule member just because he happened to be at the hotel when the Reds picked up some Thules there. He couldn't convince the Reds that he wasn't with them. The Thules, prisoners themselves of these Jew-inspired Reds, weren't about to let the Jewish professor off the hook by telling their captors that he wasn't one of them.

When Rudolf Egelhofer asked who their leader was, all the Thule members, Hella excepted, started pointing to Shansky.

"But I am not a Thule," he whimpered to them, begging for his life, "I am Jewish. How could I be one of them?"

"And how do we know you're not lying," asked the former leader of the Red Army of Bavaria, pushing him back towards the group.

But in truth Egelhofer was scared. The Free Corps were coming. He might die later that night. Why should this old man survive? And he was a snivelling liar anyway!

"It's time to make an example of someone," Egelhofer shouted. "Now who will it be? Time to make a choice – or I'll choose for you!"

The motley group of prisoners came together, then from out of their midst one was cast: Shansky.

"There he is. Our leader," they shouted.

"No," Shansky wailed. "They lie," and he backed towards them.

His only other choice was the Red maniac in front. The one with the rifle in his hands and madness in his eyes.

"Come, my little lamb," Egelhofer cooed at him, extending his arm. "You are the chosen sacrifice, it seems. Ha, ha."

He suddenly grabbed Shansky with his free hand and dragged him towards the cement wall of the large hall. It was painted white.

"Stand there," Egelhofer shouted at him.

Shansky dropped to the ground, grabbing the Red's ankle, begging for his life. Egelhofer kicked him away.

"Rise and die like a man, or stay there and be shot like a dog. I don't care which," the Red shouted down at him. "You have ten seconds."

Half a minute later Shansky still had not risen. His mind could comprehend no longer – he was in shock. Egelhofer called two comrades over, who pulled him to his feet and stood him against the wall.

"Watch and wail," screamed the Red, turning briefly to the pack of Thule prisoners before turning again to Shansky, levelling his rifle and shooting several times in succession, before the corpse had a chance to collapse to the floor.

"Who's next," he shouted, "who wants to be the next to die? Because as sure as my name is Rudolf Egelhofer, you're all going to die today. It just depends when."

"I thought they were Reds, and that we were done for when they first burst into that dining car," Einstein recounted to Wolf as they drove east through the downtown core, heading for the Luitpoldstrasse.

"I knew right away we were safe," countered Fritz Haber. "You could see from their uniforms that they were federal troops. But Albert here has no military training…"

"Of course," replied Einstein, turning a little red," and proud of it."

"And when the troopers reached us, well, they recognized my name immediately," Haber continued, "so we were escorted to the station platform right away to meet you."

"But of course," Wolf replied sardonically. "Well, belt on your holster again, Captain. I'm betting there's more action ahead for us tonight."

The Red guards paraded out the unlucky Thule detainees one by one, marching them up and placing them against the white wall, now splattered red with the blood of a professor, a painter, a prince, a baron…

Liesl, in a state of mental denial regarding the reality of her surroundings, lost track of the number thrown up against the wall and shot. Then they came towards her and, dreaming or not, she screamed; but alas, it was no dream. Hella and Liesl had been clutching each other; but now they grabbed Hella, tore her from Liesl's grasp, and dragged her forward, throwing her up against a wall still dripping wet with the blood of others.

"Just put it on and stop arguing," Haber drawled to Einstein. "It'll keep you hidden better," he continued, thrusting the black toque at him. "And smear this grease on your face."

Wolf pulled a sub-machine gun from the trunk of the car and handed it to Haber.

"I haven't seen this type before," drooled Haber.

"A gift from the American Secret Service," Wolf replied. "Latest issue from the Yank Army Rangers. My cousin Paul has some influence in the Treasury Department, which controls the Secret Service. I brought these back from New York in November."

Wolf and Haber equipped themselves with guns and explosives and, with Einstein leading, made their way up the alley towards the rear of the Luitpold Gymnasium. Einstein knew the way intimately from his youth; and he trundled up the alley now, with neither schoolbooks nor guns, but instead a tool belt.

In another part of Munich, down by the Isar River, in a glade in the Englischer Garten, Hitler lay curled up on the hard ground, tossing and turning in troubled sleep as he recalled his recuperation from the British gas attack in the closing days of the war. He was first treated at the field hospital at Oudenarde and then left by train for the Prussian Reserve Hospital at Pasewalk in Pomerania, north of Berlin, a few miles from the Baltic coast. And all along the route, the Lenin virus worked its way malignantly through the railway cars and train stations. Troops spoke openly of deserting a lost cause, bragging of their own cowardice. A veteran of four years service at the Front, Hitler was revolted.

He stared up blindly through bandaged eyes at the figure hovering above. The voice was welcome, female, a novel sound after so long in the company of soldiers. But it was faint comfort. He was sure he'd never see again.

"My eyes, they burn, fräulein."

"I know, Corporal, but be patient. The pain will go away."

"When," he pleaded, low and scared.

"Soon, soon," and the voice drifted off, abandoning him again to the darkness.

Hitler tossed and turned fitfully in his sleep. His head rolled over on the hard ground. Damn Reds! Now memories came to him of his mother's death eleven years before. She had cancer and was receiving daily doses of Iodoform, a treatment that consisted of gauze saturated with the liquid, which was pressed upon the open wound or incision. It then ate its way through the flesh to the cancer itself, hopefully then to burn away the cancerous cells themselves. The cancer was mainly in her remaining breast, the other already having been lost or burned away. The Iodoform sizzled its way through in a constant, searing pain; his mother was in terrible agony towards the end. Hitler, just nineteen, was devastated when she finally died.

The Iodoform had a nauseating, rotten odour like mustard gas. One burned through his mother's breast; the other burned his eyes.

Not only was his sight destroyed; invincible Germany as well. Bismarck's and the Kaiser's Germany.

"*Deutschland über Alles in der Welt!*" he cried out in his sleep.

Germany over all in the world!

"For pity's sake, it's four in the morning. I want some sleep. You there, shut up, or I swear I'll throw you out of here!"

The park apparently had other inhabitants.

But Hitler didn't stir. He was used to loud noises in his sleep, from shells exploding nearby. He had learned to slumber through it. The visions continued; and so too an urgent desire to restore his country's dignity, and crush the Allied armies to avenge his loved ones.

His memories returned again to the hospital at Pasewalk, in Pomerania, a blinded corporal with constant pain in his eyes and head. If that wasn't enough, he had to endure defeatist talk and Red propaganda. By the beginning of November 1918 he had regained some sight, hazy and painful though it was. He coughed hoarsely through seared throat and lungs, adding a deep, gutteral, hypnotic quality to his voice.

Hitler wanted to return to the Front as soon as possible. The war could be won if the doubters stopped whining and the workers stopped griping. General Ludendorff was right; but alas, Ludendorff had been sacked! Another shock he received while recovering.

Hitler recalled the visit to the hospital by a party of sailors trying to spread the gospel of Lenin, canvassing for recruits amidst the disintegration of the German empire. They sauntered through the wards dropping leaflets proclaiming the Red revolution in Germany.

"Where have you fought," Hitler demanded of them, "what battles have you been through for the Fatherland?"

"I don't have to bleed or die to know stupidity and waste when I see it. The Kaiser ruined this country. Only the wealthy are benefiting from the war, only the gun manufacturers and speculators and rich hoarders. Away with capitalism!"

"Such tripe. Go away. You give me a headache. You make my eyes burn."

Through his searing, hazy vision he saw the sailors stare down at him one last time and leave. Three Red swine they were, dark and swarthy easterners, probably Jews.

"We are the coming Order," they cried at him, gloating – the scene frozen in his memory as his mind drifted off.

* * *

General Erich Ludendorff returned from Sweden in the late spring of 1919, where he had fled in disguise immediately after the war's end the previous November. When he got back he took rooms at the Hotel Adlon in Berlin, initially with a fake name, and a private entrance off the Wilhelmstrasse. While there he encountered senior members of the Allied Control Commission. One morning he talked with General Malcolm.

"So you tell me why Germany had to surrender, then, if she wasn't beaten militarily," asked Malcolm.

"The Bolshevik Jew revolution in Russia was spreading westward and attacking our backside," Ludendorff replied. "It was infiltrating our troops and our population. It ate away, poisoning our troops' minds. That and the lazy cowards on the home front who were too selfish to sacrifice."

"So you were stabbed in the back by Red propaganda and slackers?"

"That's it," Ludendorff hollered, his eyes alight. "That's it. They stabbed us in the back! Those traitors stabbed my armies in the back!"

*   *   *

She had been brave. And she still was, except that she was crying too, which made her seem not quite so invincible. Egelhofer once again struck Hella full across her face. As her body went momentarily limp she was held up only by the Red guards on either side. Then he stuck his hand down her panties, and she kneed him in the groin in response. He crumpled to the ground. Rolling around, clutching his genitals, he raged at her.

"Bitch! Your death is now certain!"

She had no reason to doubt him. Liesl, viewing Hella's agony but unable to help, clutched herself and tried to hide her eyes. It was a nightmare; only it was real.

Egelhofer got up from the floor, raised his rifle over his head, and savagely hit Hella square in the face with the butt. She crumpled to the floor moaning. Her jaw was smashed, crooked and bloody. He started kicking her with his combat boots.

Hella told him to shoot her, that she'd rather be dead than be touched by an animal like him. In mad rage, he raised his rifle, took aim, and shot her three times in the face.

Liesl, disbelieving, passed out.

They were on a carousel in the Englischer Garten, she and Hella, on wooden horses parading round a ring. They were children, just five or six years old, and her mother looked on. Tiny clouds of varying shapes floated overhead, but it was mostly sunny; and she could smell the flowers nearby. Flowers of all aromas and colours. By the by a large ominous cloud floated into view, blocking the sun and darkening her mood. And then a beast, standing up and dressed in slacks, a cartoon character, appeared and scooped Hella before anyone could react. Then, before she knew it, the beast was back, menacing her…

When she came to, Liesl was being dragged by two guards across the wooden floor towards the bloody wall. At least ten others had been shot by the Red executioners under Egelhofer. It was now her turn, as they stood her up and thrust her back against the oozing, mostly red, wall.

"Any last words," Egelhofer asked in an increasingly bored tone. "Or can we just get on with it, bitch?"

Just get it over with, she thought. Egelhofer raised his rifle and took aim.

"Stop this madness at once!"

The shout came from the doorway across the room.

"What have you done, guaranteed our executions?"

Liesl looked over to see Ernst Toller, former head Red deposed by the seniors from Moscow and Berlin.

"You coward!"

Egelhofer was livid, frothing at the mouth.

"We're all going to die anyway. Or haven't you heard how the Free Corps operate?"

"But this is plain murder!"

Toller hurried forward, gingerly hopping over fallen bodies along the way, finally reaching Liesl. He stepped right in front of her and turned to confront his mad comrade.

"Move aside," Egelhofer snarled, teeth bared, "unless you wish to be next."

"I will not!"

Egelhofer, rifle pointed, stepped towards him, trying with his free arm to throw Toller out of the way. But he would not be moved, and the other comrades weren't getting involved. Finally Egelhofer stepped back and took aim.

"If you wish to die with her, far be it from me to deny you."

He cocked the trigger to fire.

"But they're murdering people wholesale," Rudolf Hess gushed to Colonel von Epp.

"We must do something," Captain Hermann Ehrhardt declared in support. "I say we move now. And if we find out those damn Reds have committed atrocities, well, heaven help them."

"There are reports they've already murdered a dozen prominent Müncheners at the grammar school by the Hauptbaunhof."

Ehrhardt took the clipboard that Hess was holding and scanned it briefly. Then his jaw dropped and his eyes went wide.

"Including the Countess von Westarp!"

"The Countess," Epp gasped. "Damn it, I've heard enough! We move now. And any Reds who oppose us, shoot them on sight! We'll brook no nonsense from these cowardly, murdering traitors."

In the Englischer Garten by the Isar, in the middle of the Munich night, Adolf Hitler's tormented dreams continued. His head throbbed, his eyes burned, and his stomach churned as he remembered back in angst and despair to his stay in the hospital at Pasewalk six months before, as the war was ending. He was coming to accept the inevitability of the coming German withdrawal from France and Belgium. He heard of desertions and mass retreats on the Western Front, and awful rumours of revolution in Bavaria under the Jew Eisner. But it was his worst nightmare when an old army pastor arrived at the hospital one afternoon to inform them that the very next day the Kaiser would abdicate and Germany would surrender unconditionally, to be demilitarized, with the chief cities of the Rhine occupied!

As Hitler stood there listening, everything went black and he was blind again. Not gas this time, but hysterically induced. He remembered – he would always remember – groping blindly, feebly, down the hallways back to the ward, throwing himself on his bunk, burying his burning head in his pillow.

Millions of German boys dead in the mud of Flanders, the Somme, the Marne. All in vain, due to pacifists, traitors, and Reds!

“Miserable and degenerate criminals,” he cried out in the darkness as he slept. “When my time comes you will all pay, with your lives!”

Siegfried's Revenge

Every person has both the ability to do amazing good and terrifying evil. No one of us can ever arrogantly say 'I wouldn't have done it'. All of us have got the capacity to be some of the most awful perpetrators.

- Desmond Tutu 1998

Germany is having a nervous breakdown. There is nothing sane to report!

- Ben Hecht
Chicago Daily News 1919

Adolf Hitler loved opera from an early age, and in Vienna he was first exposed to some of its finest. His favourite composer was Richard Wagner, a German who in the mid 19th century penned the *Ring of the Nibelung*, an epic fantasy trilogy that told the tale of the fall of the gods and the giants, and the odyssey of Siegfried, the ultimate Thule warrior.

The story begins with Wotan, the head god, offering to trade to the giants the goddess of Immortality, Freia, in return for the giants building the gods an impregnable fortress, Valhalla. He gets his fortress, but uses a ring of gold fashioned by a dwarf to double-cross, enslave and destroy the giants. The story ends, though, with Valhalla burning to total ruin – *Götterdämmerung* – the final demise of the gods. A mystical mix of epic heroism followed by ultimate destruction which the *Ring* saga portrayed became the tragic, albeit perverted, mould for the Third Reich. In 1945, Hitler led a beaten Germany down the same path.

It has been said that Wagner based dwarves on Jews, who use the power of gold to enslave the world. Richard Wagner himself was a dedicated anti-Semite who in his time hollered far and wide of the evils of the Hebrew race.

"Whoever wants to understand Nazism must first know Wagner," declared Adolf Hitler.

* * *

"This is where we make Leberwürst out of Communists."

"Reds executed free of charge."

Rudolf Hess heard these and numerous other slogans as he toured the perimeter lines of the Free Corps preparing to launch their assault against the Reds holding Munich.

It was May Day, 1919. In Red Square in Moscow it was marked by parade; in Munich, by a battle for the city. Hans Frank, a 19 year-old freebooter, was a student at the University of Munich when he was not out storming the city. Unlike his fellow student Rudolf Hess, he had not served in the war, being too young; but he had enthusiasm! As did fellow students, some of whom managed to elude Red patrols and make it to the Free Corps lines to tell of alleged Red atrocities occurring, among other places, at the Luitpold Gymnasium by the Hauptbahnhof.

Lt.-Gen. Burghard von Oven, a Prussian, was overall commander of an assault force consisting of over 20,000 federal and Free Corps troops from Bavaria, 7500 from north Germany, and almost 4000 Württembergers. The spearhead of the assault, the experienced von Oven, von Epp, and Ehrhardt Free Corps, rushed the city from all sides, the rest following. Over fifty federal and Free Corps troopers and over a hundred Reds were killed, with hundreds more wounded, in the initial fighting. The Reds were decimated, their coup toppled. But the killing was not over. Some freebooters considered themselves holy

German warriors, Siegfried incarnate, intent on annihilating the Reds and restoring the glory of the Reich.

The first Reich was the Holy Roman Empire which, in Voltaire's words, was "neither holy, nor Roman, nor an empire". It began with Charlemagne and lasted a millennium. But while there was a common language and culture, political and military power lay with the hundreds of kingdoms and smaller entities which comprised it. The empire was dissolved in 1806 to avoid letting the crown fall to Napoleon

The Second Reich was born in 1871 when King Wilhelm of Prussia, through his brilliant prime minister, Otto von Bismarck, united all of the German states to defeat France, and then in the afterglow united them politically under Prussian leadership. King Wilhelm became Kaiser Wilhelm I of the new German Empire, fated to last just 47 years. To the Reichstag in 1888 Bismarck proclaimed, "We Germans fear God and nothing else in the world!"

It was an industrial and martial society at the same time, leading the old world in scientific research and economic growth, while duelling to the death was still a recognized tradition in the army and universities. The army retained its position as a privileged caste, alongside a budding oligarchy of industrial barons.

Bismarck was such a powerful personality that he ruled imperiously, through the first Kaiser, during that period when Germany should have been instituting western-style democracy. The second Kaiser Wilhelm did no better, and their unfortunate legacy was that Germans were left with no significant experience in self-government when their new republic commenced immediately following the war.

* * *

Liesl watched Rudolf Egelhofer raise his rifle and level it at her, notwithstanding that Ernst Toller was bravely attempting to intervene. Egelhofer appeared crazy, a maniacal light shining from his eyes and froth dripping from his gaping maw.

"A pity that one so lovely has to die, my dear," Egelhofer extolled, "but take solace in the knowledge that we are all doomed anyway. The Free Corps will see to that, no doubt."

Faint comfort, she thought, as she heard the bolt click on the rifle. A shot rang out before she had a chance to shut her eyes, and she flinched, expecting the bullet to rip through her chest. But magically, it was Egelhofer who pitched forward onto the wooden floor, blood oozing from a wound in his back. And then the lights went out, followed by a loud explosion, and then two or three smaller ones. In the dark, Liesl groped the floor not knowing what to expect next. There were screams ands shouts.

“My eyes! Ow!”

“What is it?”

“I can’t breathe!”

People coughed and gagged. On the floor, Liesl was among the last to notice it.

“Gas! They’re gassing us,” a voice cried from across the room.

It now saturated her throat and eyes. In the dark, groping the floor, retching, coughing, Liesl had been suddenly plunged from one hell into another. She wasn’t even sure it was real. Perhaps she had been shot. But it wasn’t a bullet that was burning her eyes!

Rolling on the floor, coughing convulsively, from beneath her fingers which were rubbing her eyes, Liesl caught sight of jagged blips of light, enough illumination so that she could see around her for several feet. And it was a surreal scene. Her captors had collapsed to the floor, their weapons fallen away, rubbing their eyes, coughing and choking, just as she was. But it was all happening in a dim, smoky, netherworld of slow motion.

Into the hazy swirl there appeared suddenly, as if sailing through in jagged blips at lighting speed, a monstrous apparition, wearing an army greatcoat, but with the face of a ghoul. It landed, stooped quickly and grabbed her. She froze, ceased coughing, and lay stunned, too scared to breathe. Her head was forced back, and an object thrust over her face. She closed, then opened, her eyes. A mask!

She breathed in, gasped, coughed, tried to take it off. But her companion held it on.

She coughed again, and gulped. Clean air! She took a deep draught.

Then strong hands gripped her shoulders and pulled her to her feet. They could not speak, their entire faces enclosed by the masks. He grabbed her hand and pulled her along. Instantly all the fears of the day, from Hella's ghastly murder to her own near death, temporarily melted away. She knew Wolf's touch in a heartbeat.

Loping across the room, sidestepping dizzy, disoriented bodies, Wolf and Liesl, followed by a third masked figure, made their way through an eerie, strobe-lit, fog. Their progress was fast, but as they neared the doorway to the side of the room, a couple of Reds recovered their wits, and their weapons. Shots whistled across the room. Wolf pulled Liesl harder as he ran for the door. He grabbed for the knob, yanked it open, and hauled her through with him. Their trailing companion turned and lobbed a canister, this time a smokebomb. Then he stepped through the open threshold, and Wolf shut the door tight behind them.

Liesl noticed another masked figure kneeling outside the doorway. He hurriedly connected wires running from the power receptacle to the metal doorknob and frame, joined them securely with a crimper from his toolbelt, and then deftly applied some tape. Slipping the crimper back in his belt, he rose and pointed down the hallway. Wolf waved everyone on, and the four headed away from the door. From twenty-five feet down the hall, just before they turned the corner, they looked back to the doorway.

"Ow, it burns! My hands!"

"Damn! What have they done? The devils!"

"Turn it off! Ahr! Turn it off! It's sizzling me!"

Sparks jumped across the surface of the metal doorframe. If at first the door shook, it quickly became completely still. They had stopped trying to open it from the other side. Then in a moment the knob moved, the electricity crackled, followed by a familiar cry:

"Ow, it's still alive! Stop it! Pull me away, pull me away!"

The door was still again.

Wolf and his companions turned the corner and fled down the hallway to the building entrance. Once outside, they doffed their masks and looked at one another.

"Albert? Fritz?"

Liesl found her rescuers' identities hard to believe. Certainly Einstein was not the typical warrior type.

"Douse the lights in the building again, Albert," Wolf urged him. "Put them back in the dark. It'll buy us a few more minutes."

"Those lights – that was you, professor," Liesl asked.

"A little strobe effect. Quite disconcerting if you're not used to it," Einstein replied. "It confused them enough, but allowed Wolf and Fritz to make you out."

"And the electrified door – that was you as well."

"My father built and sold electrical dynamos for a living. I worked on them even as a youngster, so I know my way around electricity.

"It seems our pacifist friend has a few tricks up his sleeve," Haber noted.

"That little gas concoction of yours was spectacular too," Wolf replied. "Something to render them helpless, but non-toxic. Even Albert can't argue with that."

* * *

Rudolf Hess was wounded in the leg storming through Munich. His comrades told him later what they found when they reached the Luitpold Gym, how even they weren't prepared for the carnage within. The *London Times* reported that the killings were not done by Müncheners, but by Russian and Prussian Reds. The local populace failed to note the distinction. The freebooters found the corpses of Hella and the other Thules, shot, slashed and stabbed, and burned with cigarettes.

The Free Corps went wild in an ecstasy of vengeful wrath. Over a thousand Reds were summarily executed, many shot in the gut to ensure slow and painful death, the dead so plentiful that the undertakers couldn't keep up. The warming weather made this unhygienic, so they dug shallow trenches for graves.

Adolf Hitler, back in his barracks, head held high, let all around him know how he had stood against the Reds, and faced down three of them with his carbine.

"Siegfried's revenge shall be cruel and terrible!"

Corporal Hitler hastened the deaths of many following the Red days of Munich. A spy in the barracks, he kept a list of Red sympathizers which he now paraded before the court martial boards. Summary execution was immediate, but not without a trial first, as the army and Free Corps were quick to point out.

"I hereby summon a court-martial," began one Corps leader in typical fashion. "Members are myself, the Chief of Staff, and our Ordnance officer. Let's get on with it."

And so they did.

"Corporal Hitler, step forward and give your evidence."

"I can swear that this pig who now slouches before you," declared the hoarse, raspy, deep voice, "was a Minister in the government of the Red swine."

Hitler paused just a moment for effect.

"I myself saw him enter the Royal Residenz, which they were using as Red headquarters."

"Do you deny this, prisoner," asked the Corps leader.

"Yes, yes, I am just a businessman. I had business at the Residenz."

"Liar! Liar!"

Hitler had leapt from his chair, fist in the air.

"I saw you!"

The voice reverberated throughout the room unexpectedly loud, somehow compelling.

"We find the charges against the accused to be credible and true. The death penalty will be carried out without delay."

"But you're wrong," wailed the condemned.

"So go appeal."

But there wouldn't be time. Within minutes the Minister was dangling over the marketplace, head cocked to one side from a snapped neck.

Rudolf Egelhofer was not so lucky. He was kicked to death by his guards.

Red opposition lasted longest in the area surrounding the Hauptbahnhof and in Schwabing, but by May 6th the city was secured. As Red flags were hauled down and the blue and white Bavarian emblem hoisted up above the Marienplatz, an open air mass was held for the victorious troops; then they marched in triumph, goose-stepping by the *Feldherrnhalle*, down the Ludwigstrasse, and through the *Siegestor*, the Victory Arch, into Schwabing.

But innocents were caught in the orgy of rape and retribution.

"Two of my men approached a woman we found on the street," remembered Manfred von Killinger, Hermann Ehrhardt's second-in-command, and future Minister President of Saxony under the Nazis. "She tried to bite them. A blow on the mouth brought her to reason. In the yard, she was laid over the tongue of a wagon and hit so often with sticks that not a white spot remained on her back."

Freebooters burst into a meeting of Catholic workers at the St. Joseph Society, picked out twenty and shot them as Reds.

"It's a lot better to kill a few innocent people than to let one guilty person escape," declared Major Schultz of the Lützow Free Corps.

Müncheners came to hate the Free Corps for their savagery, and remembered why they'd been so slow to ask Berlin for help in the first place.

1919

Chained & Fettered

The Watch on the Rhine

> One pays heavily for coming to power; power makes stupid. The Germans – once they were called the people of thinkers; do they do any thinking today? The Germans are now bored with the intellect, the Germans now mistrust the spirit ... 'Deutschland, Deutschland über Alles' [Germany, Germany above All] – I fear that was the end of German philosophy.
>
> - Nietzsche in the wake of the battlefield birth of the Second Reich

It was in early May, 1919, when they left Berlin on a morning train heading west for Hannover, which they passed through in the early afternoon. A small group from Hamburg, directly to the north, containing key members of the Reparations Committee including Max Warburg, Wolf's cousin, boarded the train there. The route then swung southwest, bound for the Ruhr Valley and the Rhine River. Count Ulrich von Brockdorf-Rantzau intended to stop in Essen before they travelled on to the treaty talks at Versailles.

The Ruhr Valley is about half way between Berlin and Paris, its western border the Rhine River. It and the surrounding area were given to Prussia at the Congress of Vienna in 1815, with the intention that she should maintain a watch on the Rhine to prevent future invasion by the German *Erbfeind*, hereditary enemy, France. As Bismarck pointed out to the French emperor in 1871, France had invaded Germany on 30 occasions during the previous 2 centuries.

"We must have land, fortresses, and frontiers which will shelter us for good from enemy attack."

The valley is fairly rectangular from Duisburg at the western end to Bochum on the east, with Essen in the middle. Only thirty miles long by fifteen wide, it was a bastion of heavy industry sitting atop one large coal field. In the post-industrial era it lost importance before recasting itself as a center of the computer economy, but from the mid 19th century till the mid 20th it was the most powerful industrial area in the world. It accounted for three-quarters of German steel, heavy machinery, weapons, railway, and plane production during a period encompassing the 1870 war with France and continuing through both World Wars.

The Ruhr's geological position is unique. Coal fields run across northwestern Europe from Wales all the way to Silesia in Poland, but the best are in the Ruhr Valley. Throughout the late 19th and most of the 20th centuries the region mined as much coal as the rest of the continent combined. It has access to the ocean through the port of Duisburg at the confluence of the Rhine and the Ruhr, the world's largest inland port system.

The English discovered how to make cast steel in 1740 and kept the method secret for 70 years as the Industrial Revolution swept Britain but not the continent. In the early 1800's Alfred Krupp built a steel foundry at Essen. It grew as the Great Railway Boom took off across western Europe. In the 1840's Krupp branched out from railway parts and built his first large gun. In 1866 Prussia decisively beat the Austrians at Sadowa, using Krupp needle guns. By 1870, the Prussians and fellow Germans had about 500 Krupp cannon with which they annihilated the armies of France.

Emperor Louis Napoleon surrendered at the scene of battle in eastern France, but Paris itself refused. So two great pincers of German cannon enveloped the city. The siege began with 300 to 400 shells falling each day in the Ile St. Louis, the Salpetriere, the Pantheon, the Sorbonne, and the Convent of the Sacred Heart. The Left Bank bore the brunt of the bombardment. All of a sudden the Prussians, who to that time had greater support throughout Europe than the ever-arrogant French, were being viewed as barbaric Huns.

The French finally surrendered, in a treaty signed in 1871 at their own Versailles, at Bismarck's insistence, so that they would never forget the humiliation. At the same time the new German empire was proclaimed.

The train arrived in Essen and the visitors disembarked. Outside the station a driver sent by Krupp picked them up for the short trip to the castle. Villa Hugel, as it was called, was a massive, dull-looking structure comprising a mansion connected by a gallery to a smaller house, over 300 rooms in all, complete with hidden doors and passages. The party entered the three story building through the huge double front doors, flanked on the outside by heavy ground stone columns that supported an outside second floor balcony over the entranceway. Inside, the main staircase wound in rectangular fashion upward, graced by a spindled dark wooden handrail; the cavernous interior entrance and hallway were covered with wood panelling on the lower level and picture-painted walls higher up.

"Ah, Count Brockdorf-Rantzau, welcome," Gustav Krupp exclaimed upon the men entering the room. "And I see that Professor Haber is with you. And Max Warburg. You all know my wife."

Bertha Krupp, seated in a chair in the corner, smiled wanly at the newcomers. Eldest of two children, both daughters of Fritz, the last proprietor of the firm, she was the richest person in the empire. When Fritz died, the Kaiser had handpicked Gustav to marry her.

"You're not going on to the treaty talks, Herr Haber?"

"No, Paris and Versailles are not very good for me right now. Most likely I would be arrested by those hypocrites as a war criminal for my efforts to assist the Fatherland."

Krupp, Rantzau, Warburg, and Haber were familiar with each other. They had all worked together during the war. Krupp knew that the weapons flowing from his factories in the Ruhr would be useless due to lack of gunpowder were it not for Haber's method of extracting nitrogen from the air. Haber was here now seeking continued financial support from big industry for his research institutes in Berlin, the best in the world.

Krupp told his visitors of the effect of the war's end on the Ruhr, with the loss of weapons contracts. In Essen alone there were over 100,000 families dependant on Krupp. Haber commented on all the guards posted at the entrance to Villa Hugel.

"We're worried that the Reds will overrun us anytime," replied Gustav. "You may have dealt with them in Berlin, but let me tell you, the problem is not solved here. They're building a Red army in the Ruhr that the government appears to either know nothing or care nothing about."

"It's just that Noske's Free Corps units have been busy dealing with Reds elsewhere recently," Count Rantzau explained.

"Such as in Munich a couple of days ago," added Haber emphatically. "And they really are quite bloodthirsty."

Count Rantzau pulled Krupp aside.

"Gustav, I understand that you will be in Berlin next month to visit your offices off the Potsdamer Platz. There are some matters I would like to discuss with you when you're there."

Krupp looked back concerned. Weapons research of any sort in Germany was of course prohibited by the Allies.

"Work at the office has been greatly scaled down since the war. Not much is going on there at the present time."

"I'm aware of that," Rantzau replied. "But you should know that I am currently working on an arrangement with the Russians in which we'd be able to secretly test weapons on their soil."

"And how does that concern Krupp?"

"You will need somewhere to test the weapons that your people are currently designing at that office of yours near the War Ministry."

Krupp looked back, confirming nothing. The truth was that Berlin was safer at present than the Ruhr, close to the Allied armies, to conduct weapons research. It was unthinkable that the research should cease completely.

"An Allied occupation of the Ruhr is preferable to submitting to a system of international economic slavery," thundered Gustav Krupp. "By God, Max, you must not give in to blackmail by Clemenceau and Poincare. You must stand up to the French at these cursed treaty negotiations!"

That seemed to be the general opinion in the room. But Count Rantzau, who knew that the Allies could still invade defenceless Germany if she did not accept their terms, considered the recent history between the two nations. Back to the 1870 war, when the Krupp guns decimated the French armies at Metz and Sedan, and then moved on to lay siege to Paris; the siege and starvation of the population. First horses wound up on the menu. Then the zoo animals were served up, the prize elephants, buffalo, antelope, and kangaroos. Then they turned to dogs, cats, even rats, and then just starved. Death came as well from smallpox, flu and the like.

Paris surrendered in January 1871, but France never forgot. 43 years later, in 1914, she faced it all again. Invasion by Germany, this time her northeastern provinces turned into a cratered wasteland. Not to mention the crippling of two generations. Or that even the winners were broke and in debt to America.

Count Rantzau was under no illusions. He could expect no pity from French nor British. The Americans were the only hope for reason in the negotiations. As he and Max Warburg and the rest of the treaty team settled in the next morning for the rail journey from Essen, across the Rhine, and through the scarred landscape of Belgium and France all the way to Paris, the Count was far from optimistic.

Their train left Essen first thing in the morning without Fritz Haber, who returned instead to Berlin. The trip to Paris would take most of the day, what with going through the various towns and border checkpoints along the way, all of which they had to slow down or stop for. From Essen they travelled a short distance west to the Ruhr's western end at the Rhine River and Duisburg.

"Look at the troops, Ulrich," Max Warburg nudged Rantzau. "They're Flemish."

Troops from Belgium occupied the northern Rhine. South of them were the British, then the Americans, with the French around Mainz and Frankfurt.

The train ground to a halt.

"Do you see that, Ulrich? Those troops are boarding. What do you think they're up to?"

"They know who we are and where we're going. I don't know what to make of it," Rantzau replied.

A few minutes later there were footsteps outside their cabin and a knock. The door opened and a Belgian officer with two guards stepped inside.

"Your papers, please."

The officer spoke in Flemish. Rantzau had no trouble understanding.

"They want our identification, gentlemen," he said to his companions, then looked back to the officer.

"You are aware of who we are and where we are going, Captain. Why do you detain us needlessly?"

"I am a colonel, you German dolt. And I demand your identification. How do we know that you are who is claimed on this list your government provided us with over a week ago?"

"Colonel, I would ask that you treat me with the proper respect. I am ambassador on behalf of my country. Your rude behaviour may well be reported to your superiors!"

"Ha, ha, ha," the colonel chortled, in true mirth. Then he recovered himself and his face became stern.

"You try my patience, you German swine. You rape and pillage our country, and now you pass through on your way to judgement. And you will report me to my superiors? You are nothing but liars, all you Germans. You never stick by your word. Treaties and international borders mean nothing to you. And yet you still speak as if you had dignity. What a joke! Now, all of you, your identification, and now!"

Rantzau looked at Max, who looked at him and then at the guards who had just raised their rifles, and then sighed and pulled out his passport.

Such was their introduction to the Allied world, where they were destined to remain for the next month and a half. The train turned south to run along the eastern bank of the Rhine, first to Dusseldorf about 15 miles away, then a further 15 miles beyond to Leverkusen, where I.G. Farben had, during the last years of the war, constructed a huge factory complex to manufacture nitrates through the Haber process, so vital to agriculture as well as munitions; and to test poison gases that were partly Haber's legacy as well, and which led, years later under the Nazis, to a type called

Zyklon B. The train pushed further south to Cologne where it crossed the Rhine, and from there headed west to Aachen, or Aix-la-Chapelle, capital of Charlemagne's empire and the site of his tomb. Shortly after, they crossed into Belgium, and an hour or so later rolled into Liége. The train continued west through Namur, Charleroi, and on to Mons. It then crossed the River Scheldt and entered France, grinding to a halt at the customs office as more officials boarded.

"Monsieurs, I require your identification."

This time the Germans did not even bother argue, and produced their papers quickly.

"Have a pleasant trip to the capital, Monsieurs. Enjoy the scenery along the way. It is ever so beautiful, the result of your benevolent occupation of four years. After all, we never liked trees and grass and the like anyway. Hopefully you will be justly rewarded in Paris. Oh, by the way. So that you may fully enjoy the scenery, we are restricting your travelling speed to ten miles per hour. Have a good day!"

As the train crawled on the devastation became pronounced. A black landscape of craters and mud everywhere. The route swung southwest, to Cambrai, then through Gouzeaucourt and Peronne on the Somme. The entire region had been the scene of massive offensives and counter-offensives only a year before.

"I can finally understand why the French and British continue to starve our people," said Count Rantzau, surveying the scenery. "There is no pity left for us. I had not realized the extent of the destruction till just now."

"I just can't believe the lack of colour here," Max exclaimed. "It's all black, as far as the eye can see. There's no trees, bushes, flowers, anything green at all."

"Well, keep in mind that it is the rainy season, and it is only spring. Things will look better once the ground dries out."

"Yes, but look at the buildings, the farms. They're all flattened as well. This entire region is going to have to be rebuilt from scratch. How much is that going to cost?"

"And the roads are all blown apart, too," observed Count Rantzau. "It's pitiful. These refugees, trying to return to their homes, over roads that are nearly impassable. And then when they get there, they'll find them levelled. Their cattle won't even be able to find grass to eat."

"Who cares about that," replied Max, with a wry look. "They don't have any cattle anyway. Our soldiers ate them all when we overran these areas in the first place."

It was an excruciating slow journey at the train's snail pace, but finally they turned south at Amiens for the last leg of the journey to the capital. It was only after they crossed the Oise River and got closer to Paris that the constant succession of craters and carnage was replaced by more scenic landscape. They arrived in late afternoon. Even Paris sported the occasional sign of wartime destruction, of buildings blown up by Krupp supercannon, firing the previous summer from over 70 miles away.

Versailles Diktat

Vengeance! German people! Today the shameful peace has been signed in the Hall of Mirrors at Versailles. Forget it not! There where, in the glorious year 1871, the glorious German Reich was reborn in its ancient splendour, there German honour is today interred. Forget it not! By labour without relaxation and without flagging the German people will reconquer the place which is their due among the nations! Therefore, revenge for the ignominy of 1919!

- *Deutsche Zeitung*
June 28, 1919

This is not a peace treaty. It is a 20 years' truce.

- Marshall Foch

The peace conference to decide upon a final treaty to replace the armistice that had taken effect on November 11th, 1918, opened in Paris at the Quai d'Orsey in January of the following year. It began with the victorious Allied leaders, Lloyd George, Clemenceau, and President Wilson, hearing from various delegations seeking favour at the expense of the defunct German, Austrian, Russian, and Ottoman empires. The Allied leaders had now, by early May, 1919, decided upon the treaty terms; and they had done so without ever consulting the Germans. Hence Count Brockdorff-Rantzau, Max Warburg and the German delegation had no idea what to expect when they arrived in Paris to be presented with the terms.

What Count Rantzau did know was that France had suffered terribly during the war, much moreso than any other nation, four long years of thousands of Krupp cannon blasting the countryside into a moonlike landscape. They could imagine the costs. The French leaders trumpeted them to Lloyd George and Wilson. Germany, in contrast, suffered no damage at all to land or industry.

But the French leaders knew as well the blunt truth that France could not hope to beat Germany alone in another war. She had a much larger population that was increasing at a faster rate than France. Prussian guns had stood within sight of Paris five times within a century, and since 1870 every Frenchman had to live with the fear that the Prussians could come at any time they chose to bombard Paris again.

French Marshall Ferdinand Foch was the overall commander of the Allied forces on the Western Front during the final campaigns of the war. After its end, he wanted French and Belgium borders with Germany pushed east to the Rhine. Only that, he argued, would give France an opportunity to prepare for the next German onslaught, and to meet it till British and American help could arrive. Without that natural barrier, the next war would be a repeat of the present, the only difference being that the Germans might win. In any event, northern France would again be overrun and devastated before the Germans were stopped. The Rhine barrier was necessary to the vital security of France.

The British and Americans disagreed. Clemenceau gave in and accepted instead British and American guarantees of immediate military assistance in case of future attack. The British parliament approved the Treaty of Guarantee in 1919 on the condition that the U.S. ratify it.

But the American Senate refused to approve either it or the Treaty of Versailles, so the British guarantee was nullified.

And then there was the reparations issue. The Allies demanded that Germany pay all the Allied war costs, including pensions for families of war dead. The cost was estimated at $33 billion, in 1919 dollars. Even though Germany had suffered no damage to land or property, millions of working-age men had been killed or wounded in the war, and those left were starving and cold with little ability to pay.

* * *

The German delegation was startled by its reception.

"Do you believe that," wailed Count Rantzau as the door closed behind them, and they were alone at last in their suite at the hotel. "I thought we would get torn to pieces."

"Where were the police to protect us? I wouldn't have believed such barbarity from France, that beacon of civilization and enlightenment. Bah, they are as savage as the rest of us," exclaimed Max Warburg.

"Well, I'm not sure I want to be included with the savages," replied Rantzau.

At that there came a knock at the door. It opened to admit a French chargé d'affaires.

"Monsieurs," he said, "the government requests that you not venture outside of your hotel rooms. After the demonstration of popular ill-will expressed towards you this evening, we are not certain we can guarantee your safety outside the hotel."

"What, are we to consider ourselves under house arrest," asked Count Rantzau, shocked.

"I would not call it that, Monsieur. It is for your own safety."

"Protective custody, you might call it," sighed Max.

"Call it what you will, Monsieur. We will have meals brought to your rooms. You shall not be inconvenienced. May I count on your cooperation?"

Count Rantzau looked at the man sharply, and asked, "What if we refuse to stay in our cell here? Will we be thrown in a French jail, or will you let the mob lynch us?"

The chargé d'affaires looked back with a scowl.

"There are those who would see you tried as a war criminal and hung, Herr Rantzau," he replied. "Would you like to grant them an earlier opportunity?"

The Frenchman left. The Germans retired to sleep, but didn't get much that night. Or over the next week leading up to the meeting with the Allied leaders when the treaty would be presented.

"Are you going to press them about the continuing starvation due to the blockade, Ulrich," asked Max.

"Yes, I intend to raise that issue, before anything else is addressed. But you know what they will reply, don't you. If we sign the treaty, then and only then will the blockade be lifted."

"Those murderers," said Max. "And they call Haber a war criminal. What gall."

"What is this," screamed Rantzau, his finger poking a diagram he was perusing. "Look at the layout of the seating arrangement for the meeting tomorrow! See how they have labelled our seats!"

Max bent and looked closely. Bench of the Accused.

"I tell you, Max, if the Allies force a repugnant treaty on us, then we will make secret arrangements with others. I'm already talking to Lenin's people about using Russia for testing advanced weapons. If the Allies will not deal fairly with us, then Germany must act to protect herself. And in ten or twenty years, well, who knows what will happen if we continue to be treated vindictively."

It took some time for them to calm down. They were extremely depressed, sleeping little over the past week.

Deep bags underlined their eyes, their complexions increasingly sallow.

"Ulrich, are you sure that you're up to this meeting tomorrow?"

"No, Max. Maybe I won't go. My sciatic is acting up again, I may have phlebitis, I'm having trouble standing, and my stomach is queasy. I have a headache that keeps getting worse. No, in truth I wouldn't attend if I didn't have to."

* * *

"Would you care to fly to Paris with me, dear," Wolf asked Liesl nonchalantly as she lounged on the couch of her Munich apartment.

A quixotic smile crossed her face. He had caught her off guard.

"You mean in an airplane?"

"No. With wings attached to our arms," was his snide reply.

But remember, this was 1919 and airplane passenger travel was a novelty.

"Don't be so nasty. You could have meant by Zeppelin," she said to him.

"You're right," he replied contritely. "Anyway, how about it? Care to fly to romantic Paris? Ulrich needs some moral support, if nothing else. Max is a little concerned. He called me last night."

"Negotiations not going well?"

"They had a horrendous trip through Belgium and France to get there. Humiliated in small ways constantly. Reviled by everyone it seems."

Liesl thought for a moment. "Maybe I don't want to go if it's like that. Is there danger?"

"Only if you're German."

“That’s reassuring,” she replied sarcastically. “What kind of plane would we go on? Who’s the pilot? Won’t it be cold?”

“Don’t know, don’t know, and probably.”

“When would we go?”

“In the next couple days. Max said that Ulrich needs some spirit lifting now.”

Liesl thought for a moment, then said, “I’m game if you are, my dear. Up we’ll go into the sky, and hope to come down in one piece.”

“And think of the glorious reception that awaits in Paris,” Wolf added dryly.

* * *

The Grand Trianon Palace, Versailles, May 7th, 1919: the time had finally come for the Allies to present the treaty terms to the representatives of the vanquished nation. Count Brockdorff-Rantzau sat behind the table designated for the Germans, the 'Bench of the Accused', and stared at Lloyd George of England and Clemenceau of France.

“We are here to offer to the German delegation the terms of this, the *second* treaty of Versailles,” Clemenceau was saying.

The first treaty, they all knew, meant the German settlement imposed upon France following the 1870 war.

“Does the German representative have anything to say before the terms of the treaty are presented to him?”

With that the aged, moustachioed, Tiger of France sat down and looked to Count Rantzau for a reply.

Rantzau briefly considered standing, but just as quickly squelched the thought. He was not feeling well at all. He must be ill, he thought. He had had a feeling of vertigo on the way over from their hotel that morning, in addition to his symptoms from the night before. And his leg was bothering him. Count Brockdorff-Rantzau truthfully told himself that he wasn't sure that he could stand all the way through his speech without falling or fainting. And he'd be damned if he was going to take the chance of allowing the Allied leaders see him fall part way through. That would be too degrading a story, probably a photo as well, flashed around the world by the news services. So Rantzau did not stand as he commenced his reply.

"You must immediately lift your land and sea blockade. Since the end of the war tens of thousands of innocent women and children have starved. You, the victorious Allies, are responsible for this! You ask us to sign a peace treaty, yet you continue to kill us. You must cease this inhuman behaviour at once!"

The cavernous hall became utterly silent; an entire room too stunned to whisper.

"I expected hatred from the French and British, our blood enemies for four years; but I *am* surprised to find America supporting this *atrocity*."

Clemenceau's face went red as a beet; the letter opener that Lloyd George was holding loudly snapped, broken in two. Neither man did anything for moments that seemed an eternity. Then they glanced at each other, and Clemenceau finally rose.

In steely French, he replied, "Your remarks make what I have to say much easier. You will now be presented with copies of the *document of surrender*."

He spat out the last words.

"Your government will have fifteen days to study the treaty, and to prepare any objections. There will be no oral discussions between Allied governments and Germany over terms. Objections or proposals for alteration must be in writing, in either *Francois* or *Anglais*. *German* is unacceptable!"

The treaty returned the border provinces of Alsace and Lorraine to France; German territories west of the Rhine including Cologne, Coblenz, and Mainz, would remain occupied for at least 15 years; newly created Poland received some German territory in the east; the army was to be reduced to 100,000 men; Germany was prohibited from having tanks, poison gas, warplanes, or submarines; and reparations of an as yet undetermined amount were to be paid. Germany accepted responsibility for causing the war.

Germans were outraged. But compared to the Treaty of Brest Litovsk, forced by Germany on Russia only a year before, it was magnanimous.

In the Ruhr and nearby Rhine, the industrial magnates couldn't believe their good fortune. Krupp had expected the Ruhr to be detached from Germany, perhaps even annexed to Belgium or France. Alone it would have been a very rich nation, small, compact, a highly industrialized area abutting the borders of key western powers. French security demanded that it be taken from Germany. Without the Ruhr, Hitler would not have had the power to menace the world.

* * *

"So malignant and silly that they are futile," said Churchill, cigar in hand, commenting on the reparations provisions of the treaty.

"I know that, Winston," replied David Lloyd George, a surprise addition.

Originally it was only to be Churchill and Max Warburg meeting privately in Paris.

"But it's just too soon to expect people who have suffered so much to regain their sanity. What does it matter what is written in the treaty about reparations? If it can't be done, it will fall to the ground of its own weight. Right now we have to mollify the common folk who have suffered so much. We will, however, insert clauses that provide for review of the reparations in a few years' time. It's no good fretting about it now."

The Prime Minister looked directly at Max.

"America is really the problem in the end. You must persuade influential people over there, like your brothers, that if the Yanks would forgive the debts owed them by Britain and France, then we could think about reducing our demands from the Germans. The blunt truth is that the United States lost only 125,000 lives, compared to millions by Britain and France. But America will, through loans to one country or another, in the end receive eighty percent of the reparations paid by Germany."

"But you must halt the blockade," pleaded Max, "at once! If Germans see the Allies, and this extortionist treaty, as their greatest threat, then they'll be more hospitable to the Reds. And if Germany goes over to the Reds it's inevitable that she'll throw in her lot with Russia. Then you will have a Red empire stretching from the Urals to the Rhine. The news from Hungary proves that is no fantasy."

Churchill's ears lit up, his forehead creased, and a great troubled frown crossed his face.

"Lift the damn blockade," Max thumped his hand on the table.

"I want to, but public opinion won't let me," thundered Lloyd George in reply. "Let Germany sign the damned treaty!"

* * *

"Welcome, welcome, students. My, it is quiet. None of the usual chatter."

Professor von Müller noted the two officers among the soldiers there for the lecture. There was discipline in the classroom.

"Now, to get started, can anybody tell me who pulls the strings behind the German economy? Hands?"

A tanned, knuckled hand thrust upward from the middle of the second row.

"Yes, what is your name?"

"Corporal Hitler, sir."

"All right, corporal. Go on."

"The Jews, sir. The Jews own everything. They control all the media, and the banks, and Russia."

"Quite right. But what proof do you have to back this up?"

Hitler was momentarily stumped. Details.

"What proof do you need? I say it is so. On my word. As a German soldier."

Cheers from all around.

"And if you don't believe me, read any newspaper! They would be in power here in Munich right now if we didn't disinfect the city a month ago. Proof? There're graves galore. Just dig a few up!"

Professor von Müller, loyal Thule compatriot, couldn't agree more. Such were the sympathies of those chosen by the local military brass to lecture the handpicked soldiers of the Enlightenment Detachment of the German Seventh Army District.

"Over the last century," von Müller continued, "society has changed to one based on money rather than social class. The capitalists will tell you this is good. The best people can rise to the top. One is not trapped by accident of birth. Oh yes, a capitalist society affords equal opportunity to all her citizens: at least to those born with money! And it completely ignores noble German blood and birthlines."

"A mongrel breakfast," came the low deep, gutteral voice again. Corporal Hitler.

"The Industrial Revolution saw the rise of Jews like the Rothschilds to the top, simply because they had more money," said von Müller. "Which brings us to the issue of 'productive capital' on the one hand, and 'interest capital' on the other. Can anyone tell me the difference?"

When no one answered the professor continued, "Productive capital is real things like factories, livestock, and ships. Interest capital is money made by loaning to desperate Germans and charging exorbitant interest. Not one iota of work done by the lender, but still he gets rich on the back of everyday, working Germans. And who are these lenders?"

"Don't be shy, my lovelies," Captain Ernst Röhm barked at his troops when no hand shot up. "Snap to it, or you'll all be climbing the Obersalzberg with full backpacks for the next ten days!"

"The Jews!"

"Well, of course. Thank you, corporal," von Müller nodded to Hitler. "And in particular the stock market speculators and promoters. They're all Jews! And not just here. In America, London…"

Von Müller's history. No one cared to challenge it.

Adolf had discovered an immense truth.

"We'll separate the stock exchange money from the national economy. We'll throw out Jewish interest capital, foreign loan capital, which we have to pay back, with interest, to foreigners! We don't need it. I have the key now", Hitler crowed to Ernie Schmidt, as he turned off the sidewalk and ambled into the Turkenstrasse barracks a few blocks west of the university. "My eyes have been opened today. The first battle is not against hostile nations, but against international capital."

Ernie hadn't been ordered to join the Enlightenment Detachment, or to take the indoctrination courses at the university. But other budding Nazis like Rudolf Hess and Hans Frank had. And a few officers like Röhm, who had approved the curriculum. Hitler made his way up to his second floor quarters and opened the door. It had been a storeroom, given to him to bunk alone after two former dorm mates had complained of his repugnant 'physical habits'. Thankfully no further details were required of them other than that Adolf walked and talked in his sleep. Above his cot now was hung from the wall, by a nail and string, a swastika: the hooked cross, the future Nazi logo. It was a memento from the Ehrhardt Brigade that Hitler had picked up in the streets of Munich. Captain Ehrhardt's troops liked to wear them on the front of their helmets. And it resembled the one high on the wall behind the lectern in the great abbey church of Lambach in Austria, where he once was a chorister.

A couple of days later Hitler headed off to his next lecture. He was under the direct command of the Press and News Bureau of the Political Department of the army's Seventh District Command, located in Munich. The Political Department was new, in fact, unprecedented. Its task was to insert the armed forces' views into the political life of the nation. In the vacuum that developed in Germany following the Kaiser's abdication every agency felt it must take a stake directly in politics. And if democracy meant that everyone was to have a say, even the Reds, then why shouldn't the army?

The Seventh Army Command was thrilled with Hitler. As a stoolpigeon during the massacre of Reds in Munich he showed real flair. Many potential traitors to the Fatherland had gone to the gallows as a result of the corporal's evidence. He had zeal. Transferred to the newly formed Enlightenment Detachment for further political indoctrination, he would be trained to brainwash other soldiers.

"We must fight fire with fire," Röhm barked when pressed by his superiors. "The Reds disrupt and even attack meetings of other parties. If the army doesn't fight them, who will?"

So the Munich command, far from the spying eye of Berlin, and under the instigation of fanatical officers, Thule members, commissioned the Enlightenment Detachment.

Hitler walked into the lecture. It was early June, with only troops and faculty present. The less known publicly about the lectures, the better. Troop indoctrination was a delicate topic in 1919 Germany.

"Today we contrast Rothschild and Marx, founders of capitalism and communism. And a third way: we call it the folkish state. More about that later."

The Rothschilds had been a legend since the Napoleonic wars. Old Meyer was a Frankfurt moneylender with five sons and a plan. He sent them abroad, one to each of the major European money centers, Vienna, Paris, London and Naples, with the eldest remaining in Frankfurt. They were the best informed men in Europe. During a time when a letter from Paris to Berlin took 5 or 6 days, the Rothschilds had the information in half the time. They became official bankers to Germany and Austria. Gerson Bleichröder, the Rothschild's man in Berlin, was Bismarck's personal banker.

"Just as Rothschild epitomized capitalism, another Jew, Marx, created communism," von Müller rambled on. "Both his mother and father were descended from a long line of rabbis, but he was brought up a Christian. He claims that communism is the will of the people, who are trying to get their fair share of the pie."

Hell on earth, thought Hitler.

"But there is another way," the professor was saying. "The folkish state, our version of something new, which in Italy they call fascism."

The term was coined earlier that year by Benito Mussolini. It was a dictatorship, but right wing rather than left. Cartels flourished at the expense of small business and consumers. So long as the rich and powerful subordinated themselves to Mussolini, they got along fine.

* * *

“Yes, I’m sure you’ll both be welcome,” Max reassured them, “Paul is an old acquaintance of Baruch's, and Felix knows him too.”

“What do you know of him, Max," Wolf asked his cousin. Liesl, in a low-cut beige evening dress, stood with them. Wolf and Liesl had just flown in on a two-stage flight from Munich that afternoon. It was Liesl's first-ever plane trip, the flight itself part of her upcoming news story. They were in Paris for the week only.

"He was probably the most powerful Jew in America during the war. And he knows how to live well,” Max added, observing the sumptuous ambience surrounding them. The Ritz was one of the nicer hotels in Paris. Bernard Baruch had a three-bedroom suite there. The current soirée was in a reception room below. The main American delegation was staying at the less-elegant Hotel Crillon. Baruch had been in Paris since January as a senior economic advisor to the American delegation.

“Ah, Max Warburg. Just the person I wanted to see.”

The three turned.

“Minister,” Max replied. “So nice to see you,” he added, a little startled. And then, remembering his friends, he added, “Fräulein Liesl von Schlieffen and Wolf Warburg, meet Winston Churchill. Wolf here is my cousin.”

After some small chat, Churchill said to Wolf, "You're a western sympathizer, Herr Warburg. One of the good ones, it appears."

"What is your point?”

"Jacob Schiff and the firm he controls, Kuhn Loeb, are the biggest western money source feeding the Bolsheviks in the Russian civil war. They do so because they are determined that the supporters of the former Tsar, the Whites, will not win the war and bring back the Tsar's abominable policies towards the Jews. But we here, we are Europeans, and we can see the folly in a Bolshevik victory."

"Can we," Max asked.

"Oh, of course there will be no reintroduction of any discriminatory laws against the Jews," Churchill quickly said, "even after a White victory. A democratic government will be instituted again. As under Kerensky."

"What makes you think it will be any more successful than his," Wolf asked. "It only lasted eight months."

"Once the Reds are destroyed, democracy can have a chance to grow in Russia," Churchill replied. "But you can't spite the whole continent, and open it up to communism, just to pay back the Tsar, who's dead anyway. Do you want all your Jewish countrymen to just trade in Tsarist slavery for slavery under the Reds?"

"What do you want of us," asked Wolf.

"You must talk to Jacob Schiff. And Felix and Paul. They must not steer any more money to the Bolsheviks. In America they don't see the Red threat as real or immediate. It is an ocean away. But I tell you, the Reds must lose this war, for the good of mankind! You must convince them."

"And how do we do that? How will the eastern Jews be protected in the future, under a new Russian government?"

The British Minister of War did not answer for a moment.

"One thing at a time, gentlemen," he finally said. “Let us make Russia safe for democracy and the Jews will surely thrive, which will not happen under Lenin or any of his successors, despite what you’ve heard. The Reds too will abuse Jews, you wait and see."

* * *

They had just sat down to dinner when the troops burst through the front door of the modest bungalow in the little town of Fastov, in the central Ukraine, a few miles southwest of Kiev. It was a small, homey, comfortable house, crammed full of the varied possessions of an extended, moderately successful family of working-class Jews. Dunken von Schlieffen was thrown up against the wall along with the members of the Battel family who were present in the room, including Jonah's pregnant sister-in-law. When Jonah himself tried to intervene on her behalf he was kneed in the gut and then clubbed to the ground with a rifle butt.

"Jewish swine," said the leader of the Red Guards, "you support the White army, the Tsar's old supporters, against the Red wave. We should burn down this house right now. You consort with this German dog," he pointed to Dunken. "Do you forget how just a few months ago he and his vile countrymen lorded themselves over the Ukraine? Where are your armies to help you now," he yelled, turning suddenly towards Dunken.

The Guard commander moved swiftly across the floor and cuffed Dunken across the face, knocking him to the ground.

"Gather him up," he said, motioning two of his troopers towards Dunken.

They each grabbed an arm; the last Jonah saw of him, he was being dragged out through the splintered front door.

* * *

On June 16th, more than a month after receiving the treaty terms, Count Brockdorff-Rantzau was summoned to Clemenceau's office for an Allied ultimatum: Germany must accept the treaty by June 24th, or the Allies would invade. Rantzau telegraphed the threat to Berlin, and then he and his party departed the French capital for the journey home.

"Watch out, Max! Duck!"

Before he could react, a rock the size of a fist struck Max in the neck. The windowglass beside him shattered as another stone hit it as he was attempting to board the train. He stepped quickly inside.

Max rubbed his neck, but it felt uninjured.

"Are they mad, Ulrich," he asked, a terrified look splashed across his face. "Why do they want to hurt us? What can we do?"

Count Rantzau was shaking. He knew they were lucky. They learned later that in trying to leave Versailles Max's cousin, Dr Hans Meyer, another German delegation member, got a glass splinter in the eye, and one secretary was hit in the head with a stone, causing a cerebral hemorrhage.

The train headed east from Paris, the tracks skirting the Marne River for some distance, past Chateau Thierry, scene of the intervention by raw American recruits only a year before. It then crossed over the Marne and headed north, eventually to cross the border into Belgium and then to join up with the main line for the trip northeast to the German border, over the Rhine, and home to Berlin on the far side of the country.

After the crushing of the Reds in Berlin in March, the government felt safe enough to return to Berlin from Weimar. Philip Scheidemann, the German Chancellor, was in the hallway of the Reichstag, a few days after the treaty terms were announced, discussing them with his Minister of Defence.

"Well, Gustav, can we successfully resist an attack? Is there any chance?"

"Of course not," Noske replied. "We have Free Corps units capable of maintaining order within the country, but there is no German army that can resist an attack in numbers by Allied troops. They're already occupying both sides of the Rhine; there are no barriers. And even if there were, we have no troops manning them."

*   *   *

May 29th, 1919, saw a solar eclipse. The darkened sun passed through Hyades, a bright grouping of stars. The theory of Relativity says that light has mass, so that light rays from the stars should bend towards the sun as they come close to it, due to its immense gravity. Relativity shook man's ideas of time and space because of the mind-numbing implications. It says that time is variable, that the length of a second, a minute, or an hour actually passes slower for people in motion than at rest! We're just incapable yet of travelling fast enough to notice.

In 1905 Einstein published a spinoff to Relativity, extracting the formula $E=mc^2$, or, the potential energy contained within an object is equal to its mass multiplied by the speed of light squared. A pound of matter contains the explosive power of fourteen million tons of TNT.

"According to your theory," said Haber, "any object large enough for the eye to see would convert to an unimaginable amount of energy if released. Wouldn't that cause a large explosion?"

"If the rate of conversion was not properly controlled, yes."

"Don't you foresee this being used to create the greatest bomb in history?"

"Only you would think of that. An atom bomb? Preposterous."

But he put his violin down.

A knock at the door. Chaim Weizman preferred to meet with Einstein alone. He hadn't realized that Haber would be there; he was well aware of his attitude towards Zionism.

"Come in, Herr Weizman. I must admit, I'd forgotten our appointment. Fritz was just saying how absent minded I am."

Haber gave him a grudging nod.

"You realize that Professor Einstein is very busy. He is getting married in two days' time."

"Yes, congratulations, professor. Perhaps this isn't the best time to be asking if you've had a chance, since we last spoke, to consider our cause."

"To be honest, no."

Haber couldn't restrain himself. "Right now, Zionism is the wrong idea at the wrong time. It is the eve of the Versailles conference, and the Allies are still starving Germany."

"But what has that to do with Zionism," asked Weizman, exasperated.

"How can you even talk of Zionism," Haber replied, "when there is still a war for German survival going on? We must unite all Germans, Jews included, behind the Fatherland!"

But Einstein gave him a withering stare, and then turned to the other man. "Please continue, Herr Weizman."

"Jews will be truly safe only in a land of our own. Naturally the site should be Palestine."

"Is your description of relations between Jews and Gentiles accurate? What of the position of Jews in Germany and Austria now," Haber asked.

Einstein laughed derisively.

"What of their position in Germany at present? You are ready to ship Jewish refugees back east!"

"Come now, Albert," Haber answered. "They are not German citizens. They were not born and raised here."

Einstein glowered back at him, and was about to reply when Haber interrupted.

"What is your background, doctor? You are not German. You're a British scientist."

"That's true. I came from Russian Poland. But I escaped and settled in Britain. I'm a chemist by training. During the war I was director of the Admiralty Labs under

Lord Balfour. In a stroke of luck for me, Balfour was chosen to make recommendations on Palestine, now under British control, and I was in a perfect spot to press Zionist desires. The Balfour Declaration committed the government to try to establish a national home for the Jews."

"You know," Haber mused, "a lot of people are of the view that Jewish money bought that declaration from Lloyd George's government."

"You mean the financial contribution by western Jews on behalf of the Allies during the war," asked Weizman.

"What is so evil about that," Einstein asked.

"Only that not every western Jew thinks that the establishment of a national home is a good idea," Haber replied, his face now animated. "It could affect the nationality of every Jew who thinks he's a citizen of the country he was born and worked his whole life in. Now where do his loyalties lie? What will his fellow citizens think? Just look at the situation in Germany now. The howls that Jews are an international people; that they are not and have never been, and can never be, truly German."

"I realize that you converted from Judaism years ago," Weizman replied to Haber, "but I also know you to be sympathetic to your brethren. We have enough enemies without our own attacking us."

No one said anything for a long moment. Finally Einstein spoke again.

"I am against nationalism but in favour of Zionism. When a man has both arms and he is always saying I have a right arm, then he is a chauvinist. However, when the right arm is missing, then he must do something to make up for the missing limb."

"Why are you so caught up in this, Albert," Haber inquired. "You don't even practice Judaism."

"There is nothing in me which can be designated as 'Jewish faith'," Einstein smiled sadly. "But I am a Jew and am glad to belong to the Jewish people, even if I do not consider them in any way God's elect."

* * *

The Allies extended the deadline for acceptance of the Treaty of Versailles to June 24th after the uproar in Germany in order to allow the country to get used to it. The German delegation arrived in Berlin on June 18th, and the next day the Cabinet met.

"But how serious do you think they are, Ulrich," Chancellor Scheidemann queried the Count. "If they see that we will oppose them, that all we want is a little fairness, do you think it possible that they'll back down? Surely they don't want to invade. It would be expensive for them to occupy the entire country."

"I think they're very serious, Philip. You misjudge the depth of public opinion in the Allied countries. Their leaders are afraid of being lynched themselves if they appear soft. You must face reality," he said, exasperated.

"Our people are so nationally and morally broken that we must sign," argued Defence Minister Gustav Noske. "If we do not, and the Allies invade, the country will likely disintegrate."

"I was afraid you were going to say that," replied Scheidemann. "I think the country has no choice but to accept the conditions offered, no matter how onerous. There is not the power to resist. We are defenceless before the Allies for the present. But I cannot bring myself to sign the accursed document on behalf of our people. Therefore I am resigning."

"You're not alone," said Count Rantzau. "I'll be joining you. I just can't stomach the thought of being associated with this ultimatum, this, this," and he paused, searching for other words, "this *Diktat* fashioned in hate at Versailles."

On June 28th, the formal treaty was signed. Nobody was happy with it. The Allies thought it too easy on Germany. The *Volkischer Beobachter* in Munich labelled it the ‘Jew Deal’ and the ‘Warburg peace’. The truth was that Germany was left whole, except for some land taken on the eastern and western borders, and saddled with a huge debt. The treaty didn’t even take the Ruhr away. It just left a very resentful, still intact nation to do it all again, and next time with a vengeance.

Dark Prodigy

It was a fine morning in mid-June. For Adolf Hitler and some fellow troopers it was a day off. The grass under their feet felt soft and springy, and Ernie Schmidt bolted off across an open patch. Hitler noticed some Enlightenment Detachment classmates across the lawn. Rudolf Hess was seated on a bench talking to another officer who looked familiar. And down by the stream running through the park Hans Frank was dangling his feet in the water. Seated by him was that lovely dark haired friend of Hella von Westarp, the Thule secretary who had been murdered by the Reds. Hitler remembered her now. He'd seen her in the company of that deserter, Wolf Warburg.

Nevertheless Hitler was determined to let nothing ruin this beautiful day.

"My, what beautiful legs, corporal."

A dainty voice was teasing him. He turned to see a waitress from the Hofbräuhaus, which he and his friends had been frequenting recently.

"My cute corporal."

She loved his fiery blue eyes, which blazed when he got excited. And he was doing so more and more lately. Up on his feet in the gasthaus shouting and arguing with everyone. Which was kind of strange since she recalled that he didn't drink much. But he'd still shout louder than anyone else. And that voice! It was low, gutteral. Penetrating. And sexy, too.

"Fräulein," he said, through gritted teeth, "I would prefer if you did not call me 'cute'. It is demeaning. I am a soldier."

He talked serious, but at the same time sported *lederhosen*, leather hiking shorts, held up by red suspenders over a checkered shirt. The manner of dress was not unusual for the Bavarian foothills, but on the future Führer, his eyes ablaze indignantly and his jaw set, it looked ridiculous. She stifled her laughter, because if looks could kill…

That was wise. Hitler didn't like dirty jokes, political jokes, or, most importantly, jokes about himself. He liked boxing, or at least watching it. That was honest and manly.

"You know I am free tomorrow night, corporal. You might ask me out."

He had to think quickly.

"I'm afraid I'm busy then. We must check out some fringe lunatic organization in Schwabing. See if they are dangerous."

"Leave me alone, you animal!"

The shout came from down by the water. Hitler looked over to see Hans Frank standing by the stream with Hess and the other officer beside him. Hella von Westarp's friend was berating the officer.

"You keep your grubby paws to yourself, Captain. Keep them off me!"

Hitler couldn't hear his response. But he did see Liesl slap Hermann Ehrhardt across the face before she stalked off. After some obsequious fawning to the officer, Hans Frank excused himself and rushed after her.

Hess and Ehrhardt ambled over to Hitler.

"Did you see that, soldier," Ehrhardt asked Hitler. "What a bitch! Do you know her?"

"Her name is Liesl something or other."

"Von Schlieffen," cut in Rudolf Hess. "Now I remember. Her father's a judge here in Munich."

Ehrhardt's head snapped back.

"Then it's a good thing I didn't horsewhip her as I intended after she slapped me."

"Yes, that is a good thing, as I was trying to tell you," confirmed Hess.

"Women. Will you ever marry, soldier," he asked, glancing at Hitler.

"Never. Besides, if one wants to get ahead in life, it is better to remain single for awhile. Women get in the way. No, there is only one thing important to me, sir."

"And what is that? Say, don't I know you from those convoluted lectures at the university? You're a corporal."

"Hitler, sir, Corporal Hitler."

"You speak well, as I recall. So what have you picked up from those lectures so far?"

"Oh, that's easy, sir." His face blazed radiantly. "We must beware next time of traitors and cowards at home. Reds and Jews can't be allowed to stab us in the back. When the next war comes, Germany will emerge triumphant."

"Bravo, corporal. You're an inspiration to us all!"

Rudolf Hess' face echoed the same thought.

"Oh, by the way, corporal – just so you and the lieutenant here know – no one slaps me like that and gets away with it. I don't care who her father is. I'll have my way with that von Schlieffen bitch yet! You mark my words."

*   *   *

"Today we study the American economy," Professor von Müller began. "It rules the world now. It is incredibly unregulated, even though they purported to introduce a Federal Reserve Board just before the war to oversee the volatile swings in their money supply. Before that, any American bank could print money."

The talk then moved for the next hour through a couple of centuries of American history, exposing the Jewish domination.

"As in London," von Müller continued, "early Jews on Wall Street started as dry-goods dealers, and then moved into merchant banking. Lehmans, Goldman Sachs, Sears Roebuck. But Kuhn Loeb, under Jacob Schiff, proved most successful. In the early part of this century there was a plot by Kuhn Loeb, Lehman, and the Rothschilds to drive Morgan out of business. They met in New York to discuss it," von Müller informed his class.

There were grains of truth in the diatribe: they had met to discuss matters of common competition against the J.P. Morgan group, far and away the premier Wall Street players of the day. Before World War Two, less than 10% of all international loans floated by American firms were negotiated through Jewish-owned banks.

"Time for a break. Back in twenty minutes."

"Can you believe that Hitler," asked the soldier of Ernst Röhm. "He even reads up on the stuff during the break. We were out having a smoke, and we came back in, and he hadn't moved."

"Yes, I've noticed that," said Röhm. "Perhaps some of it could rub off on all of you slackers, eh?"

Röhm was from Bavaria, and only a couple years older than Hitler. His father was middle manager of a railway. Ernst, short and stocky, joined the army in 1906 and was promoted to lieutenant two years later. During the war he was wounded three times, had half his nose shot away, and caught a bullet in the cheek.

"Since I am an immature and bad man, war appeals to me more than peace," Röhm freely admitted.

But he had his standards.

"At least I know that the respect and affection of the men under me, not the praise of some staff officer, is the highest ideal."

Röhm was content initially to let the Reds do the work in preparing the workers of the nation for a struggle for national freedom against the shackles of the Treaty of Versailles because he figured that the right wing could co-opt their leadership later. He concentrated, rather, upon secretly stockpiling an ever-increasing cache of arms, trucks, tanks, and even planes. Of singular importance, though, would be his contribution to the rise from obscurity of Hitler and the Nazi party.

"The issue is not exactly free trade," Professor von Müller continued, "but, rather, the problems resulting from it. For by allowing free trade to continue, we will ensure that Germany is defeated once and for all. By Jewish-American millionaires. So we reject the capitalist mantra of free trade and instead protect German businesses and finance from complete takeover by the international Jews, who have over the last few decades shifted their world headquarters to Wall Street. In 1907 the Jews orchestrated a bank panic, and the stock market was shut down. J.P. Morgan had to fashion a bailout. And it was in the wake of that near-disaster that Paul Warburg wrote an article calling for a central bank of some sort. Yes, the Jews were using the calamity, which they themselves planned, as a means of establishing chains around the entire financial edifice of the United States!"

Hitler was aghast! Oh, the perfidy, the stealthiness, of the enemy. With such chains the Jews sought to bind a free people.

"Not content with just controlling most of the American economy," the professor rattled on, "the Jews engineered new anti-trust legislation, through their errand boy, Teddy Roosevelt, and in 1911 Rockefeller's mighty Standard Oil was broken up into tiny companies, on the ridiculous justification that this would foster healthy competition. Thankfully this sort of silliness never made its way to Germany."

Even after World War One Germany never developed anti-trust legislation to ensure competition.

"At the same time as the courts attacked Standard Oil," von Müller continued, "a Senate committee found that the big banks were in collusion to control the market. There were attacks in the press by Louis Brandeis, a Jew himself. This traitor – his family came from Germany – now sits on the American Supreme Court! Back at the time, he published a book called *Other People's Money – and How the Bankers Use It*. You have to admire the craftiness of the enemy," von Müller reflected, both to the class and to himself, with a faraway look. But then he turned and looked directly at the class.

"The Jew Brandeis and his protégé Felix Frankfurter both have the ear of that jellyfish Woodrow Wilson. They both say that they want to attack the big banks, the trusts. But it is all a lie. A subterfuge. And what is their goal?...Yes, Corporal Hitler?"

"It is to make fools of us, isn't it, professor? The Jews want to destroy all their competition, while steering attention away from themselves. And they think all of us dumb *Goyim* are so stupid that we will be taken in by it."

* * *

They were in a small café off the Sternstrasse.

"But you all seem so rabid about it, Hans. So – fanatical."

"Oh, I know that it must appear that way to you, Liesl. But that's only because you don't know. But our eyes are being opened right now! You should attend one of the lectures. If only you could, you'd understand."

"I'm not sure that I want to know anymore, Hans," she replied. "It just seems wrong to me, somehow. Like you're all barking up the wrong tree. You know that America goes in the opposite direction."

"What do you mean?"

"Well," she started slowly, playing with her coffee cup, "you're always hearing how they're so proud of their 'melting pot', about what a success they make of people of all nationalities and religions. Yet all I hear from you is race and blood."

Hans Frank didn't reply right away. He didn't know quite what to say. Professor von Müller hadn't dealt with it in any of his talks.

"And the Jews," Liesl continued, "my God, you'd think they were the devil incarnate, the way you speak. They are responsible for all the woes of the earth, according to you."

"It's not just me, Liesl," young Lieutenant Frank replied, the smile and enthusiasm vanishing from his face for the first time that afternoon. Liesl had temporarily burst his bubble. No one argued with the professor in class!

"Everyone believes it," Hans Frank continued. "They're the reason we lost the war."

Liesl had heard it all before. And the war had ended only months before. She was glad of the interruption that came next.

"Lieutenant, how are you this morning?"

It was Adolf Hitler, his buddy Ernie Schmidt alongside.

Hans Frank briefly returned a salute. He was much younger than the two other men, who were only thirty themselves, and still a little shy in displaying a proper snobbishness towards them. If asked later he would certainly not claim any 'affinity' with the common soldier, which Ernst Röhm was so proud of; indeed, Hans Frank knew that he was of superior makeup, both mentally and physically. True officer material.

But young Lieutenant Frank wished to be alone with Liesl, even if she was giving him a rough grilling at the moment, and even if she was a few years older than him. She was still beautiful.

“Is there something I can do for you, corporal,” he asked in a tone meant to shoo the visitors away.

“I, I just heard you and lovely fräulein discussing the Jews. Perhaps I can help.”

Perhaps you can, thought Hans Frank. Hitler was always talking out in class, and seemed to know the stuff. He motioned them to sit.

Hitler sat down beside Frank while Ernie slid into the seat beside Liesl. Hitler looked across the table into Liesl’s face.

“We have met before, fräulein. Liesl von Schlieffen, if I recall.”

He took her hand and put it to his lips. Liesl glanced into his eyes, and was caught by the fiery blue irises. She stared momentarily. This was the same soldier, she suddenly recalled, who had ranted and raved in front of her on a Berlin sidewalk last November. Yet now he was the epitome of calm. His fingernails were dirty. He wore his mustache in a ridiculous, harshly clipped style that didn’t even run the length of his upper lip. And he could use a shower. Yet he now had a presence about him.

“So what happened in the park the other day,” asked Hitler. “I could see you hit Captain Ehrhardt, but what was it about?”

“The man is a pig,” Liesl replied. “He grabbed me by the waist and pulled me towards him. He said he is used to sweeping girls off their feet. He tried to kiss me. In fact he did. So I slapped him.”

“You had better be careful, Liesl,” Hans Frank warned. “That Ehrhardt has a reputation as a real fanatic. I’ve met a lot of them over the past year, and he’s the real thing.”

“Is that right, corporal,” she asked Hitler.

“He has that reputation, fräulein. But I’m sure that he’d never do anything to harm such a lovely lass as you.”

"How gallant, corporal, but I think I'll watch my back anyway."

*   *   *

"In the leadup to the world war, Wall Street was split," Professor von Muller was saying. "Morgan was banker to the Tsar. Jacob Schiff at Kuhn Loeb hated the Tsar. Woodrow Wilson didn't want to fight Germany, but the Jews Baruch, Brandeis, Frankfurter and Paul Warburg all whispered in his ear. Wilson started off banning all loans to belligerents but then he expanded the types of securities that could be used as collateral. When the French or British now bought a bomb or torpedo or guns or ammo on credit, the security for the transaction could be the torpedo or bomb itself. Never mind that the security was meant to self-destruct upon impact. America would have lost too much money, had to write off too many debts, lost too many markets – and suffered a huge depression – should Britain and France have lost, and so she finally entered the war. By the time it was over, she owned the world."

"Can no one successfully fight the Americans," asked Hitler.

"There is a way," von Muller said, chuckling. "I read a few weeks ago that on May Day of this year Rockefeller, J.P. Morgan Jr., and other prominent Americans were sent letter bombs, but that they were intercepted by the post office. Well, next time they'll get through. The enemies of our Fatherland are not totally invulnerable. There is hope. No matter how rich or powerful these swine are as a group, they can each still be exterminated."

Captain Ehrhardt, sitting beside Röhm and monitoring the class, suddenly perked up. A lightbulb clicked on in his shell-rattled brain.

"Which brings us to the very last topic on our list," stated Professor von Müller, to the enthusiastic clapping of most of the class. "The subject is German banks. Though Jews only form 1% of our population, they hold directorships in about a quarter of our banks and joint stock companies!"

Von Müller was getting himself worked up into a dither. His numbers may have been about right. But if Jews were extremely over-represented in the upper levels of the banking profession in Germany, their numbers thinned considerably lower down the ranks. In 1925, of the 7500 bankers and brokers in Germany, only 3% were Jewish.

At the beginning of World War One, about a quarter of German millionaires were Jewish.

* * *

Lectures now completed, the troops were broken up into discussion groups. Some shy about speaking in front of a large class were now more comfortable expressing opinions. And it enabled the officers, Röhm and Ehrhardt, to learn from their spies which troops were truly loyal.

"Oh, please, sergeant, let me answer this one."

"Go ahead, Hitler."

He turned towards his fellow student.

"Have you learned nothing, Schneider? Don't you know that Jews can't be trusted? They're only trying to appear helpful so that they can worm their way into positions of power."

"But where is the evidence of that," Schneider asked.

Hitler gave him a crafty smile. The blue eyes began to burn as he gazed at the other man. Because of the small group he could now rise and stroll around the room.

"Private Schneider, it is perhaps that you are young," Hitler began in a friendly manner, "and it is not your fault that you don't remember Germany in all her glory before the war. But we do," he said, pointing to one and then another of the older soldiers in the room, "and it is our most fervent desire that our rightful place at the head of Europe be restored. My young friend," he continued, with what appeared to be a genuine paternalistic smile, "you are simply confused because you don't remember the lies that we were all fooled by at the time. Underlying all our outward glory," his right arm majestically arced high in the air, "there was, hidden close to our bosoms," and then his left arm savagely chopped the space in front of him, "vipers, Jewish snakes, all the while planning Germany's fall."

The room was silent. After a moment, Hitler relaxed and smiled again.

"Ah, my friend, would you not like to be riding on a tall horse, in a splendid uniform of the old List Regiment, with all the fräuleins throwing flowers at you? Asking where they can meet you tonight?"

Everyone in the group began to smile. Even the sergeant was remembering his early days in the service. Hitler, instinctively knowing he was on to something, threw out more images of pre-war glory, when dreams were not dashed by experience.

"If a few thousand of these Hebrew corrupters had been shot, the sacrifice of millions at the Front would have been avoided."

"That's it! Keep going," another soldier shouted.

Hitler was smiling; he was on a roll. And, really, it was just one numerically small people that he attacked. The oldest scapegoats in Europe, sanctioned even in years past by the Church; and now proven so greedy, so rich!

"Röhm, did you hear that," asked Captain Ehrhardt, signalling his fellow officer to come over.

"The professor here thinks that you have a natural orator in the Detachment."

Röhm listened to Müller for a moment, a smile building across his face. He turned to the group of soldiers milling about a short distance away.

"You, Hitler, come over here."

He hurried over and saluted.

"I'm told you have talent as an orator."

Hitler was stunned. He said nothing, briefly lost in thought.

I can speak!

On the Bodensee

They left Munich driving west headed for Landsberg and then Memmingen about 60 miles away, at which point they would turn southwest for the final 35 miles of the trip to Lindau on the Bodensee. In the Daimler touring car were Wolf and Liesl, the roof down and the breeze blowing against their faces and through their hair. It was mid-July, 1919, and in exhilaration they were leaving for a summer getaway. At least for those who were not unwelcome refugees or crippled veterans or starving ordinary folk or others still ravaged by disease, that was the feeling of many in Europe. It was the first peaceful summer since the 'glorious' summer of 1914, when all the great civilizations of the continent flexed their muscles like strutting peacocks as they girded for war. Wolf and Liesl were looking forward to seeing Einstein, Haber, and Count Rantzau. The morning passed quickly in the pleasant sunshine. They crossed the Romantic Road at Landsberg early in the day, and well before noon the touring car was cruising down the final stretch to the tiny island of Lindau just off the northeast shore of the Bodensee on the German-Swiss border.

Lindau was a narrow island running alongside the mainland, connected at one end by a narrow bridge for cars and foot traffic, and at the other by a long causeway for trains. It was already a top European tourist destination by 1900, but peaked during the interwar years. Founded as an imperial city of the Holy Roman Empire, it had many ancient buildings, including a magnificent Thieves Tower with a steeply pointed spire crowned on top with even sharper turrets. It was now the municipal museum. The town also boasted open-air cafés and terraces, and during tourist season orchestras played classical melodies outside on the promenade.

By the time Wolf and Liesl arrived at the Hotel Bad Schachen, Einstein, Haber and Rantzau were already there. Einstein's new bride, his cousin Elsa, was there too, as well as Haber's young wife, Charlotta.

"We were in Zurich for the last couple of weeks," Charlotta explained to Liesl as they settled her bags into the room. "Albert and Elsa were there for the past month. But just between you and me," she whispered, "I don't know how she puts up with it. Albert has to be there to lecture each summer. But his ex, Mileva, and their children are there too. And Albert is distracted and annoyed by that whole situation. He's been so much better since we arrived here a couple of days ago."

The Bodensee was about forty miles north of Zurich.

"How long do you plan to stay?"

"For a couple of weeks, then Fritz and I will return to Berlin. Albert has to go back to Zurich for more lectures. They won't be back in Berlin until September."

"Wolf, old chap, how are you," asked Count Rantzau, clapping him on the back.

"My dear Count. You're looking well." Considering Versailles.

"Wolf. How are you?" This time it was Albert Einstein. His hair was a shade lighter than Wolf remembered it.

"You're looking quite tanned," Wolf replied.

"Vacation on the water. Does wonders for anyone."

At forty years old lines were beginning to etch his face.

"And have you forgiven Haber yet," Wolf asked with a grin.

He was referring to Einstein's wedding. Haber was supposed to hand him the ring, but he was called away at the last minute on some business with Max Planck. Einstein paused a moment before replying.

"Well, I could have waited. But Elsa – she threatened that she wouldn't come to Zurich with me this summer unless we were married first. Ah, marriage. Hard on the career, you know."

* * *

"I don't recall him," said General Ludendorff over his drink. "But I don't know who this Charlie Chaplin is, either. So I wouldn't recognize somebody with a weirdly clipped mustache. I'll take your word for it, Captain."

"It can't do any harm, Röhm," said Hermann Ehrhardt. "We'll find out soon enough if he's got what it takes. We can always reassign him if it doesn't work out."

"What was your impression, Captain," Ludendorff asked, looking at Ehrhardt this time.

The latter stroked his glass and looked up.

"I like him. He's a real fanatic from what I can tell. And he hates the Jews with a passion!"

That was enough for Ludendorff.

"You must assign him, then. Send him out among the troops and see what kind of a preacher he makes for us."

Ludendorff wasn't in the army anymore. Many soldiers obeyed him nonetheless, hoping that he would lead a right wing coup to take the government back, bury the Weimar Republic and restore the Reich.

Hitler opened the envelope containing his orders. It was a new assignment.

"An *instruction officer*, Captain? I'm to be sent out as an instruction officer? But what am I to do exactly?"

He wanted action, fighting. But that would have meant a Free Corps brigade in Poland somewhere, since it was the only German unit actively engaged at the time.

"You're to do exactly what it says. It's your job to *educate* our brethren in the ranks about the Red-Jew danger. Now what's the matter with that?"

Hitler's head tilted back slightly and his eyes roamed the ceiling. What was the matter with it? Not much actually, now that he pondered it. In fact, he was already beginning to see possibilities...

His head swung abruptly forward, so that he faced Röhm square on; his feet came together, heels clicking; and his arm shot up to salute sharply.

"I am an obedient servant of the Fatherland! I go where I may best serve the Reich."

"That a boy, corporal," Röhm smiled and clapped him on the shoulder. "Now be off with you. You're due at Lechfeld."

Hitler turned to march sharply from the room.

"Oh, Adolf," Röhm called as he was almost out the door, "you know, we hold high hopes for you. And that's not just me. General Ludendorff is pulling for you as well."

Hitler turned away quickly so that the captain did not see the tears in his eyes.

* * *

"It's twenty-five miles or so, by water," said Albert Einstein the next morning, across breakfast coffee. "We should be there in four hours or so, have a leisurely lunch and stroll on Mainau, and then sail back here. It's a gorgeous, little island, with good restaurants and magnificent gardens all around. We'll be back by 8 or 9 tonight."

"And it'll still be light on the water then," added Wolf.

Elsa and Charlotta stayed in Lindau to stroll the area and neighbouring Wasserburg. So it was just Liesl and the four men who sailed out the harbour entrance, guarded as it was by a stone statue of the Bavarian Lion on one side, and a 19th century lighthouse on the other. The boat was a luxurious 38 footer with a cabin. Einstein was the only true sailor of the bunch. Wolf and Haber were passable since Albert had given them lessons on the Grunewald outside Berlin.

"You're sure that we can do it in one day, professor," asked Liesl as they headed into open water. "We won't be too tired later to sail back?"

Albert laughed.

"Oh, no, my dear. Once the sails are set, anyone can steer the boat on the open water, and there's little else to do but relax."

He was used to a smaller boat, like his own back on the Grunewald. But he'd sailed this size before.

The Rhine flows south from its source high in the Swiss Alps to enter the Bodensee near the southeastern end. The lake itself, in essence a great widening of the river, runs west-northwest forming the border between Germany and Switzerland. The northern shore is German; the southern Swiss; and the extreme eastern tip borders Austria. The main body of the lake is about thirty miles long by ten miles wide. At Konstanz, situated at the western end, the lake forks into two narrow fingers. The southern fork eventually narrows to form the Rhine River again, which flows west out of the lake.

"It appears that Lindau, where we came from, is on the north shore of the main lake, near the east end; and the isle of Mainau, just off Konstanz, is at the west end, about twenty-five miles away, where the lake forks in two," observed Liesl, looking up from a map spread out before her.

"That's right," Einstein replied. "I plan to sail directly from here to Mainau."

"How big is the Bodensee, Albert," Rantzau inquired.

"It's the third biggest lake in Europe, which of course isn't saying much compared to some in other parts of the world. But it is very deep. Over eight hundred feet in some spots."

Einstein paused for a moment, looking out at the scenery to the south, first the surrounding foothills, and then the Alps rising in the distance.

"I love it here," he reflected. "I was born in Swabia, just to the north, and spent my childhood in Bavaria, not so far away. But then as a teenager I crossed the Alps into northern Italy. The most cultured people in the world. And Lake Como, on the other side of those mountains, is heavenly."

He pointed south.

"And then there's Zurich," in the same direction, but just scant miles away. "That countryside – it was my inspiration!"

"For what," asked Wolf.

"Why, for Relativity, of course."

"Ah, it is all such wasted effort," moaned Fritz Haber. "You ponder these theoretical propositions that have no use here on earth. Wouldn't it be more useful," he said with a mischievous wink at Liesl, "to ponder the mysteries of beautiful women than the movement of the stars?"

The western shore was drawing ever closer as the boat made its way slowly down and across the lake.

"There's Konstanz ahead of us," Liesl pointed out in the distance.

The city lay at the western end of the main lake where it forked and the Rhine flowed out. Bordering Konstanz was the town of Kreuzlingen, where Max's older brother, Aby Warburg, had resided in a sanatorium for the last few months, a result of a nervous breakdown suffered upon realizing that the war was lost. Konstanz itself now appeared directly in front of them as they cruised close to the main wharf just south of the entrance to the Rhine. Like so many places on the Bodensee, Konstanz seemed dominated by the medieval architecture so well preserved throughout the area. What struck Liesl were the tall, narrow, sharp towers and spires on so many of the churches, cathedrals and castles.

Einstein steered the boat north and then west about five miles up the northern fork before encountering a tiny island connected to shore by a bridge. They docked at Mainau, the flower isle. After lunch, they intended to take a stroll through the luxurious gardens. When the meal was over, though, Liesl and Wolf instead decided to take a walk in the hills above the lake. They crossed over the pedestrian bridge to the mainland and started up the wooded hill. The trail had been travelled for the better part of two millennia, and was wide enough to afford a view of the lake unfolding below. He was thinking how lovely she looked. The sun was shining, and they were up high enough so that they could clearly see the island now, separated from the mainland by a long, narrow bridge.

In a glade off the main path, secluded among the trees, they made love, with the sun shining overhead. It seemed for a little while that the war was a false nightmare from the past, and that heaven had truly descended upon Europe. They lay together, naked in each other's arms, enjoying the colours and fragrance of the flora in the glade, and their own reborn intimacy.

Finally, though, Liesl broke the mood, as Wolf sensed her brooding.

"No matter how dangerous Russia is right now, I have to go there to find my brother," Liesl said as she sat up. "Dunken's been gone for the better part of a year, and we haven't heard a thing from him for almost six months. The last time from Kiev. The last of our troops there were getting ready to return home, and Dunken was going to come with them."

He had been liquidating his family's remaining business investments there.

"His last message to us was that the main body of the army had pulled out, and Reds and Ukrainian partisans were already fighting for the city. We haven't heard from him since."

"But the Whites still haven't retaken the city, and it's been over six months now since the German pullout. Can Dunken have hidden from the Reds this long?"

Liesl didn't answer at first. She pulled her swimsuit on again.

"Like I said, we haven't heard from him since the beginning of the year. My parents are very scared. I just want him back as soon as possible."

"Rantzau wants to go to Russia. He said so at lunch. Maybe he'll take a trip to Kiev and let you know what's up there."

But Wolf wasn't sure that even Rantzau really wanted to go into Russia during the height of the civil war, no matter how much he desired to speak with the leadership.

"It's my brother. I can't leave it up to the Count. I must go."

"If anyone goes to Russia to find him, it will be me," Wolf replied.

"Who said anything about you?"

Then she thought for a moment.

"But now that you've mentioned it, if Count Rantzau was willing to go to Kiev – at my family's expense, of course – I could go with him."

"It doesn't really matter. The more I think about it, there's about as much chance of Rantzau going to Kiev now, in the middle of a vicious war, as there is of a man setting foot on the moon."

They retraced their steps down the hill, over the bridge and onto the island. The rest of the party had already gathered at the dock. Einstein was anxious to be off, as the afternoon was getting late. It was nearing 4 o'clock.

"Where have you two been," Haber grilled them upon their arrival. Then he smiled and winked. "Some naughtiness, I trust?"

Liesl blushed, confirming Haber's suspicions.

"Well, fair enough," he chuckled. "But we want to get back to Lindau before the sun sets. I don't like the thought of being out on the water after dark."

Sailing east from Mainau Island with Konstanz to the south, the group could see Meersburg on the northern shore of the Bodensee, in Germany. It appeared medieval, enclosed by high ramparts overlooking the lake, with arched entrances and ancient towers. Through the binoculars Liesl could make out cobblestone lanes and castles. In Meersburg was the oldest occupied castle in Germany. They passed by the old city and continued east along the northern shore. A few miles later they rounded a tip of land as the shoreline swung gradually north and then east again, till it reached a river mouth, and the city of Friedrichshafen, largest on the lake after Konstanz. Friedrichshafen itself was an ancient town, declared a free city of the Holy Roman Empire in 1275. It became a rail junction in the mid-19th century, a resort town and ferry crossing.

"What the heck is that," asked Liesl, pointing to the northwest horizon. "I could swear there's something there, but the sun is blocking my view."

Einstein looked back over his shoulder.

"You know, you're right."

Rantzau was looking up at the sun now, using a newspaper to shade his eyes. It was helping. Wolf, under his sunglasses, had the best view.

"There's something, alright. An airship."

"But I don't hear anything," said Liesl.

"Dirigible. Zeppelin. Makes sense. The Zeppelin factory is in Friedrichshafen," Wolf continued.

“That’s right,” Haber agreed. “Graf von Zeppelin was born around here, wasn’t he?”

Zeppelin, born on the island of Mainau, off Konstanz, where the party had just had lunch, began developing rigid balloon airships after retiring from a long military career. By 1910 commercial airship service began. During the Great War they were conscripted for air raids. By the end of the war over 500 British civilians had been killed in Zeppelin raids launched from staging grounds in northern Germany. But they were slow and vulnerable to attack by planes and AA fire, so more and more were limited to stationary aerial surveillance, since they could sit for hours or days in the air at a given location to report on battles in progress. In the summer of 1919 all German Zeppelins were surrendered to the Allies under the Versailles *Diktat*, and the Zeppelin works in Friedrichshafen was preparing to turn over the last of its airships.

Liesl had the glasses trained on the Zeppelin in the sky above them. “I'd rather they didn’t get too close to us.”

“Why,” asked Wolf.

“A few of those people up there look familiar.”

“On that blimp,” Einstein asked.

“Yes. Wolf, take a look.”

He took the glasses from her and trained them on the airship.

“A veritable cornucopia of right wing fanatics. Albert, let’s give them a wide berth.”

“I’m trying. But we’re under sail, and they’re flying. And we don’t have much wind speed at that.”

“Then we’ve got a problem,” Wolf replied, “because I think they’re coming right for us.”

To her horror, Liesl saw the glint of binoculars staring back from the flying craft, which was sailing inexorably down towards them.

"Oh, my god, get us out of here," she implored Albert.

"I'm sorry, there's little I can do, my dear. What are you so frightened of? Do you think they intend us harm?"

She didn't know herself, so she looked at Wolf.

"I don't think so, professor," he said. "There's a pretty distinguished-looking entourage on board. It isn't likely they're out for a serious incident. Liesl will have some explaining to do to her friends," he nodded derisively up in the air, "when she sees them back in Munich."

"Who is on that ship, Wolf?"

Haber was insistent now, and both Einstein and Rantzau were staring at him as well.

"Alright. I can make out a few of Liesl's acquaintances from the Thule Society. There's Rudy Sebottendorff, the president. And Dietrich Eckart, a writer in Schwabing. Oh, and there's Gustav von Kahr, the prefect of Upper Bavaria. And who's this," mused Wolf from behind the spyglasses. "It's Ludendorff! Yes, for sure. That's his stepson, Heinz Pernet, beside him. No doubt about it."

"Quite a group," commented Rantzau. "What do you think they want with us?"

"Haven't a clue," replied Wolf. "Maybe just trying to scare us."

"They're doing that now," said Einstein. "They don't have to come any closer.

Ping…ping, ping.

"What was that? Why, those are shots!"

The water around the boat jumped in a few spots.

"They're shooting at us, professor," Liesl cried. "What can we do?"

"I don't know. Fritz. Ulrich. Wolf. What do we do," Einstein implored them.

"Let's get below. To the cabin," cried Haber, grabbing Liesl's hand as he headed down the entryway.

"Go with them, Count," Wolf shouted at Rantzau. "There's nothing you can do out here. Let's not give them any easy targets."

"But they'll only have the two of you to shoot at, then. I won't leave you topside to face them!"

Rantzau refused to budge. More shots pinged the water. Wolf was nervous about using the spyglasses, lest the glint draw a shot. Still, he could see Ernst Röhm chortling wholeheartedly as Hermann Ehrhardt fired round after round into the water in a ring around the boat. The shots were coming ever closer to the craft itself.

"You still think they're just trying to intimidate us, Wolf," asked Rantzau. "They're doing fine, don't you think?"

"Oh, yes. They've got me going. How about you, Albert?"

"Hm? Oh, yes. I'd be willing to admit that I'm almost scared speechless."

Both he and Wolf were rambling, playing for time to figure out what to do.

"Just so I won't feel silly later for not asking, Albert – there's no gun on board?"

"I'm afraid not. It's not our boat. So unless Haber or one of you has one, we're out of luck."

"Check the glove compartment, and any other likely place up front, anyway," Wolf said. "Count, can you check the aft? I'm going below. Be right up. And keep your heads down!"

Wolf surfaced a minute later. He climbed onto the roof of the cabin, grasping the mast. Standing erect, one hand on the mast, the other arm outstretched, he pointed at the blimp.

"What's he up to," asked Rantzau.

Haber and Liesl surfaced from the cabin.

"There's no gun on board," observed the Count.

At that moment, a shot ripped the cabin roof scant feet from where Wolf stood. It almost caught the sail.

"Wolf, get down here," Liesl shouted. "You'll be killed!"

She headed towards the cabin roof. Haber grabbed and held her. At that moment, Wolf reached into his pocket and pulled out what appeared to be a blunt, little, sawed-off pistol. He took aim at the gondola and fired. The shot hit it below the lengthy side viewing port, exploding in a bright, incandescent red, showering sparks above and below, some of which bounced off the balloon itself but did not puncture it. The party inside the gondola, however, were in consternation.

"They're running about like ants," Haber gloated gleefully. "Look at them shout and jump up and down. They're even hitting each other!"

Einstein passed the binoculars to Liesl. "It's quite a sight. Your acquaintances do not appear to be enjoying their party anymore. I do hope that you don't run into them back in Munich, Liesl." He was not smiling now. "I mean it, my dear. They look like they could do you serious harm if they ever got hold of you. They look very angry – very mean."

Wolf reached into his pocket for another flare cap. He pointed the pistol up towards the blimp again, but this time took dead aim at the balloon itself.

"Get below, Liesl," said Haber. "That balloon is pure hydrogen."

Modern blimps, like the Goodyear, use non-combustible helium.

"If he hits, it'll be the Fourth of July, as they say in America. And we're so close that we might not be around to celebrate it," Haber shouted.

But the men in the blimp had seen Wolf take aim as well. From the gondola they were all looking at the balloon immediately above their heads, and then down at Wolf pointing the flare gun at the balloon. At once the airship turned to port and headed north for shore.

“Looks like they’re turning tail for Friedrichshafen,” commented Haber.

“Thank god,” said the Count.

“Magnificent,” Einstein congratulated Wolf as he sat down beside them.

“But who were they, Wolf,” asked Liesl. “You didn’t finish telling us before the shooting started.”

“Oh, I’m sorry. They were mostly a whole bunch of senior army types, believe it or not. That’s probably how they had access to the Zeppelin. A last joy ride before they turn it over to the Allies. Or hide it. There was General von Mohl, overall commander in the Munich area; Colonel Franz Ritter von Epp, who commands his own Free Corps brigade; and there are two whom Liesl is familiar with. Captain Ernst Röhm, Epp’s adjutant. “

“And who else, Wolf,” she prodded him.

“Oh, your admirer Captain Herman Ehrhardt, ex-Imperial Navy commander, and now leader of his own brigade. The bloodiest Free Corps unit there is, I’m told. I sincerely hope he didn’t spot you on board with me, Liesl. But I think he must have. He was the one doing the shooting.”

A shudder ran down her back.

“It’s a good thing that they decided to leave when they did, though,” added Wolf. “I only had the one flare cap.”

The boat continued east towards Lindau. They passed wine towns, with steeples and spires of churches and castles towering over them, and fishing villages, and vineyards. Wasserburg came into view, a former island fortress resembling Lindau, but smaller.

Wolf talked with Haber and Rantzau about events in Russia. Einstein and Liesl sat down together.

"It's not like it looks, professor," she whined to him. "Those fanatics are not my friends."

"Are you sure you're not protesting too much?"

"No," she replied emphatically.

"Alright, Liesl. I believe you. I know you have a job to do. You're a journalist."

"Oh, Albert. I'm so mixed up. The only thing I know for sure is that I hate the Reds. They murdered Hella, in front of me."

He remembered. The auditorium at his old high school.

"That's what attracted me to all those Thule types in the first place. Well, no, actually it was Hella who took me to their meetings. And my paper wanted coverage. But they scare me. Ehrhardt, Röhm, others like them. And I know that most of what they say is bunk. Folkish ideology stuff. And everything is 'Jew this' and 'Jew that'. It's really quite revolting."

"It's not the Jew-bashing of these men that scares me, Liesl. It's their lack of human compassion. They've had it drained from them by the war. There is such a thing as simple human decency, but they seem brutalized to the point of having none left in them at all. Just a pitiless resolve."

The next morning Liesl and Wolf prepared to leave Lindau. Before they left, the trip to Russia was considered. Wolf was prepared to go if Rantzau went. But there were credible rumours of massacres and fighting on a grand scale between Cossacks and Reds, and increasing reports of major pogroms.

"I'll call you from Berlin in a week or so," said Count Rantzau, "after I've had a chance to think. It would be a dangerous trip, no doubt. So we shouldn't decide rashly."

* * *

Hitler was off to the Lechfeld transit camp, where he would get his first chance to prove what a convincing indoctrinator he was. It was late July, hot and sunny, with a slight cooling breeze drifting down from the north. Light clouds hovered above the Alps to the south.

A low platform had been built for the corporal from the Enlightenment Detachment to speak to the troops at the camp. They were returning German prisoners of war from the east who apparently had been showing Red sympathies.

"They're infected with that damn Lenin virus," Röhm said. "It's your job to delouse them."

So he stood up on the small platform in front of the dirty, decrepit, dispirited, starving troops, and commiserated.

"I know how you feel, cause I'm one of you. I'm not an officer; I'm just an ordinary soldier like you all. I served the entire war in the trenches. I survived a gas attack, and I was blinded for weeks. I earned this Iron Cross," he pointed to it proudly on his chest, "putting my life on the line for the Fatherland. I came home, fighting for my life, on a hospital train; and what did I find? That people spat on me!"

Adolf's eyes blazed as he stared defiantly at his audience. Some murmured as they felt the emotion emanating from the speaker.

"Now some of you may have already heard it in the camps you came from. Some may be hearing it for the first time. Some of you may have even been brainwashed already by the Reds into thinking otherwise. But I'm here to set you right."

He wasn't yelling or haranguing them; just a statement of fact.

"The Jew is responsible for the entire mess our homeland is in. He started the war in the first place; he fomented Red revolution in Russia which now threatens

Germany; and now he has shackled the Fatherland with that accursed treaty of Versailles."

The last word hissed from his mouth.

"Let me first impart to you a few facts about the Jews in Germany. The first ones came to our land in advance of the Romans, and even then they came as merchants. *Shopkeepers*," he said, dragging the word out.

"They were never producers; rather, they always acted exclusively as middlemen. With his millennia-old mercantile dexterity the Jew is far superior to the still helpless, boundlessly honest, Aryans, and for that reason German commerce has become a Hebrew monopoly. Money has become the god to whom all serve and bow down. The aristocracy of the sword, the might of the German army, now kneels to the millionaires. Jews publish the most prestigious newspapers, and rule the trade unions. The Jew is a parasite on the body of the Reich. Existence impels the Jew to lie, and to lie perpetually, just as it impels the inhabitants of the northern countries to wear warm clothing. No more proof is needed than the shameful, repugnant, revolting Versailles *Diktat*: it lays blame for the entire war on Germany! And then, purporting to do justice on the basis of that travesty of fact, it sweeps away all our gains in the east, bought dearly with German blood. But all that is nothing compared to what the accursed *Diktat* does to our beloved *Wehrmacht*, our German army! "

Adolf was working himself up into a fine lather, and the feeling was infectious. His audience began to murmur agreement, some clapped lightly.

"So what can we do," a soldier shouted from the audience, to the approval of others, "tell us what we can do to save the Fatherland," he implored.

"Alright, I'll tell you," Adolf began in a low voice, and then turned up the volume.

"If two million of Germany's best youth were slaughtered in the war, we have the right to exterminate these subhumans who breed like vermin."

Cheers erupted.

"And if the Hebrews try to destroy us in the press, if they don't like what we're saying, well, a thirty centimetre shell has always hissed more loudly than a thousand Jewish newspaper vipers – so let them hiss!"

They were on their feet. For the first time in years, these returning troops were given something to cheer about.

Hitler was in Valhalla

Russia

The Descent East

"I don't think there'll be regular train service east of Cracow," said Count Rantzau.

"When do we expect to arrive anyway," asked Commander Locker-Lampson, staring out the window of the train at the Polish countryside. They were in a day car, with a number of other passengers. "It really is the perfect time to travel, don't you think? The leaves are all in colour."

"We should be there in a couple hours, barring interruption," replied the Count. "So long as we're not hijacked by some roving militia. Or the Polish army itself."

"Why would they do that, Ulrich," asked Wolf.

"To flex their newfound muscle."

"And who else do we have to worry about?"

"This far west, probably nobody except a bandit militia," answered Commander Locker-Lampson. "Starving bands of outlaws or renegade Polish partisans. Maybe even some Ukrainian partisans, though they're mostly farther east. So far as I know no one else is seriously disputing Polish control over the area from here to Cracow, and a little east of there, and it's got support from the Allied leaders at Versailles. But east beyond that, look out."

It was late September as the train snaked slowly northeast, ringing the mountains to the south. The view from the opposite window revealed a landscape much flatter as the north European plain unfolded.

They were in a small section of the day car, with the seats looking towards the front and rear of the cabin. A main aisle ran up the middle of the car, with sections such as theirs off to each side.

Wolf and the Count continued to talk between themselves, reviewing their plans for the journey east of Cracow, through the remnants of old Galicia and into the Ukraine. Their destination was Kiev, where Dunken had sent his last letter from over six months before. Most of the Ukraine had been in German hands since the beginning of 1918, surrendered by Lenin's government as the price for peace with Germany under the treaty of Brest-Litovsk. Dunken had come in the late spring of 1918, with other German 'investors' in the wake of the takeover to stake a claim in Germany's newly conquered eastern territories. When World War One ended in November 1918 and it was certain that Germany would lose the new territories, Dunken at once started to liquidate their holdings. But by January 1919, when the army pulled out and headed home, he was not finished.

"How long did the Reds manage to hold onto power in Slovakia," Count Rantzau asked Wolf. "What do your sources tell you?"

Slovakia was in the mountains just to the south.

"Just three weeks."

"And what of Hungary?"

"That was longer. About three months. But the Red coup there was finally crushed earlier this month."

"And in Poland here?"

"The Reds haven't got a foothold, so far."

"What of the Ukraine itself?"

"The Reds moved into Kiev, outmuscling the Ukrainian partisans who want an independent Ukraine, after the German army left in January. The Whites are trying to win it now."

"Who is the White army made up of," asked the Count.

"What do you say, Oliver," Wolf asked, looking at the young Englishman who commanded the small band of mercenaries accompanying them to the Ukraine.

"There are lots, particularly among the officers, who support a return to rule by the Tsars. But there also are all those who want a democratic Russia, not Red or Tsar-ruled. But much of the White army is now made up of Cossacks from the Don and Black Sea areas."

This was the first real chance they had had to pick the commander's brain on the intelligence situation since they left Munich. Wolf had quietly assembled contacts who made him privy to information from the American and British secret services, as well as newspaper and business connections. But even between his sources and Count Rantzau's, there was still a large gap in their intelligence on the current situation in Russia, the battle lines so fluid and changing. And everything was rushed as they prepared for the trip, intent to be in and out of Russia before the approaching winter. It was actually Winston Churchill who had suggested Commander Locker-Lampson to Wolf when the latter approached the British Minister of War for letters of introduction to the commanders of the White forces.

"He was a flier in our Naval Air Service," Churchill told Wolf, "before he switched to reconnaissance and armoured cars. An interesting young man. His father was an accomplished poet, but not this lad. He's a fighter! Commanded armoured cars on the Western Front; and then we sent him east to train the Russians, before they pulled out of the war. After the revolution he fought against the Reds briefly. So he's quite familiar with the terrain in western Russia."

"What's he doing now?"

"Last time I saw him was at the peace conference in Paris. The lad's got an interest in politics, too. He came with Chamberlain. I'll ring up Austen and see if he knows what Commander Locker is up to right now. He might fancy a trip to Russia again."

That was only two weeks ago. Things had moved quickly, and now they were actually on their way to Kiev.

“The plan is a week in and a week out, traveling time. That will still leave us about two weeks to look around Kiev, and still be back by late October. And keep your fingers crossed that it’s not an early winter,” concluded Wolf to Rantzau.

“But what to do if we still haven’t found Dunken by that time?”

Wolf just shook his head, and turned to Oliver Locker-Lampson.

“When do they expect the Whites to win?”

“The main front right now is around Orel, a couple of hundred miles northeast of Kiev and about one hundred fifty miles south of Moscow. The White armies have been pressing the line ever farther north for a couple of months now, and after Orel falls, only the city of Tula blocks the way to the Kremlin. Lenin’s days appear numbered.”

“Anything else,” Rantzau inquired.

“Yes. There’s the Poles,” the young English commander added. “They’ve been pressing from the west against the Red armies because Lenin won’t give them a guarantee not to attempt to export his revolution there. They’re due to launch a full-scale attack at any time, and we may get caught on our way out.”

“You know, I think we’ve been a bit hasty in coming,” the Count replied. “This all sounds a trifle too dangerous.”

At Cracow the group changed their method of travel.

“We couldn’t rely on any scheduled service east of here,” Wolf explained. “We’re going into a potential war zone from now on. Even if railroads are running, they’re usually military transports or supply trains. But we should be quite comfortable,” he finished, opening the car door.

It was a 1919 Daimler touring sedan, specially prepped in the last two weeks for the trip. It had traveled, on flatcar along with their other vehicle, a small armoured troop transport, with them from Munich. Wolf, Rantzau and

Locker-Lampson traveled in the Daimler. They were followed by the troop transport carrying a dozen fighting men and supplies. They would all sleep in tents if other accommodation failed.

"The troops won't protect us from serious trouble," Wolf observed. "Only a small army could do that. We just want to intimidate any bandits that come sniffing."

And so, with the Daimler taking the lead, the party headed east down the road to Galicia.

"Tell me about Russia, Count," Locker-Lampson coaxed him. "I know little of the history. Just that before the war she was thought to be strong militarily, due to her population if nothing else."

"Ever since Napoleon's debacle in the Russian snows, Germany and Austria-Hungary have slept with a nightmare on their doorstep," said the Count. "The Russian behemoth might gather all her forces and move west."

"So Germany and Austria built up huge armies to protect themselves from the Russian threat, and in turn France built a huge army in case Germany should look west," Wolf interjected. "The continent of Europe became an armed camp. The assassination in Sarajevo just happened to light the fuse."

"That's right," Rantzau replied. "Russia, west of the Urals anyway, is heavily populated. A hundred million hungry, envious peasants to draw armies from."

Commander Locker couldn't help but notice how comfortable his seat was. The upholstery was tan, plush and warm. The ride was smooth too, considering how pitted the highway was, thanks to the heavy duty shocks installed the week before. There was continual refugee traffic on foot heading west, although lighter than they'd seen elsewhere. It struck him how little traffic was going east.

"At least we're making good time," Wolf said to Rantzau. "We could be in Lemberg tonight at this pace."

"Something will slow us down along the way, I'm sure," replied the Count, ever the optimist.

The commander passed coffee from a thermos to Wolf and Rantzau.

"Tell me of the Cossacks, Count," Locker-Lampson asked. "The Tsar's Cossacks!"

"'Cossack' means 'freebooter', the same term we use for Free Corps troopers. They were folks who left Lithuania, Poland, and Russia a few hundred years ago and went south to the steppes by the Black Sea. They considered themselves free peoples, and eventually united to defend themselves against the Russians and Poles. Their first great leader was Bogdan Khmelnytsky, who united them to throw the Poles out of the western Ukraine. But they ended up under the thumb of Moscow instead."

""Where did they learn to ride like they do?"

"A gift from the Tatars, and the Mongols before them. The horsemen of the endless steppe that runs from the Black Sea all the way to China. It made the Cossacks feared throughout their history. The great Russian peasant revolts all began as Cossack revolts which swept north towards Moscow."

Their tiny two-vehicle convoy was now passing through Tarnow, with Lemberg in the distance.

"The Tsars decided to co-opt the Cossacks by making them into a warrior caste with special privileges," said Count Rantzau. "Then they fought for the Tsars. They kept their masters in power during times when even Russian units couldn't be trusted to protect the autocracy. "

"And the Tsars used them against the Jews," said Wolf.

"Right," confirmed the Count. "Alexander II was assassinated by a Jewish revolutionary in 1881, and the last two Tsars went after the Jews right up until the revolution."

"Why?"

"They believed that most of the revolutionary leaders were Jews," answered Wolf this time, "because they were usually the only ones who could read and write. And hence the beginning of the modern pogroms."

"You never told me where you got our little troop of mercenaries from, Wolf," mentioned Count Rantzau as they rolled along the highway east, headed for Lemberg, not more than a couple of hours away in good traffic. Today the trip might take longer, blocked as they were now by heavier refugee traffic heading west. They snaked along the road, pedestrians parting for them slowly.

"The commander looked after that."

"I hired them in Munich," Locker replied. "Mostly Free Corps troopers who served in the east during the war. So they all know some Russian and Ukrainian."

Along the side of the highway further evidence of the recent war surrounded them. Broken down vehicles, both military and civilian, regularly littered the ditches.

The commander looked out the window at the endless line of ragged Slav peasants, interspersed with groups of black-robed Jews, and the flotsam and jetsam of war strewn along the roadway.

"You were telling me about Russia, Count."

"I think we left off about the turn of the century," Wolf reminded him.

"Right. The 20th century blew in with revolutionary pressures within Russia about to explode. The Tsar wanted the benefits of industrial progress, but to continue to rule by divine right. He continued to repress everybody, in particular the Jews, which caused many to support revolution. Meanwhile, literacy in Russia continued to rise, and the more literate the people became, the more they realized how truly repressed they were, and they wanted change."

"Literacy leads to revolution," commented Wolf.

"And pressures just kept building in Russia," Rantzau continued. "Any attempts at western-style agriculture meant consolidating properties, throwing families off the land. They had nowhere to go but the cities, and even though jobs were opening up, they couldn't keep pace."

"It sounds like the Tsar would have welcomed a war to take the pressure for reform off his government," Locker said.

"He did when the war began," Rantzau confirmed, "but by 1917, with Russia losing, and all his troops away at the Front, he couldn't stop revolution at home."

"But it was a democratic revolution," observed the commander. "Kerensky's government wasn't Red. So what happened? How did Lenin hijack the revolution?"

"You were here," observed Rantzau. "It was because the new government continued the war, which lost them the support of the people. Lenin then moved against Kerensky."

A highway sign indicated Lemberg only thirty kilometres away.

"Tell me," Locker asked, "is Lenin Jewish? I keep hearing that so many of the Red leaders are."

"Not as far as I know, although their enemies would love to be able to prove it. Of the inner circle, Trotsky was born Jewish, although he says he's an atheist. Zinoviev and Kamenev are Jews. Stalin, the youngest, isn't."

"If Lenin was, they sure could label the Red cause as a Jewish plot to destroy society," observed Wolf. "Even though Jews are held responsible for capitalism as well."

Lenin's ethnic background was actually quite diverse. Besides Russian blood, his grandmother was from a wealthy Lutheran family from Germany, while his grandfather was partly Mongol. And his great grandfather was a Jewish merchant from Volhynia who married a Swede.

"It looks like we're in Lemberg," Count Rantzau noted. "I'm told this used to be a pretty city. But it took some punishment in the early part of the war."

"Didn't a pogrom happen at the end of the war," Wolf asked.

"Why are the Jews so despised here," Locker pressed him.

"The local peasants couldn't compete economically. They were illiterate, while every Jew, even women and children, could read and do at least simple math. Jews dominated business and trade in Poland and the western Ukraine out of all proportion to their numbers."

Lemberg was the biggest city on their route through the western Ukraine to Kiev, so it took them some time to drive through town. Finally they left the congestion of the urban streets and headed out on the highway east to Kiev.

"What's the next town, Count," asked Wolf.

"I believe it's Brody. Not too far up the road."

"A lot of Jews there too?"

"Oh, yes. This whole area from here to Kiev and the Dneiper is fairly infested. Tiny in comparison to the Ukrainian and Russian populations, but large by western standards. They form over a tenth of the population, for sure. Some say higher than that, particularly in Poland. But they control half the commerce! Or at least they did, before the war."

"And the rest of the population is very resentful," observed Locker-Lampson.

"The Russian Jewish community, including Poland and the Ukraine, is five to seven million by best estimates. Since the assassination of the Tsar in 1881 and the resulting pogroms, there's been huge emigration to the west, particularly America. But that still leaves many here. Over a quarter of the western Ukraine may be Jewish. And up north, over half of Minsk province. It's due to the insane Russian policy of restricting the areas where Jews can live.

This huge country, and the government seals them within the western provinces. So what happens? The numbers concentrate in relation to the local population. And they're so good at business anyway…"

"You mean they're the only ones that could read," said Wolf.

"Whatever," continued Rantzau, "the fact still remains, like I said before, that over a tenth of the population is Jewish. That's roughly a hundred times the concentration of Jews in France. They took over Budapest and Vienna. Imagine what would happen in Germany if we had that many!"

"Oh, I don't know," said Wolf. "I saw New York City, and there are more Jews crowded into the Lower East Side than anywhere else in the world. Over a million and a half stuffed into a little corner of Manhattan Island. But many have prospered," Wolf exclaimed.

"To whose benefit," asked Rantzau.

"Everyone's."

They were all silent as the highway rolled by outside. It was overcast, a gloomy day but not raining, a boon for the refugees trudging by them in the opposite direction.

"It's quite a contrast," Rantzau continued after a while. "While the Tsar was banning Jews from Moscow and St. Petersburg, America drew them to her bosom. Which country prospered more?"

"How could the Tsar have acted so stupidly," asked Wolf. "And that wife of his. She was German, for pity's sake."

"That's a bizarre tale, from what I've heard," the Count replied. "And who knows what is true."

"Tell us what you know," the commander prodded him, as he cast a glance outside. "The scene never seems to change. How depressing."

"We're coming into Brody now," Wolf commented. "The battle line in 1918, when the Russians surrendered.

No fighting took place east of here, at least not between Germans and Russians."

They passed through Brody and continued east towards Kiev.

"There's a civil war going on in the heart of Russia and the Ukraine," Wolf said. "All the fighting is east of here – east of Kiev hopefully; and there's lots of it, according to the last reports."

"So there's a chance we can get in and out of Kiev without entering an actual war zone," mused Rantzau hopefully.

"Let's be clear, folks," the commander said, "we're in a war zone right now."

Neither Wolf nor the Count replied.

" You were going to tell us about Nicholas and Alexandra," Wolf finally said.

"Ah, yes," replied Rantzau.

He wanted to stop thinking about the danger ahead as well, so he turned his mind to the Russian royals.

"You really have to begin with Nicholas' childhood. One of his earliest memories was of watching his grandfather die at the hands of terrorists. He was the victim of a bomb, and his tattered body, still barely alive, was brought back to the palace where young Nicholas could view the end. His father, who could bend iron bars and had a scary temper, was committed to retaining absolute rule in Russia. He died young, when Nicky was in his mid-twenties. Alexandra was Queen Victoria's granddaughter, and the Kaiser's cousin. Trouble was, she was more like the Kaiser than the Queen, and she wanted Russia to remain an autocracy."

"And then there was the Kaiser's contribution," Wolf added.

"Yes. He whispered in Nicholas' ear that rule by divine right must be preserved. "

"And don't forget Rasputin," said Wolf.

"The mad monk," replied Rantzau. "Made indispensable by the crown prince's hemophilia."

Inherited from Queen Victoria, who carried the gene but didn't suffer from it.

"The family tried to keep it a secret – it wouldn't do for Russia to know that its next Tsar could die from a nosebleed or a bruise."

"I heard about it," said the commander. "But I thought it was another ridiculous Russian rumour."

"His blood doesn't clot," continued the Count. "So when the blood vessels bleed internally, in a bruise, they can fill a body cavity or a lung or a joint. At the very least he swells severely before the vessels have a chance to repair themselves."

And his parents refused him painkillers because they were afraid he might get hooked on morphine. So Alexandra watched while her child suffered.

"And then Gregory Rasputin came along," the Count related. "He was a *starets*, a travelling peasant holy man. He had visions. He was gross and lecherous, although some say he was impotent. And he exerted complete control over the royal family. Or at least over Alexandra, who in turn controlled Nicholas."

"But why," asked the commander. "What power did he exert over them?"

"It was his seeming ability to control the crown prince's hemophilia. Or at least the pain associated with it."

"How?"

"No one is quite sure. Perhaps a fraud; perhaps hypnosis, I suppose. His eyes were magnificent! Have either of you ever seen a picture of him?"

"I met the man just once," Commander Locker replied. "The eyes just jump out at you. So big and penetrating."

Modern testing provides some evidence that hypnosis can help control internal bleeding.

"I'm sceptical," said Wolf. "Nicholas was just stupid. He blundered into the war by being as stubborn as the Kaiser. Two dinosaurs whose final act was to plunge all Europe into war."

"You may be right," the Count conceded. "Because with Nicholas off at the Front, Alexandra was left to run the government. And she had no experience! So who did she rely on?"

"Rasputin," muttered Locker.

"Of course. Then Rasputin began to give Nicholas advice on how to run the war. But it couldn't go on. The papers openly speculated on what hold he had over the empress. Was she sleeping with him? Even their relatives tried to rid them of Rasputin, and appoint a ministry responsible to the legislature."

"So he was finally assassinated. By a Russian prince, if I recall," said Wolf.

"Yes. Prince Felix Yussoupov, the richest lad in Russia. A young man. Do you know the story, Wolf?"

"Not the details."

"Well, this is what was reported to us, though it sounds incredible," Rantzau continued. "They invited the holy man to the prince's estate one night. The prince poisoned him with enough cyanide to kill an elephant, but it didn't have any effect. After two hours the prince shot him in the back. A doctor there pronounced him dead, but a couple minutes later he leapt up off the floor and grabbed the prince by the throat. The prince managed to break free and ran away screaming, which alerted the others, who then shot Rasputin again. They dumped him through a hole in the ice into the Neva River."

Wolf looked sceptically at the Count.

"Could be," commented Commander Lampson. "In fact, I heard a similar story from an acquaintance of mine on the Grand Duke's staff. What's the name of this place," he asked, looking out the window as the tiny convoy slowed to a crawl through the village streets.

Wolf looked up from his map, one hand on the wheel.

"Pavolochka," he replied. "Kiev's not too far from here."

"I have a feeling," said Count Rantzau, "that we are quite definitely in the wrong place at the wrong time."

Dzerzhinsky's Lair

> Woe unto the people which will behave in a Christian fashion, in an era where a struggle has begun for the possession of the earth.
>
> - Ernst Wachler in *Der Hammer*

> History is a cruel stepmother, and when it retaliates, it stops at nothing.
>
> - Lenin

The direct antecedent to the violence and direction of the Holocaust occurred two decades previous, in 1919 in Russia. The civil war was a bloody affair that violently displaced every segment of society; it took place in a poor, starving country in which major food-producing areas had already been destroyed by four years of world war. Society was at its most despicable as the civil war blew Cossack armies west over the Dneiper and through the Ukraine, lands with large Jewish populations. And a sadistic, horrific, internal security agency, the chief instrument of Stalin's future terror, and the model for the SS, spawned from this same cesspool.

"Just call me 'Torquemada'," said the giant in khaki, sleeves rolled up, whip handle firmly clenched in his right hand. "It is my job to question you. Now you say that you've already answered me, but I have to make sure you answered true. You can understand that."

Dunken looked up from his bunk, wire mesh with a sheet thrown over it. The mattress had long since disappeared, either stolen or eaten away by the vermin. His eyes were hollow, reflecting his general exhaustion from lack of food, sleep, and warmth. Bruises covered his body. But he was too tired now to display real fear of the whip. The large man pulled him roughly off the bunk and threw him sprawling to the floor.

"Move, ingrate. You Germans are not so high and mighty now!"

With that he kicked Dunken hard in the rear, exhorting, "Get on with you, or you'll feel my lash!"

* * *

"It's time we picked up a local guide," said Wolf, as they cruised slowly through the village of Pavolochka.

"Who are we looking for," asked Commander Locker-Lampson. "And what will he tell us?"

"We have to know what it's like in Kiev right now," Wolf replied. "We have to check both the police records and local grapevine for news of Dunken."

"Do you think it will work? Why will anyone recall him in particular," asked Count Rantzau. "He wasn't the only German in the Ukraine."

"But there weren't that many silly enough to hang around after our troops pulled out. Or to leave it until the last minute. Whether he's still alive is another story."

"And which 'police' do you propose to check with," asked the Count. "The military authorities, or the secret police?"

"Whatever," Wolf replied. "They may be the same thing. There's a good chance he's being held by the Reds, if he is still alive, so we'll just have to ask them."

"And don't you think that might be a little dangerous," inquired Commander Locker.

"Very," Wolf said, "but the bigger danger is from the lower level comrade who decides to shoot us before reporting our existence to his superiors. If we can make contact with the Red leadership, our chances of success rise."

"Why," Locker inquired.

"Because I am a Warburg, and my name carries some weight. My cousin Felix and his father-in-law Jacob Schiff have been supporting the Reds financially against the Tsar for years. They need that continued support to fight the civil war."

They had been driving around for about twenty minutes when Wolf suddenly motioned for Commander Locker to pull the car over. He got out and crossed the street to a lorry parked facing the opposite direction. It was a dirty white colour, and had 'JDC' printed on the side in large black letters. Three men and a woman, all dressed in fatigues with JDC logos, stood around. They were speaking English.

"I thought the JDC had pulled all of its personnel out of Russia for the time being," said Wolf to the group. "Excuse me, my name is Wolf Warburg. I'm a cousin of Felix."

The American Jewish Joint Distribution Committee was a charity, based in New York and headed by Felix Warburg, responsible for distributing food and supplies to Jews throughout war-torn eastern Europe. The group Wolf encountered explained that they had been frightened by fighting which erupted between Reds and Whites south of Kiev three days before when the Whites invaded from the south. It was only a matter of time before the White armies, reinforced by weapons and supplies from the western Allies, overran Kiev and headed north for Moscow. It looked like the Reds would lose the war after all.

"I'm looking for a German civilian who got trapped in Kiev last January," Wolf explained. "It's possible he's in hiding, or that he's been arrested by the Reds."

"We do have some contacts among the local Jewish population," one of the JDC party confirmed. "They might know something. If he's been arrested, though, he's likely dead already."

"This is Jonah Battel. He lives in the village of Fastov, a few miles east of here, on the way to Kiev. Believe it or not, he knows this person you are looking for," smiled the exultant JDC agent later that afternoon. "It really is quite a coincidence."

"I bring sad news, though," said Jonah as they sat down. "Dunken was seized from our home in Fastov almost two months ago by the Red terror police, and we haven't heard from him since."

"The 'terror police'," inquired Count Rantzau.

"The 'Cheka'. They torture and kill – they're more horrible than you can possibly imagine. No one ever returns from a Cheka jail, from the stories I've heard. There's someone you should meet who can tell you what it's like in there – what they do to people."

The dictatorial state in the modern world, with a repressive secret police network to enforce its will, was born first in Russia, in the Tsarist state of the 1880's. The revolutionary movement was gaining force, and in 1881 the Tsar was assassinated by a terrorist. His son, intent on revenge and stomping out the revolutionary movement, unleashed his police. They in turn, aided by communication and transportation advances of the Industrial Revolution, were for the first time able to create a tight, nationwide police network connected by radio and then phone with headquarters in St. Petersburg. Before the Nazis, Germany never had a police state comparable to that of the last Tsars or the Red regimes which followed.

"I spent part of the war in Vienna, at the headquarters of the Union for the Liberation of Ukraine," said George Leopke. "There were many of us from Dneiper Ukraine there. We were engaged in propaganda work among the prisoners of war in Austria. After the Russians pulled out of the war and surrendered the Ukraine to the Germans, I returned. But it was short lived. When the world war ended, the Allies forced Germany to give up the Ukraine. The Reds have held it for the last six months now, but the Whites are moving up from the south, overrunning everything in their path. Cossack armies could be in Kiev by the end of the week, they say."

"And what do you know of the Red prisons," inquired Commander Locker.

"I spent two months there. After that I spent a month as a Cheka 'recruit' before escaping. I've seen and heard enough to make you cringe."

In Russia before World War One there was a long history of violence and cruelty, unalleviated by any acquisition of wealth as occurred in western Europe, where torture had for the most part gone by the wayside. In Russia there was not the desire to jail peasants, always an expensive proposition since they then had to be fed and housed; though Siberia was always an option. It was useless to fine most of those convicted since few had any money. So physical beatings were still standard punishment for most offences.

After the coup of October 1917 Lenin set out to mirror the secret police apparatus of the former Tsarist state. The Cheka was founded in late 1917, and within a year branches spread across the country. The only real control over it was the Central Committee. Lenin intended to disband the Cheka after the civil war ended. But the terror it employed was returned by its opponents, so the Red leadership deemed it necessary to retain the secret police, who eventually became the KGB.

"Let met tell you a little about the Cheka," said George Leopke, "which really got under way after the attempt on Lenin's life a year ago."

Lenin had taken two bullets, in the arm and neck. Fanny Kaplan was the Jew responsible.

"After that, the Cheka got nasty. Nothing was more important than the survival of the revolution and the destruction of opposition," Leopke continued. "Each local operation has its own special torture. It's own unique flavour, so to speak. Some force their victims to watch family being raped and tortured. Others bury victims alive, or even better, alongside a corpse in the same coffin. Last winter they poured water on naked people until they froze solid outside. In Kharkov they employ the 'glove trick' – boiling the victim's hands until the skin can be peeled off to make a pair of human gloves."

Count Rantzau was visibly blanching. He'd heard rumours of the savagery of the civil war, but this was beyond belief.

"The Cheka in Tsaritsyn saw their still-conscious victims' bones in half," Leopke continued relentlessly. "In Voronezh they roll them around in barrels studded with nails. And in Armavir they crush skulls by tightening a leather strap with an iron bolt around the head."

Wolf listened surreally as Leopke described how the Cheka in Odessa chained their victims to planks and pushed them live into the furnace or a tank of boiling water. He imagined what Dunken might have gone through.

"And what is the specialty of the Kiev Cheka," he asked.

"They fix a birdcage to you, opened against your stomach. Inside is a rat or two. They heat the bottom of the cage with a torch. The rats will do anything to escape, including eating their way through your guts."

* * *

Kiev was the Russian holy city. Far older than Moscow and St. Petersburg, former capital of the ancient state of Kievan Rus, it was the original seat of the Russian Orthodox Church. The number of Jews living there had always been restricted and immediately before the war there were only about 5000 there, or one percent of the population. Still, that was more than in Moscow or St. Petersburg. In sharp contrast, in western Russia overall there were 100 times as many Jews in relation to the rest of the population than generally existed in western Europe.

Wolf decided that the direct approach was the best. A scout was sent to contact the local Reds and pass a message that Wolf would be coming into the local Cheka office in Kiev. The Reds responded the next day confirming the place and time. So here they were, driving down the main street of Kiev, which was mostly deserted since everyone was scared of the approaching White army. A Red evacuation was imminent. Meanwhile, it was eerily silent save for the sound of far off shelling to the south and east. The Daimler touring car, with the troop truck following, pulled up to a large structure presently serving as local Cheka headquarters.

Two armed Reds accompanied Wolf and Count Rantzau into the building. Commander Locker and the troopers remained outside. The two were escorted down a long hall, up a short flight of stairs, down another hall to an office at the end. A secretary sitting at the wooden desk nodded to them.

"This one says he has an appointment to see the commander," one of the soldiers told her. "He says it's all arranged. I told him no one *wants* to visit us, but he insisted."

"You may go inside," said the secretary, an older woman with her hair wrapped above. "Just so you know, Comrade Dzerzhinsky is in there. And he is expecting you," she hissed in warning.

The two Red soldiers who were escorting Wolf and Count Rantzau both gasped audibly.

"I didn't even know *he* was here," one of the soldiers blurted out.

"May God have mercy upon both of you," said the other one to Wolf and Rantzau as he escorted them forward. He opened the door and, with his rifle tip, pushed the two ahead into the inner sanctum.

Felix Dzerzhinsky was seated behind a stately, worn, wooden desk. There was a lamp on one corner and piles of documents covering the rest. A short-handled black whip lay there as well.

"You should feel honoured, Herr Warburg. I came all the way from Tula to meet you. At Lenin's instructions. It seems you are a valuable commodity. The leadership wishes no harm to come to you."

Dzerzhinksy was lean and clean-shaven with scars on his face.

"Do you know my personal history, Herr Warburg," he asked, fondling the whip handle at the same time. "I was expelled for speaking Polish in my dormitory in Poland. I spent most of my adult life in Russian prisons, and I was in the Orel," one of the most notorious Tsarist prisons, "for over three years until the revolution freed me a couple of years ago. There is something you should see."

With that Dzerzhinsky removed his own shirt to reveal extensive scars, cut marks, all over his torso and arms.

“This is the Tsar's response to my leading a hunger strike."

"But it must have been more than that to merit such torture," Count Rantzau blurted out.

Dzerzhinsky looked over at him for the first time, smiling slightly.

"And who have we here?"

"I am Count Ulrich von Brockdorff-Rantzau, formerly of the German government. Your superiors will have heard of me."

Dzerzhinsky's lips snarled momentarily.

"I am in charge here. Perhaps you do not know who I am. My word carries life and death in Red Russia. I am more powerful than anyone besides Lenin. You live or die by my command," he shouted, raising the whip with his right hand.

"Ah, the infamous Count Rantzau," a voice boomed from the doorway to Dzerzhinsky's right side.

In walked a familiar figure with a mustache and goatee.

"We meet again, Count," he said, extending his open hand towards Rantzau.

"Thank God. Your arrival is better late than never, Commissar Trotsky," the Count replied in relief.

Leon Trotsky was dressed in a grey greatcoat, still fully buttoned despite the heat. He had a dark blue cap on.

"How are you, Felix? Our esteemed Comrade Lenin directed me to travel here immediately to assist you with our guests. Herr Warburg comes from a most important family. But the Count – we didn't expect to find him here. How is that, Herr Foreign Minister?"

"I hold that position no longer, as you are surely aware. There are matters I would discuss with you, nonetheless. Off the record, so to speak. It is fortunate that you yourself attended here."

"And Herr Warburg," Trotsky asked, "what is your mission here?"

"I am looking for someone. He may be in one of your cells."

Trotsky looked over at Dzerzhinsky.

"I would know nothing of such things," Trotsky said. "Felix is responsible for security services."

"Who is he," Dzerzhinsky asked.

Wolf's description of Dunken was given to the secretary to pass on to the guards below.

"You realize that if this von Schlieffen has done anything counter-revolutionary in nature, he will have to be punished," warned Dzerzhinsky. "That is, assuming we even have him."

Wolf looked over at Trotsky.

"It is Lenin's principle," Dzerzhinsky continued, "that it is better to arrest a hundred innocent people than to allow one enemy to go free."

"I am not here to talk about your revolution," said Count Rantzau suddenly, to change the topic. "Commissar Trotsky, I am here as a secret emissary from the German government and private commercial interests, including Krupp, to propose cooperation in the testing of advanced weapons. They would be tested secretly on bases here, far from western eyes."

"Why should we want to deal with you, who we've been fighting for four years?"

"Because it will help both our countries. Russia will have access to advanced weapons. Germany will be able to test the weapons, which we are barred from under the Versailles Treaty."

"Comrade Lenin and I have travelled widely and we can see your usefulness," Trotsky stated slowly, "but there are those who are not so inclined. They do not see the value of international connections and foreign money and assistance. You are the enemy. They would kill you immediately. Those such as Felix here," he motioned to the scowling man pacing the floor, "and Comrade Stalin as well, who are, shall we say, less travelled. I think Lenin sent me here just in case you happened to annoy Felix by mistake. You'd best be polite to him while we consider your offer."

The Whites were invading Kiev; the shellfire could be heard all round. The telephone rang. Dzerzhinsky answered, then whispered briefly to Trotsky, who got up to leave the room.

"Come, Herr Warburg. We may have your man – if he's still alive. Hurry."

"What about me," wailed Rantzau as Wolf rose to leave.

"You stay here and keep Felix company," Trotsky smiled. "And Felix," he added, looking over at Dzerzhinsky, "behave yourself. Comrade Lenin will be most unhappy if the Count here is harmed."

Dzerzhinsky smiled back crookedly. More cannon exploded, closer and louder.

Dunken was lashed to a column that stood in the center of the dungeon-like room supporting the ceiling. It was a circular column about three feet in diameter, and Dunken's back curved nicely to fit it. White braided cord half an inch thick and lashed round his torso and arms strapped him firmly to the column. His huge captor, Torquemada, tugged at the ropes to test them.

"Tight enough," he commented. "You can struggle all you want, but you'll not escape."

He had a crazed look in his eyes that scared Dunken even more than he had been.

"Now comes the pièce de résistance," the big man added. "You're going to love this, you German swine."

Torquemada laughed maniacally as his assistant brought a birdcage from the counter by the wall. Dunken looked at the cage as it was carried close and handed to Torquemada. In it was a good size rat, perhaps six inches long, with a black, hairless tail the same length. Torquemada opened the door of the cage, but before the rat could escape he pressed the open entrance against Dunken's stomach. The other Red then threw more rope round the cage, Dunken, and the column, attaching them all tightly together. Horrified, Dunken peered into the cage, noting the rodent's two long, narrow, sharp front teeth, each over an inch long. They were two sabres, waiting to gnaw anything in their path. What did his tormenters have in mind?

The cage itself was metal; Torquemada lit a piece of wood, and held it under the bottom. The rat became agitated as the heat increased. It pressed against the bars, moving round the cage, searching for a way out. Finally it reached the doorway, which was open but pressed firmly up against Dunken's stomach. It sniffed, then began to gnaw gingerly at his shirt. Dunken, terrified, began to struggle against the ropes holding him. He could feel teeth ripping his shirt, shredding it. Then a tingle against his bare midriff, and a sudden stab of pain as the skin was torn. He began to scream.

"It'll eat right through me! Stop, please, I'll do anything!"

Torquemada laughed mercilessly, as Dunken hoped to pass out.

Leon Trotsky and Wolf Warburg hurried down the hallway in search of the Guard commander. They were now in the basement, where the Cheka conducted its most intense interrogations. Already they could hear screams and shrieks from various cells along the way. Trotsky had been told that Dunken was in the hands of Torquemada, a particularly sadistic debriefer who extracted confessions where none were usually to be had. The Reds had given the German to him to break and then bury, so Trotsky knew it was a race against time. And now the order had been given to abandon Kiev and evacuate the city. What was to be done with the captives in the building? Trotsky was glad that that was Dzerzhinsky's problem. Most would have to be shot, and he didn't want the responsibility, even though he'd seldom been squeamish about such things in the past.

But he wanted to rescue Dunken von Schlieffen. That was a valuable connection that neither he nor Lenin wanted sabotaged. Western funding was crucial, so it was plain stupid to alienate the Warburgs. Trotsky and Wolf flew from door to door in the building depths while shots echoed from various quarters, from different cells where Wolf imagined prisoners were being tortured and executed. They would have been hunting their captors before nightfall if allowed to go free. Red comrades were now scurrying towards the stairwells, anxious to escape the city before the Whites arrived.

"Where is Torquemada? I must know," Trotsky screamed as he corralled a pair of comrades in a hurry.

"You've come to the right place," one replied. "That's his usual abode."

They were deep in the bowels of the building, by the furnaces near the center of the lowest level. Wolf stared at the heavy wooden door in front of him. Were they in time? He reached for the handle, turned it, and pushed. Nothing happened. It was bolted from the inside.

He knocked heavily, skinning his knuckles, and cursed.

"Who's there," bellowed Torquemada from the other side.

The giant pulled the burning faggot back from under the birdcage. The animal inside stopped squealing, pulled back and sat still, its teeth dripping blood.

Again there came knocking at the door.

"I said, 'Who's there?'," the giant bellowed again.

"It is I, Commissar Trotsky. Open this door!"

Wolf heard nothing for the longest time, and Trotsky was just about to shout again when a large bolt shot back from the other side. The door opened, and they stood facing an ogre.

"You are Torquemada, I presume. I am here to inquire after a prisoner."

"I really am quite civilized," mused Felix Dzerzhinsky to Count Rantzau. "I just can't stand aristocrats. And all those who were formerly 'upper class'."

And where do I fit into your view, wondered Rantzau, who was in a very vulnerable position until Trotsky returned.

"I hold the power of life and death here," Dzerzhinsky continued.

"But no one disputes that," the Count replied. "You certainly have nothing to fear from me."

"Ha, ah ha," chortled Felix. "But you have much to fear from me. What will I do with you?"

"Why should you want to do anything," asked the Count.

"Because you are a capitalist and an aristocrat. An enemy of the revolution. But Lenin thinks your friend is too valuable to allow to be harmed."

"We are on your side," the Count said. "Wolf's cousins, and Schiff, are helping your cause."

"That's just to help the Jews," Felix countered. "You'd be aiding the Whites and reactionaries otherwise. You're all capitalists, and we are out to destroy your society. We'll eventually end up fighting each other anyway."

The Count agreed deep down.

"What can we do," he asked instead.

"I don't know, Herr Rantzau. And that's the problem. We have to evacuate the city, and we're disposing of all the prisoners right now. Trotsky won't find Warburg's friend still alive. Now, what to do with you, since I have to be leaving. It's stupid to leave you alive, to shoot at us later."

"And what will you tell Trotsky – and Lenin," asked the Count.

"White snipers took you outside the building. No one will question that."

"But what if witnesses tell a different story," he countered.

"And who will see me put a bullet in your brains here?"

The room fell silent as Rantzau prayed silently for Trotsky's quick return. Suddenly Dunken's fate was not uppermost in his thoughts. Dzerzhinsky played with his whip handle. A few minutes later the phone rang, and he picked it up.

Ka-blam!

At that moment the building was rocked by a thunderous blast. The receiver dropped from Dzerzhinsky's grasp.

"Get my jeep ready," he shouted into the receiver after retrieving it from the floor. "I'm not waiting any longer to get out of here."

Standing up, he pulled out his revolver and aimed at Count Rantzau.

"It's a pity I must do away with you. Such are the fortunes of war."

"Hold on there, Felix!"

The door had just opened to re-admit Trotsky. Behind him came Wolf, and leaning on him was a broken-down shell of a man, smelly and filthy.

"I give him to you as a gift, comrade," said Trotsky. "Rosa Luxemburg spoke highly of you. Get out while you still can."

Turning to Count Rantzau, he said, "We'll let you know about your offer – assuming that we win this war."

So, with Rantzau and Wolf supporting him, Dunken limped out of the building and into the waiting vehicles. They headed west, anxious to leave Kiev before the arrival of the Whites invading from the south and east, bursts of artillery reverberating in their ears.

Invitation to a Party

> The Marxists taught – If you will not be my brother, I will bash your skull in. Our motto shall be – If you will not be German, I will bash your skull in.
>
> \- *Mein Kampf*

Summer passed and the population sizzled in Munich, as elsewhere across Germany. Discontent seethed everywhere, due to lack of food and other basics, a creeping inflation, and, as a result of the onerous provisions of the Versailles *Diktat*, a general lack of hope for the future. The war was over, but Germany was defeated and destitute. The fact that England was broke as well, in hock to its teeth to America, wasn't something Germans knew or cared about. The only bright spot was the new political freedom. Myriad fledgling parties sprouted, all seeking the support of the German middle class.

In 1919 the Reds had very experienced organizers used to fighting the union busters of the steel barons before the war. They now employed the strong-arm methods of the union busters against any new right wing or center parties that came along. They tore down posters advertising meetings, heckled public speakers, and, in the end, sent thugs into meetings to break them up. By late summer and early autumn this was commonplace in Munich. But since the Reds and right wing had been openly killing each other in the streets there only three months before, it was a definite improvement.

"A lovely day, Colonel," Ernst Röhm commented as he held the door for Franz Ritter von Epp entering the Vier

Jahreszeiten hotel for a mid-afternoon meeting in early September. A bright sun was arcing overhead to the west and a cool breeze fluttered by. The two made their way to the second-floor suite where two other officers awaited them. They saluted General Ludendorff who nodded back. Though no longer in the army, let alone in command, he was the idol of the right wing.

"I was just saying that the time has come for us to back a political party, to really get into the action. We have to build so we are ready to take power come the next election," said Hermann Ehrhardt

"Hogwash," barked Ludendorff. "We should just roll a few tanks through the Brandenburg Gate and down the Unter den Linden. Rattle the windows of the Chancellery and the Reichstag. The people need discipline. The people want discipline!"

Ludendorff banged his cane on the floor.

"You are right, of course, General," said Hermann Ehrhardt. "But we're not ready for that yet. We're not strong enough. At least that's what Röhm here tells me. He says we must wait. Bide our time."

"And he's right," agreed Colonel von Epp. "The Allied armies would crush a military government in an instant. We have no armies to resist them."

"Damnation," cried Ludendorff. "What have we come to? Where is our honour?"

"Lost at Versailles, General. Read the newspapers. We are the world's pariah," drawled Ernst Röhm.

Ehrhardt shook his whip handle at his fellow officer.

"You have some respect for the general," he said menacingly.

The room was silent for a moment.

"Relax, Captain," Ludendorff finally said. "Unfortunately Röhm here is correct."

Ehrhardt calmed down.

“What about the German Workers Party,” Röhm asked.

Ludendorff looked puzzled.

“It had its first meeting in January. At the Fürstenfelder Hof. I’m told that about two dozen attended, railway workers from Anton Drexler’s shop. They’re a small workers party looking for just the right program to support.”

“And the Reds haven’t infiltrated them yet,” added Hermann Ehrhardt.

“It had the backing of the Thule Society,” said Röhm. “Or, at least, Dietrich Eckart’s taken a personal interest in it.”

“We are all agreed on the need for the army to control a political party that will fight for Germany’s true interests,” said Franz Ritter von Epp, who commanded federal army troops in southern Bavaria along with his own Free Corps brigade. “If the left wing gets elected they’ll starve the army of money. So for the good of the country we have to get involved in politics.”

“Eckart wants soldiers to attend the party meetings, anyway,” said Röhm “He wants them to protect the speakers, who are usually intimidated or even attacked by Reds trying to break up the meetings.”

“We must fight back against the strong arm methods of the Reds,” commented von Epp. “But how can we even be sure that this German Workers party is as you say it is,” he asked Röhm, his adjutant.

“We should check it out further before we commit,” suggested Ernst Röhm.

“Exactly,” von Epp barked. “What do you propose?”

“Why not send a man over to the next meeting,” said Ehrhardt.

“Suggestions, Captain,” asked Colonel von Epp.

They thought for a while.

"What about Corporal Hitler from the Enlightenment Detachment," offered Röhm.

"Of course," Ehrhardt agreed. "I remember him. A real speaker too. Worships a greater Germany. Despises the Reds. Maybe he'll liven up the meeting for them."

"Just what we need," bellowed General Ludendorff with a smile. "A real patriot, if I hear correctly. Just what the doctor ordered."

"It's settled then," agreed Colonel von Epp. "Röhm, take a message to Major Hierl for me. Have him draft orders for Hitler to attend a meeting of this German Workers Party, and to report back to us."

"But have him go in civilian clothes," Ehrhardt put in. "He'll draw less attention that way."

It was the night of September 12th, 1919 and Adolf Hitler, in an old suit and tie, turned off the Im Tal and onto the Sterneckerstrasse, headed for the Sterneckerbräu. He entered the building and looked for the Lieber Room. Inside, he removed his overcoat and fedora and sat down towards the rear of the room so that he had a view of most of those in attendance. There were about thirty-five people, an assortment of shopkeepers, students, clerks, teachers, tradesmen, the odd professional, and one young woman whom he recognized: Liesl von Schlieffen. It was a small meeting because Karl Harrer, the national chairman, and Anton Drexler, chair of the Munich district, hadn't advertised at all due to fear of Red provocateurs showing up to disrupt it. Dietrich Eckart, the nationalist writer from the Schwabing district of the city, was supposed to speak, but he pulled out at the last minute due to illness.

"My name is Dr. Gottfried Feder, and I am a professor at the university."

He sported a clipped mustache like the one Hitler now wore.

"I am pleased to be able to speak before you today in Herr Eckart's absence. He sends his regrets on failing to attend. The title of my talk today is 'How and by what means is capitalism to be eliminated?'"

Hitler had heard it before at the university. Fine, he thought; now he'd be free to concentrate on the people there. There weren't too many in suits like he was. That's good; most Germans didn't go to work dressed in suits. The workers were who they wanted, the bulk of the nation whose support they meant to capture; the same constituency as the Reds were going after.

Feder droned on, Hitler knowing the text by heart. It was much the same drivel as he had spoken only days before to an Enlightenment Detachment trainee, tutoring him on the Jews, something which Hitler was rapidly developing a reputation within the troop as an expert upon.

"He burrows into the democracies sucking the good will of the masses, crawls before the majesty of the people but knows only the majesty of money.... His activities result in racial tuberculosis of the people."

The German Workers Party appeared to be an acceptable candidate for financial contributions by the Wehrmacht in southern Bavaria. Never mind that it was illegal for soldiers even to take part in politics, let alone the brass investing army funds in political parties of their choosing. Now, if we posted a couple of guards by the door, Hitler thought, and a hall monitor to roam around inside, that should be lots of security until the Reds come calling. And if they do, then we'll be ready for them too. A few large off-duty troopers in civvies, with wooden clubs by their sides.

Hitler's eyes wandered the crowd. That one looked like another professor. He was dressed like Feder, and Hitler for that matter. And he had that know-it-all look on his face, contemptuous of Feder's remarks. Adolf could sense it, and he had more and more confidence in his own instincts. The eyes, the sight painfully restored bare months before, continued to rove the room. They fell upon the graceful curved figure seated in the third row, a tight sweater hugging her body. Liesl von Schlieffen – a German fräulein of class. If only Adolf could get her alone for a couple hours, he'd straighten out her thinking. She was a little confused in her circle of friends, but who wasn't these days? Her friend Wolf Warburg though – he should have his heart cut out while still alive and screaming to watch.

What was she doing here anyway? It was a good sign, no doubt. Hitler's newfound oratorical skills would pull her back into the German fold where she belonged.

"But the final aim must unquestionably be the irrevocable *Entfernung* of the Jews," Feder said with a rise in his voice.

"What does that mean, professor?"

"Ah, my dear Fräulein von Schlieffen. So nice to see you. And a good question you've asked. It means the removal, the complete expulsion, of Jews from German life."

"But what if other countries won't take them? I understand that America has choked off immigration."

"A wise policy. They saw it as necessary for the ultimate salvation of their nation. So why should Germany do any less? But if the other countries won't take them, what do we do with them? I leave that up to the people to decide. What should we do with the Jews," he suddenly asked the audience, his voice rising, "if no one else wants them?"

"Drive them into the Baltic!"

"Or back into Russia – let the Cossacks have them!"

This will do fine, thought Hitler.

Liesl knew the Reds might show up and cause fighting, but she went anyway. She'd attended Red meetings; now it was time for the German Workers Party. Rumour said that the military brass in Munich were contemplating investing in a political party to further their own agenda, and this one was high on the list.

Feder concluded his lecture. He was now taking questions from the floor. Surprisingly, not everyone agreed that the Jews were responsible for everything evil in Germany.

"I agree with most of what you say, professor. But there is one area you haven't discussed, and it's essential to any analysis of the economic woes Bavaria is currently experiencing."

"And you are, mein herr?"

"I am a fellow professor. My name is Baumann."

He doffed his hat to Feder and his fellow guests.

"And what is it that we haven't discussed," asked Feder, somewhat perturbed. He liked to be thought of as the most educated man in the room.

"We cannot improve the economic situation unless we clarify our politics. It doesn't make a wit of difference if we free ourselves from Jewish and American moneylenders unless we first free ourselves from our true oppressors. The Prussians! We must cast off the yoke of Berlin. The Prussians, who dragged us into that monstrous war."

What!

"Let's rid ourselves of Prussia and throw in our lot with the civilized Germans in Austria. Cultured Germans, unlike the swine to the north of us."

"Never," Hitler cried and rose to his feet.

Adolf Hitler was in a rage even before he reached his full height. A giant shiver ran through Liesl. Until then she didn't even know he was there.

"Never," he cried again. "What, did we die for the benefit of loan sharks," he thundered. "Do you know what you're saying? Did you fight in the war? I'll bet not! Another professor," he sneered. "Well, did you fight?"

The other man was taken aback by Hitler's vehemence. "Well, no, I, what has that got to do with it?"

"I knew it," Adolf exulted. "And have you ever lived in Austria? In that mongrel agglomeration? The Austrian army was useless in the war. Worse than useless! It was a chain around the neck of the mighty German Wehrmacht. It drained our resources to continually support them. In Galicia; in Italy; in Romania; everywhere they went. The same story. A rotting empire, a mongrel army. Now, if Germans had been in charge throughout Austria, as in the days of old, in the days of Habsburg glory, then Austria would be an ally worth joining. But now? You would have us spurn Prussia, and join our fortunes to that putrid Austrian state? By the ghost of Bismarck, not while I live!"

Hitler's eyes blazed wide, a brilliant blue, his right fist held high. Baumann quivered in the chair in which he had sunk, not daring to rise or reply.

"Well, you know what I would do," Hitler continued finally, his voice low, his right arm and forefinger extended above. "First I would purge our universities of all professors who spew such tripe for our young people to consume, and then", his voice rising to a crescendo, his left arm sweeping the evils away, "I would hang all such traitors who spout treason against the Reich. Germany must be cleansed!"

The audience, at least most of it, erupted in a rapturous applause. Hitler beamed. He had found his calling.

And as for Professor Baumann?

"He left the hall like a wet poodle, even before I was finished," Hitler later related to Captain Röhm.

Anton Drexler, chair of the Munich district of the party, was ecstatic. This one, Hitler, he has what it takes. We must have him!

Liesl was aghast. In awful awe she sat in shock, gaze transfixed, entranced by something in Adolf Hitler.

The meeting was breaking up. Some folks pressed Hitler's hand as he prepared to leave. As he headed for the door, Drexler caught up to him.

"What is your name, mein herr?"

Hitler was nervous at first. Did his superiors really want him identified?

"Hitler. Adolf Hitler."

"Well, Herr Hitler. You are needed here. You must help us get our message out to other true, patriotic Germans."

"I don't know…"

"Here, take this," Drexler coaxed him, pressing into his hand a thick pink pamphlet. "Read it and give me your thoughts. I think you'll agree with most of it. Now, where can I reach you, Herr Hitler?"

Hitler gave him a number and address. A soldier, Drexler thought. But not an officer, despite the suit and tie. He could tell from Hitler's manner of speech that he was a man of the common people.

Back in his cubbyhole at the barracks, Hitler sat up well into the night running over his triumph. He had sent that damned professor scurrying with his tail between his legs. Just through the power of his voice. Hitler looked at the pamphlet given him on his way out. Authored by Drexler and forty pages long, *My Political Awakening* had a writing style about as appealing as the pink cover, but its basic premise was on point: rid Germany of Reds, Jews, and international loan capital.

He rolled over but couldn't sleep. A mouse crossed the floor and he fed it bits of bread. A German trench veteran, Hitler too knew what it was like to starve. At five in the morning still he lay awake. The next day his report to the captain recommended support for the German Workers Party.

Hitler was surprised and a little annoyed to find in his mail a week later a letter from the German Workers Party telling him that he had been accepted for membership, since he couldn't recall applying. The letter went on to request his attendance at a committee meeting the following Wednesday at the Altes Rosenbad on the Herrnstrasse. Ernst Röhm, upon being informed of this by Hitler, instructed him to attend.

"What exactly did Drexler say to you," Ernst Röhm pressed him the day after. "He wants you to join?"

"That's the short of it. And they're pressing me for a decision. So what do I do?"

Two days later Hitler's commanding officer was able to report that, "To please Ludendorff, whose wishes were still respected in the army, I ordered Hitler to join the German Workers' Party and help foster its growth."

1919

Pogrom

For when a minority is punished, it is guilty in the eyes of the masses.

- Konrad Heiden

As the violence of the Thirty Years War finally ended in central Europe in 1648, it shifted east to Poland and the Ukraine with major pogroms occurring a decade later. Unimaginable savagery and butchery, unless one remembered what had occurred between Roman Catholics and Protestants in the religious wars in Germany in the years immediately previous.

The Nazis did not perpetrate the major actions of the Holocaust on German soil. There weren't many Jews there. It was to the east where they instituted the massive extermination camps of Poland and Galicia, such as Auchwitz, where they killed with gas and then burned the bodies; and the execution pits of the Ukraine including Babi Yar, just north of Kiev, where they simply machine-gunned millions and buried them in mass graves. Areas that had already experienced large-scale violence, especially against the Jews, in the civil war only two decades before. The older population, whether or not they approved of the violence against Jews, were not seeing it for the first time. It was the scale and thoroughness of the Nazi operations, typical German thoroughness, that made them so incredibly hideous and novel.

* * *

The two vehicles sped southwest from Kiev along the main highway, the Daimler roadster followed by the troop truck carrying Locker-Lampson's mercenaries. In the Daimler, Wolf, Rantzau and the commander discussed the upcoming trip back to Germany. Wolf said something about stopping in Fastov to say goodbye to the Battels; Rantzau and Locker were concerned about any delay.

"Listen to the cannon fire," the commander pleaded, stroking his mustache and chestnut-hued hair. "It can't be more than a few miles east."

Dunken meanwhile was huddled up in the back seat with blankets wrapped around him, shivering. But he was beginning to calm down, and a small feeling of security emerged for the first time in months, ever since he had been seized by the Reds and dragged off to the Cheka prison in Kiev.

Even now Dunken didn't know for sure if it was real or a desperate dream. Was he still back in the Cheka torture chamber, the sadistic giant with the torch heating up the birdcage that was fixed to his stomach, with a terrified rat set to eat through his innards, and his mind just couldn't face that reality anymore? Or did Wolf Warburg suddenly burst into the chamber with Leon Trotsky, second only to Lenin in the Red leadership, to save Dunken from the big man, and the rodent gnawing at his stomach? Wolf Warburg! Here, in Russia, unannounced, unexpected, to save his life and carry him out of hell. Please, God, don't let it be a dream.

"Dunken, Dunken, what is it?"

A pair of hands shook him gently. He opened his eyes and saw Wolf sitting in the back seat beside him.

"What is it, Dunken? You were calling me, but you looked like you were sleeping."

"Thank God," Dunken gasped, tears flowing unexpectedly, as he leaned forward to hug Wolf. "I just can't believe you're really here – that I'm out of that hellhole."

"Relax, my friend," Wolf said gently, "we'll get you home safely. The worst is over."

There was silence in the car for several moments. Not one of the travellers really believed that they were out of danger. Not with the constant sound of cannon in the distance. It was Dunken who finally spoke.

"But we're still in deadly peril," he said. "If we get caught by the Whites or a Ukrainian partisan group, we could still all be shot. And you, Wolf – for God's sake don't let them know you're Jewish if we are caught or questioned."

"And why is that?"

Wolf knew the answer anyway.

"I've been with two completely different types of Jews in the last few months," Dunken replied, "the Battels in Fastov who were the salt of the earth; and the Jewish butcher in charge of the Kiev Cheka. They both have one thing in common: they are terrified of the coming White army. The rumours say that it is made up of Cossacks who rape, murder, and loot the inhabitants of every Jewish village they pass through."

"Pogroms," said Wolf, teeth gritted.

Austrian anti-Semitism, by and large and by comparison, was virulent but not violent; in the Russian empire it was a different story. 'Pogrom' is a Russian word for 'devastation'. The modern age of pogroms was ushered in with the assassination of Tsar Alexander II in April 1881. Little of substance had occurred since the Haidamak raids from the southeast in the mid-1700's, and before that Bogdan Chmielnicki a century before, in the years following the Thirty Years war. In April 1881, in the wake of the Tsar's death, it began with a dispute about the Blood Accusation in a tavern in Elisavetgrad, and spread to the Ukraine like wildfire. Claims of exploitation by the Jews, in addition to the old ritual murder stuff.

At Elizavetgrad, in the south central Ukraine, the message from the imperial government was clear to the local police chief:

"If, God forbid, a Jewish pogrom should occur, you will not be guilty, you would not be involved in it, and you do not have it in your power to foresee an unexpected explosion of popular indignation due to the economic exploitation by the Jews. And, after all, they are Jews. But if the mob begins to rob rich Russians, Germans, that is a different kettle of fish – this is entirely negligence and the police are guilty."

Malicious rumours, that officialdom generally refused to deny, swept through the population.

"The Tsar Alexander Alexandrovich is not a real Tsar, because he still has not been crowned, and therefore he cannot send out an edict to kill the Jews, but only to destroy their property. After his coronation, then he will send out an edict to slaughter Jews, because they killed his father and drink our blood."

Hundreds of pogroms blew across the Ukraine, and the entire Jewish Pale of Settlement including Russian Poland, from 1881 through 1884. They spread from the cities to the country, with seasonal workers returning home along the new railway lines of the slowly budding Russian industrial revolution, and fuelled by peasants resentful of Jewish economic domination. While the government didn't arrange them, it refused to intervene once they were underway, even instructing soldiers that to do so would incur disciplinary measures. Pogromists knew that for the most part police and soldiers would look the other way. They generally intervened only when the degree of anarchy appeared to be reaching dangerous levels. The government did not wish to foment a revolution. In 1882 the minister of the Interior, Count Ignatieff, brought in "temporary measures" which continued to forbid Jews from settling outside the Pale, from buying or leasing land, and restricting the types of work they could do for a living.

"Jews themselves are guilty of the pogroms," said Count Ignatieff to a St. Petersburg rabbi, "since by siding with the revolutionaries they deprive the government of the possibility of protecting them from violence."

Still, certain government officials including Ignatieff did try to curb the pogroms, and his successor, Count Tolstoy, warned police that those found guilty would be dismissed.

They reached Fastov without incident and drove to the Battel residence. Jonah and his family were truly surprised to see their German visitors return.

"We thought you were all done for once you placed yourselves in the hands of the Cheka," Jonah told Wolf over the meal that was laid out for the guests. It didn't consist of much: some sort of meat which could have been anything from dog to who-knows-what. No one tended to ask; no one really wanted to know. But the visitors were all appreciative of the fact that whatever it was, the Battels had paid dearly for it. Food of any type was an expensive commodity in Russia in 1919.

Dunken revelled in the familiar, friendly surroundings in which he had spent a few months earlier in the year, hiding from Red and White alike. The discussion turned back to the civil war and the coming White armies from the east and south; but also of the Partisan bands all around who could operate with impunity in the vacuum between Reds leaving and Whites arriving.

"But it is we Jews who have the most to fear from the Whites coming," said Jonah. "We've suffered a lot from the bands of Ukrainian bandits that have passed through here since the Tsar's government was overthrown in 1917, but this coming army is supposed to be huge. And it's made up of hungry, angry, killing Cossacks. They say it's going to be worse than the pogroms of fourteen or fifteen years ago."

Fourteen years ago, thought Rantzau. And then it dawned on him - the violence that swept the Russian empire following its humiliating loss to Japan in the war of 1905.

From 1885 through 1902 there is no record of significant pogroms in Russia. And then they flared up again, more virulent than ever. It began in 1903 in Kishinev in the Russian province of Bessarabia, now Moldavia, which borders Rumania to the west. Rumania itself had a reputation as perhaps the most anti-Semitic place in Europe; but it was a tiny country. In Russia the Tsar's policies affected millions of Jews, some fifty thousand in Kishinev alone, a third to half the population of the city.

Pavolachi Krushevan was an anti-Semitic publisher in Kishinev, the former editor of the *Banner* in St. Petersburg, now publishing the *Bessarabian*, which had some influential readers including police, army, church, and government officials, as well as middle class merchants resentful of Jewish competition. He was determined to put the Jews in their place. Rumours were circulated that a young Jewish doctor had tried to extract blood from a young girl for the matzah for the Jewish Passover, the ancient so-called Blood Accusation in which Jews were accused of killing Christian children for this purpose. Krushevan imported thugs from Albania and Macedonia, armed them with steel bars and gave them the addresses of Jews. The police were slow to suppress it, so it gained momentum, allowing some real atrocities to take place such as driving nails into peoples' eyes, disembowelling pregnant women, and the rape of women in front of family members. About 45 Jews were killed, and about 500 injured, more violent by far than anything that had occurred in the pogroms 20 years earlier.

Krushevan was never charged with anything. Before Kishinev, he had published one of the first known versions of the *Protocols of the Elders of Zion*, a tract that would resurface in Germany in late 1919 to eventually cause untold misery to the Jews of Europe.

In 1905 the Japanese chose to test Russia. With that war going on in the east, the bloated noble class in Russia could no longer rely on the army to quell dissent at home. To divert the attention of the underprivileged masses, major pogroms were encouraged throughout the country, including Zhitomir, Nizhnii Novgorod, Baku, Odessa, Kiev, Kishinev, Minsk, and Kursk, to name the largest. In Odessa in 1906 some 800 Jews were killed, more than 5000 wounded, and thousands more left homeless. Police printed pamphlets to incite, then organized and armed the looters, supplied them with vodka, and directed them where to go.

Leon Trotsky reminisced on occasion of his days in Kiev and St. Petersburg in 1905 organizing self-defense groups against the pogroms. Trotsky remembered the rumours first spread by the instigators that the Jews were going to attack the local church and destroy its sacred icons. So a 'patriotic' procession of ordinary local folk was organized to march towards the Jewish quarters, to systematically loot and terrorize the population. And all the while the police stood by to prevent any organized effort at self-defence by the Jews.

It was getting towards evening.

"I don't think you should be out on the roads after dark, what with the Partisan bands and other bandits about. Stay with us, at least through the night," Jonah implored them.

After some discussion the group decided to stay.

"Jonah, you said some of your family left Russia for the west. Where did they go," asked Wolf.

"To America. And Canada. Before the war. Back in 1911; and some before that."

The conversation returned to the civil war, and the Blood Accusation as fodder for anti-Semitism.

"What about the Beilis case, Jonah," asked Count Rantzau. "What do you know of it, having lived so close to Kiev throughout the whole affair?"

Thirteen year old Andrei Yustshinksy was murdered in the spring of 1911 outside Kiev. The true killers may have been a woman named Bera Cheberiak and her gang of petty thieves. The theory is that Andrei was murdered because the gang suspected he was about to betray them. So they tortured the lad, and when he died they moved the body and tried to make it look like the work of some perverted Jewish cult. Sure enough, the Double Headed Eagle Society distributed a pamphlet alleging:

“Every year before their Passover, the Yids torture to death several dozens of Christian children in order to get Christian blood to mix with their unleavened bread (*matza*)…The official doctors found that before the Yids tortured Lushchinksy, they stripped him naked, tied him, and then slaughtered him, stabbing him in the principal veins in order to get as much blood as possible.”

The local cops and most of the local prosecution, except for one reactionary, wanted to drop the case against Beilis since it was so weak. But the local anti-Semites would raise a storm, so the prosecution pressed ahead.

"I remember the case well," Wolf commented. "All of us civil liberty types read all of the newspaper accounts we could get hold of. It had to be the biggest anti-Semitic legal spectacle in Europe since the Dreyfus affair."

"So what was your read on it," Rantzau quizzed him.

"The government and security forces felt boxed in. To release Beilis would be to risk major unrest, probably a pogrom. To try the case would be to look ridiculous internationally, and there was a risk of losing it even in a

Tsarist court. And to lose the case would hurt the government domestically, since it was already laughable to many. But to not go ahead could also send a message that the government was so inept that it couldn't find and prosecute the killers."

"So what did they finally do," Rantzau pressed.

"The government decided to try to 'win' the case in the court of public opinion by getting the jury to decide that, even if Beilis did not conclusively do it, a ritual murder had occurred nevertheless. In other words, in 1913, the Ministry of Justice wanted to get a jury decision that ritual murder occurred in modern day Russia," smirked Wolf. "The theory they advanced was that two outside Jews had come to the local Hasidim headquarters on land owned by Beilis to do some ritual killing in anticipation of Passover. Expert evidence by some professor of Hebrew at a Catholic academy in St. Petersburg was that ritual murder was outlined in the *Talmud*."

"And was it," asked Commander Locker.

"In a way, yes," replied Wolf. "The defence rebutted it by showing that he was referring to sections involving the slaughter of cattle. And in the end, the jury acquitted Beilis. Though it also found that the boy had indeed died by Jewish ritual murder."

They were outside the house, loading the trunk of the Daimler, when the first news came. Jonah came trotting up, returning from an early morning trip to the market square.

"They're killing Jews, looting their homes, in all the villages east of here," he cried, out of breath.

"We must go *now*," exclaimed Commander Locker. "We have no time to lose. I knew we shouldn't have stayed the night!"

Rantzau was already climbing into the Daimler.

"We must move, Herr Warburg," the commander stressed.

Wolf just stood, looking off to the east. The cannon fire was ever more immediate. He was having second thoughts. Rantzau and Locker and Dunken had no qualms about leaving right away, but Wolf was feeling guilty. He felt deep down a duty to stay, to help defend the village from attacks by Whites or Partisans.

"We are too few, Wolf," Dunken argued.

He was terrified of being captured again. Or worse. His quota of bravery for the next decade was used up.

"Tell me what it was like around here after the war began in 1914," Wolf said to Jonah.

His companions all groaned aloud, but Wolf just could not budge himself into the Daimler.

Jonah related how during the world war Jewish soldiers with beards served in the Russian army; the brass was willing to accept Jews as fighters even if they refused to shave. It didn't change an underlying anti-Semitism in the officer corps. For the Jews, the war created a dilemma. They preferred the Germans over the Tsar's medieval policies. But it turned out to be a brutal German occupation in which everyone was hungry. The Pale of Settlement died during the war as Jews were sent east, away from the frontier areas where their sympathy for Germany created a security threat. After the first revolution in February 1917, Kerensky's provisional government did away with the restrictions on residence altogether. Jews began to appear all over Russia for the first time, many as agents of the new Bolshevik government after the Red coup of October 1917.

Communications to the village had by now been cut, and rumours poured in of a huge White army on the way.

"The Cossacks of the 2nd Brigade from Tersk, commanded by Colonel Belogortsev," Jonah's neighbour was telling them. "Their arrival is imminent. Everyone must start to make plans about what to do."

"I must meet with their commanders, to make sure that they do not let their men commit any atrocities here in Fastov," Wolf stated.

"You can't be serious," Rantzau gasped at him, aghast.

"Don't be a fool," Commander Locker-Lampson implored him. "You're sure to be killed."

"But I cannot just do nothing."

The whole village around them was scampering to prepare for the White invasion. Most expected to huddle in their basements, praying that they would be spared a pogrom, and escape with their lives.

"At least we'll be better defended than most," Jonah soliloquized. "Commander, we should lay out your men in positions on the main floor of the house. We haven't much time!"

Locker looked up at him. He realized his duty; commands barked forth. None of them had ever experienced a pogrom before. On the other hand, they had all been through trench warfare. Locker's troop ran into the house to set up their gun positions.

Count Rantzau gave up trying to get Wolf to leave. As they waited the arrival of the Whites, Wolf asked Jonah about his family across the Atlantic.

"They are mainly on the Canadian prairies. Winnipeg, Calgary."

"But what's it been like here, since the Bolsheviks took power," asked Rantzau, more interested in their current situation than what was happening across the ocean.

"In the anarchy following the revolution, there were pogroms, particularly in the provinces south of Moscow for some reason. After the Bolshevik coup, I think many ordinary Russians, who are now starving, blamed everything on the Jews. Since the civil war began, there have been thousands of minor incidents of anti-Jewish violence, and many serious ones. Most around here have been done by local partisans or bandits. But this Cossack army on its way – that is a different story," Jonah concluded, worriedly shaking his head.

The battles of the Russian civil war in 1919 reached epic proportions, with hundreds of thousands involved, including the use of tanks, planes and even armoured trains. Neither side tended to take prisoners. As far as the Jews were concerned, the pogroms of 1919 had two peak periods. The first, in May, were perpetrated primarily by Ukrainian partisans and other outlaws, and involved the looting of much Jewish property. But the armies tended to be tiny, so the devastation was not so overwhelming in comparison to that which occurred when the Cossack armies invaded from the southeast in the summer and early autumn, as they now were.

"They're coming," the lookout yelled from his horse as he came galloping back into town. The streets became quickly deserted. The Battels, along with Dunken, still extremely weak from his time with the Cheka, headed down into the cellar, while Locker's men occupied their gun positions on the main floor. Count Rantzau remained in the house while Wolf, Locker and Jonah took a furtive stroll around town. Wolf had in his jacket a letter from Winston Churchill, which made him feel a little safer in case of a run-in with the Whites.

From behind a tall thicket the trio observed the Cossack army as it began to roll into town. It was a huge sight, a vast serpent uncoiling itself over the village. Fastov was a fairly large town, with 3000 or so Jewish families and more than twice that many Gentile. It had suffered some during the war, but was still relatively intact, though hungry. The Cossack soldiers began to make themselves at home, senior and junior officers strolling into the shops and knocking at the doors of the nicer homes, ordering the inhabitants out, unless they were comely females. Not one shopkeeper was silly enough to argue, but many unfortunate husbands were, resulting in a rifle butt or blow, or worse to those who still would not yield. Wolf and his companions headed silently back to the Battel house. Wolf decided for the time being against approaching the White commanders.

"I just can't believe they'll turn that army lose to ransack the Jewish quarter," he said. "They can't be that uncivilized."

"I'm not so sure," Commander Locker-Lampson bluntly noted. "These easterners can be very primitive. It's in their nature. Hell, it's in everyone's nature, if you strip away enough of the veneer of civilization."

"But why are they so focused on the Jews," Rantzau wondered. "It all seems so medieval."

"It's a lot to do with propaganda," Wolf argued. "The Whites claim that Trotsky is a mass killer of the Russian people and that Jews are prominent in the Cheka. They certainly are in Kiev. This allows them to condone or even encourage pogroms."

"But why would they want to create this image, if it wasn't true in the first place," asked Commander Locker.

"The whole country is starving; there is little food; first the world war, and now the destruction of the civil war. The spoils of the pogroms are perfect rewards for the White generals to offer their followers, since they have nothing else to give. Rape and pillage the Jews," Wolf concluded, "since they're all Red supporters anyway."

The officers partied it up at balls with local woman and prostitutes while their troops were allowed free reign to plunder and kill Jews. The booty was then loaded onto trains to take home, to the Don, Kuban, or Terek regions.

Sir Eyre Crowe, a senior official in the British foreign office, had to reply to his government about the alarm bells raised by Chaim Weizman regarding Russian pogroms.

"What may appear to Mr. Weizman to be outrages against Jews, may in the eyes of the Ukrainians be retaliation against the horrors committed by the Bolsheviks who are all organized and directed by Jews."

But elections to the constituent assembly showed that Bolshevik support came from the armed forces and the cities of Great Russia, not the Pale. Less than 1000 Jews joined the Bolsheviks before 1917.

But it was a vicious circle in the civil war. Whites killed Jews for being Reds, so the Jews had to embrace the Reds for protection from the ravages of the Whites, thus fuelling the belief of the Whites that the Jews were all Reds. The true motive of the White leadership in allowing the pogroms was to offer their followers booty and reward.

"Churchill has a pretty low opinion of the White forces," Wolf was saying. "He thinks they're all corrupt. But he also can't accept either communism or the return of a Tsarist-type government to Russia. Deep down he believes the greatest danger at present are the Reds, which means that the western governments must support the Whites, no matter how corrupt. The pogroms sicken him, but he doesn't know what to do about them."

The leaders of both the White armies and the chief Ukrainian partisan bands, both receiving support from the west, disavowed the pogroms. But their followers did not believe them, and they were never truly discouraged. The leaders had nothing to offer them but Jews' property and a good time with their women. Jews who initially fought in the White armies naturally lost their enthusiasm for the cause.

"The Bolshevik leadership, on the other hand," Wolf noted, "fights pogroms because they are aimed at Reds as well as Jews."

During the civil war, the pogroms by the Cossacks and the lacklustre opposition by the White army leadership to violence against Jews cost the Whites any significant Jewish support. At least the Red leadership battled anti-Semitism as counter-revolutionary. And Trotsky, Kemenev and Zinoviev, all members of the inner circle and all Jewish-born, were in positions to give orders combating it as well, as opposed to the White leadership in which there was simply no Jewish participation.

"I still can't decide whether to directly approach the White leaders and warn them against a pogrom," lamented Wolf.

"I say we just stay here and keep our heads down," piped up Commander Locker.

"I agree," chimed Rantzau emphatically. "They might simply kill you along with the rest of us."

A knocking came at the door, a series of raps in the form of a signal. They opened it to admit a slender, clean-cut, but furtive-looking fellow with a small grey skullcap on his head.

"Welcome, Avrum," Jonah said. "What can you tell us?"

"There have already been several random attacks and beatings. A pogrom in its early stages, basically," he replied.

* * *

In September 1919, General Denikin, overall commander of the White forces, ordered his armies from the Volga to the Rumanian border to advance north towards Moscow. The second stage of the pogroms of 1919, which took place as the Cossack armies marched north and west through the Ukraine, saw the most brutal and savage attacks on Jews to occur before the Nazis. Typically, officers would allow the soldiers a couple of days to rob and kill Jews. So at the same time as Adolf Hitler was attending his very first meeting of the German Workers Party, the White army in Fastov was perpetrating a pogrom.

Newspaper reporters such as Ivan Derevensky filed stories on the pogrom from Fastov itself within a week of its occurrence.

"You see," exclaimed Hitler to his beer hall buddies back in Munich, "they mass kill Jews in the Ukraine and the world refuses to intervene. And the world will do nothing when we string up all the Jews in Germany!"

* * *

Fastov was finally in sight.

"Not much to look at," commented Alexei Golubov as he rolled a cigarette between his fingers, his horse ambling slowly beneath him.

"No," his companion in arms, Dmitry Kozlov, acknowledged, "but it's big enough."

The regiment had disembarked, horses and all, from the train a few miles southeast of the town itself. In case there was any Red resistance left in Fastov, it was better to approach at the ready from outside, rather than step off the train in the middle of town to a hail of machine gun bullets. And this way they were spread out as they entered town, so that an ambush would not find them an easy bunched-up target.

Alexei took the canteen hanging off the horse's left side, threw his head back, and took a long draught of water.

"So long as the vodka is plentiful," Dmitry commented, the late summer sunshine beating down on the pair. It was mid-afternoon, and the regimental caps on the Cossacks' heads were not enough to counter the stifling heat. They had been on the road only for an hour and a half since disembarking, and had suffered much worse over the course of world war and then civil war during the past five years, but at this particular moment both were anxiously looking forward to the party to come that very night.

"I hear there's a sizable Jew population," Dmitry said. "And the wife has sent me a shopping list," he added, patting the left lower pocket of his fatigue shirt and smiling.

"What difference does it make," commented Alexei Golubov, "I'll collect my due no matter who lives here. I'll take from the Ukes just as easily," he said matter-of-factly.

"But everyone gets so much less upset if it's just Jews complaining."

"That's because they deserve it more," said Alexei. "Most of them are flaming Red. If not for them, my own farm and family wouldn't be suffering now. What are we supposed to eat over the winter?"

"You're not alone, brother."

Both Cossacks recalled to themselves the previous year in the Kuban, just south of the Don region far to the east of Kiev. The civil war, first between Reds and Tsarist forces, then the dissatisfaction under brief Red rule, and then the Cossacks rising against the Reds, had sown destruction and death across the Cossack lands in the Don River and Kuban River regions. Whichever side controlled the region demanded that most of the local men join its army, if they had not already done so; there was continual requisitioning of food and supplies to the point that the Cossacks feared for food over the coming winter; there was mass billeting of rude and intrusive soldiers in the local residences, which was an experience in itself; there were arbitrary searches of homes for draft dodgers, deserters, food, weapons, horses, and supplies; land was trampled over and crops ruined. In addition, the Whites and then the Reds took vengeance on those suspected of being officers in the other army; as the civil war intensified and became more vicious, with more loss of life, both sides started shooting anyone even suspected of collaborating with the enemy. All these situations proved quite impossible for the ordinary person to cope with, since as the battle lines shifted back and forth so did the government of the moment. To not cooperate with that government would mean instant death; but to cooperate would mean that as soon as the other army and government returned, death would be meted out for cooperating with the prior regime.

In the late afternoon of September 10th, 1919, Alexei, Dmitry, and the rest of the army rode into Fastov. Breaking off into squads, the occupying force swept first across the central core of the town, then spread out all over. Once the officers were informed where the better parts of town were, they moved off to inspect them and select billets for themselves in some of the nicer homes. Other buildings, particularly the larger ones in the small commercial core, were occupied for staff command and security purposes. The officers were provided with information as to where the supplies in town, including livestock, grain and tools were located, and special squads were set to guard them against both the town inhabitants as well as the Cossack troops.

Dmitry and Alexei bedded down their horses for the night in an open stabling area in the town stockyards. Foot patrols were set and, after dinner, the two Cossacks took their turn.

"Why should we have to sleep out in the open on the ground when there are so many houses all around us," asked Alexei to his companion as they stalked up the street. "What makes this town so special?"

"Some of the rich locals have met with our officers and bought them off," replied Dmitry. "They say we shouldn't be allowed to billet in their homes. And so certain homes are spared."

"We'll just see about that," Alexei said, his tone hardening. "So our officers think we should sleep in the street so the Hokhols and Jews can be comfortable. Or so that the officers can loot them at their leisure over the next few days, while we get nothing. Well, we'll see how long we put up with this for," he drawled, taking a long swig from the vodka bottle clamped in his right fist.

Most of the Cossacks, the bulk of the army, began their binge, which was to last for the next three days. It only took a few hours for them to get worked up enough to decide that sleeping out in the open was simply not good enough. There was an entire town full of perfectly adequate huts for them to billet in. And the ordinary locals certainly were in no position to object.

Alexei and Dmitry selected billets in a run down hut, though not so bad by local standards, northeast of the center of town. The Ukrainian family, a father, mother, one older daughter and two younger ones, huddled together in one tiny room. The parents emerged to wait on the Cossacks and then quickly returned to their children.

"Come, sit with us," Dmitry commanded the woman as she filled his mug again with vodka. "We frighten you so much you have to hide?"

He pulled the woman down beside him on the bench. Her husband bit his tongue and kept quiet for the moment.

"See, we're not so bad," Dmitry drawled, leering at the woman, spittle running down his chin.

"Tell us where you're from," said her husband, in an effort to distract the Cossack from his lusty thoughts.

"We are from Tersk, 2nd Brigade," Alexei Golubov replied from across the table.

"And who is your commander," the Ukrainian asked.

"Why are you so curious," asked Dmitry, scowling at the man, his right hand reaching down slowly, obviously, to grip his sabre. "Are you a Red spy?"

The Ukrainian's face went white.

"No, no," he quickly cried. "Please, it was an innocent question."

Dmitry laughed. "Relax. I believe you."

He took another swig and banged his mug down on the table.

"We are commanded by Colonel Belogortsev. A reasonable enough fellow. He's told us that we can have a party in Fastov for the next three days."

The Ukrainian looked scared still, but asked, "And what does that mean?"

"That means: where do the Jews live," Alexei laughed, from the other side of the table. "We are permitted by headquarters to have a little fun with them. After all, the Jews aid the Bolsheviks."

"But that is not so," the woman blurted out, and then quickly shut up as they all looked at her.

"What do you mean, woman," Dmitry prodded her. "Come on, speak up now."

She would not speak at first; she was too scared, and tears began to stream down her cheeks.

"It is only that the Jews hid in their homes along with the rest of us when the Red army passed through," she finally replied. "But then, what do I know anyway. It is as you say."

"Ah, keep quiet, woman," Dmitry growled, and lightly cuffed the woman across the cheek. "Those Jewish commissars jeering at our faith," he continued, gulping down more vodka. "Get me more drink, woman!"

"They have ordered us to do it," Alexei said to his hosts. "Maybe to cover up their own looting of the better parts of town. But would you rather we loot you, the common folk, instead of the Jews?"

"We have to feed our families. Our homes have been looted and picked clean," Dmitry took up the argument. "Why shouldn't we *have a party* in the Jewish quarter?"

In the Jewish quarter, Wolf and his companions were crowded around the common table in the main room of the Battel residence.

"Did you hear that," Tova Zindstrum moaned despairingly. "What are they screaming about? What can be happening?"

"Relax," said her brother-in-law, Jonah, stroking his beard. "They are way across town. No one seems to be bothering us here."

In his mid-thirties, with a small skullcap on his head, Jonah had a heavy shawl wrapped about his shoulders, more for warmth than anything else.

"But for how long," asked Yeleva Battel, Jonah's wife and Tova's sister, looking up from her sewing.

"So you have family in Canada, you were telling me," Count Rantzau piped up, to distract the women from their fears. "On the western prairies, is it?"

"That's right," Jonah replied gratefully.

He too was scared of what was to come, and appreciated the distraction.

"It has a similar climate. Hot in the summer, cold in the winter. Lots of snow. And people don't hate Jews there."

"Well, not so much, anyway," Wolf agreed.

He had spent a little time in the United States and imagined Canada was quite similar.

"Maybe it's because there aren't as many Jews there as in Russia," he added.

The next day, the occupying army picked up where it had left off the evening before. Alexei and Dmitry were roaming through Fastov, ostensibly under orders to patrol the town and flesh out any Red resistance, and to 'pacify' the population; but they also expected to supply themselves for the coming winter from the town's resources. Expensive but compact loot was preferred, to take back home for trade purposes over the coming winter. They were moving throughout the middle class neighbourhoods, but looking forward to the Jewish sections because they felt freer to pillage there. At first they just stopped Jews in the streets and searched them, abused them a little and let them go with a mild roughing up. But the Cossacks were hung over from the night before, and the second day saw more violent incidents in the street than previous.

And what were the officers up to in the meantime?

"You know very well, Dmitry," Alexei replied. "They are searching the better sections of town for the best loot, to load on the train for back home. That is why they tell us, 'rob the Jews, they deserve it,' so that we will leave the better sections of town alone. We take the attention off them while they're robbing the rich types."

"That's right," Sergei Vulgarin, a Cossack corporal, remembered. "That's what our colonel said. 'Do what you like with them. Have a party. Strip them bare.' And it was just an attention getter so they can pillage the richest residences in town."

"What of it," asked Alexei. "This is news to you? It has always been that way. Even in the days of old. That is the way of the warrior. Of the Viking. Of the Cossack. The officers receive the richest spoils. What of it? Be satisfied with your share."

So they accepted their lot, their station in the pecking order, and started to strip search Jews in the street to look for weapons, property, money, and, with the women, sometimes just to grope them. They extorted people by threatening them with hanging. And then they hung and shot some anyway, and certainly those who resisted.

Alexei and Dmitry happened by as four of their mates were harassing two middle-aged Jewish men who they had pulled out of a store that they were hiding in. Now the Cossacks were threatening them for their gold. They would be killed unless they paid up.

"They deserve it," both Alexei and Dmitry thought. All they had to do was remember back over the previous year, to their homes in the Don and Kuban that were robbed and pillaged, sometimes in the name of the state by requisitioning brigades. They remembered how the Reds confiscated and divided up the lands and property of the rich Cossacks. Not that that necessarily bothered Alexei or Dmitry, who had little land themselves.

"It's rich against poor, not Cossack against Russian," Dmitry told his friend in an honest moment.

But then the Reds began killing ordinary Cossacks for either supporting the Whites or just for not fully supporting the Reds. The Cheka made itself known and feared. So the Cossacks rebelled and threw the Reds out. But then the tide reversed, and the Reds were on their way back. And in fear of the Red revenge, many Cossacks fled their villages with just the possessions they could carry. Alexei and Dmitry remembered all the property that their own families lost. And with everyone off at war, the crops were lost; what would happen this winter, without lots of booty to barter for food and scarce supplies?

But the damn Jews liked to argue. And the Cossacks were drunk and ornery, now after more than 24 hours of straight partying. So they had little patience, as Sergei Vulgarin confirmed in an exchange with one unfortunate band of Jews, a group of 3 men pulled from their hiding place in a shop cellar.

"I have no property. It has all been taken by the Reds," said the first.

"You lie, Jew. You are a Red. You are all Reds."

Sergei swatted him across the face.

"The next time it will be with my sabre. Now where is your gold?"

"I told you. It has all been taken. I have none left to give."

The Cossack whipped out his sword, and placed the tip at the Jew's throat.

"One more chance. Before I cut your throat."

The Jew looked scared. But still he said," If your lack of humanity compels you to kill me, then do so. We knew the Cossacks to be uncivilized butchers, anyway."

There was momentary silence, and then a gasp as the supreme insolence of the prisoner dawned on the group. Then Sergei Vulgarin shoved him backward so that he fell to the ground, flat on his back. Kneeling quickly on top so that his knees pinned the Jew's arms to the ground, the Cossack grabbed the man's chin with his left hand and turned the face towards him; with his right, Sergei took his sabre and brought the tip to the man's lips

"Open your mouth, you filth, so I can cut your tongue out!"

The Jew opened his mouth and screamed, briefly. Until the Cossack blade drove deep down into the open gullet. The head was pinned to the ground as the sabre stabbed through the back of the man's skull into the earth below.

"Murderers," gasped one of his companions. "Cossack heathens!"

Losing control, the Jew launched himself at Sergei Vulgarin, who was trying to dislodge his sabre from his victim's throat and skull. But he didn't get far. Dmitry Kozlov, revolver at the ready, shot him in the stomach. He collapsed to the ground, blood and intestines gushing out the gaping gut. Dmitry had used a dumdum bullet. The Jew commenced to scream, a long, drawn out, howl of agony, which was at last mercifully choked off by the blood that began pouring from his mouth a moment later.

"Shut that man up," the Cossack corporal, Sergei Vulgarin, shouted a minute later, pointing to the remaining Jew, whose hands were covering his ears and sobbing to himself in Yiddish. "It's repulsive."

"You there, shut yourself up if you know what's good for you," Alexei warned, prodding him with his sabre. "What's your name, Jew?"

It turned out the man's name was Markman. He sobbed that he couldn't stand the sound of his friend's screams of agony, so he just had to cover his ears.

Sergei Vulgarin, wiping blood from his sabre blade, burst out laughing.

"You want agony? I'll give you something to cry about!"

He rushed over, knocked the man down on his back, and pushed his head to the ground, his left hand gripping the man’s chin as he had his companion. This time, though, with the sabre in his right hand the Cossack deftly and quickly sliced off Marksman's right ear. Before the stunned and mutilated man could react, the Cossack swivelled one hundred and eighty degrees around on his left palm, which was still planted squarely upon Marksman's chin, so that he was now in a position to quickly slice off the other ear, which he did without hesitation. Then he jumped to his feet, releasing the poor man.

Blood streamed from both sides of the head where the ears had been. In shock, mouth open and eyes glazed over in horror, the man already looked dead.

Alexei and Dmitry rode on. All about them ornery Cossacks were breaking into homes up and down both sides of the street. Their horses' saddlebags were becoming fat with choice booty.

"Ah, finally we sow the rewards, eh Dmitry?"

"It is our due. And not soon enough. But still, it doesn't make up for what we've lost. Not what the civil war has cost us."

It was not just the loss of property that embittered the Cossacks. Alexei and Dmitry remembered the bitter details of how life in Russia had been gradually reduced, through world war and then civil war over the past five years, to a state of brutality and sadism. The earmarks of civilized culture disappeared. Neither side in Russia could afford the supplies and manpower necessary to run prison camps. Typhus, diphtheria and starvation were already running through the villages. Lice were ever-present everywhere. In the end, prisoners could not be held for extended periods; they had to be executed or otherwise disposed of.

Dmitry recalled the effects of the civil war in particular on his own village. All males from sixteen to sixty were now mobilized. There were no men at all to assist in the planting, let alone the fall harvests. Amidst impending starvation, on top of all their other sufferings, the villagers now lost trust in one another. Rich against poor, Red Cossack against White Cossack, and both against those other Cossacks who wanted no part of either. Women and children were arrested by Red Cheka units or White discipline brigades if they or their menfolk were suspected of aiding the enemy. Friends put the whip to former friends and neighbours.

"And do you recall how the Red bastards burned our neighbours' homes," Alexei said out loud. "It could just as easily have been mine. I helped the Reds back in 1917, as did most of my village. But that was because they wanted to end the war, and the old government was intent on fighting on against the Germans. And getting more Cossacks killed while our family slowly starved. But once the war against Germany was ended, well, we haven't helped the Reds since then. They wanted to take my land, my farm, and divide it up among the peasants. Cossack land that our ancestors fought for!"

"But that wasn't the worst of it," Dmitry commiserated. "In our town the Red Cossacks, some who I'd grown up with, took to shooting and maiming friends of mine. And don't forget how they raped the wives and sisters and daughters of those suspected of aiding the Whites. I have little pity for the Reds. Or their Jew masters."

With that the two Cossacks paused to look about them as they walked slowly down the street, leading their horses now weighted down with booty. Ukrainian villagers were being thrown out of their homes; but the scene was gradually moving into the Jewish quarter. Cossacks broke into residences, with the occupants moments later running out screaming. Sometimes a women or girl would be grabbed by the arm or hair as she tried to escape, to be hauled back inside the house. Alexei and Dmitry regularly heard screams as they passed by the homes, but they felt no pity. They had none left to give.

They heard the sound of a train whistle.

"The officers must be moving the baggage cars, starting to load their loot up," commented Dmitry. "And we are left with what we can carry home in our saddlebags."

* * *

The second night of the White occupation fell upon the village of Fastov. Wolf and Locker ventured out under cover of darkness with a couple of their troopers. Staying to the side streets and back alleys, they still had trouble avoiding the many Cossacks drunkenly cruising all through town. The foursome spotted a furtive-looking figure slinking through the night as well, and they stopped him. He turned out to be a terrified Jew who related how just a short time ago, within the hour, his home had been broken into, for the second time, by Cossacks. They had been there earlier in the day and had ransacked the place and left. But now they had come back looking for his wife and daughter. The last time he saw them the Cossacks had dragged them both off to a room, while another couple Cossacks turned to the task of torturing Shlomo, for such was the man's name, and his teenage son before they killed them. They ran a blade down his son's chest, slicing the shirt open as well as the skin. When the lad screamed, a Cossack pressed the point of his sabre home through the boy's heart. Shlomo went crazy, wresting himself from his captor's grip and jumping through the window, shattering the glass as he made his way out and ran madly down the street into the dark.

Wolf and his companions saw the flames rising from numerous houses close by and all over the town.

"Maybe we should be making our way back," Wolf said. "They'll be breaking down the Battel's door pretty soon."

And what are we going to do then, they all wondered.

"I don't think we can get out of town at this point," said Commander Locker-Lampson once they were back inside the Battel home. "There are just too many drunken Cossacks wandering around town for us to make our way through without alerting anyone. And once we're discovered, we'll likely be strung up right away."

"I say we just lay low," said Dunken von Schlieffen.

He had had enough danger for awhile.

"But if we stay here, we'll likely be caught like rats in a trap," moaned Count Rantzau. "We're damned both ways. All we can do is wait, and hope they pass us by."

No one said anything, but they all knew that there was little chance of that. And the longer it took for the Cossacks to discover them or make their way to this home, the more ornery and drunk they would be when they finally got there. No one got much sleep as intermittent screaming, shots, and fires continued through the night.

* * *

Alexei and Dmitry strode down the street, swaying slightly from side to side. It was now the third day of the occupation, and the Cossacks were very ornery, and very disoriented after three straight days and nights of drinking; but they were still capable of inflicting great damage even in their inebriated states. They had whips, guns, sabres, and nooses. Needless to say, any villager silly enough to mouth off was summarily executed.

But in some cases the pain was just too great to bear, and a mother or father broke down and wept, yelling profanities at the executioner of their son or daughter or spouse. The litany of terror became ever more savage and primitive. In a house on the corner of Torovey Square, where from the night before much screaming had issued, this morning they found the bodies of fifteen young Jewish girls, dead after being raped. In the square in front of the synagogue, twenty Jews were stripped naked and shot.

"Look there," pointed Dmitry.

Alexei looked and saw, across the square, a middle-aged Jew with a noose around his neck, from a rope hanging over a tree. The man stood on a fence post. What was unusual was that it was a young boy who appeared to be tightening the noose. They strode over.

"Welcome, comrades," said Sergei Vulgarin. "This is young Boris here," he said, pointing to the lad.

The boy was miserable. So was his father as they looked into each other's eyes. The father was mouthing something to his son that Dmitry Kozlov took to mean "Do it."

"I've told the boy that if he doesn't hang his father, we'll hang the both of them together. The old man, good father that he is, had kindly instructed his son to carry out the sentence. Ha, ah ha, ha," he chortled.

Dmitry thought back to his village, only a couple months ago now, just before he left as the tide of war swept north. It was brother against brother, cousin against cousin, father against son, father shooting grandfather. Yes, it had all happened. Even the last, when his cousin Mitka Gorshenkov returned to the village, now an officer in the Red Guard, and had himself ordered the division of his father's estate among the peasants. Old man Gorshenkov had come out of the farmhouse with a rifle and shot at his son. Mitka then hacked his own father to death with his sabre.

Damn Reds, thought Dmitry to himself. Damn the Jews for starting this revolution. So Dmitry had little pity as he watched young Boris, being prodded by a sabre, forced to push his father off the fence post, thence to choke on a taut noose. He remembered, rather, how the Reds had burned entire Cossack villages, of the mass executions, of the rumours that the Reds had now decreed the killing of all Cossack males from age six to the very oldest.

The drunken Cossacks in Fastov knew that this was the last day of the party, that they were due to move north, to more fighting, either that afternoon or the next morning. So they had to get what loot they could without further delay.

"Where is your jewelry, gold, valuables? Let's cut off your fingers and see what you say then."

People lost limbs, noses were sliced off with sabres. One man was sawed in two.

The Battel home was finally broken into. Except for the family, Wolf and the others were hiding in the root cellar which, amazingly, was not searched at first. But then they were discovered and there was a small firefight. After dispatching the Cossacks, Wolf and his companions decided to flee before more Cossacks returned to avenge their comrades. But Tova, Jonah's sister-in-law, was very pregnant and couldn't be moved. In their haste the group reasoned that she would be safe even if discovered by the Cossacks, since they would have no desire to ravage a woman in her condition. In any event, she would likely be safer than caught in a firefight with the rest of the group. So they camouflaged the entrance to the root cellar where Tova lay hidden, the bodies of the Cossacks covered up in a corner of the cellar, and left.

The Cossacks returned in short order, Alexei and Dmitry among them. At first they found nothing, but a diligent search uncovered the root cellar.

"Where are your men, the killers? Where did they go?"

"Give up your gold, Jew bitch. Which is more valuable, your gold or your child," they threatened Tova.

Then they discovered the bodies of their comrades, all shot up, and they lost control. One of the number threatened to cut the baby out of the womb. Tova screamed. Dmitry and Alexei were told to hold Tova's arms while Sergei Vulgarin stood ready with his sabre near her belly.

Dmitry remembered back again, then to the immediate future: impending starvation or deprivation in the coming winter, since the Cossacks had not been able to plant grain in the spring. Alexei thought to himself, as he looked down at the Jewess, about to have her belly slit open, that there was nothing left to call civilization anyway.

"Tell us where your gold is, bitch," he half-pleaded with her. "The Reds stole everything we have. Now we need gold to trade over the winter for food. And all because you Jews had to have this revolution. You couldn't be satisfied with your lot. Now see what you have brought us all to!"

No one had either the capacity or the time for frail emotion, for pity. Faith in God had disappeared; in a few it became, rather, a new fanaticism. God wanted them to take revenge on the Jews, who had killed Christ anyway. The Reds were the result of allowing Jews to live among Christians. Even women and children were desensitized; they began to inflict the most base violence on fellow Cossacks. Bands of captured Red Cossacks were marched through the villages and set upon by the women and older children with pitchforks, crowbars, pieces of wood, pipe, and whips to exact punishment and revenge.

It was now a fight for survival, survival of the fittest! That meant taking possession of all one could, including the booty of conquest, to be traded over the winter and spring for food and supplies to live on.

"My house may be burned down by now," raged Sergei Vulgarin at Tova as he drove the knife into her belly and then began working it in a circle as she shrieked in agony. "We won't burn down your house, bitch, but you'll pay nonetheless."

Her own fault, thought Dmitry. She could have just told us where their gold is hidden. Then he remembered his ambushed dead comrades, and that her husband or brother was among the killers. Pity was not a factor in any equation anymore.

* * *

From the root cellar of the house across the street and one door down, Wolf and Commander Locker squinted out the wooden door. The crack was just big enough so that the two could see the Cossacks emerge from the Battel house and ride off down the street. Wolf and the group emerged gingerly from the cellar and made their way cautiously back across the street. When they entered the house, Jonah started to scream but then had the good sense to bite his tongue. Blood seeped from his mouth. His eyes, fixed wide, stared in horror across the room at where his sister-in-law lay dead and mutilated on the floor. His own wife was already weeping over her.

"We should never have left her," Jonah said bitterly through his bleeding tongue. "I am a coward."

Wolf tried to comfort him, but was afraid he was right. They had all been cowards. A dangerous resolve took root in him.

"Not so," protested Locker and Dunken.

"There was nothing we could do," Locker continued.

But Dunken was silent thereafter.

"Where are you going," asked Locker-Lampson as Jonah picked up a rifle and headed for the door.

"Jonah, no," his wife screamed. "You will leave me with no companions. You'll only be killed."

Wolf blocked the way. "We will do something, Jonah. But let us plan a response."

So they held a council of war.

"Desperate measures must be taken," Wolf argued. "We have a responsibility to do what we can to save as many lives as we can. And if that means getting killed in the process, so be it."

"But it doesn't mean suicide," Locker answered back.

"It appears to me, Wolf," said Count Rantzau finally, "that you have turned into one of them without realizing it. Revenge is all you want now. Don't you see?"

In the end, Wolf more or less told the others that he and Jonah would attack the Cossacks nonetheless, picking off as many as they could, when they could, from hiding. The others were free to join or not. It was finally decided that half the squad would remain behind to protect those who stayed. So in the late afternoon Wolf, Jonah, Commander Locker and a half dozen guards slipped out of the house moving furtively, from hut to hut, up the street. Before long they killed their first unlucky group of ransacking Cossacks, a party of four caught unawares amidst their plundering. Quickly dispatching them, the group moved on surreptitiously up the street.

In these latter stages of the White rampage, fires were set wholesale to Jewish homes, sometimes to cover up the corpses and evidence of looting.

"Look," whispered Jonah, eyes wide, pointing across and down the street.

Wolf trained his spyglasses in that direction. There, in front of a burning home, two Cossacks held a man.

Dmitry had him by the right arm; Alexei held him by the left.

"One more time, Jew. Where is the gold? Roubles? Kerensky notes, even. Give us anything, and we'll let you go."

"I have nothing," the man replied miserably. "You have burned it all."

"But you told us there was nothing," Dmitry yelled at him. "Now you say that we burned it! Well, you go in and get it for us. Now!"

And with that, they hurled the man through the doorway back into his burning home.

Dmitry suddenly pitched forward, sprawled on his face on the ground. Blood spurted from a small hole under his left shoulder blade.

"You shouldn't have done that, Jonah," said Locker in a low but stern voice.

"It wasn't me," he replied. "But I should have done it. Let me take that other Cossack bastard out."

"It's too late," said Wolf. "He's already running for cover. And we'd better get out of here before he gets help."

Over two hundred buildings were burned by the Cossacks, almost half of them houses. The smell of roasting human flesh emanated from many. But at least the synagogue was spared, unlike Chernobyl, north of Kiev, where the local temple was filled with Jews and burned to the ground.

"That was you who shot the Cossack," Commander Locker asked Wolf in a low voice as they walked down the alley. "Understandable," he continued, "Let's hope it doesn't cost us, though. The other one will definitely let his fellows know that we're here somewhere."

"They're all too busy burning and looting everything left standing before they pull out," Wolf replied. "They haven't got time to deal with us small fry."

He was right. As they turned the corner, hugging the side of the building, a group of Cossacks was putting the torch to another building, this one a large commercial barn used for livestock sales.

"They've crammed it full of Jews," Jonah blurted out from behind his binoculars. "I can see them through the door. There're over a hundred people in there. We must get them out!"

"How can we," asked Locker-Lampson.

After a moment, Wolf said, "I'm going to talk to them. Maybe one of their officers is still semi-human."

"Don't be a fool," hissed Locker, grabbing Wolf by the shoulder as he started walking towards the Cossacks.

"You'll be killed. You can't do it," Jonah agreed unexpectedly.

Wolf stopped for a moment, wavering. Then an image came to him, of Tova's mutilated body and a dead fetus lying beside. All because Wolf and the others had been scared to face the Cossacks.

"I just can't let them burn all those people alive. Not without at least trying to stop them. I'll tell them that I know Churchill. That the Allies will withdraw their support if the Whites murder people like this."

"They won't listen, Wolf," Commander Locker pled with him. "They'll just see a German, and shoot you right away."

Nevertheless Wolf shook free of Locker and Jonah and strode quickly across and up the street.

"Who's in charge here," he shouted at the Cossacks.

Everyone was stunned; a momentary silence descended over the immediate area. Then Jonah and Locker and the squad jumped back into the shadows, content to watch the drama unfold at a distance. For their part, the Cossacks didn't know what to do. The figure walking boldly towards them was not a local, that was clear. He might not even be Russian; in fact, his language was clumsy with a definite German accent. And he was well dressed, in new tan combat fatigues. The rifle was non-threateningly slung over his shoulder. He seemed to present no immediate danger, so the Cossacks let him approach, though they held their rifles on him.

"Where is an officer," Wolf asked.

"Who wants to know," Sergei Vulgarin asked.

"I am Wolf Warburg. I carry messages from Winston Churchill. In the name of the Allies, I must speak to an officer of yours immediately. You must not burn these people in this building!"

"And why not? What business is it of yours," asked Corporal Vulgarin.

"What is going on here," said a voice from over Wolf's right shoulder.

Looking up at the mounted figure behind him, Wolf knew it was an officer by the epaulets on his shoulders.

"I am Lieutenant Ilyushkin. You have documents?"

Wolf took a folded letter from his left breast pocket and handed it up to the officer. Ilyushkin was blond, middle-aged. He read the letter, then got down from his mount.

"Come over here, Warburg. I wish to talk with you. Corporal," he said, eyeing his Cossacks, "you will do nothing until I return. You understand me?"

Wolf and the officer wandered off across the street and into a small store. Ilyushkin motioned Wolf to sit.

"You come from the west, bearing a letter you expect to pull weight here. I am sympathetic to you. The problem is that we Cossacks, indeed, all Russia has descended into barbarism, and I fear we can't just stop it here and now. We may both wind up dead."

"But you will try, lieutenant?"

"I will."

They went back outside, and the officer approached his men, who were deep in discussion near the barn.

Lieutenant Ilyushkin ordered them to retreat, to allow the Jews inside to go free.

Suddenly Sergei Vulgarin wheeled and pointed his rifle at the officer.

"You are not giving orders anymore. What were you two discussing in there? Some German plan? Or are you both Reds? That's what I think."

"Either way, it doesn't matter," shouted Alexei Golubov, who had joined the group of Cossacks while Wolf was talking to the lieutenant. "You deserve death. In fact, we'll roast you along with the rest of your Yid friends. Into the barn with them!"

As the Cossacks tried to grab Wolf and Lieutenant Ilyushkin, Wolf swung the rifle from his shoulder, trying to bring it level with Sergei Vulgarin. But as he did so his body was jerked backward and to the right. A second shot knocked him clean off his feet, leaving him bleeding silently on his back on the hard ground.

"That's for Dmitry, you German butcher," Alexei smiled, lowering his rifle.

"He's been shot," Jonah wailed.

"Is he moving? Is he getting up," pressed Locker-Lampson, raising his own binoculars to his eyes.

"They're throwing that Cossack lieutenant into the barn with the Jews," Jonah continued. "And they're torching it! Oh, my God."

1500 to 2000 Jews were killed in the Fastov pogrom. Over five hundred were buried in the local Jewish cemetery, but most of the bodies, burned and mutilated, were never recovered for proper burial. Similar events occurred throughout the Ukraine, western Russia, and Galicia in the civil war causing somewhere between 150,000 to 300,000 Jewish deaths.

The Cossacks vacated Fastov in the early evening. Count Rantzau would not rest until the squad had returned to the area immediately in front of the burned barn to recover Wolf's body, which had escaped the fire. One bullet had dug about an inch into his left breastplate; Locker fished it out with a knife. The other had lodged in his cranium, by the left temple. Locker, at Count Rantzau's insistence, gingerly and gently fished that bullet out as well, and sealed the entry wound with candle wax.

They wrapped the body in white silk, the best the Battel household had to offer, and placed it in a hurriedly made, plain wooden coffin. The next morning, early, so that the Germans could leave Fastov just after first light to head west for home, they buried Wolf in a shallow grave with a makeshift marker. After saying prayers in both German and Yiddish, they said their goodbyes to Jonah and the remaining members of his family. Then the party got into their vehicles and started west, Dunken von Schlieffen not relishing the news he was bringing home to his sister, Liesl.

Thule Winter

Protocols of Deception

I have read the *Protocols of the Elders of Zion* – it simply appalled me. The stealthiness of the enemy, and his ubiquity! I saw at once that we must copy it – in our own way, of course... It is in truth the critical battle for the fate of the world.

- *Hitler Speaks*

A theory is the more impressive the greater the simplicity of its premises is, the more different kinds of things it relates, and the more extended is its area of applicability.

- Einstein

What's breaking into a bank compared with founding a bank?

- *Threepenny Opera*
Bertolt Brecht, 1919

The Red threat, the Great Depression and the Nazification of Germany in the thirties ended the Weimar democratic experiment. During the lifetime of the republic, though, great benefits occurred, along with the street fighting and political deadlock. Freedom of speech and expression blossomed, and Germany experienced an artistic explosion. This was both good and bad, of course, depending on whether one liked a particular movie, song or book. There were always two Germanys: the 'enlightened' absolutism of the north, and the poets and philosophers of the liberal south. It is obvious which won out under Bismarck in 1871 and continued, expect for the fourteen-year Weimar interregnum, until the demise of Hitler. It then arose again under the guise of communism, to smother East Germany for another forty-five years.

There was little government censorship after the departure of the Kaiser. Classics such as *All Quiet on the Western Front* and *The Magic Mountain* were published during Weimar. There were also racist novels like *Sin Against the Blood* and *Volk Without Space*. In art there was Dadaism, a child of the despondency of war, intended to portray the meaningless nothingness of life. In 1919 George Grosz painted a Dadaist 'happening': a sewing machine operator worked at top speed, producing nothing, racing against a typist typing garbage, beneath a pig dressed up in a Prussian army uniform and hanging from a tree. A parody of meaningless sacrifice. A Dadaist painting depicted Ludendorff and Hindenburg dressed up, with fangs, as "vampires of humanity". Officers, industrialists, and aristocrats were shown eating and whoring while the populace starved. Rhinemaiden fingered their genitalia. The "toad of possession" was not the distorted image of the Jew; rather it was the bloated Prussian industrialist.

Berlin was home to the most gaudy, satirical, and risqué theatre in the world, while other cities such as Hamburg, and Schwabing in Munich, followed suit. Bertolt Brecht penned the *Three Penny Opera.* Marlene Dietrich blossomed in theatre and films like *Pandora's Box* and *The Blue Angel* before moving on to Hollywood in the Thirties. Early masterpieces of film horror included *The Cabinet of Dr. Caligari*, *The Golem*, and the original vampire movie, *Nosferatu*. Germany produced more films than the rest of Europe combined during Weimar. As in America, many actors, producers, directors, and screenwriters were Jewish.

And there were the cabarets of Weimar Germany, where the costumes and dance strove to outdo each other in creativity. The wit was bawdy, no topic sacrosanct. The Nazis couldn't match the wit; so occasionally they beat up the comics instead. Weimar was glorious in its freedom, even if extremists from both right and left injected some violence into the mix.

* * *

On September 23rd, 1919, *V Moskvu,* a reactionary Russian magazine, published what it claimed was a United States Secret Service report stating that the Bolsheviks had received millions of dollars from Jacob Schiff on behalf of New York bankers Kuhn, Loeb and Co. The article also reminded its readers how instrumental Schiff had been during the days of the 1905 revolution in spreading lies to the American government about supposed pogroms inflicted on Jews in Russia. America itself in 1919 was not immune to the same gossip. It was Max Warburg in Germany, so the rumours went, who was Lenin's chief financier, while Max's brother Paul sat on the board of the U.S. Federal Reserve, controlling the American money supply; and brother Felix was Schiff's son-in-law, a conduit for passing both U.S. government and Wall Street money to Max Warburg in Germany to pass on to Lenin and the Bolsheviks to take over Russia.

And in fact Schiff and many other Jews were aiding the Reds with money, because the Reds seemed the best of a bad lot in protecting Jews in Russia during those days of war and revolution.

In October 1919 a group of financiers and economists including Paul Warburg and British economist John Maynard Keynes drafted a warning that excessive reparations threatened the German economy and would hence harm creditors as well. Future presidents Herbert Hoover and William Taft, and banker J.P. Morgan Jr., also signed the appeal. But it was ignored, and the reparations tab was set at 132 billion gold marks, or 33 billion American dollars.

Winston Churchill became Secretary of State for War in January 1919. It was his first real contact with Russian problems, and it happened when there was intense pressure to demobilize. In May the Allies professed support for the White cause in Russia, provided that meant opposition to the Reds and the installation of a democratic regime. In the autumn of 1919 Churchill was the most strident advocate of intervention.

"It is a delusion to suppose that all this year we have been fighting the battles of the anti-Bolshevik Russians," argued Churchill in September, about the same time as Wolf was buried outside Kiev. "On the contrary, they have been fighting ours, and this truth will become painfully apparent from the moment that they are exterminated and the Bolsheviks are supreme over the whole vast territories of the Russian Empire."

Churchill warned that certain influential Jews must rein themselves in if they did not wish to destroy the goodwill that existed between them and the government. They risked jeopardizing the Balfour Declaration, in which the British declared support for a Jewish state in Palestine; on the other hand, if influential western Jews would curb their contributions to the Bolsheviks, then the British could much more easily forgive some reparations.

"What has one to do with the other," Max Warburg queried Churchill.

"If Britain and France didn't have to spend so much helping the Whites against the Reds in Russia," Winston replied, "then they could afford to forgive some reparations."

John Maynard Keynes was incensed at Woodrow Wilson's support for exorbitant reparations.

"The greatest fraud on earth," he labelled Wilson, and then wrote *The Economic Consequences of the Peace*, which helped block ratification of the Versailles Treaty by the U.S. Senate. Keynes knew that the reparations demands would fuel outrageous inflation.

"Lenin was certainly right," he warned. "There is no subtler, no surer means of overturning the existing basis of society than to debauch the currency."

* * *

By its very nature the memorial service for Wolf was a sad affair, but it was so much worse due to its unexpectedness. Everyone knew there was danger in going to Russia during a civil war, just as there was danger for soldiers during the world war. But no one really contemplated Wolf or Rantzau not returning; they just doubted that Dunken would be with them. So when Dunken returned, his family was of course ecstatic; but the loss of Wolf was a hard, unexpected blow to the gut, and it sucked the spirit out of those who had been close to him. Liesl, who had lost her best friend Hella just a few months before, was verging on a nervous breakdown. The way she viewed it, in the distortion of her misery, was that she had deliberately sacrificed Wolf to save her brother.

Supported by Einstein on one side and Dunken on the other, Liesl faced the memorial marker for Wolf, next to his father's, in the Jewish cemetery on the outskirts of Munich. Fritz Haber and Count Rantzau came down from Berlin as well, along with Hugo Haase. Max Warburg came from Hamburg, devastated at the news of his favourite cousin's death.

"It's good to have friends around at times like this," said Count Rantzau to Haber and Hugo Haase. "One needs their support to get through this. There's plenty of time for private grieving later."

Liesl was doing that in any event.

"But it wasn't supposed to turn out this way," lamented Einstein, joining the group. "Wolf and Liesl were just becoming close again. Life was beginning to run a positive course. It's almost as if we're cursed. Our friends continue to die young."

"Oh, don't be so morbid, professor," Hugo Haase spoke up. "The Kaiser is gone, and we have a republic, so some good has come of the whole mess."

"But how little gained at such a price," lamented Rantzau to Einstein and Haase. "You just watch your backs, my friends. You're both prominent, Jewish, and leftist, and those seem to be dangerous earmarks to be carrying right now."

The Thule Society kept a list of those who attended the Warburg memorial service, and some old friends of Wolf such as Willy Frick and Franz Gürtner decided it was better not to be there. The right wing press called Wolf a middleman between the Jewish bankers and the German government, just as Paul was in America. They labelled Max the 'Secret Kaiser', who pulled the strings behind Germany's economic subjugation by the Jews of Wall Street. Max, who secretly controlled all the banks in Germany, was himself controlled by brother Felix and Felix's father-in-law, Jacob Schiff, in New York.

Back in America, auto magnate Henry Ford linked the Federal Reserve Board and Paul Warburg to the international Jewish cabal. Ford ranted that Paul and Max had concocted the Versailles treaty, even though Paul wasn't even at Versailles. He was on the outs with the Wilson Administration at the time.

"As has been recounted in the press the world over," Ford's *Dearborn Independent* reported, "the brother from America and the brother from Germany both met at Paris as governmental representatives in determining the peace. There were so many Jews in the German delegation that it was known by the term 'kosher', also as 'the Warburg delegation.'"

It was actually the Morgan group which generally provided and controlled the financing of reconstruction and reparations in Europe following the war. Even the Nazis eventually grudgingly accepted this, but then claimed that the House of Morgan has changed its name from Morgenstern to cover its Jewish roots.

At the same time, Adolf Hitler attended further meetings of the German Workers Party in downtown München.

"In the former Sterneckerbräu in the Tal," Hitler later recounted in *Mein Kampf*, "there was a small vault-like room which had once served the imperial councillors of Bavaria as a sort of taproom. It was dark and gloomy and thus was just as well suited for its former purpose as it was ill-suited for its projected new use. The alley on which its single window opened was so narrow that even on the brightest summer day the room remained gloomy and dark. This became our first business office. But since the monthly rent was only fifty marks (then an exorbitant sum for us!), we could make no greater demands and were not even in a position to complain when, before we moved in, the wall panelling, formerly intended for the imperial councillors, was quickly torn out, so that now the room really gave more the impression of a funeral vault than of an office."

There was a small seven-person organizing committee which met regularly on Wednesday nights and Hitler quickly became integral to the group, his powerful personality emerging, combined now with the confidence that comes with experience and age. He was much more now than the young man in his early twenties who used to spend time arguing politics back in the men's hostel in Vienna before the war; he was more than the young soldier joyously discovering his own bravery in the trenches during the war. He expressed his views ever more cogently, willing to compromise less as his *Weltanschauung*, his world view, hardened in its mould. It was a terrible mould, though: Germany prostrate before the western powers, the Rhine occupied and the Jewish bankers squeezing the economy dry, while the Reds, Jewish minions themselves, threatened Germany from the east. Like peeling the layers off an onion, Hitler felt that he was moving inexorably closer to exposing the methods by which the Jews, through their manipulation of all the major nations of the world, had brought Germany to her knees.

And it was only a year ago that he had suffered through the British poison gas attack, with the initial blindness, and then hysteria and pain which followed, only to recover his vision to learn that Germany had surrendered; it was only a few months now since the bloody events in Munich which saw the Reds first take over his beloved city, and then the brutal butchery of the right in throwing the Reds out. The lesson that Adolf Hitler's disturbed mind picked up from Munich was that the only way to deal with Reds and Jews was to kill them all. Caught in a vise between the Red threat from the east, and the Allied armies occupying the Rhineland in the west to enforce the monstrous reparations payments, Hitler's mind searched for the common thread which would lay bare the conspiracy to subjugate Germany. And the Jews were behind it all: he felt it, he knew it. But how to prove it?

In a café on the Marienstrasse, not far from the Isartor, Adolf Hitler sat with a new acquaintance whom Dietrich Eckart had introduced him to. Alfred Rosenberg, a portly young man with glasses, came from a middle-class family of German descent, which may have had some Jewish blood, and which lived in Estonia on the eastern Baltic. He received an engineering degree from the technical college at

Riga, and then studied architecture at the University of Moscow. Hitler recalled his own earlier interest in architecture.

"I had to flee Russia," Rosenberg related, "when the Bolsheviks threatened me. They didn't like anyone with education. They couldn't very easily convince the educated of the truth of that Lenin or Marx nonsense. They used to separate those with a degree or diploma of any sort, along with the doctors and lawyers and other professionals, and send them off to the Cheka jails. The ignorant peasants and factory workers were their favourite recruits, the type of people who get easily confused at their false slogans."

"Will they win the civil war there?"

"It seems to seesaw," Rosenberg replied. "The Whites took the offensive and they've been driving towards Moscow, so we're led to believe that it's all over for the Reds. But the White armies are stretched pretty thin about now, and the Bolsheviks have hunkered down in their power base in the center of the country. And the Poles are ready to attack the White armies in the rear, is the rumour, because the Whites won't promise that they won't try to reclaim the land the western Allies gave to reconstitute Poland. The Reds, on the other hand, have now promised not to touch Poland."

"Too bad," said Hitler. "We are forced to fight a secret war to stop Poland from taking more land from Germany, and the Poles don't have to worry about the Reds attacking their rear."

"Never fear," exulted Rosenberg as he raised his mug again and took a hearty swallow.

His companion across the table stuck to coffee.

"You can't keep German blood down," Rosenberg went on. "The Poles cannot defeat us unless we allow them to. Germans are the master race, it is in our blood, the ultimate gift from our ancestors. It is the sacred right of

Teutons, by virtue of their innate natural superiority, to rule the world. We recognize the beauties of violence and war."

His face grew animated, and not just his; Hitler, too, glowed keenly. Then Rosenberg put his mug slowly but forcefully down on the table, and in a lower voice cautioned his companion.

"But let us not forget the role of the Jew and the danger he represents. All the important Reds are Jews; oh, there might be a few that aren't, but the Jews control them all anyway. Beware of the biological and spiritual inferiority of the Jew, and his debilitating effects on Christian love and humility," he concluded with a knowing glance of his eyes.

"You think we need more Christian love and humility," Hitler asked his companion, concerned for the first time after they had been getting on so well.

But Rosenberg put his table mate's fears to rest.

"No, what I meant was that the Jews foist this love and humility crap on us Germans so that we will not put up a fight when they come to finish us off. What we really need is a pagan-Nordic religion based on the dynamics of heroism, on the Nordic gods of old. Wotan. Thor and his hammer, ready to destroy all!"

Hitler's heart soared as he listened enthralled. And, sitting there in his chair in the small café, the veil of darkness was finally lifted from his eyes. Alfred Rosenberg revealed to him the secret war being conducted by the Jews to complete their final enslavement of the world.

"There is an ancient and continuing battle between Aryans and Jews for mastery of the globe. The real culture of the world has radiated out from the north, borne by a blue-eyed blond race which in several great waves determined the spiritual face of the world. Against it was, still is, pitted the Jew. Dark, swarthy, crafty and cheating, he is the antithesis of the honourable Aryan. The Jew seeks profit and mastery for its own sake, while we Aryans seek the spiritual essence behind life. But never fear," Rosenberg zealously continued, taking another swig, "we are returning to the old way, the true faithful among us. And the Thule Society is one bastion. It is in our blood that our salvation lies, Adolf. Do you see that?"

"Yes," Hitler heartily confirmed, his fist rising in the air, "we must have the faith to defend our blood. It is our divine essence."

"Well said!"

There was a short silence in which both men just smiled at each other in blissful comradeship.

"Have you ever heard of the *Protocols of Zion*, Adolf?"

Hitler indicated no.

"Actually they're the *Protocols of the Elders of Zion*. That's the proper title. And they're a revelation. They detail the Jewish elders' plans to complete their conquest of the world!"

Hitler was flabbergasted.

"I've never heard of such a thing," he said, "Such a monstrous plan to enslave the world! I knew it. It had to be. Tell me more, quickly!"

The original *Protocols* may have been a treatise from the end of the 18th century that blamed the French revolution on a secret conspiracy of Freemasons. It didn't take long before it was altered to include the Jews. Then a pamphlet written by French satirist Maurice Joly in 1864, entitled *Dialogues in Hell Between Machiavelli and Montesquieu*, cast the dictatorial new emperor Napoleon III in the villain's role. Thirty years later it was altered by the Ochrana, the Tsar's secret police, perhaps General Rachovsky, head of its French division, to again cast the Jews as devil incarnate. Extreme factions in Russia published similar texts, the most popular being one by Sergei Nilus in 1905 during the bloody but unsuccessful revolution in Russia that year. There was then a lull until the Red revolution in 1917, and the *Protocols* appeared in circulation en masse across Russia after that. They were carried abroad in 1919 by fleeing Russians, and by Allied troops evacuating the country. Alfred Rosenberg was among the first to bring the *Protocols* to Munich. It was this revelation that he bestowed on Dietrich Eckart, who, enthralled, then asked him to have a talk with his budding protégé, Hitler. The book gained a wide circulation in Germany in late 1919 and sold over 100,000 copies the following year.

"Do you know much about the Zionists, Adolf?"

"They're Jews who think that they should have a land of their own in Palestine. Good idea, I say. Send Germany's Jews there – and good riddance to them."

"That's right. They were officially formed into an organization only twenty years ago, in Basel in 1897. Under Herzl. You may know that."

Hitler nodded, even though he didn't.

"But what was going on behind the scenes is more important. They weren't there just to form a society dedicated to Jews moving to Palestine. The true purpose was to allow their ruling members from around the world to come together as a group – without suspicion of their true business. Jews from Germany, Britain, America, Russia – all gathered together in one place to decide their course for the next hundred years."

Hitler was beginning to understand.

"They were there to plan their final conquest of the world? Is that it?"

"Precisely."

Rosenberg proceeded to read Hitler some extracts from the pamphlet he had pulled from the inside vest pocket of his overcoat.

"...we shall create an unprecedented centralization, which will unite all powers in the hands of government... Around us will be a whole constellation of bankers, industrialists, capitalists and – the main thing – millionaires because in substance every thing will be settled by the question of figures."

"Diabolical," Hitler replied, astounded and dumbfounded.

"Yes. Everything comes down to gold for the Jews," Rosenberg said. "The *Protocols* are proof that the Jews have burrowed into all the countries of the world and control their economies. But we had no idea up to now that they all were working together."

"Tell me more," pleaded Hitler, animated and rubbing his hands in glee, a broad smile splashed across his face.

"Adolf, you sound like a man after my own heart. What makes you believe that this is nothing but a big lie? The Jews say that it is, of course."

"But it sounds so real. It makes sense."

"You were expecting something like this, weren't you, Adolf? Deep down you believed that there was a Jewish conspiracy, anyway."

"No, not quite," Hitler replied. "I didn't have enough facts. Take these Zionists, for example, and their meeting in Basel. I suppose that I should have made the connection earlier. It seems so obvious, now that you've pointed it out."

"Yes, that's what the *Protocols* do," confirmed Rosenberg.

Hitler was ecstatic, the last piece of the puzzle filled in.

* * *

In Berlin in mid September, Colonel Reinhardt, commander of the troops in the city, called the government a "pack of rascals" in front of his assembled troops. Reinhardt, like his fellow right wingers in the military, wanted a stronger stand taken against the Reds in Germany and against the Poles trying to take land from Germany on the eastern border. Philip Scheidemann, the ex-chancellor, demanded that President Ebert dismiss Reinhardt. Defence minister Noske, still fearful of another Red rising in Berlin, pressured Ebert to leave Reinhardt be.

"I shall not think of dismissing him," Ebert finally told Scheidemann. "Even if they are a bit extreme, those captains and colonels are all that stand between us and the Red hordes."

"The anniversary of the armistice is just a month away, as is the second anniversary of the Bolshevik revolution in Russia," said Count Rantzau to Liesl over the telephone in early October. "Those were both tragic events for the right wing in Germany, and they're itching to take it out on somebody."

"But I want to come see you and Albert and Fritz. I've been through danger before, it's part of my job. Berlin can't be that bad."

Liesl desperately wanted to see her friends. With them she could share common memories of Wolf. Her heart was breaking, but she tried not to show it.

Einstein took the phone.

"Stay at home for now, my dear. It's too dangerous here, the tension is too high in the city."

"Beware! The enemy is on the Right," shouted Philip Scheidemann the next day, rising from his seat in the Reichstag.

He immediately became a lightning rod for every right wing extremist in Germany.

"He's not a Jew, I'll grant you that," Captain Hermann Ehrhardt replied to his companions at the gasthaus on the Im Tal, in downtown Munich. He finished reading from the afternoon tabloid and looked up at his three companions, all fellow officers or non-coms from his barracks. "But he's in the pay of the Jews. As is most of the Reichstag, of course. He'll get his just rewards, mark my words, even if it takes a little time."

"Why does it always have to take time," asked Manfred von Killinger, Ehrhardt's second-in-command, from across the table.

The dark stained wood of the walls, with their ornate patterns, blended well with the dingy light coming in through the small, square windows around the room. It was the right pitch for meetings with dark purposes.

"We should kill him now," von Killinger continued. "Don't leave it to others like we did Kurt Eisner earlier this year. Remember how that half Jew Arco-Valley managed to get to him before we did. Damn embarrassing!"

They agreed that the *Feme*, just created to dispense their version of right-wing justice, should carry out the next Red-Jewish murder. The waitress in the shorts and black leg hose who was serving gave them a quizzical look, but continued about her work.

"But who should our first victim be," asked Ehrhardt of his companions. "I want targets!"

"How about Hugo Haase, the senior Red in the Reichstag," suggested von Killinger.

Haase had been a member of the first government after the fall of the Kaiser, before he resigned in protest after Ebert and Scheidemann allowed the army to storm the Royal Schloss in Berlin the previous Christmas. And Haase was a Jew to boot!

"And he was at Warburg's funeral," added von Killinger. "What about it, Hermann? Famous Berlin Jew dies for his sins against the Fatherland."

Alas, their planning was all for naught. The very next day, as he approached the Reichstag, Wolf's old friend Hugo Haase was shot. He suffered severe injuries and lay critically wounded in the hospital. The assailant was a deranged worker not connected to the Feme. At his trial, he would be found insane, and sent off to an asylum. The center and left wing were angry that the perpetrator got so light a sentence, while the extreme right were angry for other reasons.

"Again we are embarrassed," raged Hermann Ehrhardt, stalking around a sparse office in the barracks. "How can we be so jinxed? We were just talking about him yesterday. And some crazy person beats us to it. Where is the glory for us in that?"

"Humiliating," they all agreed.

"The only consolation, I suppose, is that the nut wasn't successful. I mean, he failed to kill Haase. He's still breathing. If we'd done the deed, he'd be gone for sure. This I pledge," declared Ehrhardt, standing suddenly still and dramatically placing his right hand over his heart, then extending it out in front, as if greeting Caesar. "The next Jew that raises his head high in this country it will be our turn to erase."

Time Unhinged

> Napoleon and the other great men of his type: they are makers of empires. But there is an order of men who get beyond that. They are not makers of empire but makers of universes… Ptolemy made a universe which lasted 1400 years. Newton, also, made a universe which lasted 300 years. Einstein has made a universe, and I can't tell you how long that will last.
>
> - George Bernard Shaw

For two centuries the Industrial Revolution slowly unfolded across Europe, rolling relentlessly from west to east, modernizing the continent as it went. In the endless lands and people of Russia it ran up against the last two Tsars. Never forgetting nor forgiving the assassination of Alexander II in 1881, they ran reactionary regimes that for the final thirty-six years of the empire adamantly refused to allow political modernization to accompany the inexorable economic revolution.

These policies, especially those of the last Tsar, made an eastern European conflagration inevitable. The Reds then failed dismally to halt the societal meltdown already in progress in Russia when the revolution occurred. In food production, the basis for any stable society, the grain harvest fell by 1919 to less than half what it had been two years before. Famine and starvation became widespread, and by 1922 America stepped in to feed ten million Russians a day.

Not that the Red leadership suffered noticeably. By 1918 there was already a special dining room for Lenin and his associates. And then came special villas, accommodations, hotels, family privileges, exclusive shops, special hospitals, entertainment, servants. The Soviet leadership picked up all the perqs that the old Tsarist brass had enjoyed, a result ridiculed years later in George Orwell's *Animal Farm*.

Not so with the rest of the population. Food brigades became the order of the day for both Red and White armies. They searched the countryside high and low for stores and caches, intimidating, confiscating, and sometimes killing as they went. Mothers screamed in terror, afraid that the Red food brigades would carry off their children in order to blackmail the parents into revealing their hidden supplies. The peasants fought back. Five thousand members of the food brigades were murdered in 1919, and it was higher the year after.

Famine and starvation reached such proportions and duration that some turned to cannibalism. Beginning in the last days of the world war in the west of the country, it peaked in the east with the Volga famine of 1921. People began to like the smell of blood; once having consumed human flesh, even such upstanding citizens as doctors could experience persistent, gnawing cravings for it. Families refused to give up their dead because they needed the flesh to live upon.

It became very dangerous for the young to venture out after dark. Youngsters were especially tender, their flesh particularly sweet.

There was also the reverse problem of millions of orphans roaming the streets and countryside in packs, as many as nine million, most not even teenagers, since many of the older ones had already been killed fighting. These gangs preyed on young and old alike.

Over eleven million died in Russia from the revolution, civil war and famine, which resulted in a burial problem. There was usually not enough wood for coffins. In 1919 the Bolsheviks pledged to build the biggest crematorium in the world, but never went ahead since it ran contrary to both Orthodox Christian and Jewish beliefs.

So people continued to be buried in Russia; and in their desperation and depravity driven by circumstance, one band of orphans happened upon the village of Fastov outside Kiev in the wake of the pogrom that occurred there in mid-September 1919. The day after the last of the Cossack troops and hangers-on left the village heading north, and night fell over the razed neighbourhoods of the village, they crept through the streets and alleys, by the burned buildings, passing in and out looking for food and booty. There was little; it had already been picked clean for the most part by the departing army or the remaining villagers. The orphans, not for the first time, then took to searching the graves. The conditions of some of the bodies they uncovered are best left undescribed. Others were in good condition, even dressed in quality wrap, and on occasion a bonus, a pocket watch or jewelry; such was the case when they dug up and carried off the still-warm body of Wolf Warburg.

*　　*　　*

Count Rantzau and Albert Einstein were seated in the latter's study, located in a corner turret of his apartment block at No. 5, Haberlandstrasse, in the Berlin suburb of Dahlem. Reached by a small staircase, and looking out over the rooftops, it was Albert's private reserve, where he did his best work. Count Rantzau had unfolded a map and spread it out over the table in the window alcove, shuffling a stack of notes and papers to the side.

"It's so far away," Einstein commented, "almost Kiev itself. Another world. Civilization seems to end at the Russian border."

He reached up on top of the bookshelf, and pulled down a cigar box, from which he took a cigarette and lit it.

"Wolf lies in the ground outside Kiev; and now Hugo Haase lies in hospital close to death. Where will it end?"

Count Rantzau shook his head to indicate he had no idea.

"How about you, Albert? You've decided to stay in Berlin," the Count finished, smiling hopefully.

"Yes, I'll be staying. I turned down the offer from Zurich. I'll stick around to see how our new republic conducts itself."

"Good for you," Count Rantzau responded gregariously, slapping Einstein on the back.

They were both silent for a few moments.

"So you don't think he suffered at all? He fell quickly?"

"Yes, Albert. The Cossack cut him down from behind before he knew what hit him. He was likely dead before he hit the ground."

"Poor Wolf," Albert said softly. "And we thought the deaths would end when the war was over. But they just seem to continue."

"True. You can imagine how tough it was for Dunken and me to break the news to Liesl. How does one explain it? It seems there's no God, no justice."

Einstein thought for a long moment, all the while smiling his inscrutable smile.

"Don't blame this mess on God. Or, if you must, only blame him because his creation has gone wrong."

Did Einstein believe in God? He believed, in his words, "in Spinoza's God who reveals himself in the harmony of all that exists, not in a God who concerns himself with the fate and actions of men."

"I will tell you what it does convince me of, though."

"What's that, Albert?"

"Wolf's death, I mean. A pogrom – in the 20th century, for pity's sake! And who is there to protect the

Jews in Russia? Only the Reds? Would you trust your future to them?"

"What are you getting at, Albert?"

"Did you know that I said I was busy when they called me from some committee last year that was trying to raise funds to help the Russian Jews who had fled to Berlin as a result of the war, when their villages were destroyed? They wanted me to play my violin at a benefit at the synagogue. I laughed at them."

"But you were busy," said a supportive Count Rantzau.

He still couldn't figure out where Einstein was heading.

"I am convinced now of the necessity of the Zionist movement, to reconstitute a Jewish homeland in Palestine. Other nations, other people, can't or won't stop the pogroms; Jews can only really be safe in a land of their own. Deep down even the Reds are hostile to Judaism, since Marxism is contemptuous of all religion."

"And the Reds are creating a problem for the Zionists," said Count Rantzau.

"What do you mean?"

"You know who Winston Churchill is, the British Minister of War? He told Wolf that the support of some western Jews for the Reds is jeopardizing British support for the creation of a Jewish state in Palestine."

"The world war is over, and Britain doesn't need the Jews anymore – so he can afford to discard us now."

In mid-October, 1919, at about the same time as Einstein and Count Rantzau were commiserating together in his study in Dahlem, Zionism was being discussed at a meeting of a different sort in Munich. As a result of advertising for the first time in a newspaper, at Adolf Hitler's insistence, this meeting of the German Workers Party saw attendance hit triple figures for the first time.

"I see you out there," Corporal Hitler was saying from the podium, a battered lectern on a well-worn stage, "in your military fatigues, your old coats, your hats shiny from wear; I see your boots and shoes with patches, with holes in the soles; and I see the cudgels you carry in your hands, 'walking sticks' to protect you from the Red swine who accost decent folk in the streets. I am one of you," Hitler fired his point across, raising his voice in punctuation, "and we are all together in the war against the Reds and Jews. You know that the Jews want to control the world. They say that they just want a home for themselves in Palestine – and we dumb *Goyim* are content with that answer, when in truth we are allowing them to build a satanic stronghold that will be a haven for convicted scoundrels and a university for budding crooks."

A few moments before, the small audience was passive, but now the speaker was galvanizing them. His delivery was strident, his timing impressive.

"It is not enough that the Jews have spawned the Reds and the Zionists; now their western bankers control all the reparations payments. Their plan now is to finish Germany off, not on the battlefield, but by bleeding us dry financially. That was a part of their strategy. That is, of course, unless their present plan of starving Germany to death fails."

Albert Rosenberg sat with Dietrich Eckart at a table in the rear.

"You can hear the man easily. His voice carries perfectly."

"The voice of a war veteran," Dietrich Eckart replied. "Exactly the type that the masses will trust. They won't listen to the politicians anymore."

"And rightly so," said Rosenberg, lighting a cigarette. "You're dead on about Hitler. A frontline soldier who seems to cut to the heart of the matter. For someone with such a harsh voice, he's very pleasant to listen to."

Liesl von Schlieffen, attending the event as an observer for her paper, noted that several others had the same impression, and were clapping enthusiastically. At the back of the room, Liesl recognized Ernst Röhm, an adjutant to the division commander, along with, to her chagrin, Captain Hermann Ehrhardt. Military personnel weren't supposed to be attending political events; perhaps that was why the pair lingered in the shadows at the rear.

I wonder what they're talking about, she thought, noting how upset Ehrhardt looked. She hoped he wasn't aware of her presence.

"I tell you, it's embarrassing, Röhm. And I simply won't allow it to happen again. Next time," Ehrhardt said, thrusting his finger dramatically out in the air in front of him, "we will be the ones to do the killing. The next Jew who lifts his head high in this country…"

His hand made a slicing motion across his throat. Liesl, spotting the gesture, once again hoped that Ehrhardt was not talking about her. But then his eyes met hers.

Captain Ehrhardt, his companion Röhm trailing reluctantly behind, slid into the chair behind Liesl, and leaned over her shoulder, his lips touching her hair.

"So nice to see you, Fräulein von Schlieffen. You've made my night. You must have a drink with me after the meeting."

Liesl felt ill. And she told him so.

"It has nothing to do with you, Captain," she assured him. "It must have been something I ate."

Röhm was tugging at his companion's coat. Liesl picked up on it.

"May I report in my newspaper that you are here in support of the German Workers Party, Captain," Liesl asked Ehrhardt.

The smile immediately vanished from his face. A stern demeanour replaced it, and he stood away from her.

"No – no, fräulein. We are only here – investigating the party. Yes, that is it. Part of our duties – to protect the security of the State. Please, do not report it in your paper."

Röhm, hearing the conversation, was aghast.

"What have you done, Ehrhardt? You fool!"

Army support for the German Workers Party was supposed to remain secret. Röhm pulled his fellow captain away, and then turned to Liesl.

"I entreat you, fräulein, to forget about this incident. It is for the good of the country."

Liesl hesitated. But Röhm was not the type to be toyed with.

"It would be good for *your* health, as well as for that of the Fatherland, Fräulein von Schlieffen," he smiled savagely back at her. "Many have died defending Deutschland over the last five years; more may yet follow."

With that he turned and, tugging at his companion's belt, pulled Ehrhardt along as he headed out the exit at the rear.

"I had high hopes for that bitch," Ehrhardt mused to Röhm on their way out, with a backward glance towards Liesl, "but she's been a major disappointment. Never fear, though – you know how I deal with my disappointments."

Liesl did not hear him. She was entranced by the speaker with the tiny cropped mustache, the one who had ranted crazily at Wolf on a Berlin street the year before, and who now raged gamely from the lectern in front of her.

"We have now the proof of the Jewish conspiracy – it is laid out before us in the *Protocols of the Elders of Zion*! They may deny it, they may claim that these *Protocols* are but a forgery. But we, through experience, know better; indeed, we suspected it all along. But fear not," he shouted, his fist stabbing upwards, arm fully extended in the air. "Once this book becomes known by our people, the Jewish menace will be shattered forever!"

The audience, a few souls excepted, jumped to its feet, erupting in applause.

Hitler, sweating and smiling, face red and beaming, drank in his due.

*   *   *

"Planck and Haber are so relieved since you assured them you're not leaving Berlin," Count Rantzau told Einstein, seated across from him by the small alcove in his study. "They were both beaming when I saw them this morning."

"They do me too much honour, you know," Albert said. "They deserve more praise themselves."

"I agree," said the Count. "Did you know that Haber has been asked to speak before the Reichstag next month?"

"On what?"

"The government war effort – the last days of the administration – the surrender. That whole inquiry, you know. The same one that Hindenburg and Ludendorff are supposed to appear before."

"You don't think he'll be shouted down as a Jew?"

"Fritz is a war hero. Besides, this is Germany, not Russia, Albert," the Count replied. They committed pogroms in Russia.

The two looked at each other. Rantzau spoke from bitter experience; but Einstein's gut told him Germany wasn't particularly safe, either.

"Albert, what do you hear about the eclipse results? I thought they were confirmed last month."

On September 27th Einstein received a telegram informing him that the photographs of the eclipse taken in May by Eddington confirmed the theory of Relativity.

"That's right. But I never doubted it."

The photos of the eclipse taken by Arthur Eddington and his associates on May 29th, 1919, from Principe off the coast of West Africa, were developed on June 3rd. Einstein had predicted that gravity would cause the light rays to be deflected 1.75 seconds of an arc; the actual measurements from the photos showed a 1.64 second deflection. Close enough! The final results weren't released until late September to a select few scientists. At the beginning of November still, Einstein was unknown to the world outside a small community of physicists.

November 7th was the second anniversary of the Bolshevik coup in Russia. Defence Minister Gustav Noske, expecting trouble, ordered the Wilhelmstrasse in central Berlin blockaded and all traffic stopped.

The same day, Wolf's old friend, Hugo Haase, died from the injuries he suffered when shot a month earlier near the Reichstag. After an elaborate and very public funeral the next day in which over 10,000 attended, he was buried with honours next to Wilhelm Liebknecht, revered founder of the German Social Democratic Party, and the father of Karl Liebknecht, who had died along with Rosa Luxemburg in January.

Scant days later, November 11th, was the very first Remembrance Day. One year before, on the 11th hour of the 11th day of the 11th month, the armistice took effect ending the First World War.

These two anniversaries, November 7th and 11th, evoked painful memories for the extreme right. What they didn't need was another famous Jew popping up in their faces.

On November 6th, Arthur Eddington finally presented the findings of his eclipse expedition to a meeting of the Royal Astronomical Society at Burlington House in London. The next morning, the *London Times* crowed, "Revolution in Science; Newtonian Ideas Overthrown."

Albert Einstein woke to find himself famous the world over. And to this day, he has remained the universal symbol of genius. Two of his ‘discoveries’ stand out: the power of the atom, and the Theory of Relativity. He didn’t split the atom, but his formula $E=mc^2$ led to it. It was Relativity, though, with its predictions about the manipulation of time, which instantly awed people the world over.

He was described in the papers as a genius, a nutcase, a pacifist, and a Zionist. And while most Germans couldn't travel to Paris or London without fear for their safety, Einstein was invited everywhere. Even at home he quickly became an adored and worshiped figure.

“Strange people these Germans,” said Einstein. “I am a foul smelling flower to them, yet they keep tucking me in their buttonholes.”

But a sinister few held less benevolent intentions towards him.

The Secret Court

> The illicit organization became notorious for its revival of the horrors of the medieval *Femegerichte* – secret courts – which dealt arbitrary death sentences against Germans who revealed the activities of the 'Black Reichswehr' to the Allied Control Commission.
>
> \- *The Rise and Fall of the Third Reich*

> …the term *Feme* cropped up with alarming frequency. It meant a kind of kangaroo court; people who were charged with some offence against the community but refused to attend a self-constituted citizens' 'court' were outlawed, liable to be killed by anybody who found them.
>
> \- *Weimar Eyewitness*

A week after Einstein broke upon the world the German Workers Party held its second advertised meeting, and the attendance was well over a hundred. It was held at the Eberlbräukeller, and they even managed to convince some who attended to pay a small admission fee 'for the cause'.

"My friends," Corporal Hitler began his address to the crowd, "look what's occurred over the past week. We've had two anniversaries. It's been two years since the Bolshevik coup in Russia; and a year since the armistice in the west, when the new government betrayed us to the Allies."

The hall was quiet. Hitler's voice had a way of cutting through noisy rooms and catching people's attention, a strange, compelling mixture, both gutteral and sweet.

"On the good side, a prominent Jew, Hugo Haase, a Reichstag leader, died earlier this week."

There was clapping from some in the crowd. Hitler frowned and held up his hand for silence.

"But as soon as we get rid of one, another pops up," he added. "All of a sudden there's this Einstein, a professor from Berlin, who's now acclaimed a scientific wunderkind. Re-invented gravity." Hitler smirked. "And the world adores him! All other Germans are shunned while this Jew is fawned over everywhere. Is there no end to how they humiliate us?"

A week later, Generals Hindenburg and Ludendorff, Germany's unofficial rulers for the last two years of the war, testified before the Reichstag committee investigating the debacle called World War One.

"Long live Hindenburg! Down with the Jew Republic! Down with the investigating committee," hollered reactionaries as the generals entered the building.

"Down with Ludendorff! Long live Ebert," others shouted back.

Inside, Hindenburg declared his position, carefully considered over the course of a year.

"An English general has with justice said that the German Army was stabbed in the back. Where the guilt lies requires no proof."

"In spite of the superiority of the enemy in men and material, we still would have won," Ludendorff argued, "if only there had been unity between the army and those at home. But traitors – Reds – infected both soldiers and civilians, eroding our will to conquer. In the end, the home front no longer supported us!"

"We had the best scientists, the most sophisticated weapons, the most advanced petrochemical, explosive, and pharmaceutical industries in the world," Fritz Haber pointed out when it was his turn to speak. "Yes, as the General says, we could still have won, despite the Allied superiority in manpower and supplies. But we were stabbed in the back by the cowards, slackers, and Reds."

"And the Jews," came a cry from the gallery.

* * *

The Versailles treaty allowed only a small German army. Germany could not count on the Allies to stop Poland from attempting to take more land from her along their border. So the Germans created the Black Reichswehr, an underground army to guard the frontier. The Ehrhardt brigade briefly served there, as did other Free Corps formations. Since the army was illegal, and had to be kept secret, its officers relied on *Femegerichte*, secret courts, to ensure that no one spoke of it to the Allies. The *Feme*, as these secret courts became known, and of which Captain Ehrhardt was a charter member, pronounced death sentences on those they found guilty of harming Germany.

By late November, 1919, Rosa Luxemburg, Kurt Eisner, and, most recently, Hugo Haase, all prominent Jewish leftist leaders, had been killed by right wing assassins. Albert Einstein was now suddenly the most adored German in the world; as a pacifist Jew and declared Zionist to boot, he became an irresistible target for the Feme.

"Pure drivel," Professor Gottfried Feder commented, taking a good swig from his glass.

They were in a small gasthaus off the Im Tal in downtown Munich.

"This charlatan must be silenced," argued Manfred von Killinger. "His 'Relativity' theory is nothing but a Jewish plot to undermine German science. Just like the Jews are secretly plotting to destroy the German economy with these massive reparations. And the inflation."

"'Relativity' says that a person who leaves on a journey through space travelling at very high speeds for a hundred years would return after that time having aged little. What do you make of that," asked Ernst Röhm in response, looking up from a copy of the *Volkischer Beobachter*, a tabloid he was reading.

"Sheer lunacy," Professor von Müller replied. "Even worse, some respected scientists, whom I had thought intelligent up to now, support it. Despicable!"

Some prominent German scientists lined up against Relativity when it first burst upon the scene in 1919. A few had motives other than scientific. They spouted Nazi race theory, and became known as the 'Anti-Relativity Company'. There was Philipp Lenard, 1905 Nobel Prize winner in physics. A younger one was Johannes Stark, 1919 Nobel winner in physics. The spotlight that year was stolen from him by Einstein and the eclipse results. Resentful, petulant, and greedy, Stark accepted money from extremists to discredit Einstein and Relativity, referring to modern theoretical physics as "Jewish physics", and advocating removal of Jewish professors from universities.

"Something must be done about this Einstein before he makes a laughingstock of German science," exclaimed Gottfried Feder.

"Something will be done! The verdict is guilty, five votes to zero," Hermann Ehrhardt pronounced of Einstein. "What is the sentence?"

"I leave that up to you," said Captain Röhm. "I have to get back to the barracks for a meeting with the colonel."

Ehrhardt looked to his remaining companions.

"What about it, Manfred?"

"There is no doubt," von Killinger replied, setting his mug down on the table. "German honour requires that he removed. But let's get it done before anyone else beats us to it this time."

The night of November 27th saw another meeting of the German Workers Party, this time at the famous Hofbräuhaus in downtown Munich, albeit not in the main hall; that was too large. Featured speaker: the budding firebrand, Adolf Hitler. There was another rise in attendance as Hitler's fame spread locally.

"If you are going to lie, make it a big one – the bigger the better. The more incredible the lie, the more it will be believed! What, you don't believe me," Hitler laughed, at one with the crowd. "Consider," he continued, his arms gesticulating to the cadence of his speech, "this theory of Relativity. It says that a person who goes off in space at high speeds will come back in a hundred years hardly having aged at all. And we're told, by these scientists from Berlin – with straight faces – that we should believe this. But when we are shown proof of the Jewish conspiracy to rule the world, as the *Protocols of Zion* does – we're told by the same know-it-alls from Berlin that the *Protocols* are just a big invention. Now you tell me who is lying."

The room exploded into applause and shouting. Liesl von Schlieffen was trying hard not to be noticed as she took mental notes of events from the rear of the room. Her concentration was still distracted by the information that she had picked up earlier from her young admirer, Hans Frank. Apparently the Feme, a budding organization of right wing extremist killers, had decided to kill Einstein. He was currently at the top of their list.

* * *

"You've done well, my boys," the old woman cooed. Three of them, all around 10 or 11 years old, looked back at her hungrily. "We'll eat well tonight," she assured them. "Now run along. You know you're not allowed in the kitchen when dinner is being prepared."

The kitchen in this instance was a dilapidated room in a small hut in the country. The old woman shooed the lads, all orphans, out of the room and then turned to her companion, an equally old man, who was filling a large cauldron with water.

"I'll be outside. But remember, old man, those children aren't to see you preparing dinner. It's bad enough that they have to rob graves and handle corpses. And even though they know what they're eating, I just won't allow them to actually see other human beings cut up and cooked."

This old couple had banded together with the orphans out of necessity, but in the old woman a certain maternal attitude had arisen. The old man wondered to himself how the strange morals of this time and place, in the midst of starvation and death, would look to other people in a time of peace and plenty. Not very kindly, he was sure. But what could they know? Then he poured more water over the naked body in the cauldron.

* * *

"But now he's left the country again," Fritz Haber raged at President Ebert. "We had just convinced him to stay in Berlin, and now he's scared he'll be killed. This is intolerable!"

Haber slammed his fist down on the President's desk, got up from his chair and started to pace the room, cane in hand. Ebert wasn't sure how to respond to this distinguished scientist, a national icon and war hero.

"He is right, Herr President," said his companion, Max Planck, in a soft voice, remaining in his seat. Planck was a slight man, impeccably dressed. His shadow would fall over the world of physics for the rest of the century. Ebert could not ignore these two foremost scientists in the nation.

"But why is he so special," Ebert pressed them meekly. "You liken his possible departure to a national tragedy."

"And it would be," Fritz Haber exploded. "The man is a genius, the greatest scientific mind of our time."

"You should listen to Professor Haber," Max Planck added. "He is not one to bestow praise easily."

Ebert looked over to Haber, who was still pacing the room.

"Albert Einstein has single-handedly rearranged our most vital notions of space and time," Max Planck continued. "Where the practical implications of his work will take us is difficult to imagine now – but they will be stupendous. Space travel, lasers – who knows?"

"What is a 'lasers'," Ebert asked.

"Don't ask," was the reply. "It would take too long to explain. Just believe us when we say that we can't afford to lose him, Herr President."

"If he leaves for Switzerland or Belgium or France," Fritz Haber took the argument up, waving his cane about the air as his hands spoke as well, "or even America, other German scientists will follow. To be close to him, to consult, to interact with him in his research. Right now we have the greatest scientific talent in the world collected right here in Berlin. At the institutes in Dahlem. You know the effect that Einstein has had around the world over the past couple weeks, the prestige he has brought to German science. Would you risk him leaving?"

President Ebert thought for a moment.

"But how can I stop him?"

"You must catch these criminals who put a bounty on his head," Haber exploded again, whacking his cane against the leg of the chair. "You must send such a message to these right wing crackpots that they will be scared to harm a hair on his head."

* * *

A dull awareness grew slowly as a great fog slowly lifted. His first sensations were of great warmth, then gradually a growing pain as the water heated up. Then, finally exploding into consciousness, he awoke to a stabbing, searing pain in his left thigh. He opened his eyes to find himself stark naked, curled up in a cauldron in a small dilapidated room, the water painfully hot, and an old codger prodding his thigh with a fork.

Acting instinctively, he grabbed the chef's head with both hands and yanked it forcefully towards him, ramming his cranium into the cauldron rim, cracking the man's skull, who then fell backward, dead. He jumped out of the vat.

Clothing, the first order of business – he was freezing. That happened when one was caught naked in a Russian winter. He ended up undressing his dead captor and donning the frayed and tattered attire.

Looking furtively out the door, he found that he was in a small hut in a farmyard on a vast northern plain. It was late afternoon from the look of the sun, getting dark early at that time of the year. There were a number of children in the yard, but none had yet noticed him. An old woman was moving about, preparing a barbecue pit that had three large tables next to it. It appeared that a picnic was being laid out.

He huddled in the shed for the next while, fearing that someone would venture in. It was getting nippy as the sun set, and the light from the barbecue provided the only illumination. He couldn't chance waiting any longer, since they would be coming soon for the main course for the grill. With a peek out the door to make sure it was clear, he darted out, turned the corner round the side of the building, and slunk away, half crawling, half running, through the faltering light. If not for the lateness of the day, he might not have made it.

He kept moving, not knowing where he was, which way to go. Hours later, exhausted, he fell to the ground, crawled into the bushes, and fell into a deep sleep. The next day he awoke, remembering the events of the day before. Famished, he immediately foraged for food, but there was none to be found. So he spent another miserable night in a dank, marshy swamp, and by morning his physical and mental reserves were near gone.

It had dawned on him sometime the day before, during one of those moments when the pangs of hunger and cold temporarily subsided, that he didn't know who he was. But he was lucid enough to know he was ill.

The next day, when a pair of troopers came riding close by the bushes where he lay hidden, he crawled out and threw himself in their path. Whatever his fate, he figured it preferable to a slow death by starvation or cold.

But he wasn't so sure a few hours later when, compelled by lash and rope, he stumbled along on aching, blistered feet, his hands bound and tethered to one of his captors' mounts. At the end of the day, on a still empty stomach, his head swimming and body aching, he finally fell to the dirt in the main yard of his new home, a Polish POW camp bordering the Pinsk marshes.

* * *

Ernst Pöhner was not happy. The message that he had received from the leader of the Bavarian state government was unequivocal: no effort must be spared, no stone left unturned, in locating and putting an end to the threat to

Albert Einstein's life. If Pöhner felt himself incapable, or undesirous, of carrying out the task, then someone else would be named to replace him. Pöhner was livid, as his associate, Wilhelm Frick, head of the political section of the Munich Police Department, could attest. Pöhner had called him into his office earlier that morning to hear the news.

Ernst Pöhner just wanted to do his job, and that was protecting Munich and Bavaria from danger. The chief danger at that point in time was the Reds. Their leadership was basically Jewish, so Jews were generally undesirable. Particularly those who were famous and influential, such as Albert Einstein. It was nothing personal.

Wilhelm Frick wasn't quite so sure. Some Jews, such as Wolf Warburg, were really quite admirable in many ways. But he was beginning to see the overall picture. The Reds had now taken over a large country, Russia, and Germany was next up on their list. The Red leadership contained far too many Jews in proportion to the population in general. And now the *Protocols* was evidence of an international Jewish plot. Well, maybe that was bunk; but how did one explain away the monstrous reparations payments under the Versailles *Diktat*? There was indeed a plot to destroy Germany, only now it was to ruin her financially. And who were the best, the most insidious, financiers in the history of the world?

"Do you believe this trash," Franz Gürtner whined, walking into the office where Pöhner and Frick were seated.

Gürtner had just come from his office at the Ministry of Justice.

"I just got this memo," he continued, pacing, reading from the document that he had pulled from his vest pocket. "It says that we're supposed to arrest and interrogate all the leaders of right wing military and paramilitary groups in southern Bavaria. Does that include the army? This is ridiculous! Why has this Einstein suddenly become God anyway?"

Gürtner, too, was livid. If he had doubts as to Jewish control of the backrooms of the country, or their hold on the government in Berlin, they were dashed now. The Ministry of Justice and the police had been ordered to arrest military leaders? Who would guard the country against the Reds?

"These Jews are the ones that need to be reined in," said Ernst Pöhner. "Did you read about this 'Relativity' nonsense? That time stands still if you run fast enough? It is as this new speaker, Hitler, says – the bigger the lie, the more easily people swallow it. And now they have bamboozled the government!"

"I'll not order the arrest of Colonel von Epp, nor General von Oven," said Franz Gürtner. "I won't prosecute such a case."

"There's no need to arrest anybody," Pöhner said flatly, his rage now spent. "But Ehrhardt and his group must keep a low profile. I've been threatened with removal from my post if the danger to Einstein is not removed. So I'm passing that threat along to you, Willy," he said, eyeing his subordinate. "Like it or not, you make Ehrhardt and Killinger understand – they are not to touch Einstein!"

"Do you think they'll listen," Frick asked back.

"They had better," Ernst Pöhner responded. "I've never seen the Berlin government in such a tizzy. Nothing like it since the Red risings a few months ago. There are other Jews – just leave this one alone."

"Whether we like it or not, this Einstein is sacrosanct. That's the bottom line; it's all I've been told."

Hermann Ehrhardt was more than upset as he delivered the news to his associate, von Killinger.

"Feme operations are shut down for the time being. That's what Röhm said Colonel von Epp told him," Ehrhardt continued. "The Berlin government has threatened to cut all funding to the Munich military district if a hair on Einstein's head is touched. Röhm said that von

Epp was even threatened with removal from his command if he can't guarantee Einstein's safety. Do you believe it? The German army is now charged with the task of guaranteeing the life of a Jew."

There was pressure as well from the Allied Control Commission, which was itself pressured by Woodrow Wilson and Lloyd George. In the end, the Feme had to accept that Einstein was inviolable. At least for the time being.

"I want to know how they found out," Ehrhardt seethed through clenched teeth.

"We'll float a reward," declared Killinger, "in Yankee bucks, to find out who betrayed us. And when we do, that person will pay!"

The meeting of the German Workers Party on December 10th, 1919 was at a hall on the Dachauer Strasse, northwest of the city center. Adolf Hitler had by this time become the de facto chief of propaganda for the budding party. He was its chief draw, and was already honing his craft, exploring the art and science of public speaking. He liked to keep the audience waiting, to build the suspense. Sometimes he just stood silent for a few moments. He started off slow and quiet, and then all of a sudden erupted. His hand gestures were like those of a conductor. The first part of a speech was soft and exploratory; then, once connected with his audience, he switched to 'march time', building to an ultimate crescendo in the final stages. He seemed possessed of a bottled rage, and no one doubted his will to murder.

"He is very good," commented Professor von Müller to Dietrich Eckart, as they admired their protégé from the wings. "The masses seem to rouse him, give him strength. That pale face with those burning eyes – he seems possessed! He speaks of murder, but makes it drip with honey. He's got them hypnotized."

“He is wonderful,” Eckart gushed. “The future of our movement, I’ll wager. And it is my job to make sure he is educated correctly now.”

Hermann Ehrhardt slid up to the table at that moment.

“You have some news for me, Herr Eckart,” he asked.

“Why, yes, Captain. Have a seat. You know the professor.”

“You wanted to know who tipped off the Berlin government to the plan to kill the Jew, Einstein. You have some money for me? I believe it was to be in American dollars.”

“Get on with it,” Ehrhardt said impatiently. “If your information is as promised, you’ll get your money.”

He pulled an envelope from his coat pocket and set it on the table, his hand on top, and waited for Eckart to tell his story.

“Colonel Reinhardt heard it from Ebert, who got it from Scheidemann, that it was Liesl von Schlieffen.”

“No,” cried Ehrhardt.

He still lusted for her.

“It’s true,” Eckart continued. “She called her friend Count Brockdorff-Rantzau, who called Scheidemann, who called Ebert. Then Max Planck and Fritz Haber, both friends of Einstein, pressured Ebert as well. Apparently Fräulein von Schlieffen knows them too. Colonel Reinhardt was told this by Ebert himself, who had no reason to lie. He didn’t know it’d get back to us.”

Hermann Ehrhardt’s jaw muscles worked themselves silently. He seemed to be chewing his lip for a few moments.

“Take your money, Eckart. It’s well worth it to me to have the bitch’s name.”

* * *

"We know that you're German, that's obvious," said the Polish inquisitor hovering above him in the prisoner of war camp near the Pinsk marshes.

It was mid-November, and he had been there for the better part of two months. His biggest problem was not his incarceration. Even if he was free, he wouldn't know where to go, because he had lost his memory. His only recollections were those acquired since he regained consciousness to find himself in a vat, being stuck with a fork. The first month of his captivity was spent regaining his health, from physical exhaustion and hunger, and from bullet wounds to his chest and temple that he couldn't explain. The second was spent trying to convince his captors that he wasn't faking amnesia.

"You are a German spy; why do you not just admit it," the blond major with the hooked nose pressed him, coming so close that one could smell the onions on his breath. "We have been patient with you so far, due to your injuries, but no more! I, for one, never believed this loss of memory nonsense for an instant. But the colonel did…"

The major re-commenced pacing round the room. He then stopped abruptly in front of his captive, suddenly bringing the riding crop in his hand down, with a swish and then a loud smack on the table beside him.

"You know, my German friend, you should consider yourself fortunate. I am in a good mood. The armistice celebrations of the past couple of days – a year since the Germans were defeated. And look what has happened since: Poland reborn after more than a century of extinction."

Major Sidulski slapped the prisoner across the back heartily, knocking his entire chair forward.

"Come, let's be friends. You tell me who you are, and maybe you get out of here."

His captive just stared back at him blankly.

"You are a spy," said the major. "Germany needs information on the Polish army. That's what I think."

Poland was reconstituted by the victorious western allies in 1919 from land taken back from Russia, Austria, and Germany. But the Poles wanted more, and Germany wasn't prepared to give any. But how to protect herself from incursions by the growing Polish army, what with the restrictions on the German military imposed by the Versailles *Diktat*?

"Are you a Jew? A Red, maybe," the major pressed him further. "A German Jew, perhaps?"

He couldn't remember a thing. The major spoke some Yiddish. He answered back.

"So you are a Jew, yes," the major pressed him further. "You must be if you understand their language."

"Perhaps. But I really don't remember."

"Enough!" Suddenly the riding crop came down hard across the prisoner's thigh. "You're circumcised, we know that," the Pole screamed, shoving the tip of the crop into the man's groin. "No more lies! Admit your mission, or you will be shot."

He doubled up in pain. Sidulski returned to pacing the floor, then stopped by the table and picked up the newspaper lying on top.

"There's something in here about a German Jew – he's become quite a sensation recently. Let's see if you know him." The major leafed through the pages and found the story. "'Berlin physicist proven right in his new theory of gravity. Professor Albert Einstein, whose controversial theory of Relativity predicted the bending of rays of light from the sun during the solar eclipse this past May, had his work proven correct when his predictions for the deflection of sunlight from its expected path were confirmed in photographs taken by English astronomer Arthur Eddington.' What about it? You recognize this Jew,

Einstein? You're German. You know Yiddish. He's a famous German Jew – what about it?"

His brain was in turmoil. Albert Einstein – Relativity – Einstein…

"What about it, my lying friend? You recognize the name, don't you?"

The major unexpectedly slapped him on the back with his riding crop.

"You remember?"

And all of a sudden, he did! A deluge of memories flooded his consciousness.

"Yes," he said, slowly at first, then again, with more conviction, "Yes, I remember now. My name is Wolf Warburg. I am a lawyer from Munich. I came to Russia, to Kiev, to rescue a friend held by the Reds there. We got him out – but I can't remember much after that."

Major Sidulski had stopped in his tracks. He was eyeing Wolf closely, scrutinizing him.

"And what has brought on this sudden revelation?"

"Einstein – you mentioned him. He's a friend of mine. You said he was in the newspaper. May I see it?"

The major was taken aback. He hesitated, then stooped and picked up the paper off the table. He held it out to Wolf, who was about to take it when the major suddenly pulled it back, and threw it on the ground.

"Liar," he cried, slapping Wolf savagely across the face with his crop. "I know that you are a German spy, trying to steal information on our troop strength and locations. Don't deny that you are spying for the Black Reichswehr. You think me a fool?"

Major Sidulski suddenly stopped his rant, and after a moment leaned over, bringing his head close to Wolf's, where blood trickled down his cheek, cut by the lash. Then, with a wicked glint in his eye, the Pole hissed in Wolf's ear.

"We shall see which of us is the fool."

* * *

She continued to beat herself up over Wolf. Her eyes were constantly drawn now, her skin pale even allowing for winter. She rarely smiled, and then just wanly. Her zest for life was gone – buried with Wolf Warburg in a grave outside Kiev. Every scenario that she now imagined involved only drudgery and duty. She soldiered on with life because she didn't know what else to do.

"You must steer clear of the Munich right," implored Albert Einstein, when he spoke to her from Zurich. "If they found out it was you who reported their plot to kill me, you'll be a target yourself."

"Of course I'll steer clear," she answered back, with no intention of doing so.

Journalism was the only thing that made life bearable. It was therapy for her. Danger had something to do with that. She had sacrificed Wolf, sent him into mortal danger; why should she now spare herself. So whenever anyone warned her about threats to her safety, she agreed politely, but in practice ignored them.

Liesl was very slender now, eating little for the most part. Time on her hands invariably brought back thoughts of Wolf; so she allowed little spare time. She covered the dangerous Munich political scene not with zest, but with experience and perceptiveness. Her articles were insightful and sceptic, too much so, for she skewered both the Reds and the Right. The Reds knew that she hated them for killing Hella. The right wing, which had initially welcomed her, hissed now in surprise when she belittled their spiels about Jews and the Weimar government. And after her exposure of the Feme's plot to murder Einstein, she should have been more careful. But that would have involved her caring about her own safety, and her behaviour indicated she did not.

Back at the barracks, in a speedy trial, sentence was pronounced. This time there were only two judges: Hermann Ehrhardt and Manfred von Killinger.

"I don't care if she is the daughter of a judge," Ehrhardt raged, "and her uncle is a distinguished general, and she's friends with a whole bunch of Berlin bigwigs. She has betrayed us, and must answer for her crimes."

His companion pulled out a revolver from the holster at his side, and cocked back the bolt.

"Don't worry, Hermann," von Killinger purred, caressing his weapon, "this time I will attend to matters personally."

"No," Ehrhardt shouted unexpectedly. "Just find her and bring her to me. I want the satisfaction of dealing with this one myself."

1919

Resurrection

> The victory of 1870 and the subsequent commercial and industrial success... have established a religion of power... I am firmly convinced that only harsh realities can stem this confusion of minds. These people must be shown that they must respect non-Germans as equals and that, if they are to survive, they must earn the confidence of other countries.
>
> - Einstein during WWI

> Particularly our German people which today lies broken and defenceless, exposed to the kicks of all the world, needs that suggestive force that lies in self-confidence. This self-confidence must be inculcated in the young national comrade from childhood on. His whole education and training must be so ordered as to give him the conviction that he is absolutely superior to others. Through his physical strength and dexterity, he must recover his faith in the invincibility of his whole people.
>
> - *Mein Kampf*

"We cannot afford to do without him," said Anton Drexler emphatically, setting his mug down on the table. They were at an outdoor café south of the Marienplatz. Dietrich Eckart was with him, as was Karl Harrer, leader of the German Workers Party. Drexler led the Munich chapter of the party.

"He's such a wonderful speaker," Eckart pointed out. "Listen."

It was a Sunday afternoon, and Hitler stood out on the corner shouting his harangue to all who would listen. A small crowd had gathered.

"He's got such strong lungs," noted Anton Drexler. "That's what I mean – he is the best speaker I've ever heard. And he's been drawing crowds to our meetings like never before."

"Then you must control him," Karl Harrer said. "This anti-Semitic rhetoric of his, and the socialistic attitude towards big business – he must give those up."

"What do you mean," Eckart challenged him. "What's that about his attitude towards business?"

"He keeps saying that he'll nationalize this industry and that, and he wants huge contributions from others. Sounds like a Red platform. It'll scare off business support for us," finished Harrer.

"I think I can get him to tone that down, once I've explained," said Anton Drexler. "Hitler's really quite practical where money is concerned."

"Fine," said Harrer, getting up to leave. "And make sure he drops that drivel about Jews. It'll only drive intelligent workers away."

With that, Harrer took his leave.

"You really think Adolf will tone it down," Drexler asked Dietrich Eckart, as they listened to him shout his message to the crowd.

"Like you said, I think he'll be practical about not scaring big business contributors away from the party."

"And what about dropping his attacks on the Jews?"

Eckart stared across his beer at the other man.

"You tell him," Eckart finally replied. "But I advise you to have him tied up before you make the suggestion."

Drexler looked at his companion and smiled.

"So what do we do, then? Hitler is our chief fundraiser. They come to the meetings to hear him speak. He's the one that draws in the paid admissions."

"It appears, then," replied Dietrich Eckart, "that it is Herr Harrer who will have to step back, rather than Hitler. Perhaps the party needs a new chairman. How about it, Anton, are you up to the job? Could you put up with this slander of the Jews?"

"What slander?"

* * *

"We checked with Berlin, Herr whoever-you-are," Major Sidulski eyed his unfortunate prisoner, who was tied down with ropes to a wooden chair. "Wolf Warburg is buried in some village outside Kiev. In a box. You probably killed him. You're trying to steal his identity now. Even if you are working for the German government, they're officially denying your existence. So you have no friends – and no identity. Unless you confess fully, immediately, you will be shot without delay."

Wolf had no reply. He couldn't understand why his government wouldn't help him – unless this Polish major was lying. And it didn't really matter, because if the Pole was intent on killing him, there was little he could do about it.

They beat him about the body and face. Then they cut the ropes and he slid to the floor in a heap. The blond major commented on how valiantly he protested his innocence, even in the face of torture. Then they dragged him from the interrogation chamber over the stone floor, up some rough stairs and out into the sunlight. It was December and the sun shone in the southern sky. Trees were snow-covered across the way, but the exercise yard was bare. It was a large open space in the middle of several two-storey wooden structures with white paint peeling off. The side of the building that Wolf was dragged over to and stood up against had a metal siding attached to it, about ten feet high by a dozen across. It was thick enough to stop bullets, its intended purpose. The grey sheet metal was streaked and splotched with blood of differing hues, some dry and some still dripping.

Wolf ruminated on how it had all come to this, finally, after having passed through so many trials. With the war over, he had hoped to resume his relationship with Liesl, get married, have a family, and live happily ever after. A new democratic regime would bring peace and prosperity. But instead, the Allies sought revenge, and Germany tore itself apart in civil war. In Russia, where hell itself had ascended the earth, Jews were butchered in medieval pogroms.

It just didn't make any sense. Was there meaning to life? Apparently not – at least not if it ended like this.

"I am truly sorry," Major Sidulski sympathized. "Don't get me wrong – I won't lose any sleep over you. Millions have died, and you'll just be one more corpse. But you seemed a nice enough sort, Warburg, or whatever your name really is."

* * *

For the next meeting of the party, a few days before Christmas, 1919, Ernst Röhm let it be known that he would look favourably on all of the men in his command who attended. Never mind that the Allied Control Commission frowned upon army participation in politics. The influx of soldiers caused party attendance to rise to over two hundred, the highest ever. And it gave Hitler the opportunity to win more converts through his speeches.

Ernst Röhm, who would be indispensable to Hitler and the Nazis over the next fifteen years, had other methods of encouraging German patriotism. He liked to take a small troop into the beer hall. Every fifteen minutes or so they'd have the band play a patriotic song. If someone didn't stand up for it, they'd answer to the troop.

But it was as security for party meetings that the military proved elemental to the Nazi success, and allowed it to flourish, even against Red agitators who broke up other large political gatherings. And it allowed the Nazis to set the agenda in their own meetings.

"No one begged the audience graciously to permit our speech," remembered Hitler in *Mein Kampf*, "nor was everyone guaranteed unlimited time for discussion; it was simply stated that we were the masters of the meeting, that in consequence we had the privilege of the house, and that anyone who should utter so much as a single cry of interruption would be mercilessly thrown out from where he came from."

On the night of December 20th, Liesl decided to attend the advertised meeting of the party. It had become a bit of a habit over the last three months, as part of her duties to report such things for her newspaper. But she had to admit that she was getting more and more interested in the rising star of Adolf Hitler. At this particular meeting, he was speaking of the unique birth and baptism of fire of the Second Reich, in the shadow of the victorious German armies at Versailles in 1871. And now, Versailles had become a place synonymous with German defeat and subjugation.

"The progress and culture of humanity are not a product of the majority, but rest exclusively on the genius and energy of the personality," Hitler shouted to the crowd. "You are offered a choice of Jew democracy, where numbers alone decide everything; or Bolshevism, again founded by a Jew, in which numbers mean everything. But what about the extraordinary man, perhaps a reborn Siegfried? Shall intelligence and superiority count for nothing? What about me – shall my word count for no more than that of the ignorant rabble?"

Hermann Ehrhardt, surveying the crowd from the back of the hall, couldn't believe his good fortune. Tapping

Manfred von Killinger and Rudolf Hess, he motioned them to follow.

"If she won't come nicely," he instructed, "take hold of her and move quickly out the door. No one will hear; Hitler's too loud. And we're among friends," he concluded, noting the troops in attendance.

Liesl saw Hess and Killinger making their way towards her – and then she saw Ehrhardt behind them. Panicking, she looked around for a place to run. She couldn't make it to the doorway before Ehrhardt did, so she stayed where she was.

"There's something we wish to talk to you about, but it's too loud in here," Rudolf Hess whispered as he arrived by her side. "Please accompany us outside."

He smiled at Liesl and tipped his cap. She smiled nervously back. Killinger was now by her other arm. Ehrhardt circled in back.

"Hello, my dear," he whispered over her shoulder. "So we meet again. There's a matter of small concern that I would discuss with you."

Right arm extended, Killinger motioned her outside. She hesitated, but strong hands grabbed her and moved inexorably towards the doorway. She suddenly realized that she was very scared. Perhaps she did care if she lived.

"Stop or I'll scream!"

"To no purpose. These are all friends of mine," Ehrhardt replied.

"Help!"

Killinger squeezed hard on her wrist, causing her to yelp louder. Some members of the audience glanced towards the rear.

"The woman is a Red provocateur," Ehrhardt barked at them.

They wrestled her out of the meeting room and into the foyer, where Ehrhardt promptly clamped his hand over her mouth. As she was carried from the building, Liesl could still hear the featured speaker drone on.

"Any man who is not attacked in the Jewish newspapers, not slandered and vilified by them, is not a decent German!"

* * *

Wolf was standing in front of the blood-smeared metal wall, his hands bound behind him.

"That cigarette you promised me, Major?"

"You don't normally smoke, man. What's gotten into you now?"

"I'll be dying shortly. Don't you think that's reason enough?"

The Pole pulled the cigarette pack from his vest pocket, opened it and removed one. He placed it between Wolf's lips. He closed the pack, put it back in his pocket, and then proceeded to pull out a box of wooden matches from his trouser pocket.

"I'm going to untie you so you can enjoy your last smoke, man. But any wrong moves, and those two over there will shoot you immediately."

In response to the major's nod, the two-man firing squad smiled back at them from 30 feet away.

Wolf couldn't believe his ears. They were going to untie his wrists! He thought quickly.

"What could I do, Major? You carry the gun. And it is loaded, I presume?"

"Of course it is loaded, Warburg, or whoever you are – what is your name, damn it! You're about to die. What is it to you to prolong the secrecy now? And it is so annoying!"

"All part of the game, I suppose, Major. I keep telling you, my name is Warburg, but you still won't believe me."

The major pulled a small folding knife from his pocket. He turned Wolf around and cut the rope binding his hands. Wolf turned again to face the major, and his two executioners in the distance.

"It is not my choice to die," Wolf told his adversary as a desperate hope emerged in his mind. "I don't believe I can accept it."

"You'll just have to accept it, no matter what," declared the major, laughing in response. "It appears to me that you have no choice in the matter. Now – do you want this last cigarette, or are you going to make me die laughing?"

The major pulled a match from the tiny box, closed the container and stared straight at Wolf.

"Enjoy your last smoke, German spy."

He struck the match against the abrasive edge of the box and watched it flame. He lifted it to the cigarette dangling from his prisoner's mouth.

"If it was me," the major intoned, "I'd relax and enjoy *my* last cigarette."

The major put the match to the cigarette, his free hand cupping the other to protect the tiny flame from the wind.

"Perhaps you should have the cigarette, then," Wolf said from pursed lips.

He suddenly hugged the major, pulling him close and squeezing hard. He simultaneously spit out his cigarette, and grabbed for the gun in the holster around the Pole's waist. Finding it, he pulled it out and levelled it at the two riflemen, whose weapons were both trained on him. Shielded as he was by the major's back, they hesitated to fire. Wolf did not, and one of riflemen fell dead immediately from a bullet through the nose. This caused his partner to fire back. Two shots struck the major between his shoulder blades as Wolf continued to hug and use him as a shield. The major slumped forward, still, against Wolf, who fired back at the remaining trooper, catching him thrice in the chest and knocking him down on his back, where he lay coughing, spurting blood. Wolf then let go of the major, who slumped lifeless to the ground in a sprawl.

It was fortunate for Wolf that the firing squad consisted of just two troopers. Since shots were expected, no one deigned to check them out. Switching into the major's uniform, he made his way gingerly across the open courtyard to the other side. His luck held, as he quickly came across a small panel truck. Hotwiring the engine, he headed for the main gate.

"But it must be there," Wolf argued with the gatekeeper. "I arrived just this afternoon. My business is concluded and I am now leaving. I must be in Warsaw by tomorrow morning. The guard here this afternoon must have forgotten to note my arrival."

"That would be strange," the gatekeeper mused. "It is required procedure to note down all arrivals and departures. Major Warski, is it?"

"Yes, Corporal. And I am in a hurry. Let me pass. Open the gate."

"Wait until I call up to main reception desk and see if they have a record of you. I'm sure you checked in there on your way to visit the colonel."

"No," Wolf answered back quickly, "I went straight to his office."

"Well, let me check there," answered the persistent gatekeeper.

Wolf waited for what seemed an eternity, his right hand fondling the gun in his holster. Fortunately for the gatekeeper, there was no answer at the other end.

"On your way," said the corporal after some anxious moments. "Have a safe trip back, Major, and watch out for bandits along the way."

With a salute, Wolf was gone. He hoped it would be a while before they discovered any of the bodies he'd left behind. He carried enough gasoline for the entire run to the German border, he reckoned. And he had a fair chance, since he was in a Polish uniform in an army vehicle.

Finally on his way, Liesl's face flared up in his memory. It was the first time he'd allowed himself that luxury since being sentenced to death, when he vowed he would only think of her if there was a chance of holding her again.

Even in the barrenness of the winter landscape, Wolf marvelled at the majestic expanse of the white Russian plains, occasional patches of trees breaking through the generally white background. He imagined the fields of wheat, oats, barley, that would sprout once peace returned, the bushes displaying their various shades of greenery, the flowers gushing forth in myriad colours.

Wolf reached Cracow without incident and continued southwest without stopping. He had driven ten hours with just a brief break, and was intent to go on. He couldn't shake a gnawing feeling that Liesl was in danger. He promised himself that once they were home safe together, nothing would ever part them again. If only he could reach her now.

Wolf pulled off to the side of the road and gassed up from the reserves he'd brought from the prison camp. Later, in the no-man's-land between the Polish border and the Austrian frontier, he shed the Polish army uniform for civilian garb he had picked up along the way. The Austrians had a record of him having passed through in the opposite direction a few months before, so he passed back in with no difficulty, even without a passport. Bandits had taken it, he told them. Reaching Vienna, he turned west for the final leg to Bavaria and home. He tried to get comfortable, to enjoy the mountain scenery to the south, and the majestic Danube as the highway paralleled it. But that nagging sense of foreboding about Liesl pressed him on.

*　　*　　*

She was enthralled by a beautiful dream. It was a memory of a sunny summer afternoon, in a rowboat on the river Isar, drifting lazily downstream, just her and Wolf. The banks were shaded by large, old trees of varying shades of green, while the smaller vegetation displayed a variety of bright colours. They drifted by stately bridges, viewing them now from the water beneath. Most seemed ancient, while a couple were obviously newer. Dragonflies skimmed lightly over the water in search of grub, and the occasional fish rose in a shaded pool to grab for the insects hovering above. Boat traffic was light, with other voices far off. Liesl and Wolf were in a world of their own. It was their last afternoon together, before he set out for Russia to find her brother. The current drifted slowly northward as the river wended its way through the heart of the city, on its way to the far-off Danube. The mingled fragrances of the flowers, along with river breezes, wafted through the lovers' nostrils. All the time wasted over the last few years, that was in the past, or so they thought. The only thing necessary to complete Liesl's happiness was the safe return of her brother. Or at least to know what had happened to him.

On that last summer afternoon, Wolf and Liesl were determined to make the most of it. Fully reconciled, ready to devote themselves to each other, perhaps for the first time in their lives, Liesl looked forward to tranquillity and joy. She'd seen enough war, enough killing, to last forever; and the memory of Hella intruded her fragile cocoon. But she was determined to move forward.

They hadn't floated down the river together in years. The cruise started out south of the city, near the zoo, where they put the rowboat into the water, along with a picnic lunch, beach towels, and a large umbrella. An hour and a half later, they were in the city center, cruising under bridges and by the parks abutting the banks. They skirted a couple of long narrow islands in the middle of the river, and finally, on the left bank as they floated north, was the Englischer Garten. Wolf steered the boat to shore and beached it. They took the basket and towels, along with their umbrella, and strolled into the park. Finding a secluded spot by a narrow stream, the beach towels were spread, along with their lunch; the umbrella was set up to block out the sun, and spying eyes.

Liesl continued to dream, to remember. It was better than the reality of her captivity. They were under a large umbrella, sipping red wine after a sumptuous meal, lying amidst a grove of gentle, swaying trees. Wolf slowly undid the buttons on Liesl's blouse, and she willingly shed her clothing. Wolf did the same, and the two spent the next while in ecstasy. She could recall it all in exquisite detail, the feel of Wolf's body next to her, inside her. His kisses smothering her face and breasts. And his whispered declarations of love for her. Liesl thought of him now, begged for his return – but knew it could not be.

The lights suddenly went on in the room where she lay captive. Her dream turned into the nightmare of reality.

Hermann Ehrhardt had no desire to do away with Liesl. He rather liked her. But she seemed to leave him no choice. She was argumentative, disagreeable, and refused to stand aside for the Feme to do its work.

"What are we to do with you, my dear," he asked, as she lay tied to the bed, spread-eagled and helpless. "You have been treated well, I hope? I gave instructions that you not be harmed."

Ehrhardt sidled across the room and sat down on the bed next to Liesl. He removed the gag from her mouth.

"Your screaming was just upsetting everyone. None would have helped you, though. We're on a private estate outside the city. You're on your own."

His hand stroked her cheek, and she tried to bite it. He slapped her lightly on the nose.

"Be nice," he barked.

"What do you want of me," Liesl pleaded. "You've kept me here for two weeks now. What are you waiting for? Surely if it's money…"

"No. I'm sure there are many people who would pay a king's ransom for you. You're very beautiful," he said, leaning over so that his breath stroked her face, causing her to recoil.

"Don't be so cold, my dear. You may need a friend here to get you out alive."

"If that's what it takes…"

"Careful what you say next, fräulein."

"…then kill me now," she declared.

Ehrhardt pulled himself up and off the bed.

"Bitch. There's no one to save you now. Your boyfriend, Warburg, is dead in Russia. You've no friends here anymore; so who's going to come? Next time I see you, my dear, you will have a noose around your pretty neck. Call me if you change your mind."

He waved goodbye, opened the door, then stopped and turned.

"I nearly forget. Merry Christmas, my sweet."

He blew her a kiss, turned out the lights, and slammed the door shut behind him, leaving her all alone in the dark once again. Struggling against her bonds, her façade cracked, and she was about to cry, but didn't. She was altered from the woman who had spurned Wolf during the war because he shrank from fighting; or from even a year ago, when Adolf Hitler raged at him outside the Hotel Adlon, and she was still embarrassed by his wartime 'cowardice'. Since then she'd seen death and destruction at home. Hella had been shot in front of her eyes. Liesl knew of violence first-hand, that it was something to avoid in all but exigency, because violence breeds violence. Not a mind-boggling revelation; but one that Europe forgot in 1914.

Liesl again chaffed at her bonds. As for Ehrhardt, she could handle him. He hadn't raped her – yet; and she didn't believe the bit about the noose. So she told him that she'd rather die, but which way would she choose with a knife to her throat?

Normally her will to survive would win out.

But right now her zest for life was gone. She had sent her love off to Russia to die, and never would see his smile again.

* * *

It was Christmas, 1919, and Adolf Hitler was at the home of Anton Drexler, the latter's young daughter on Hitler's lap as the two adults planned the party platform. Hitler had to take the tram from the barracks downtown to Drexler's place, by the Nymphemburg palace in the western part of the city.

"I would rather have a hundred ignorant ruffians," argued Hitler, "than a thousand politicians, when it comes to a good street fight. And a political meeting is just the same. The ruffians don't stop to disect your words. They accept them and follow you. You take your professors and politicians – give me the street people, and I'll build you a movement."

"Fine," agreed Drexler, "but we're going to have to simplify our message then. They'll only be able to remember a few simple themes."

"Yes," Hitler said, "common repetition of the same simple messages. The Jewish threat, the shackles of Versailles, the formation of a Greater Germany."

Hitler thought for a moment.

"And no compromising with the enemy," he continued, as Drexler wrote down the agenda. "I will never agree to Harrer's way. There is no making deals with Jews. And the people will only view a halfway position as a sign that we're not certain we know what we're shouting about."

"Adolf, why do you hate the Jews so deeply," asked Drexler. "I get the unmistakable impression that you want them all dead."

"Maybe from something I've said at one time or another," replied Hitler wryly.

"Oh, lots of people say it, but you really seem to mean it. Is it just an act – I mean, you're a very good actor. That's part of your skill as an orator. But I'd like to know – deep down – what you really believe, and what you say for effect."

Hitler looked straight at Drexler, his steely eyes catching the latter man and holding him.

"Believe me, Anton, when I speak of what I would do to the enemies of the Reich. The Jews created the Reds; or at least they lead the Reds. The Reds are the greatest threat to Germany. They could come sweeping from the east to engulf us before we know it. The British and French and Americans can't appreciate this. Suffice to say that I would kill every Jew in Germany in an instant if it would safeguard our country."

"You'll have to tone it down in any event for public consumption," Drexler noted.

"I know," replied Hitler. "And for the time being it will suffice if we stop further immigration from the east. Then we can work on tossing out the Jews who have invaded us since 1914. And after that we can see about cutting back on the Jewish influence in German society. One step at a time. I am a most practical man. You will see."

"Uncle Dolf got funny 'stash," cooed Drexler's child as she played with the sharply clipped growth under Hitler's nose.

Hitler smiled down at the little girl seated on his lap. He held her tiny hands to his mouth and kissed them tenderly.

"Ah, this is what we do it all for, eh, Anton? Our children are our future. Strong, young, clean, healthy Germans."

"Why don't you get married and have kids, Adolf? I can see that you love them."

"Who knows? Right now it is the farthest thing from my mind. The building of our party is the first priority. Women can come later, once we are established!"

"Well, I admire your commitment, Adolf. And we all think that you have a wonderful future in politics. You've certainly livened up our party so far."

Hitler smiled appreciatively.

"When do you want to announce the new platform," asked Drexler. "Harrer won't agree to it, but Eckart and Röhm are in your corner."

Hitler looked off into space, as he imagined the event in his head.

"I will do it soon, at a night time rally," he finally proclaimed, rising from his chair with the child in one arm, eyes wide, as though gripped by revelation. "That is when people are the most receptive, the time when they are most easily won over. During the day their willpower and stubbornness are greatest; but at night they succumb more easily to an emotional appeal to their patriotism."

* * *

It was Christmas at the von Schlieffen residence. Dunken, Count Rantzau, and Commander Locker waited for some news of Liesl to break. It was a mournful affair, the three men sitting about, plagued with trepidation at every ring of the phone or knock on the door. It was half past eight, on the evening of December 27th, and the snow was falling outside. Frost built up around the edges of the windows, and icicles hung from the trellises. Finally a knock came.

"I'll get it," Commander Locker volunteered, setting down his rum toddy and rising from the couch.

He left the room, heading down the hallway towards the front door. After a couple of minutes, Dunken mused, "I wonder who it is."

"Indeed," agreed Rantzau.

Still they waited, and Locker did not return. Dunken called him, and Locker answered back, a strange tone in his voice, beckoning them to the door. The two rose from their chairs and strode down the hallway.

They found Locker standing silent by the door, stunned, like a deer caught in headlights. His eyes were glued to a man dressed in farmer's boots and a worn old overcoat. He sported a dark, ragged beard under a heavy, brown cap which had bits of torn fir trim. At their approach the cap was doffed, and they were greeted by a friend who they all thought they'd lost.

"Hello Ulrich, Dunken," he said with a smile, and then added, "It's been quite awhile."

There was silence for a long moment as the newcomer surveyed Rantzau in his shock.

"What, no 'where have you been', or 'it's about time you got back'?"

"As I live and breathe," exclaimed the Count, finally managing to exhale. "How is it possible? We buried you outside Kiev!"

Thank heavens, thought Rantzau. Life was not just conflict and loss; against hope, Wolf Warburg had come home.

Gasthaus Orator

The Russian civil war reached its climax in the late autumn of 1919. Marching north, on September 20th the Whites captured Kursk; then moved on to Voronezh on October 6th, Chernigov on October 12th, and Orel the next day. The next target, Tula, was the last large city before Moscow. At the same time, it looked like St. Petersburg would fall to other White armies. But then the whole picture suddenly changed. The Whites were stretched thin, having taken so much territory in so short a space to time, and the lands taken being heavily populated. At the same time, the Red armies were massing in the dense heartland surrounding Moscow for a major counterattack.

The White lines were shattered when the blow came, and the entire seven hundred mile southern front fell into retreat. Within days Orel was lost, within a month, Kursk, and by Christmas the entire Ukraine. The White forces were squeezed and crowded like rats into the Black Sea ports, scrambling to evacuate before capture by the Reds.

By mid-November Lloyd George declared publicly that the Reds couldn't be defeated by force of arms and that Britain couldn't afford to fund "so costly an intervention in an interminable civil war." The British followed the French and started pulling their forces out. Instantly White morale throughout the south, the Ukraine, plunged at news that the Allies were quitting the cause.

In normal times, there would have been a population gain. Instead, since 1914 Russia suffered over eleven million deaths from combat, epidemics, and famine. Between 1917 and 1920 Moscow lost half its population and St. Petersburg two-thirds. By 1921 Russian industrial production was less than a fifth of pre-war levels. Millions of Russians fled abroad; the educated elite left in droves. It was the first large-scale cultural exodus of the century; the second occurred in Germany during the first few years of Nazi rule. These two migrations fundamentally altered the scientific and intellectual balance between Europe and America in favour of the latter for the remainder of the century.

By the end of 1919, Russia had finally fallen, for the next seventy years as it turned out, to the Reds. The civil war was virtually over, except for mopping up in the south. Germany was now on the front line; just a thin string of newly formed states stood between her and Red Russia. Citizens of the West, in Britain, France, and particularly America, could not appreciate the paranoia engendered by living so close to the Russian colossus. Hitler and his cohorts were grimly determined that Bolshevism would not conquer Germany.

Attendance at German Workers Party rallies continued to climb as 1919 ended. As numbers approached three hundred, it was decided by the propaganda chief, Hitler, that a larger hall was needed. Arrangements were made for a giant rally in a month's time in the main hall at the Hofbräuhaus, which could seat over a thousand.

Karl Harrer, the overall chairman of the party, knew that his days were numbered. It was taking a direction, under Hitler and the army elements with him, that Harrer couldn't support and was unable to check. He rejected the racist course, and thought that its radical tone would alienate support from business.

"But who will take Harrer's place," asked Gottfried Feder.

"Drexler will become national chairman," replied Dietrich Eckart. "But he'll just be a figurehead anyway. He's officially leader of the Munich chapter now, but Röhm and I call the shots. Besides, we can't afford to lose Hitler, and he and Harrer just don't see eye to eye."

"And do you think you will be able to handle Hitler? He's becoming a little intolerable lately. A real know-it-all. I grant you he's an excellent speaker…"

"Leave Hitler to Röhm and me," Dietrich Eckart replied. "He's a real volcano on the podium, but he's not so bright in person. Oh, there he is now. Hitler," Eckart shouted across the room. "Adolf. Over here."

Adolf Hitler was in the midst of conversation with an older, buxom breasted female of the Munich upper crust. It was a minor society affair in the better part of downtown München, in one of the fancy luxury apartment buildings close by the Isar. Hitler instinctively adopted a different persona here. No longer the harsh gutteral sounds as he spoke; rather, gentle deep purrs emerged, which to some bespoke a pent-up power. Those more familiar, or had seen him speak, knew of the smouldering volcano inside. Hitler charmed the elite crowd here, particularly the women, many of whom seemed enamoured of his husky Austrian accent and fiery, emotive eyes. On this night, Hitler was dressed in a new suit and tie, sparkling white shirt and black scarf, all recent gifts from Eckart, who was intent on trotting out his budding star in front of as many wealthy potential contributors as possible.

Eckart made his way over to Hitler.

"And what have you and the lovely Frau Belcher been discussing this evening?"

"Adolf and I were just talking about this political party of yours," Frau Belcher told Eckart, whom she was familiar with. "He feels that Munich is big enough to support at least ten meetings each week. But he says you need more money for advertising. You know," she said smiling, reaching out at the same time to pinch Hitler on the arm, "he's really very persuasive. He's as gentle as a pussy cat, really, although you wouldn't know it from some of his speeches, I'm told."

Eckart gave Hitler a knowing smile. Not only could his protégé overwhelm many from the podium, he also seduced them as he worked the room. Hitler was selectively well read in German history, including Clausewitz, Frederick the Great, Wagner and the German heroic myths. He read novels, viewed certain erotic works of art, and loved classical music. He would imbibe alcohol only occasionally, but liked coffee and chocolate. And he could be very gallant, offering flowers to women he was trying to charm.

"But why do you hate them so much," Frau Belcher was asking Hitler.

"Because they are trying to enslave us. They want to marry all our women and thus dilute the true blood of the Aryans. They are insidious. With satanic joy in his face, the black-haired Jewish youth lurks in the wait for the unsuspecting girl whom he defiles with his blood, thus stealing her from our people. "

"Oh, Adolf," cooed Frau Belcher. "You have such a way with words."

"Jews who marry German women should be jailed for a few years, and executed for a second offence," Dietrich Eckart agreed. "I myself have a young daughter, and must think of her future welfare."

"I respect the Jew more than most," soliloquized Hitler. "That they have kept their race virtually intact for two millennia is proof of the fact that nowhere in the world is the instinct for self-preservation developed more strongly than in them. What people has gone through greater catastrophes and emerged unchanged? They are, without a doubt, the most potent threat to Aryan civilization today."

Dietrich Eckart and Adolf Hitler wandered off to talk to a small circle of army officers dressed in their best uniforms, enjoying the unexpected opulence that was so different from barracks life. Ernst Röhm, Hermann

Ehrhardt, and Manfred von Killinger toasted each other over glasses of champagne.

"You're certainly coming up in the world, Corporal," Röhm commented.

But his voice was tinged with a new measure of respect.

"I ran into an old acquaintance this morning," Eckart interrupted, changing the subject. "Dunken von Schlieffen, returned from a Cheka prison in Kiev this past autumn. Says it was Wolf Warburg who got him out."

"That coward," Hitler shouted, as if on cue. Just mention that name and it set him off like a fuse.

"Oh, calm down, Adolf," Eckart added quickly. "You know that Warburg was killed outside Kiev, cut down by some Cossack."

Hitler's demeanour softened. He settled down, stood still, and straightened his tie.

"At least the skunk got what was coming to him," Hitler concluded.

"How do you know Schlieffen," interrupted Hermann Ehrhardt, "and what did he want?"

"Old friend of mine," replied Eckart. "We used to do some serious drinking together in our younger days. He knew the clubs of Schwabing just about as well as I did."

He looked at Ehrhardt suspiciously and then over at Killinger.

"He was devastated," Eckart continued, smiling wickedly. "Seems his sister has recently disappeared. You wouldn't know anything about that, would you?"

* * *

"It was a strange conversation," said Dunken to Locker-Lampson and Wolf, as they sat in the latter's office in downtown Munich, overlooking the snow-covered banks of the Isar. "Eckart told me that he was hearing about

Liesl's disappearance for the first time, but I had the distinct impression that he wasn't surprised at all, that he knew about it. He was asking too many questions. Just a little too interested."

"You know who his friends are," Wolf said. "He'd likely know if it was the Feme that's got Liesl."

No one spoke it, but they all knew that she might already be dead.

"If it was that group, we should be watching Ehrhardt and Killinger, to see where they go," said Commander Locker.

"Let's do it," declared Wolf without hesitation, grabbing his coat and heading for the door.

The surveillance picked up Manfred von Killinger as he exited the Turkenstrasse barracks. Now they were on the Dachauer Strasse heading south. His vehicle took a right and then a minute later turned left down the Goethestasse to head south once again. There were three units involved in the surveillance, nondescript cars and panel vans. Wolf and Locker-Lampson trailed behind them, all connected by radio.

"Looks to me like they're headed out of town," said the commander a few minutes later. "There's no reason for Killinger to head this way otherwise. He doesn't live in this part of town."

"I think we're on the right track," muttered Wolf. "Who else would kidnap Liesl? No doubt they found out about her blowing the whistle on their scheme to eliminate Albert."

The trunk of the staff car they were driving was a munitions warehouse. There were new sub-machine guns, a miniature flamethrower, grenade launcher and powered grappling hook, all state of the art from the British and American secret services. They had hardened vests underneath officers' uniforms, capable of stopping light shrapnel and soft bullets. They were ready to swing into action immediately.

The route continued further south, then swung west, and then south again, finally leaving the city limits. The surveillance units changed positions as they turned corners.

"If Dunken is right, the Rüchtstein estate should be half a mile ahead. The road jogs twice more before we get there. The guy is a committed right wing sympathizer. Heavy contributor to the Thule society. He's hiding weapons there, too. They say," Locker-Lampson continued, "that he may even have an airplane or two broken down and hidden away on the property."

"All I care about is Liesl," Wolf said grimly, "and if they've harmed her…"

"We don't even know that she's there," replied Locker-Lampson.

The surveillance units dropped off on instructions from Wolf, and they all stopped down the road from the estate gates. It was a beautifully wooded, rustic Bavarian country road. The Alps stood out to the south, the sunshine just above their rim, shining directly into Wolf's eyes. He looked away, and towards the castle-like gothic structure set well back into the grounds of the estate.

"We can sneak in through the woods to the right," the commander said to Wolf. "The group can follow us," he added, nodding towards the surveillance units.

"I don't like it," said Wolf. "There's too much danger that we'll be seen. The more we are, the greater the danger."

"But the bigger our force, the better."

"All it takes is one bullet to kill Liesl," Wolf replied grimly.

He turned and faced the rest of the group.

"Drive a mile away and await further instructions. Head south, where there's less danger that someone coming from town will run into you. We'll call if we get in trouble. Be ready!"

They turned away to deploy accordingly.

"Oliver, we'll approach the chateau head on," he said, turning back, "and as quickly as we can, before they have a chance to react. In our uniforms we should be able to get by the guards without problem. Once we're inside, we'll have to wing it."

They already had a map of the house from the source who tipped them off to its current use by the Ehrhardt Free Corps to store weapons. Herr von Rüchtstein was vacationing on the Dalmatian coast, so the house should have been unoccupied except for staff. But there was a beehive of activity, and food and supplies constantly arriving at the estate. And rumours of a female guest kept against her will.

"Supposedly some woman was heard screaming upstairs," said Locker-Lampson to Wolf as they drove up the main road towards the imposing structure. "It would have to be towards the rear, since all deliveries are made there."

"It was a deliveryman who heard the shouts?"

"Apparently."

They reached the front of the building and continued, without stopping, up the driveway along the side and then round the corner to the rear.

"I'm betting one of those rooms up there," said the commander, nodding towards the windows directly above the double back doors of the sprawling chateau, as they turned into the rear courtyard. "She may even be looking down at us right now."

Wolf appreciated the commander's optimism, which he knew was for his benefit. Up ahead, though, he spied what looked like a noose.

In the rear courtyard of the chateau on the sprawling estate outside Munich, a rope was thrown over the yardarm that extended from the building. The tell-tale hangman's noose, with the gigantic knot to break the victim's neck as she dropped, hung from one end of the rope, while the other end was tied to a hook extending out from the building.

Liesl had a gag in her mouth and her arms were tied behind her back, but her legs were free so she could move around the room. From her second-floor window overlooking the courtyard, Liesl had witnessed the preparations being made that morning. So when the knock came at the door, and it opened a moment later to admit her captor, she retreated to a corner of the room, as far away from Hermann Ehrhardt as she could get.

"My patience has run out, my dear. If you won't have anything to do with me, why should I let you live? It's not like you won't run straight to the police or your friends in Berlin as soon as I let you leave."

Liesl said nothing; she felt terror.

"It is not like you can do anything," Ehrhardt continued, "what with your arms bound behind your back and your mouth gagged. But it's your fault. Every time we remove it you begin to scream out the window. And I keep telling you that there is no help within shouting distance."

In the courtyard below, she saw two Ehrhardt Brigade troopers hitching a horse to a wagon sitting directly below the hanging noose. She would be stood up on the wagon with the noose tight around her neck; the horse would then tear away with the wagon, leaving her to dangle. An army staff car was rounding the corner, coming into the courtyard. There were two officers inside, though she couldn't make out who they were. It didn't seem to matter much in any event.

"So you see, there is no reason to struggle anymore, my dear. Your life is forfeit. Unless, of course, you care to reconsider your feelings towards me. I'm really quite loveable, you know."

Liesl nearly choked on the gag in her mouth. Worse still, Ehrhardt was moving towards her. She tried to elude him, but the room was confined. He easily corralled her, and then picked her up bodily, carried her over to the bed, and threw her down. She tried to bolt up and off, but with her hands tied behind, his left arm easily held her down. With the right, he reached for his belt buckle, undid it, pulled it off. Then he grabbed the front of Liesl's blouse and ripped it open, exposing the bra

"I was thinking this morning, why should I dispose of you without first doing as I want? It would be an inexcusable waste of German beauty."

Suddenly there was thumping and banging outside. It was loud enough to interrupt Ehrhardt. He stopped moving; Liesl also lay still. Getting up, Ehrhardt dragged her by the hair to the window. In the courtyard below, all was quiet. The horse stood lazily chewing blades of grass sticking up through the cracks between the well-worn, red bricks that paved the courtyard, where the snow had been brushed away. The noose hung undisturbed. The troopers were nowhere in sight.

Ehrhardt surveyed the scene for a moment, then dragged Liesl back to the bed and threw her down again. With her hands still bound behind, he now tied each foot to a corner post at the end of the bed, so that her legs were spread apart. He unzipped his trousers and began to remove them. Liesl struggled to rise, but the back of the officer's hand struck her savagely across the mouth.

"Back, bitch. You're not going anywhere."

Commander Locker-Lampson steered the roadster, converted to resemble an army staff car, to a halt in the courtyard behind the chateau. The pavement was clear of snow, having been shovelled earlier in the week. Wolf stepped out of the passenger door and approached the guards working on the hangman's device.

"You will go to the trunk of my car and unload equipment and supplies," he ordered the two.

"But we have been told that this must be completed urgently, mein Colonel," one of them argued.

"Do you wish to end up on the Polish frontier, you impertinent swine? You will do what I say immediately!"

The two meekly stopped what they doing and followed Wolf. Locker-Lampson, meanwhile, had gotten out of the driver's door and followed behind. Wolf stepped back to allow Locker-Lampson to make his way through with a key to open the trunk. He did so quickly, and then stepped back and motioned the troopers forward. Then both he and Wolf pulled their revolvers and stuck them in the troopers' backs.

"Where is the girl hidden," Wolf demanded. "What room is she kept in? Tell me quickly or die!"

Locker-Lampson thrust the gun hard into the trooper's back.

"I know nothing."

"Tell me now, or I'll kill you," Wolf hissed. "We know that she's here. You have five seconds, and then I shoot you to make an example to your friend here."

The freebooter thought for a moment.

"She is upstairs. In a room overlooking us now."

"Don't look up," Locker-Lampson jabbed the trooper he had custody of. "Just keep moving normally."

"Okay," declared Wolf, "we're all going to go inside and visit that room."

They closed the trunk and started moving towards the main entrance to the house. Reaching the door, they knocked and it was opened by a servant. The party started to make their way in when the servant noticed the guns held in the troopers' backs. He started to scream. But before he could get out more than a double note, Locker-Lampson pulled a knife and slit his throat, severing the larynx and windpipe. The dead man's eyes stared forward, frozen, as did the two troopers who looked on in shock.

"Get him into the closet there," Wolf exhorted his companion.

The commander opened the closet door and motioned for the two freebooters to drag the dead man in. They did so without argument. Then Locker-Lampson clubbed one over the head with his revolver so hard that the man fell to the floor unconscious.

"He'll be alright," the commander assured the remaining freebooter as the two stashed the fallen man into the closet as well. "I could have killed him – which is what you'll get if you don't cooperate!"

"Where to from here," asked Wolf.

The trooper hurriedly pointed to the stairs midway up the hall. The trio ascended slowly and lightly. At the top, the trooper led them off to the left and down a dim passage. Around the corner came an officer.

"Von Killinger," Wolf gasped.

Indeed it was him. He stopped dead in his tracks, about to shout. But Locker-Lampson, gun in hand, pointed it straight at his face.

"One word, one move, and I splatter you all over the walls."

Von Killinger never doubted it. His hand froze in its path towards the covered holster at his side.

"Where is she," Wolf demanded in a low but steely voice. "Which room?"

Killinger pointed down the hall.

"There at the end," he said softly. "But Ehrhardt is in with her now."

He was staring hard at his captors.

"You're Wolf Warburg, aren't you? You're supposed to be dead."

"I've returned. An avenging angel, you might say. Especially if you've harmed Liesl."

Killinger was quickly regaining his composure. The initial shock of events had worn off. "You know," he said after a moment, "if you harm me, your girlfriend will die. Ehrhardt will see to that. If you leave now, though, I'll put in a good word for you."

Locker-Lampson was livid. Wolf was impressed by Killinger's audacity, especially in the face of weapons trained on him.

"Let me silence him now," Locker-Lampson pleaded with Wolf.

"Go ahead – try it," Killinger smirked. "Then the captain will be alerted and the Schlieffen bitch will die."

Wrong move – it enraged Wolf.

Von Killinger's eyes were glued to a hesitant Oliver Locker-Lampson. Wolf suddenly reared back, and then sent his right fist crashing into Killinger's solarplex, slamming him backward and to the ground. There he lay, flat on his back, the wind knocked completely out of him, unable yet to breath or move, unable to shout out. The commander, seizing the opportunity, then quickly clubbed him into unconsciousness with his gun.

They dumped Killinger into an empty room, and bound and gagged the remaining trooper. Hurrying out, they headed up the hallway to the room at the end. Wolf put his ear to the door.

'They're in there, all right,' he mouthed to Locker-Lampson.

"What now," came the whisper back.

Liesl was stunned by the blow from Ehrhardt. She couldn't move for a few moments, during which time he fondled and kissed her all over. It brought little reaction. Then, patience wearing thin, he finally ripped off her bra. That brought her back to life. She tried to scream, but the gag stopped her. She strained to break the ropes holding her arms behind and under her; but they held tight. Her legs were spread-eagled, her feet tied to the posts at the end of the bed. On top of her, she could feel Ehrhardt as he began to get excited. Then came a knock at the door. Ehrhardt stopped still.

"Go away," he shouted. "Come back in ten minutes. The bitch will be ready to hang then."

For a moment there was silence; then more raps on the door.

"I said go away," Ehrhardt screamed. "Go away or I'll shoot you!"

Silence. Outside the room, the sound of boots trundled off down the hallway. Ehrhardt waited a moment to make sure all was silent. Then he turned back to Liesl, his hand reaching down to her panties.

"Time for these to come off, my sweet, and then I will have my way with you," he hissed gleefully.

Somehow she managed to spit out the gag; but still lay powerless under him as her hands and legs remained tied.

"Stop," she hollered, struggling. "Get off me, you animal!"

At that moment there came from the corridor the sound of running boots, then a heavy thud that shook them, and the sound of splintering wood. Looking up from the bed, from under Ehrhardt whose head cranked right around, Liesl saw the solid wooden door fly off its hinges, back into the room and onto the floor. Following close behind were two officers, whose shoulders together had just burst the door asunder. Oliver Locker-Lampson fell sprawling on top of the fallen door. Wolf, retaining his feet, turned towards Liesl and her captor.

After a moment she gasped, eyes wide, face white. "Wolf!"

"Warburg?" Hermann Ehrhardt exclaimed, "No, it's not possi…"

Like a whirlwind Wolf jumped to the bed, and, a growl escaping his lips, flung Ehrhardt off Liesl and into the wall six feet away. He smacked head-first, and crumpled silently to the floor.

In disbelief Liesl looked up to see Wolf's face hovering above, smiling.

"Better late than never," he said, sinking down on the bed to kiss her.

* * *

"Now that we have a new chairman, let us deal with the other changes I have proposed," said Adolf Hitler.

"What have you got in mind," Anton Drexler, the new chair, asked his chief of propaganda.

"We need a new name," Hitler argued. "And a flag, for that matter. And our own special uniform. Those are the symbols that will make us stand out from the crowd. The flag must have lots of red in it, just to antagonize the Reds. And in it we'll incorporate the swastika that Captain Ehrhardt's troops already use as their insignia," and which they had borrowed from the old Teutonic Knights.

"And as for a name," Anton Drexler asked him, "have you decided on that too?

"As a matter of fact, yes," Hitler replied without hesitation. "The *National Socialist [Nationalsozialistiche] German Workers' Party*. It's designed to attract both the nationalists and the Red supporters, which will infuriate the Reds."

"But isn't that name a little long?" drawled Dietrich Eckart.

"The press will shorten it down soon enough," Hitler shot back. "Within a week we'll be known as the *Nazi* party."

Eckart thought for a moment, staring off into space.

"I like it," he finally said, slapping his thigh. "It's got an edginess that just makes you take notice."

"And if it doesn't, I will," Hitler promised emphatically. "We have already booked our next rally, and I expect to see thousands attend."

"You dream mightily," Drexler said, shaking his head.

And so it was that the first mass meeting of the Nazi party took place in the Festsaal, the main room of the Hofbräuhaus in Munich in the first days of 1920, with almost two thousand people in attendance. The trouble was that half of them were Reds.

But the Nazis were ready. Burly freebooters and army troops in civilian garb served as security, battling it out in the seats and on the floor as the Reds tried to disrupt Hitler's speech. People were thrown about and knocked down while others sat trying to listen to the speaker. It was the same sort of battle that would be fought countless times between right wing and Red forces across Germany over the next fifteen years. Sometimes the Nazis would be carried out by their mates, or thrown out on the street by victorious Red supporters; and on other occasions Hitler and his cronies would prevail.

On this particular night in the Festsaal at the Hofbräuhaus, Adolf Hitler was determined to present the newly refined Nazi party platform to all Munich.

"This is our *Weltanschauung*," declared Hitler from the podium. "We are in a fight for our national and racial existence against the Bolshevik-Jewish international world conspiracy. So we demand the following: Firstly, that the Versailles *Diktat*, and its reparations provisions, and its limits on German military power, be torn up, for we reject it totally."

There were cheers from the house.

"Only Germans can be citizens of Germany. All non-German immigration is to be stopped, and foreign workers expelled."

More cheers.

"And no more Jews!"

Some mixed support. Hitler expected more.

"All Germans in surrounding countries must become part of a Greater Germany!"

The cheering continued. Hitler reveled in it, coveting more. He returned to his own pet theme.

"We must expel the Jews," Hitler shouted. "And why must we do this?"

He paused for a moment to let the tension build.

"Because without the Jews, there would be no Reds!"

Pandemonium erupted as Red supporters threw chairs and mugs, while others tried to storm the podium. Hitler continued unabated.

"The Jews are behind the Reds in Russia! The Jews sold us out at Versailles!"

The fighting continued, but gradually the trained troops acting as Nazi security got the upper hand over the Red agitators. More and more were tossed physically from the building, so that the thinning crowd largely supported the speaker. Applause won out over the Reds' howling curses.

* * *

"It is the fight of our time," argued Wolf, "elitism and racism versus the politics of inclusion of all peoples. Which way will the world go? That of the West; or that which the Right extremists rage about, a German racist world view?"

"To the West, then, and the Weimar Republic," said Albert Einstein, hoisting a glass of sparkling wine in his right hand while his left played with a suspender strap running down his chest. "May she bloom and prosper, a true German enlightenment," he said, beaming optimistically, so glad to be back home after his forced absence.

"Do you really think we've won," asked Wolf. "Sure, we're still alive, we're healthy and we live well among friends. But it's all so fragile, and maybe temporary. Red Russia is a monster just beyond our borders waiting to gobble us up; and at the other end are the extremists on the right who would sacrifice all tolerance for democracy and minorities in the name of protecting us from the Reds. Either way we end up with a dictatorship."

"Or we're picked clean by the western bankers for reparations," declared Haber, sitting in an armchair, his arm crooked, stroking his partly greying beard.

"So we skate the middle course while we may," offered Count Rantzau. "Democracy is fragile, but better than any alternative."

"But how long can it maintain itself with such pressure from both the left and the right," asked Wolf again. "You think Ehrhardt or Killinger or any of the other extremists are through? And my old nemesis, Hitler – what do we make of him? I used to think he was just an annoying crank. But I've seen him speak recently – and I think I've underestimated that devil."

Liesl draped one arm around Count Rantzau, the other around Wolf's shoulder; she kissed him on the cheek, and softly recited a melancholy rhyme:

O love, while still 'tis yours to love!
O love, while love you still may keep!
The hour will come, the hour will come,
When you shall stand by graves and weep!

- Ferdinand Freiligrath